BLUE NUMBERS

Also by Bruce Goldsmith
Strange Ailments; Uncertain Cures

BLUE NUMBERS

a novel

BRUCE
GOLDSMITH

MERCURY HOUSE
300 Montgomery Street, Suite 700
San Francisco, California 94104

Published in the United States by
Mercury House
San Francisco, California

Distributed to the trade by
Consortium Book Sales & Distribution, Inc.
St. Paul, Minnesota

Mercury House and colophon are registered trademarks of
Mercury House, Incorporated

Manufactured in the United States of America

Library of Congress Cataloging-in-Publication Data
Goldsmith, Bruce, 1947–
   Blue numbers : a novel / by Bruce Goldsmith.
   p. cm.
   ISBN 0–916515–53–2 : $19.95
   I. Title.
PS3557.03854B58   1989
813'.54 — dc19
                           88–7848
                            CIP

Again, for Sally

1

A7549653.

Sandy Klein studied the numbers: *A7549653* — such neat blue lettering, yet so confusing.

It was exactly seven o'clock on a blazing hot morning, June 19, 1973. A metallic click from the clock radio by his bed signaled the beginning of the CBS national news. Directly outside his window, chirping birds only added to the irritating noise reverberating from hundreds of cars speeding over the canyon road, just one block away, on their way to work.

It seemed to Sandy a routine Southern California summer morning except for that one horrendous item: *A7549653*, vividly stenciled on the pale skin of his forearm a third of the way between his hand and his elbow. Suddenly, for unfathomable reasons, Sandy's flesh now bore exactly the type of number the Nazis had used thirty years earlier to identify their slave laborers at Auschwitz.

How had such an abomination come to be? Sandy asked himself, still lying in bed. It was revolting, degrading, humiliating — a nightmare. Yet the thing on his arm was also a transformer, converting him from an emotionally depressed, spiritually alienated, bitter outsider into a vivid incarnation of the all-time victim of history — the Jew condemned to the death camps.

Who could have done such a thing to him? Sandy searched his memory but could recall nothing about the preceding evening except the first few drinks he and Billy Hoyle, his only real friend, had downed at the bar of the El Padrino Room. Everything else about the past ten hours was lost in a long dark tunnel with no recognizable walls, reflecting not the faintest glimmer of light. Whoever had inked on those vile numbers could only have done it when his brain cells were one hundred percent unreceptive. Or so he wanted to believe. *Was I unconscious?* Sandy asked himself. How did I get home? The fact that he had no answers was driving him crazy. It must have been the booze. *Why the fuck did I ever try to keep up with Billy?*

Staring at the numbers, Sandy felt rage. For the first time in years he wanted to scream, to attack, to injure — even to murder — whoever had mocked his Jewishness by writing those numbers on his arm. The only thing stopping him was the acute pain pulsing through his head with the power of a Caterpillar diesel at full throttle. Too much booze, Sandy told himself, sitting up in an effort to reduce the blood pressure in his brain.

Elevation helped only momentarily as the pain shifted straight down his throat to a more horrible residence in his stomach, where the fire in his belly was paralyzing — as if some angry revolutionary had crammed a burning Michelin-X radial down his esophagus through to his bowels. The inferno quickly distended his abdomen with pain. Was it an ulcer? Forget ulcers, his body shouted, this was either a heart attack or the terminal stage of stomach cancer.

Sitting on the edge of the bed without moving, Sandy tried to meditate the pain away. If Filipino mystics could do psychic surgery, why couldn't an American Jew do psychic anesthesia? But the waves of pain not only refused to recede, they built up rapidly, erecting an impenetrable wall between himself and the world, silencing even the news broadcast reporting John Dean's decision to make a deal with Sam Erwin and the Senate Investigation Committee and to testify in public about President Nixon's role in the Watergate break-in.

As the furnace in Sandy's belly and throat snaked its way down through his ileum into his large intestine, he tried deep breathing. Thirty-two years old was too young for such a sudden, undeserved death. It wasn't as if he were a murderer, a robber, a rapist, or even a drug dealer — he'd just had a few too many drinks. Should he phone an ambulance? Before he could move, the inferno within made a sudden shift downward and a tidal wave of pain paralyzed him. Nothing he'd ever experienced had hurt so terribly; Sandy had no choice but to recognize that he was about to die.

Leaning forward, he reached for the phone. As he was about to dial the operator and call an ambulance, the fire in his chest and belly exploded up, down, and out. From his throat came a bitter, burning, sulfurous belch while his rectum issued forth a long, rumbling fart rivaling the blow-out of an off-shore oil rig mainlining a pocket of million-year-old-swamp gas. Four times Sandy's intestines vividly demonstrated Bernoulli's principle by painfully shooting gas at high pressure and speed through the narrow orifice. Cramps, terrible rushes of agony, bursts of relief—and then, to Sandy's amazement, the pain vanished so suddenly and completely that it was almost impossible to believe it had ever been there.

Getting out of bed, Sandy padded into his small white-tiled bathroom and turned on the tap. As the hot water worked its way from the heater in the garage of his 1930s clapboard house, he examined himself in the medicine cabinet mirror. On the top of his head he saw a pale, shiny bare scalp where only a few years before there had been an impressive bush of electric, sixties-style hair. Under his bloodshot eyes hung dark bags of sagging flesh. His once baby-faced complexion was now an unhealthy gray-green, highlighted by blotches of finely etched red capillaries. The successful young man of the late sixties, the once bright light of New Age journalism, looked like a seriously worn, suffering soul long past his peak, in appearance easily ten years older than his chronological age.

After considerable hammering from the pipes, an anemic flow of scalding water finally issued from the spigot. It took only an instant for Sandy to mix in the cold, then thrust his left forearm under the water. But as much as he soaked the numbers and as hard as he scrubbed with a washcloth and soap, all he accomplished was to irritate the already tender, swollen, and reddened flesh surrounding the Auschwitz numerals. It wasn't enough that the anonymous artist had used a waterproof pen; from the considerable swelling and tenderness it was obvious that the ink itself was causing a severe allergic reaction. The longer such an irritant remained on his flesh, the worse the contact dermatitis would get. Sandy knew from previous experience that if he didn't want a swollen arm the size of a blimp, he had to get the ink off immediately.

Over the kitchen sink he upgraded his attack, first trying 409 and then shifting to Comet. Nothing was achieved except further inflammation of the skin. What the fuck kind of ink had the son-of-a-bitch used?

Grabbing the phone off the wall hook, Sandy speed-dialed a number that rang repeatedly without an answer. *Billy, Billy, Billy, pick up the god-damn phone,* he screamed in his mind. If anyone knew what had gone on last night, it would be Billy. As bad as the pain in his stomach had been, as frightening as the ink on his arm was becoming, none of it approached the panic inspired by that ten-hour hole in his memory. Had he given himself a chemical lobotomy? First a night was gone; next it would be a missing year. Soon he'd be a slobbering idiot wandering around a nut house, another mind lost to Alzheimers. How could a few too many glasses of scotch turn someone so quickly into a human vegetable?

"God damn him," Sandy screamed aloud, slamming the phone down on the hook. It wasn't as if Billy weren't home. Sandy knew for a fact that the son-of-a-bitch was asleep with his phone shut off.

Spinning on his heel, Sandy stomped through the side door into the connecting garage and searched through a stack of cans until he located a gallon of paint thinner and an equally large quantity of acetone. *Let's see the fucking indelible ink survive these chemicals,* he chortled to himself.

Back in the kitchen, standing over the mottled white sink, even massive applications of these two potent solvents did nothing to the appearance of the numbers. All that was accomplished was further irritation of the already raw skin under the delicate blue lettering. As much as Sandy hated to face it, the reality was undeniable. Those numbers weren't simply inked to his arm. *A7549653* hadn't been rolled on by ball point. Not only wasn't it washable, it was permanent, serious, and grim. *A7549653* was for real, just like the identification on the slave laborers at Auschwitz. The characters were now part of him, not *on* his flesh but *inside* the cells themselves. Those blue numbers and letter constituted the worst of all fears, more frightening to a Jew than death itself — a concentration camp tattoo, indistinguishable from the authentic, Nazi-created original.

A7549653. The number was like a beacon to Sandy, commanding attention, vivid and permanent, branding him with a nightmare, turning his flesh into that of a human steer. Who could have done such a thing? And why? Even worse was the question of how he had permitted it to happen. But try as he might to uncover its secrets, *A7549653* divulged nothing.

After another futile attempt at reaching Billy by telephone, Sandy flew into action, throwing on clean slacks, dark blue shirt, and his sleek Italian silk and cotton sports coat. Then he slipped on his custom-made, weird — but comfortable — orthopedic shoes, stuffed his wallet and keys into his pockets, and ran out of the house.

2

"Go, go, go!" Sandy screamed through the windshield at the crawling line of bumper-to-bumper commuters. They have to do something about Beverly Glen, he raged to himself. It's just a shitty little two-lane road, but people use it as a main thoroughfare. Another disgusting failure of leadership. I mean, what are we paying the mayor and the planning commission for?

"Get these cars off my street!" Sandy howled, knowing as always that no one was listening.

Everything at that moment was funneled into the bottomless maelstrom of his frustration and rage. Even the car didn't seem to be running right. Had it not warmed up yet, or were the engine's throwback British SU carburetors hopelessly out of sync once again? Those two little mechanical dinosaurs were the only real problem in his otherwise wonderful but clearly oddball automobile, a Volvo 1800 ES. To most people the car embodied conflicting concepts — a two-seater sports car bolted to a station wagon rear end. To Sandy, its weird curves and specific Swedish strangeness endowed the machine with charm and character. But to Sandy's father and boss, Nathan Klein, the damn thing was an embarrassment. This was a leased car, a company car, the old man had argued so many times; it represented the company in public, as did Sandy. "What does that car say about the company?" Nat demanded. "A *mishugena* company." A corporate *mensch* would drive a Cadillac. Or a Lincoln. Even a Volvo sedan would have been acceptable. But a pile of crap, a little of this, a little of that, a curved and square piece of hard-to-service Swedish steel, this was not the machine for a young executive on the rise. And Nat was right, which was precisely the reason Sandy loved the car. It was the last symbol of his long-vanished passionate past, his one connection to the time when his career had been totally outside of the family business and had sparkled with success. Life had felt vivid then, and every day had brought new excitement. The

6

Volvo was like a nostalgic drug, a tranquilizer, softening, if only slightly, the humiliating, colorless, everyday grind of being the youngest son working for and enslaved by the family-owned Vita-Line factory, the third-largest manufacturer of solid, gelatin capsule vitamins in the entire United States.

As the endless line of automobiles idled toward Sunset Boulevard, Sandy felt as if some sadist had arranged the worst traffic jam in history just to drive him over the brink and kill him. Any other day he wouldn't have cared. What difference would a small delay have made? If anything, it would have improved his mood by promising to shorten his twelve-hour sentence at the vitamin factory. But on this June morning, Sandy needed not only to move but to fly. If that weren't possible, then he wanted to ram the car in front of him. Instead of a Volvo I should have bought a fucking war surplus Sherman tank, Sandy lamented, fantasizing about stomping on the throttle, climbing over and crushing any shithead stupid enough to get in his way.

Then he noticed the virtually empty northbound lane on the other side of the forbidden double yellow lines. The fading paint in the center of the street seemed to call out, Shoot out over me and pass all those idiots; why be a dumb sheep and wait in line when the road is open for a man gutsy enough to take risks? But before he had time to consider such an impulse further, the traffic surged forward and Sandy broke free of the near gridlock, turning left onto Sunset Boulevard.

Mashing the accelerator to the floor, Sandy stressed the little four-cylinder engine to the limit and, with the grace of Sterling Moss in his prime, began snaking the Volvo in and around the eastbound traffic. Within moments the palm trees of Beverly Hills vanished from his rearview mirror as West Hollywood surrounded him with the flash of Sunset Strip. At Sunset Plaza Drive, Sandy flicked on his turn signal, cranked a radical left, and accelerated up through the manicured neighborhood lining the narrow, curved street. As the elevation increased, the houses became more secluded and rustic, less suburban. Near the top, where Sandy again flipped on his left-turn signal, the character of the street changed into something almost junglelike, with huge pine trees and overgrown vegetation concealing the houses as well as their occupants from the curiosity of passersby.

With a twist of the steering wheel, Sandy guided the Volvo off the road and down a long, narrow asphalt driveway. He braked to a halt in front of a small, white, glass and stucco California bungalow in the style pioneered by architect Richard Neutra. With a twist of the ignition key, Sandy was out of the Volvo and banging on the shiny black enameled front door. But knock and pound as he might, no one answered. Big surprise.

In seconds, Sandy shifted his attention to the side of the house, where he climbed the wooden gate into the tiny grass-covered yard and worked his way around the living room to the steel-framed sliding glass windows, which he knew were always left unlocked. With one back-breaking shove, the floor-to-ceiling sheet of glass rolled open. Without the slightest hesitation, Sandy slipped inside and hurried past the black Steinway grand piano and racks of professional recording equipment.

As Sandy had expected, the bedroom door was closed. And, of course, another loud series of knocks elicited no reponse. So Sandy twisted the knob and pushed open the door. Inside, the heavily curtained bedroom was as dark as a crypt, and Sandy stood without moving for nearly thirty seconds while his eyes adjusted. What he finally saw was hardly surprising. On the king-sized bed lay Billy, alone and asleep, snoring up a storm.

"Billy," Sandy said softly.

But the man didn't move. Sandy knelt down and gently tugged at the thin arm hanging out over the sheet.

"Billy," again he muttered softly, "I need to talk to you."

Grasping the dangling arm, Sandy gave it the kind of forceful shake a corpse would have had trouble ignoring.

"God damn it, get up. I don't have time to screw around. I have to talk to you!"

Slowly one eyelid opened halfway to reveal a bloodshot eyeball. The brain, only marginally connected to the eyeball, sent a reluctant message to its vocal cords: "What time is it?"

"Almost eight."

Billy groaned, slammed shut the eye, rolled over, and buried himself, face down, in his pillow. "Sandy, it's the middle of the god-damn night; get out of here and leave me alone."

Sandy nodded that he understood, walked to the curtains, and yanked open the double-layer blackout fabric. Through the enormous floor-to-ceiling picture windows, intense June sunlight blasted into the bedroom, transforming it from a dark cave into a brilliant, over-exposed hothouse.

"Why are you doing this to me?" Billy wailed as he tried to escape by burying himself under his pillow.

"We have to talk."

"Please. Close the curtains. Let me sleep a few more hours. Be reasonable."

"No, I need to talk *now*."

Sandy did not have to wait long for the pillow to slide off Billy's head. Slowly the half-asleep man dragged himself up into a sitting position and squinted against the bright light, trying to get a better look at his friend. The anguish in Sandy's voice had aroused Billy's curiosity.

"So, I'm listening. Happy?"

"I want you to tell me, moment by moment, everything you remember about what we did last night." Sandy spoke in the tone of voice a professor would use to intimidate a lazy student.

"You're kiddin' me."

"No . . . I'm . . . not."

"*No . . . I'm . . . not?* Who shoved a bug up your ass this morning?"

"Look, I want you to tell me what you saw happen last night."

Billy stared at his friend. The question, no matter how it was viewed, just didn't ring true. "Wait a second. You're trying to tell me that instead of going to work you came here and woke me up in the middle of the night just to gossip about what I saw happen a few hours ago — which you already know all about. What the hell is wrong with you?"

"Listen, I have my reasons. Just go along with me."

"You had a blackout, didn't you?" Billy spoke sympathetically, as if suddenly his friend's crazy behavior made sense.

Sandy shook his head. "I'll explain my reasons later. Just tell me, from the time I met you, what you saw me do." He had to hand it to Billy. For a skinny, pale, out-of-shape thirty-five-year-old both inspired and damaged by an extended overindulgence in Russian vodka, the son-of-a-bitch was damn perceptive.

"You've never had a blackout before, have you?"

Sandy admitted nothing.

"All you can do is relax, forget about it, and stop beating yourself up. It comes with the territory. If you choose to remain serious about boozing, blackouts happen."

"I still want to know the details of last night."

"You drank too much."

"Asshole, that I know. What I did *while I drank too much* is what I want to know."

"What's the last thing you remember?"

"The El Padrino Room and two JB, rocks."

"You have no memory of leaving the Beverly Wilshire Hotel?"

Sandy shook his head.

"We got in our cars. You followed me up to Sunset."

Sandy obviously drew a blank.

"Sneaky Pete's?"

Again Sandy came up with a zero.

"How about driving down Melrose?"

Again nothing came to mind.

"Does the Studio Bar and Grill mean anything to you?"

"You're kidding."

Billy shook his head. "You just had to go there. What a disaster."

"Why?"

"It was bad enough last night — don't make me go through it again. You don't want to know. Trust me."

"The fuck I don't want to know. God damn it, Billy." Sandy exploded in anger. "Why do you think I came over here? I want to know. And I want to know *now!*"

Impressed by Sandy's uncharacteristic passion, Billy nodded, then slowly drew himself up out of bed. "Lemme take a piss first. Then I'll give you every gory detail I know."

Sandy followed Billy into the spacious carpeted bathroom. Not a word was spoken as the naked Billy stood over the toilet bowl, trying unsuccessfully to pee. Sandy couldn't help wondering if the last few years had been as cruel to his own body as they obviously had been to the gaunt package of skin and bones that called itself Billy Hoyle.

"Would you mind leaving me alone for just a minute? I mean, I'll tell you what I know, but I need to piss in peace."

Sandy nodded, left the bathroom, and stood just outside the door. Seconds later the sound of streaming water broke the silence. Billy peed and peed. Enough fluid seemed to flow out of him to fill every reservoir in the city. Such a thing just can't be true, Sandy told himself. Seconds stretched out into hours. A cup of liquid became an ocean.

"Do you remember meeting a woman?" Billy called out from the bathroom.

Instantly Sandy was standing by the sink as Billy flushed the toilet.

"What woman?"

"She was Danish. Good looking. Tall, with long, dark brown, very straight hair. Tan. Bone thin, like a model. She wore blue jeans and a jeans jacket over a very thin, very tight black silk shirt. On anyone else the clothes would have looked hippylike. But on her, talk about sexy — I mean, if you like cold women. And we're referring here to a high-output Frigidaire with no defrost cycle. Chill and glamour, with skin made of pink stainless steel, the epitome of cool. Any of this coming back to you?"

Sandy could recollect nothing.

"Her name was . . . was . . . Let me think . . . Yes . . . Erica. That was it. With the i pronounced *eee*. Er-*eee*-ka. She made us both repeat it until we got it right. You don't remember that either?"

Sandy shook his head.

"She was sitting beside you at the bar with her back to us. I thought she was with the man next to her. Maybe she was. But he left and she stayed. You were into one of your Auschwitz harangues. Really into it, going over all the horrors. In fact, you were so into it you didn't notice her until she interrupted you with the remark that in Denmark her grandfather hid Jews on his farm throughout the war. There was a meat shortage, which he got around by raising rabbits. All Erica ate as a kid was rabbit. That's what she remembers about the Jews and the war — rabbit eaters. She thought it had something to do with kosher. Only when she was a teenager did she understand the real reasons. This interested you a lot. Now are any bells starting to ring?"

"Zero."

Avoiding any hint of judgment, Billy nodded, quickly rinsed off his face, then led Sandy back into the bedroom and dressed while continuing to talk. "The two of you really hit it off. Anyone else would have called it love at first sight, but I knew the truth — it was love at first gas chamber. All you could talk about was death camps. The Holocaust. Nazis. You kept drinking, I kept drinking, she kept drinking. This discussion about torture and death seemed to make you hot for each other. It was such a passionate connection that it made me a little jealous. The only reason I wasn't a lot jealous was because I could see that Erica was a deadly serious person. Women without a sense of humor bother me, as you know."

Sandy nodded for him to go on.

"Anyhow, she seemed real interested in your spiel about the Holocaust being 'the most significant and meaningful event of the twentieth century.' But what fascinated her even more was the way you were so obsessed by it. You don't remember this either, hm?"

"Go on," was all Sandy could say.

"It didn't take a clairvoyant to see that something about your preoccupation aroused some really weird part of her. Like I said, the vibes I felt coming off of Erica weren't for me; but you were gone, off with her on a marathon verbal romp through all the concentration camps. The more she talked, the more I was sure she was into some very strange stuff, like whips, chains, and leather. Not *my* sort of style. But I'm not one to judge."

"The fuck you're not," Sandy blurted out in anger before he regained control of himself and waited for his friend to continue.

"I just don't know what to think about your preoccupation with all this death camp stuff. Yes, it's interesting. Yes, it's important. But I mean, shit, it was thirty years ago. You were only a baby. It just isn't right that you spend so much time going over and over all those horrors. Honestly Sandy, what it is in you that's so drawn by Auschwitz I don't understand. Think about it. You connect with a humorless, sadistic woman. All you talk about is torture and mass deaths. Is it really so outrageous for me to jump to the conclusion of you being into whips and chains?"

"I think you're right," Sandy replied sarcastically, "I've got to be a masochist to have you as my only friend. I care about things. I have interests. I try to see the world in the big picture. And you have the mind of a cesspool."

"Sandy," Billy began, attempting to placate his friend's rage.

"Go *Sandy* someone else. Don't you understand? I see the whole fucking culture collapsing around us. Things bother me. *Little things* like the Nazis not being punished for their war crimes. Thirty years ago those Germans butchered Jews by the millions, but today you and everyone else sees it as ancient history, like some atrocity committed by the pharaohs in Egypt. Well, it is *not* ancient history. It was fucking yesterday. And, contrary to your mathematics, both you and I were alive, here, while six thousand miles away the SS was converting living Jews into fertilizer. So just because you don't care, don't fucking mock me for what I believe. Is that clear?"

"Yes. I'm sorry." Billy spoke after a brief hesitation. "You're right. Forgive me. But you do have to understand you woke me up and you want to have a serious discussion when I'm too sleepy to remember my own name."

"Yeah, well, you've done pretty good so far. What happened after my conversation at the bar with Erica?"

"You left."

"With her?"

Billy nodded.

"Where did we go?"

"I assumed your house. Or was it hers?"

"Do you know where *hers* was?"

Billy shrugged his shoulders.

"You really don't know?"

"Honest to God, Sandy. The two of you walked out the door and that was the last I saw of you until ten minutes ago."

Sandy didn't move. It was an apparent dead end. What could he do now? He was beyond frustration, beyond grief, into the familiar territory of paralyzing despair. As much as he wanted to act, to find out, to uncover the culprit and obtain justice, he simply did not know where to turn.

"Look," Billy advised sympathetically, "don't worry so much about the blackout; it's the cost of drinking. You want to avoid 'em in the future, ease off on your intake. And as a serious boozer who knows, let me tell you, you're not cut out to be a drinker. It's just not you, no matter how many scotches you tossed down last night. Slow down and you won't have a problem. It's really not so serious."

"The blackout is not what's bothering me; it's what I did *during* the blackout," Sandy confessed grimly.

"What's the difference? If you can't remember, it doesn't matter."

"I remember enough," Sandy said quietly.

"Hey," Billy tried to be cheerful, "you went to a bar, picked up a beautiful woman, and went back to her place and fucked her. You had a good time. She had a good time. No one got hurt. It's not like you haven't done it before. So what's suddenly so horrendous?"

Sandy studied his friend. As close as they were, as long as they'd known each other, the truth was too humiliating to admit.

"It's not something I want to talk about," he answered after much hesitation.

"Sandy, this is Billy here. Your friend. If you can't talk to me, you can't talk to anyone. *Capice?*"

"That just may be."

"Aw, come on. It can't be that bad."

"Can't it?"

"Listen bozo," Billy grinned, "I've lived all my life in Hollywood. Nothing surprises me. What is it? Heroin? S and M? *Ménage a trois?"*

Sandy said nothing.

"I know. Back at her apartment your woman had 'a friend,' and your one night stand turned into a homosexual experience. Hey, Sandy, it's okay. I understand these things, believe me. You were drunk as a skunk. It's perfectly understandable. That's why you're unable to remember — you're unconsciously trying to protect yourself by blocking out your actions."

"Billy, don't be a jerk. I did *not* have a homosexual experience. Or any of those other things. No, what I did was much worse. Truly."

"Oh, now I understand. Yes. You were drunk, and you were driving. You hit someone, didn't you? A pedestrian. You got scared, panicked, and ran, is that it?"

"I only wish. That I would understand."

"Well, what is it? I'm your friend, remember? I want to help you. Won't you let me?"

"You'll be disgusted and make fun of me."

"Never." Billy shook his head with convincing gravity, assuaging Sandy's fears.

"Okay. I'm going to show you something. But you must never tell anyone about it. Do you promise?"

"My word of honor."

"What do you think of this?"

Billy waited as Sandy unbuttoned the cuff of his shirt, rolled the material back, and thrust out his forearm.

"When I woke up this morning, this is what I found."

For some time, Billy stared at the tattooed numbers.

"I don't understand."

"It's a tattoo," Sandy whispered.

"That I can see."

"Well, the fucking thing wasn't there when I met you last night at the El Padrino Room!" Sandy's voice had a definite hysterical edge.

Billy remained calm while continuing to examine the tattoo. "You really don't remember where you got this?"

"If I did, what the hell do you think I'd be doing here this morning?"

"*A7549653,*" Billy read aloud. "What do the numbers stand for?"

"You don't know?" Sandy was incredulous. Was his friend stonewalling, or had he suddenly become retarded?

"If I knew, why would I ask?"

"Jesus, for a guy the commercial directors keep calling a musical genius, sometimes I really worry about you."

"You worry about me?" Billy asked sarcastically. "Who's the one that doesn't remember where he got the god-damn tattoo on his arm?"

The truth punctured Sandy's self-righteousness. "You've really never seen one of these?" he asked.

Billy shook his head.

"What you are looking at is an exact copy of the numbers the Nazis tattooed on their slave laborers at Auschwitz. This is a concentration camp identification number."

Uncharacteristically somber, Billy once again studied the neatly tattooed blue numbers and letter. A strange contortion of his jaw indicated that he was undergoing a serious reappraisal of the situation. Patiently, Sandy waited for an option. Even the slightest clue would be a godsend.

But instead of volunteering information, Billy looked up at Sandy's face, then suddenly turned, bolted from the bedroom, charged across the living room, and disappeared into the kitchen.

This bizarre behavior puzzled Sandy. Was Billy suddenly sick? Sandy had known drinkers who woke up in the morning nauseated, occasionally vomiting. But it could also be that Billy was suffering from a psychic disgust and moral revulsion prompted by the blasphemy of the tattoo. That made more sense; simply put, Billy was grossed out.

Adopting his most humble and least frightening demeanor, Sandy prowled quietly through the house. If a person is hysterical and panicked, he told himself, it's essential to behave calmly. Reassurance was the order of the day, no matter how crazed he himself felt. The bottom line, as his father was always pointing out, was to get what he needed, which in this case was the help of his one and only friend.

In the kitchen Billy stood with his back to the open doorway, gulping from a tumbler of tap water. Although his face wasn't visible, Sandy had no doubt from Billy's posture that he was experiencing unbearable anxiety — the man was scared.

"Billy, listen, I'm sorry. I didn't mean to make you crazy. I know it's shocking. That's how I felt when I woke up this morning. It's why I came over. Just take it easy for a minute and you'll get used to the idea. But don't run away again. I need your help."

With his back still to Sandy, Billy turned on the tap, let the cold water run for a moment into the deep stainless steel sink, refilled his glass, and quickly drank it down.

"You're doing the right thing. Have another sip of water. Let the news digest. It's not as bad as it seems. It's like any other horror in life. Remember when Kennedy was shot, how terrible that seemed? I thought I'd never get over it. For months I anguished over that wonderful man with a bullet through his brain. Who really did it? And why? Was it Oswald, the KGB, Castro, or the CIA? Over and over I reviewed the facts, the Warren Commission, the various conspiracy theories, yadda, yadda, yadda. Today it's history. Everything shocking eventually becomes history. Just like the concentration camps. One day this tattoo will be nothing. So go easy on yourself."

"I'm trying," Billy muttered. "If you only knew how hard."

Sandy waited as Billy took another deep swallow, then turned to face his friend. Instead of terror, Billy's face was contorted with the expressions of a man working to suppress an absolutely uncontrollable fit of hysterics.

"I want to be serious," Billy spoke through a mouthful of water. "But I can't." With that remark, the bizarre and ridiculous nature of Sandy's predicament flooded through him and Billy involuntarily coughed, spraying Sandy with a mouthful of water, then began a howl of spontaneous, primitive, gut-wrenching laughter. "It's so fitting," he spoke between convulsions of glee, "a fucking concentration camp tattoo."

As the memory of that blue, hand-lettered image took hold of Billy's imagination, the volley of giggles escalated into a roar that seemed to Sandy to mock his very existence. What could he say to a reaction so unexpected, so insulting, so bizarre?

"For a solid year now that's all you've been talking about," Billy continued, regaining control of himself. "Auschwitz, the SS, Dachau, Bergen-Beldson . . ."

"*Bel*sen," Sandy corrected his pronunciation.

"*Bel*sen, okay. Thank you. That's just the beginning of the list. The Brown Shirts, selections, the Angel of Death, the Irgun, the Displaced Persons Act; I could go on for an hour. Every book you 'discovered' I had to hear about in detail. Every book was a *must read*. How long have I been telling you to drop this obsession?"

Sandy, stunned, said nothing.

"But you wouldn't listen. No, you went further and further, digging your way into that nightmare. And now look what you've done to yourself." Billy gestured at the tattoo.

Sandy remained silent.

"Enough is enough." Billy wiped tears from his eyes, regaining control of his rebellious, embarrassing emotions and speaking seriously. "Look, I more than anyone know what you've gone through the last few years. No one should have to suffer like you have. But Sandy, the past is the past and you can't keep living in it. End this focus on death. As much as I hate to say this again, I'm going to, and for the five hundredth time — Rachael is dead and gone and no matter how much you keep driving yourself to hook up with the nature of mortality itself you're *not* going to bring her back. Drop this death camp obsession. And do it today." Again he pointed to Sandy's tattoo. "You see where it's leading. Take that as a warning."

Infuriated by his friend's presumption, Sandy hesitated before speaking. Running through his mind were all the fun and exciting ways he could murder Billy. Which would be most enjoyable? Fifty rounds from a machine gun? Hack him to death with an axe? Squeeze him against a building with the bumper of a dump truck? Such fantasies did their job, and Sandy's reason returned relatively intact.

"You can't tell me anything else about last night?" He spoke in a calm, affectless tone of voice.

"If I knew something, you know I'd tell you."

"Thanks, you've been a really great friend," Sandy said sarcastically. "Next time you need help, remind me how useful and sympathetic you were this morning." Without waiting for an answer, he swiveled and headed out the front door.

"Sandy! I'm sorry," Billy yelled. "Have a sense of humor."

Fuck you and your sense of humor, Sandy fumed as he slammed the door shut. Crossing the oil-spotted driveway to his Volvo, Sandy heard a distinct volley of that revolting, uncontrolled, hysterical laughter briefly erupt from Billy's kitchen. Torch the asshole's house and turn it into a fabulous, two-thousand-degree, flaming funeral pyre, he fantasized as he shifted the stiff transmission into reverse and cranked the steering wheel in preparation for backing up the steep, narrow driveway. But as he was about to engage the clutch, the blue numbers on his arm again caught and compelled his total attention.

A7549653 — the reality of the thing demanded answers. What the hell was it doing there? More than a drunken prank, worse than a public disgrace, to a Jew those numbers and that single letter constituted a crime of unparalleled proportions. It couldn't be laughed off as a joke. Nor could it be explained as some aberration of postadolescent rebellion. Playing games with such a tattoo was the equivalent of urinating on the memory of each and every one of the six million Jews slaughtered by the Nazis. What was on his arm wasn't art, a fashion statement, or even the bitter humor of a drunk. As Sandy stared at the pale blue brand he knew exactly what the encoded message cried out to him. SUICIDE, it translated.

Attempting to obliterate this terrible insight, Sandy tried to focus on the physical nature of tattoos in general. In truth, he found them disgusting — self-mutilations acted out by masochistic, antisocial losers seeking pathetic mechanical routes to perverse senses of individual identity. Show me a tattoo, Sandy believed, and I'll show you someone who hates himself. Unfortunately, this train of thought led him straight back to the very thing he was trying to avoid. It didn't take a genius to see that his self-esteem was at an all-time low. Did he view himself as one of life's losers, a wino in an Italian sport coat, a Hell's Angel in orthopedic shoes? A sociologist might be happy with that explanation, but not Sandy. Depressed? Yes. Thoughts of suicide? Certainly. What sane person didn't have them? It wasn't as if life was so wonderful for anyone. No, the explanation for the tattoo had to be more complex. Perhaps, he told himself, he was looking at the thing in the wrong way. Instead of a curse, maybe the little letter and numbers were actually a key capable of unlocking the mystery of his long-standing grief, despair, and depression.

Such a promising idea gave Sandy enough of a lift to let him rebutton his shirt sleeve, back up out of Billy's driveway, and accelerate down Sunset Boulevard onto the freeway toward Glendale and the Vita-Line factory.

During the twenty-minute drive Sandy worked hard to deny Billy's observations. Instead of behaving like a trusted friend, he had acted like a sadist. The remark about Rachael had been particularly offensive — useless advice from an alcoholic pop musician and twisted amateur psychiatrist. How could the bastard have mentioned Rachael, Sandy's brilliant, beautiful daughter who had died three years earlier when a five-thousand-pound Buick Electra slammed into her tricycle? Was he just supposed to forget that the police investigation had called it "an accident," and said that no one was at fault, that Rachael had simply shot out of the driveway into the street on her new, over-sized tricycle just as the Buick was speeding by? Could Sandy dismiss the fact that he had bought her that trike only one week earlier? According to Billy, even the question of blame was to be forgotten. How could Anne, Sandy's wife and Rachael's mother, ever be forgiven for her gross lack of attention? She had been home, on the phone, and had let Rachael ride that damn tricycle alone in the driveway, "Just for one minute." No, Billy was asking too much.

3

By his father's standards, Sandy's ten a.m. arrival in the parking lot of the Vita-Line plant would be yet another in a long line of embarrassments that he had caused the family. Nat Klein was from the old school; he believed that the two sons who worked for him — Sandy and his thirty-nine-year-old brother Ed — should set an example for the rest of the employees and be at their desks at least fifteen minutes before the first shift started at seven-thirty a.m.

This was no trouble for the goody-goody Ed, who hit the parking lot each morning at seven. But Sandy had informed Nat long ago that it was crazy for him to roll in that early when none of the distributors ever phoned before nine. Sandy had argued that it would actually be destructive to plant morale for him to sit around for an hour and a half eating doughnuts and drinking coffee, waiting for the phone to ring. It would only lead the other employees to believe that what counted at the plant was not productive work, but merely putting in time.

Nat's angry response had been to demand that Sandy arrive at seven-fifteen, go into his own office, shut the door, and at least *give the impression* that he was busy. This, like so many other issues, resulted in a father-son stalemate, one more small unresolved skirmish on an enormous battlefield of long-standing differences. As a result Sandy seldom pulled in before seven-thirty, and Nat's never-ending irritation percolated just below the boiling point.

The business of the Klein family was vitamins — A's, B's, C's, D's, E's, and the latest rage, megadoses of B-12. Two brand new, state-of-the-art, incredibly expensive, custom engineered and constructed, computer-controlled, stainless steel marvels of automated machinery punched out solid gelatin capsules at such an extraordinary rate that this one plant was able to supply twenty percent of the entire country's vitamin needs. Nat Klein had

21

taken a huge financial risk in funding the development of these innovative machines, and the gamble had paid off. Because he owned the patents, no other pharmaceutical company could compete. As a result, Nat's unit costs on vitamins were the cheapest in the world. Eighty-five percent of the plant's production run was contract work, manufacturing capsules sold on the retail level through major pharmaceutical corporations under well-known national brand names. This work — the lucrative corporate contracting — was Nat and Ed's special domain. The other fifteen percent of the plant's output was Sandy's exclusive responsibility — Vita-Line Vitamins, a private label line of supplements marketed nationally by a network of distributors and sales reps through health food stores and independent pharmacies.

What a time to be in the forefront of the vitamin manufacturing business! With the health boom engulfing the country, orders were pouring in at such an unprecedented rate that Nat, Ed, and Sandy would have had to be complete incompetents not to benefit from the windfall. And since all of them were quite capable, profits accumulated out of all proportion to the accountants' most optimistic forecasts.

For Sandy, the massive success of the business was both good and bad. On the positive side, he received a small but much-needed salary increase. In addition, the exploding sales figures had an exhilarating effect on Nat's emotional state: Instead of bullying Sandy all the time, over the last six months the old man had reduced his agenda to intermittent torture. The bad side of the deal was that, given the dramatic increase in orders, it would only be a matter of months until the plant moved from two shifts into round-the-clock production. At that point Sandy feared the last remnants of his personal life would be over — that he would have to give up his house, set up a cot in his office, and kiss off any activity other than work.

A glint of brilliant sunlight reflecting off the highly polished chrome of Nat's gleaming white-on-white Cadillac De Ville awakened Sandy from his reverie. He was still sitting in his Volvo, late and daydreaming. Opening his door carefully, he slithered out from between his own car and Nat's block-long Cadillac replete with every option from continental kit to 1920s wider-than-wide whitewalls. In Nat's eyes the car had real class. To Sandy, his father drove a ghetto pimp's dream machine.

Parked on the other side of the Caddy was Ed's compromise with luxury — a powerful, prestigious, and highly unreliable British-built Jensen Interceptor — a model of Anglo engineering that would overheat at the merest hint of bumper-to-bumper traffic. In his heart, Ed lusted after a Mercedes. Even a BMW would have been preferable. But Nat had an iron-clad rule that no Klein could ever break: Never, ever buy, lease, or rent anything manufactured, sold, or in any way touched by anyone in or from Germany. If it was German, it was forbidden — no exceptions permitted, no discussion possible.

Nat's absolute hatred of Germany was not mysterious. It was the country where he had been born and the nation that had murdered most of his family during World War II. If it had been up to Nat, Germany would have been isolated forever under armed-guard prison-camp conditions and prevented from ever dealing with or pretending to be part of the civilized world. The Second World War had proven that the Germans had no place among the decent nations of Western democracies. Next to them, Attila the Hun looked like an innocent *bar mitzvah* boy. No, Nat would argue, the Germans now held the record for the most barbaric, disgusting, and inhuman behavior of all time. No country had butchered more women and children or committed more atrocities against innocent civilians than the once-exalted culture of Germany. When put to the test, they had displayed their true nature with twelve unrelenting years of rape, slaughter, torture, and mass murder.

And what did the free world do to punish this nation of criminals? Nat had so often raged. After the Nuremberg trials a few German generals were hanged from the gallows. *Big fucking deal.* Fifty-five million human beings were killed during World War II. Six million Jews were exterminated amid a grief, suffering, and pain virtually unimaginable. And for all of this a handful of old German generals were publicly put to death. It was all just too god-damn disgusting.

Apparently in the minds of Eisenhower, Churchill, Stalin, and Truman, the few executed Nazi leaders cleansed the German nation of its crimes and cleared the way for the Marshall Plan to flood the reborn Deutschland with truckloads of cash. Did rebuilding and modernizing the bombed-out industries set an example for the world that would prevent other nations from emulating the Nazis in the future? *Some punishment.* In Nat's view, it was all one overwhelmingly sick joke. In real life, he would ask, what were the consequences of the Nazis' crimes other than establishing a line of credit long enough to completely rebuild and modernize all of Germany's industries, from factories to mass housing? It was a variation on the old "crime pays" idea. In this case, the lesson read: Kill enough Jews and the free world will rain cash on your nation. Could a logical person come to any other conclusion?

Not only did Nat never buy anything German, he personally tormented anyone who did. Among his friends and business acquaintances, Nat's anti-German diatribes were so well known that those who owned German cars always drove the family Chevy station wagon whenever they gave him a ride. God forbid they should show up in a Mercedes. Not only would Nat not get in the car; after a long harangue he would force the friend into the Cadillac and lecture him on twentieth-century German history. Hearing Nat postulate that Hitler's Mercedes was upholstered in tanned Jews' skin did nothing to relieve the tension of a long freeway business trip.

Sandy often wondered if Nat's diatribes ever really accomplished anything other than to aggravate his friends. The way they put up with Nat always amazed Sandy. But he was thankful that at least some of Nat's rage siphoned off in the direction of the Germans and away from its usual target, his youngest son. Sometimes Sandy felt almost grateful for the Nazis' brutality. Had the SS not existed, there would have been nothing to deflect his father's aggression.

His thoughts reminded Sandy of the tattoo. After checking his shirt sleeve to make sure that the cuff was securely buttoned,

Sandy knew he could no longer avoid facing the music. He was late, and Nat would make him suffer for it.

The Vita-Line building was immaculately white and modest in appearance, a one-story concrete block structure erected in the 1950s, indistinguishable from thousands of similar industrial constructions. From its exterior facade, no casual observer could have determined its purpose. It might have housed anything from a printing plant to a condom factory. In fact, it contained a highly sophisticated, carefully monitored laboratory environment — the air filtered, the humidity rigidly maintained, the water purified, the temperature fanatically regulated. And talk about cleanliness: Every room and office was swept, washed, and sterilized to antiseptic, surgical theater standards. The walls were soundproofed; air locks divided the production area from the office and shipping departments. From the chemical labs to the palleted drying vaults, everything was up to the minute and state of the art. Despite all this technology, the place reeked of the sour odor of freshly manufactured gelatin capsules. To Sandy, entering the plant from the street was a sensory experience rather like taking a plunge down the throat of an ulcer victim who'd just gulped a pepperoni and anchovy pizza.

That particular morning with his burning, tattooed arm, head pounding from the hangover, and stomach still protesting the periodic attacks of needle-sharp gas pains, the shock of entering the plant nauseated Sandy. It took every ounce of his diminishing self-control to keep from vomiting.

"Good morning, Mister Klein," the receptionist called across the empty waiting room.

Sandy smiled mechanically, swallowing the rising lump in his throat, and hurried toward the air locks protecting the environment of the inner plant. To slow down would mean chit-chat and gossip with Irene, who at fifty was his father's longest-serving employee. She might also notice something wrong. Were that to happen, the news would pass at the speed of light to Nat, with who knew what nasty consequence. Irene had her good points (honesty and loyalty), but she also had massive drawbacks as far as Sandy was concerned. Rumor had it that she rented a nest somewhere near the plant where she slept, lacquered her hair, and applied her makeup. But if he hadn't known better, Sandy would have assumed she never left her seat at the reception desk switchboard. Irene arrived every morning before Sandy and stayed long after he went home. Maybe she has no apartment, he reflected. Maybe she just sleeps on the reception room floor like an old family dog. All she talked about was the Klein family. And she knew everything, which was another reason she worried Sandy. Irene behaved as if she were his mother, entitled to every detail of his and everyone else's private life. Were she to find out about the number on his arm, she would flash that information to the world faster than he could walk down the corridor to his cubbyhole of an office.

With a satisfying clunk, the air locks sealed the door shut and he was safely out of Irene's reach, inside the working plant. The cool, dark, dry hallway always reminded him of a desert night, a kind of nocturnal indoor Palm Springs. Opening an unmarked door, Sandy slipped into his small, sparsely decorated, windowless office. Aside from his gray metal desk, telephone, and wall-to-wall files, he was absolutely alone. With no view, he had nothing to look at except his work. (Nat didn't believe in the distraction of windows.) On most days, arriving in this mushroom farm of an office was grim. But this morning, Sandy was just grateful to have made it in without running into his father or brother. It wasn't much, but it was the first good news of the day.

On his desk, an intimidating stack of orders and invoices awaited Sandy's verification and signature. As he dug in, he thought of the bizarre and irrational market he was serving. Across the country and around the world, human beings had gone vitamin crazy, frantically swallowing the pretty capsules by the handful. Obviously the fuel for this fever was the wish to live not simply healthier but longer, perhaps even forever. "Take megadoses of vitamins and never die" was the unspoken fantasy. Never fucking die, what a joke, Sandy muttered to himself. Vitamins or not, everything died; hadn't the general public heard of entropy?

In the popular unconscious, vitamins had taken over the place once dominated by religion. Instead of a *hereafter,* the priests of health promised a far more vivid and interesting eternity in the concrete *here.* "Eat right, exercise, and you too can live for a hundred years." Even better for the Kleins, heaven and the afterlife were now produced at the family plant in Glendale, approved and regulated by the FDA. "Immortality for only $19.95 a month," Sandy had once joked, mocking a more cautious advertising slogan of the Vita-Line megadose multivitamin.

Unfortunately, all this cynicism was not useful in helping Sandy get down to work. Ten o'clock crawled eventually to ten-ten. After what felt like hours, his next glance at the clock revealed the time to be ten-fourteen. His mind was racing and his concentration shot. As he struggled to verify an invoice against an order, all the letters and numbers on the pages began to dance in front of his eyes, blur, and lose all meaning. No matter how hard he tried to focus on the invoices, the only figures he could understand or remember were those in the sequence he so longed to forget, the terrifying *A7549653.*

Quickly unbuttoning his sleeve, he rolled back the cuff. Staring up at him from his forearm, exactly as he had anticipated, was that horrible enigma, *A7549653,* as blue, vivid, and frightening as ever. Contemplating this vision, Sandy felt overcome by a compulsion to head for the nearest hardware store, purchase the largest, sharpest butcher knife available, and liberate himself from that offensive, alien tattooed arm. But a heavy footstep from the corridor and the sudden opening of his door interrupted his self-mutilation fantasies. It was his brother — barging in, as usual, unannounced.

"Well, well," Ed gloated, "if it isn't his majesty himself, finally out of bed. I hope whoever she was, she was worth it and you humped her good because Dad's been waiting to talk to you since seven-thirty and he's pissed off."

In one smooth move, Sandy leaned down under his desk, pretending to pick something up off the floor and throw it in the wastebasket, while surreptitiously buttoning his cuff to conceal

the tattoo. Sitting back up in his chair, he faced his brother.
"What's so important?"

"He wants you to hear it from him."

"You wouldn't like to help me out with a little preview?"
Slowly Sandy's heart rate descended from an adrenaline-induced
machine-gun rate to a more normal idle of seventy as he realized
that Ed had seen nothing. Sandy's brother might be hostile,
competitive, and a fundamental lifetime rival, but at least he
wasn't observant. In fact, Ed had little awareness of almost
anything other than money, as his conventional appearance
reminded Sandy—white button-down shirt, charcoal tie, and
immaculately pressed gray cotton slacks. He was a walking ad for
Brooks Brothers, California-style.

"Sorry." The word and gesture of open hands meant nothing,
certainly not an apology.

"Ed, gimme a break, will you? I had a lot of problems this
morning. Help me out for once, why not?"

"This isn't about me—this is Dad. Now he's waiting; you
coming?"

"Do I have a choice?"

Ed grinned with sadistic pleasure, swiveled around and led
Sandy out into the corridor and down the hall. At the heavy,
vault-like, walnut door labeled "Nathan Klein, President," Ed
stopped, knocked once, swung the door open, and gestured for
his brother to enter. At that moment, being forced into the gas
chamber at Auschwitz would have aroused only slightly less
pleasure in Sandy.

4

At the far end of the impressive office, behind an enormous, hand-carved desk, the old man himself sat with his back to the door. Nat Klein was on the phone, passionately *hondeling* over some minor negotiation while staring at the huge photo-mural mounted on the wall behind his desk. It was a gigantic, beautifully lit, superbly hand colored enlargement of Ansel Adam's spectacular, fog-shrouded photo of Yosemite's Half Dome, a remarkable image of the wilderness at the peak of its beauty and ruggedness. The incongruity of this particular picture never failed to strike Sandy. Who did his father think he was kidding? Old Nat would have been no more comfortable backpacking in the woods than he'd have been sweating in a steam bath in some gay West Hollywood massage parlor. But obviously somewhere deep in that gruff, battle-hardened mind, beyond business, was a private corner of Nat that loved that picture. Of course, it didn't hurt that the scene conveyed a vital, organic, healthy image that reflected positively on the company and its products. But the meaning of the photograph went deeper than money; it penetrated into Nat's heart in a sentimental way that Sandy couldn't quite figure out. Behind that ten thousand dollar desk sat a German-Jewish refugee from the Nazis who'd never in his life gone on a camping trip, or ever lived anywhere other than the most urban of neighborhoods. Nat's life was his business and his business was his life. It was inconceivable for Sandy to imagine his father in a high Sierra setting. Nat in hiking boots, down parka, and backpack was an image simply incomprehensible — about as likely as a Storm Trooper in Auschwitz converting to Hassidism and showing up for work in a *yarmulke* and *tallis*.

Before Sandy could speculate further on the meaning of the picture, Nat bellowed one last command into the phone, slammed the handpiece down, spun his chair around, and stared angrily at his youngest son. "Good of you to make time for me this morning. Or is it afternoon?"

"Morning, Dad," Sandy answered calmly, refusing to rise to the bait.

"Sandy, you punched in at nine fifty-four. You forget what time we open for business here?"

"I'm sorry," he spoke quietly and sincerely, "I had a little problem this morning. I got here as fast as I could."

"Two hours I've been waiting for you. What kind of problem could keep your father waiting two whole hours?" Although Nat spoke with virtually no trace of his original German language, the cadence of his speech was distinctly Eastern European.

"Dad, I'm not going to waste your time boring you with my petty troubles. What is it you want to see me about?"

Nat glanced at Ed, then nodded once to himself, as if to say, "I'll let it go one more time." However, the momentary Nat-to-Ed exchange confirmed what Sandy had already guessed—his father and brother were in collusion against him. The nature of this complicity was so subtle as to be unprovable to an outsider, but Sandy was forced to recognize once again exactly where he stood with both of them.

"Sit," Nat finally gestured.

Sandy sat across from his father while Ed took a seat to the side and behind, out of view.

"Sandy, I've been giving you a lot of thought lately. I'm concerned about what's happened to your life in the last couple of years, and I think I've finally figured out what the problem is."

"Dad," Sandy went rigid with anger, on full alert, "I'm here because I thought you wanted to discuss business; if and when I want to talk about *my problem,* as you call it, I'll make an appointment with a psychiatrist, thank you very much."

"You know," Nat spoke calmly, "for a smart man who prides himself on his abilities to communicate, sometimes you amaze me. Why is it so difficult to talk to you? Don't you understand that you're my son and that I care about you? Ed's your brother; he cares about you too. We're a family, Sandy. As a family we have a duty to be honest with one another. To be *honest* requires being *involved,* that's the key word this morning. That's why I wanted to talk with you. Even if you're not involved now, from your reporter days you must know what that word means."

"No, I don't have the faintest idea," Sandy replied sarcastically, rising from his chair. "Now if you don't mind, I've got to catch up on the work I missed this morning."

"Sit down; I'm not finished."

Nat's serious tone made Sandy hesitate.

"This isn't going to hurt; I guarantee it," the old man shifted gears, slipping into his most charming voice. "Sit down. What I have to tell you is a good thing, I promise."

Knowing it was only a matter of time until he had to hear it, Sandy reluctantly sat back down.

"As you know," Nat continued, "my entire life has consisted of three ingredients — the family, the community, and the business. All are separate, yet all are interdependent. Take away one and the rest mean nothing. What holds them all together is my *involvement;* what gives my life meaning is that involvement. What I figured out last night, and what troubles me, is your total *lack* of involvement. Ever since you and Anne split up, all you've done is drift. And I'm not talking here about other women — that I understand; it takes time to find someone you can really care about. No, what I'm addressing is your relationship to the family and the community. You're isolated — a hermit. You come to work, put in your time — you're hard working and responsible, that I don't deny — then you vanish. To what? To where? Who the hell knows. But I'd bet every penny I own it has nothing to do with the family or the community. Am I right?"

"Dad," Sandy smiled in his most uncombative manner, standing up again, "I appreciate your concern, but I really do have work to do."

"God, are you jumpy; what's gotten into you? Sandy, will you please sit down and have the courtesy to hear me out?"

Slowly Sandy eased himself back into his chair.

"Thank you. Now what all this is leading up to is your mother. Remember how we've talked about doing something to honor her memory?"

Sandy nodded, intrigued in spite of himself.

"Well, I finally figured out what that should be. It's something she'd be proud of, something big and important. Memorable. But I need help with it. What I want to know is, would working on a project like this interest you?"

Sandy's brain did an emotional backflip. What a question his father was asking! The old man knew that the subject of his mother was hardly neutral. For Sandy, Florence was the real thing, the greatest mother a son could possibly have had. Her death in 1967 from liver cancer had come at a terrible time for him. In a family that viewed him with both jealousy and contempt, she had been his only ally. A bastion of support, both emotionally and financially, Florence had encouraged him to dream, take chances, and live out his unconventional impulses. She had believed in risks and backed him in his efforts to break out of the mold, into a life of excitement and passion. He still felt that if she hadn't died, everything would have turned out differently for him. Would working on a project that honored her memory interest him?

"You know it would; what kind of thing are you planning?"

"It's more than a *thing,* Sandy; it's a sensational project, an institution everyone's going to admire. But it's going to take a lot of work. And that means time. If I involve you in this, will you be able to commit the kind of hours out of your busy schedule to see your mother's memorial through to completion?"

"Whatever it takes, Dad, I'll do it — you have my word. What is it you want to build?"

Nat grinned with pride at his spectacular plan. "A new wing at Beth-Israel: The Florence Klein Cancer Research Center. We're talking a state-of-the-art medical facility here — the best in the world. It's something she would have been proud of, don't you think?"

"Sounds incredible." Sandy was surprised and a little intimidated by the scale of his father's plan.

Nat nodded. "I brought it to a vote yesterday at the Beth-Israel board meeting. They loved the idea. My plan calls for us to build it and them to staff it."

"I'm impressed. I mean it."

"I hoped you would be. Your mother was a great woman. Whatever we do has to be equal to her memory."

"Tell me how I can help." As he spoke the words, an almost subliminal flash of eye contact between Nat and Ed announced to Sandy that he'd made a big mistake. This was not a spontaneous meeting after all, but another carefully rehearsed manipulation, complete with the usual intrigue and hidden agenda.

"Okay then, I have a commitment from you?"

"You do."

"Here's what I was hoping for. The way the business is growing, I'm up to my *touchus* in obligations. My big problem, as you know, is time, which I don't have any of. And that's exactly what's needed if the Florence Klein Cancer Research Center is going to move from idea to reality. What I'm proposing, I want you to consider seriously before you answer."

Sandy nodded for Nat to continue.

"Ed came up with this idea and I think it's a brilliant solution. That is, if you agree."

Sandy said nothing, but every alarm in his brain went off at the mention of his brother's name.

"Instead of me being the organizer of the cancer center, why don't you take charge of it? *You* meet with the hospital and the doctors. *You* discuss it with the board. *You* find the architect. *You* make it your baby and carry the ball for the family. If you think it needs more money than I'm contributing, *you* raise it. What I'm suggesting is that you see the whole thing through to completion. Would you be willing to do all this for your mother?"

Sandy nodded, both flattered by and wary of the authority suddenly being offered to him.

"You understand the ground rules," Nat continued. "This is the family name we're talking about here. I want absolutely no screwing around. If you can't commit to a hundred and ten percent effort I don't want you getting near the project, is that clear?"

Again Sandy nodded. "I'd be proud to do it. You don't have to worry."

Nat shook his head in disagreement. "I worry most when someone tells me I don't have to worry."

"Dad, this is me, Sandy, your son, making a promise. Isn't that enough for you? I mean, don't forget, she was my mother. I want to do something wonderful for her."

Nat appeared to weigh his son's commitment. "What's at stake here is also money. I've pledged a contribution of one million, five hundred thousand dollars, and I don't want one penny of it going to waste."

"One million, five hundred thousand dollars?" Sandy was startled by this gigantic sum of money.

"Over fifteen years. A man has to give generously when the community has been so good to him. It's a sacrifice that's going to require some real belt-tightening for all of us. But to build something really useful in your mother's name will make it all worthwhile, won't it?"

Sandy nodded in agreement. His real feelings, however, were wildly in contradiction. One and a half million dollars! How dare the son-of-a-bitch! When I needed just forty-eight thousand the old man cried poverty and sent my whole life down the drain.

"I ask two things from you," Nat spoke warmly. "One, do it right. And two, give me weekly updates on your progress. Otherwise it's all your baby. And use me and Ed if you have to. Any problems, we're always available. Ed knows all the details so far; let him start by filling you in on the personalities and politics at the hospital. And don't fear," Nat concluded in a theatrical, intimate tone of voice, "I have every confidence in you."

"Thanks, Dad," Sandy muttered as he stood up to shake the old man's hand.

To an outsider, Sandy imagined that the scene would look like a Norman Rockwell painting entitled "Immigrant Who Made Good Turns Over Big Business Responsibility to His Youngest Son." But Sandy knew that something was being concealed from him. What exactly that something was, he couldn't yet figure out. But it was there, floating in a subterranean reality beneath his father's every word and gesture.

Back in his office behind a locked door, Sandy reviewed the situation. The fact that the Florence Klein Cancer Research Center had Ed's approval could mean only one thing—his brother wanted and expected Sandy to fail, thereby requiring a public last-minute rescue to save both the family name and its tax-deductible money. It didn't require a genius to formulate such a hypothesis; this was a pattern that had repeated itself in uncounted variations since the moment of Sandy's birth.

Unlike his two considerably older brothers, Sandy's birth had been unplanned. Charlie was the oldest, born nine years before Sandy. Ed was number two, twenty-five months younger than Charlie. And that was supposed to have been it for the Klein family. But then came Florence's third pregnancy, which Nat attributed to a quality control problem at the Anchor condom factory. Apparently Sandy owed his existence to a microscopic pinhole in one of his father's rubbers. Perhaps the fault lay with a careless worker on the Anchor assembly line who inadvertently dropped a hot cigarette ash on one of the sheets of elastic feeding into the molding machine. Or possibly the life-giving perforation originated in Burma with a diseased rubber tree. In any case, the final product had been defective. Nat had even briefly considered a lawsuit. But facts were facts, and Florence was pregnant. Fortunately, by then the vitamin business was providing a living, and a third child wasn't the financial burden that Nat had feared. But did the Anchor condom company, Sandy's true spiritual father, even bother to send a baby present? No. Except for his mother, no one wanted him. As Florence showered Sandy with affection in an attempt to compensate for the lack of fatherly interest, the situation only became worse. Nat, Charlie, and Ed reacted to the new baby as an intruder and an enemy, a parasite and resident family alien. The more the men resented him, the more support Sandy drew from Florence, which only made Nat, Charlie, and Ed abhor him further.

Inspired by the memories of Florence's love, Sandy vowed to triumph over the petty revenge his brother and father were anticipating. *Fuck them if they expect me to fail.* He would show everyone the kind of job he could do with the Florence Klein

Cancer Research Center. Just let them try to attack the labor of love he would create. The cancer center would be the best, most efficient, useful, beautiful, and cost-effective research facility ever built in the world. That would shut them up, once and for all.

The loud buzz of his private outside telephone line startled Sandy out of his reverie.

"Sandy Klein?" a deep male voice inquired in a thick German accent.

"Yes."

"This is Gunther here."

"Gunther, yes. Hello. How's it going?" Sandy tried to speak calmly.

"Good. Yes. Very good. Everything you require through today I've found. You'll be very pleased with my lists. Where shall we meet on Thursday?"

"The Brown Bagger?"

"No, absolutely not. Two times at the same place is risky."

"You think someone's watching you?" Sandy's voice betrayed his concern.

"What's the point in taking foolish chances?"

"Gunther, this isn't the Manhattan Project we're talking about here."

A momentary silence. "What is this Manhattan Project?"

"Forget it. Where would you like to meet?"

"Do you know Ship's Restaurant in Westwood?"

"The coffee shop with the toasters on the tables?"

"Exactly. You bring your half of the deal, I'll bring mine. Eight o'clock after work, ya?"

"Fine. See you then."

Sandy smiled grimly as he hung up. At least something was going according to plan. But the plan, which included Gunther and Germany, also reminded Sandy of the tattoo. Those little blue numbers and letter had to go. But who should remove them? He couldn't just nip in to the family doctor for a referral; that would be as effective as taking out an ad in the *Los Angeles Times* and announcing his private nightmare to his family and to the world at large. No, what he needed was a plastic surgeon with absolutely no Jewish connections, someone to whom removing a tattoo would be a simple, unemotional job. The problem was where to find not just a non-Jewish surgeon but an *excellent* one. The last person he wanted cutting away at his arm was a butcher whose sole credential consisted of possessing a foreskin.

Pasadena hit Sandy in a flash of inspiration. Pasadena, the haven of conservatism and breeding ground of old Los Angeles wealth. Not only was it proudly and distinctly non-Jewish, Pasadena was a collection point of prejudices ranging from segregationist-level racism to (happily for Sandy at the moment) serious anti-Semitism. Pasadena was the modern day Deutschland of Los Angeles County, the perfect place to find a non-Jewish surgeon. Sandy picked up the phone and buzzed the front desk. The receptionist answered promptly. "Yes, Mister Klein."

"Irene," he asked casually, "do you happen to have a Pasadena telephone book?"

Of course she did. Sandy hung up the phone, overjoyed, momentarily ignoring the difficulty of locating a qualified surgeon solely through a phone book. He had a plan; with that plan came a future. Remove the tattoo, go cold turkey on the booze, and clean up the mess of his life. The fact that the plan was so simple gave Sandy confidence. Perhaps the tattoo was actually a beneficial thing, just the kind of shock he had been unconsciously seeking to shake himself out of his rut. *A7549653* was a watershed number; either he would be able to root out and overcome the inner impulses that had led to its presence on his arm, or those same impulses would eventually lead to his death. It was kill or be killed.

After three years of drifting, an end had finally been reached. Now it was time to get his house in order — cut out booze, begin a regular exercise program, go to sleep early, get up before dawn, bust his ass at work, and make a real success out of the Florence Klein Cancer Research Center. For a moment Sandy actually felt not only relaxed, but bursting with joy. Then his private line rang again.

"Hello?" he answered cautiously.

"Thanks for calling me back." The woman's familiar voice spoke sarcastically.

"Vikki," Sandy attempted to placate her. "Give me a break, will you? I didn't get in until after two. I mean, did you want me to wake you up?"

"You could have called me this morning."

"I could have, yes. But I was in meetings until five minutes ago. In fact, I was just about to dial your number."

"Right." She obviously didn't believe him.

"Vikki, listen, I'm tired. I've had a very difficult morning. And I don't have a lot of time to talk. Just tell me straight what it is I can do for you, okay?"

"You didn't even listen to my message on your machine, did you?"

"Jesus, I forgot all about my machine. Sorry."

"Boozing again, huh? With Billy?"

"Vikki, I really don't have time to talk. Can I call you later?"

"As I told your stupid machine," she ignored his attempt to rush her, "last night I turned out a big batch of lasagna with that pasta maker you bought me for my birthday. Why I called was to invite you to dinner tonight. Just you and me, a quiet evening together. I mean if you're not too busy for me anymore."

Sandy attempted to seem pleased. "That sounds great. But it's impossible. I've got a business dinner tonight." His automatic lie covered his real plan for the evening.

"I see." She obviously didn't believe him.

"Vikki, hey, relax. I just had a marathon meeting with my father this morning and he's assigned me an incredibly important responsibility. It's an opportunity I just can't turn down. I thought you wanted good things for me."

"I do, you know that." Her voice softened. "Okay, tonight's out because of work. How about tomorrow? Lasagna's always better the second night."

"Sounds great. I'd like that, really. But I'll have to let you know in the morning. It's just possible there'll be meetings in the evening for days."

"Listen, Sandy," the chilly tone returned to Vikki's voice, "if you don't want to see me, you have no obligation, okay? Just tell me."

"No, no. I want to see you. It's just that with all this stuff that's come up here, I don't know my schedule yet."

Despite the way he was treating her, Sandy did actually like Vikki — in small doses. She was just not someone he could take very seriously. In his mind Vikki was an "interim woman," the latest in a sparse line of interim women he had known in the years since his divorce from Anne. Interim women liked him; interim women tried to please him, largely because he had all the credentials to be a good catch. The only problem was that Sandy wasn't able to connect with any of them except on the most basic of levels — flirtations, occasional mutual enjoyment of food, a passionless semblance of sex, and a superficial friendship, all adding up to a temporary easing of his loneliness and depression. All he wanted was a hiding place from the pain of Rachael and Anne. The women, of course, never understood that. And why should they? he had asked himself more than once.

"What are the odds on dinner tomorrow?"

"Fifty-fifty," Sandy admitted.

There was no response. Sandy knew he wasn't being fair to her, and it bothered him. Vikki was a good person. She cared about him and tried to get closer to him. And what did he offer in return? An occasional kind word, a few good bottles of wine, once in a while dinner and a movie, and, infrequently, someone to screw. Maybe he should take her more seriously, give her a real chance. Perhaps she could be part of his planned self-reformation. Just possibly she could help. It was true that on the surface she behaved like a princess, but perhaps that was only a deception, a psychological protection. Deep down she might be very different. A good man would find out, he told himself.

"How about seventy-five, twenty-five?" Sandy compromised.

"From you that's a commitment," Vikki softened. "You think I should freeze the lasagna or leave it in the refrigerator?"

"If you freeze it, you're covered both ways, aren't you? It'll only take a minute to defrost in the microwave."

"It tastes better if it hasn't been frozen." The disappointment in her voice was obvious.

"Then refrigerate it."

"But if you don't show tomorrow, it'll be ruined."

"Vikki, I'm trying. Really I am. But the best I can do is seventy-five, twenty-five. You're just going to have to take your chances. Now I have to go back to work. I'll talk to you in the morning."

"Sandy, I'm going to trust you and refrigerate it. Don't disappoint me."

"I'll do my best. Talk to you mañana."

"Bye."

As Sandy hung up the phone, he felt a pang of guilt. Why hadn't he just accepted her invitation? Unfortunately, he knew the answer. He had to leave her hanging for twenty-four hours because of the tattoo.

5

"If either of you even opens your mouth, I'm calling the police and having you arrested. Now turn around, walk out that door, and stay the fuck out of here, understand?"

To overcome this reception, Sandy slipped two brand new twenty dollar bills across the polished oak counter to the bartender of the Studio Bar and Grill. After a suitable interval, considerable flattery, and another two twenties, Billy was able to persuade the bartender to restrain his rage and tell them exactly what he had witnessed the night before with the Danish woman named Erica. It was a horror story worse than anything Sandy had imagined.

The bartender did not mince words. He didn't like Sandy or Billy, and he was even less fond of Erica. Not that he knew her — he'd never seen her before. She was one of those sadistic women, he informed them, who enjoyed nothing more than provoking men. And the barman had had a ringside seat with an unobstructed view of her effect on Sandy. What at first had appeared to be a simple pickup turned, through Erica's genius, into a raging argument about Nazis, the Holocaust, and the whole world of war crimes and concentration camps. At some point, according to the bartender, she had so angered Sandy that he began screaming a long, itemized list of horrors committed against the Jews by the Germans.

This behavior created a problem in the restaurant, a one-room affair consisting of fifteen small tables fanned out around the bar. All dining stopped as the customers were forced to listen to Sandy's drunken ravings. The last straw was an extended, gory story about SS officers whirling Jewish babies overhead like kosher lariats before smashing the infants' heads against stone walls, splitting open their skulls like discarded cantaloupes. As the bartender pointed out, this was not the kind of entertainment that kept a restaurant popular; people paid their hard-earned

41

money to eat and have a good time, not to be grossed out by a lunatic obsessed with Nazi perversions.

The bartender's recollections stunned Sandy. It wasn't as if he thought of himself as a man at peace with his own soul; he knew he was a tormented person. The part that frightened him was his loss of control, his inability to keep his pain to himself. His behavior in the bar was a verbal equivalent of the tattoo on his arm, a public announcement of his tortured, grief-ridden inner life.

It didn't take much imagination to guess what would have been his father's reaction to the scene at the Studio Bar and Grill. Instead of putting him in charge of the Florence Klein Cancer Research Center, Nat would redirect his youngest son to the psychiatric ward and pay cash to have him locked up forever in a straitjacket.

The bartender's revelations reinforced Sandy's earlier resolve to get his life back on track. But as much as he wanted to turn his back and forget the whole mess, Sandy knew he had to face up to his inner devils and come to grips with the mysterious circumstances that had led him to be tattooed. For this he needed Erica. Unfortunately, the bartender knew nothing more about the Danish woman; even the promise of two more twenties elicited no additional information.

Sandy and Billy shifted to plan B, canvassing all the local tattoo parlors in hope of finding the one he had visited. The two tattoo joints on Hollywood Boulevard were so sleazy that simply entering them made Sandy want to shower. Neither Charlie's Tattoos nor Hollywood Skin Art had any helpful information. Sunset Boulevard Tattoos, the only other shop in the area, suggested that Sandy and Billy try the tattoo emporiums in San Pedro adjacent to the U.S. Navy and Merchant Marine facilities.

The long drive from Sunset Boulevard to the waterfront streets of San Pedro was bad enough dead sober; Sandy couldn't imagine negotiating the complicated route while drunk at two in the morning.

After driving half an hour in silence, Billy came to the same conclusion. "Look, since we both think it's virtually impossible for you to have made it down here last night, why don't we quit wasting time, kiss off plan B, and turn around?"

"If there were any alternative I would."

"Your best option that I can see," Billy responded without missing a beat, "is to hit the doctor's office tomorrow, have the stupid thing removed, quit boozing entirely, and write off the whole episode as the irrational behavior of a drunk. Which is what it was."

"That's a cop-out, not an alternative," came the rigid response. "I have to find out *why* I did it."

"Please. You know why you did it. I told you this morning. The fact is you're very depressed. You've got to give up this living in the past; can't you see how it's killing you? The present is all there is. Live for today; forget all the bad that's happened, and life will take care of itself."

"And how am I supposed to do that?" Sandy asked quietly.

"I know this is out of fashion these days, but the concept is called *will*. You're thirty-two years old; in anyone's book you're still young. Quit thinking of yourself as half-dead; you've got forty or fifty years ahead of you. All kinds of wonderful things can happen."

"That's good advice."

Billy grinned, pleased that he had finally gotten through.

"But we're still going to San Pedro," Sandy announced with conviction as he pushed his foot down on the accelerator.

Twenty minutes later he guided the Volvo off the San Diego Freeway, down the Long Beach connector, and exited onto the main drag of San Pedro, the rough, waterfront community surrounding Los Angeles harbor.

Big Al's Tattoos was located in a one-room, clapboard shack, apparently unpainted since its heyday during World War II. "Ask For Our Special Serviceman's Rates!" read a faded red, white, and blue cardboard sign propped up in the grime-covered window. As Sandy and Billy entered, a brass bell over the front door sounded. Across the room, the proprietor—a bony, wheezing, seventy-year-old geezer—was hard at work. Time had turned him from what once must have been an impressive waterfront character into someone who could now more honestly have called himself "Little Al." The frail man bent over his work, carefully bonding a classic all-American fighting eagle to the arm of a pale Marine private who was obviously in pain.

As Al colored in the eagle's feathers, Sandy explained what he hoped to learn. But after a quick glance at *A7549653,* it was clear that Big Al could tell them nothing.

Half a mile away they found a clean stucco bungalow fronted by a neon sign reading "Maurice's Tattoos." Sandy sensed pay dirt—something about the place felt very familiar. Walking up the concrete steps gave him a shivery sensation of *déja vu.* Maurice's flash of surprise, followed by an evasive glance, confirmed his feeling.

"Can I talk to you for a minute, Maurice?" Sandy spoke in a low friendly tone, presuming a prior acquaintance.

Maurice was about forty, six foot five, two hundred and eighty pounds—a muscular black tattoo artist of Mister Universe caliber. He coolly continued his lettering on the chest of a drunken Navy petty officer sitting bravely on a low stool.

"This is a paying customer, mister—you'll have to wait," Maurice muttered in a businesslike voice, as if he had never seen Sandy before.

Apparently nothing was going to distract Maurice from his work. Over the sailor's left nipple, the word *Hot* was tattooed in red ink. Above his right nipple, in blue ink, Maurice was completing the final letter of the word *Cold.*

Sandy felt like laughing. The fucking idiot had turned himself into a human water faucet. Why anyone would mutilate himself like that was simply incomprehensible. But were the *Hot* and *Cold* logos really any weirder than a concentration camp number? *Hot* and *Cold* had no greater meaning than a joke. Tomorrow, the petty officer would laugh hysterically with his shipmates over the silly words he had bonded to his chest. "Boy, was I drunk," Sandy imagined the man explaining through his tears of laughter. What would otherwise have been simply one more dim, drunken day off, after months at sea, had instead become a night immortalized forever by Maurice. The tattooing of the sailor's chest was a battle cry against oblivion; it was a memory, a capturing of time, that nothing but death or a surgeon's skill could ever take from him.

After the last needle prick, Maurice set down his tools and swabbed the sailor's chest with alcohol. "Take a look." The big black man pointed to the wall-mounted mirror, just as a barber might at the completion of a haircut.

The petty officer staggered to the mirror and studied Maurice's handiwork. To Sandy, the style of the lettering bore a distinct uncanny resemblance to the blue tattoo on his own arm.

"Far out!" The drunken seaman was delighted. "You're a good man, Mau-reese." The sailor held out both his hands, palms up, for Maurice to slap in brotherhood.

Feigning sincerity, the tattoo artist obliged his customer.

"Be sure to keep them clean; use an alcohol wash twice a day for the next week. We don't want no infection, do we?"

The petty officer nodded gravely, pulled on his shirt, honored Maurice with a drunken salute, and staggered out the door into the night.

"What can I do for you?" Maurice spoke without apparent recognition as he disassembled and began cleaning his electric needle.

"I wanted to ask you a question about this tattoo you did on my arm last night," Sandy replied in a confident, friendly, matter-of-fact voice.

"Hey, man," Maurice answered, "I just did what you and your lady friend asked. No more; no less."

"Maurice," Sandy continued in a disarmingly gentle manner, "I came down here because I wanted to thank you properly. You did a great job. And last night I know I wasn't exactly in the best condition to appreciate the really superb work you do."

Billy stared at his friend with respect, impressed by the effective and unexpected tactic.

Relieved, Maurice swung around. "Thank you. I'm glad you like it."

"I do, yes. Very much. I, uh, also wanted to apologize. I know I was pretty looped last night. I hope I wasn't too nasty."

"Forget it, man; you were fine."

But it was obvious from Maurice's evasive glance that whatever had gone on was far from fine.

"Maurice, you know and I know I wasn't. I'm sorry."

"Mister, forget it. I seen a whole lot worse, believe me."

"Worse than my lady friend?"

Maurice smiled broadly. "I like to say nice things about my customers; don't make me change my policy."

"Tell me something else. How did I pay last night? Was it by credit card?"

The big man shook his head. "Cash, the lady paid. I don't take plastic."

"Did I tell you my name?"

Maurice shook his head.

"Did she?"

"Nope. And that's the way I want to keep it. You don't have to be a bagel eater to know what that number's all about. Like I told you last night: I don't want to have anything to do with it. I don't know you. I don't know her. And this is the last conversation we're going to have on this subject, understand?"

"Maurice, tell me something . . ."

"Man, don't you understand," Maurice interrupted, "what 'last conversation' means? You don't look retarded."

Although Billy was beginning to fidget at the threat in the man's voice, Sandy wasn't fazed.

"Please, one last question, Maurice. It's important, okay?"

"Okay," Maurice allowed after a moment's reflection. "One more, and then that's it. And I don't want to hear no more about Nazis, concentration camps, or them ovens. Last night was all I could take."

Sandy nodded. "That woman I was with, Erica, she's disappeared. Is there anything you remember that might help me track her down?"

"You want my advice," Maurice said carefully, "you'll forget that one. She's a bad-ass ball breaker, you ask me."

"She didn't say anything that might tell me where to find her?"

Maurice played dumb. "Mister, I don't know who you are or why you're here but I don't have time for no more questions. *Comprende?*"

"I think he wants us to go," Billy interjected, alarmed at the menace in the big man's voice.

"You got one smart friend here." Maurice gestured in Billy's direction. "Listen to the man."

Sandy nodded; it was obvious that he was talking to a wall. "You may be good at your work, Maurice, but you sure have something to learn about public relations."

Without waiting for an answer Sandy spun around and led the way out of the bungalow.

Back in the Volvo, Sandy started the engine while Billy stared warily at the front of the tattoo parlor as if expecting a blast from a shotgun.

"Jesus fucking Christ, you didn't have to insult the guy. Didn't you see the size of those arms?"

"Sometimes I really wish I owned a gun. The bastard knows where she is. I *know* he knows."

"Sandy, drive the car, will you? Let's get the hell out of here before he comes after us!"

"What do you think? If I went in there and offered him some bucks, would he talk?"

"No. And you wouldn't be alive two seconds after you walked through the door. Now will you drive, please?"

"What if I came back with some really big friends?"

"Sandy, stop with the bullshit, okay? Not only do you not *have* any really big friends, but other than me, who do you know that you can even talk to about this?" Glancing at the tattoo parlor, Billy gasped in alarm. "Maurice is watching us from the window. C'mon, before things get any worse, let's go."

Sandy shrugged and didn't answer. Could he just let the whole thing drop? Maybe Billy was right. Maybe he should just see the doctor, have the tattoo cut out, go cold turkey on the booze, and straighten out his deteriorated life.

"Sandy, god damn it, he's picking up the phone. Stick this Swedish piece of shit in gear and go. Now!"

Finally facing reality, Sandy engaged the clutch and headed the Volvo home.

6

At work the next day, Sandy tightened the screws on himself and labored like a demon. Arriving twenty minutes ahead of Nat, he actually used his own key to unlock the front door of the Vita-Line plant. Driving himself at a nearly impossible pace for ten uninterrupted hours, even forgoing his usual hour and a half lunch break, by the end of the afternoon he had cleared out the entire backlog of invoices stacked on his desk—work that would normally have taken him days to complete. In addition, he wrote pages of notes in preparation for a series of meetings he scheduled with the doctors, researchers, and administrators who were contributing to the basic concept of the Beth-Israel Hospital Florence Klein Cancer Research Center. By quitting time, even Nat was impressed by his youngest son's sudden productivity. For the first time in the old man's memory, Sandy was behaving like a model executive.

As good as his efforts looked from the outside, Sandy's true motivation sprung from his terror of succumbing to another flare-up of despair. Forget the Danish woman, forget the tattoo, forget everything but work and the future, he repeated to himself over and over during the day. Moving forward was the key to life. Auschwitz and the past didn't matter. It was 1973, not 1941. The goal wasn't fighting the Nazis but proving his value to the company and earning his father's respect.

Sandy still wasn't sure how he could achieve that last objective. If it came down to simply earning large sums of money and achieving power, only Charlie, the eldest son, was worthy of Nat's approval. As an attorney, Charlie was independent of the family. Through his skill at engineering all sorts of complicated corporate acquisitions, Charlie was riding high on a wave of merger mania. But even that level of success wasn't enough for the oldest brother: More than once Charlie had bragged to Sandy of impressive profits made from stock trades based on untraceable insider information. Nat knew the same facts, yet still respected Charlie even though the Securities and Exchange Commission would have considered him a crook.

Ed was an even more difficult case. Here was a man who had dropped out of college to work full-time for his father. The middle brother had known no other life than well-paid employment in the family business. Ed wasn't particularly bright, enjoyed bullying subordinates, was selfish, conventional, boring, weak, and a yes-man for Nat. As far as Sandy knew, Ed had only two worthwhile qualities. First, he was loyal to the point of having no inhibitions about carrying out dirty work for Nat, such as firing a long-time but unproductive employee. And second, Ed had a dogged capacity for repetitive, boring tasks that no one, including Nat, wanted to perform. What did Nat respect about this? Sandy could never come up with an answer that made any sense.

Despite his concerns, it was an amazing day for Sandy, who exercised more will power than he'd been capable of generating in years. Even the phone call setting up an appointment with a Pasadena plastic surgeon went without a hitch. As a referring physician, Sandy had simply used the name of the chief of internal medicine at Pasadena Memorial Hospital as listed in the yellow pages. Sandy the energetic reporter was back in action. Eventually the plastic surgeon would find out about the deception, but by then the tattoo would have been removed, the bill paid in cash, and the whole situation made untraceable by the fake name under which Sandy had made the appointment. It had been a good day, no question about it.

At home after work, as he showered and changed clothes for his lasagna dinner with Vikki, he couldn't help fantasizing about his new self and the possibilities of the future. He was on a roll, for the first time in years. How could he maintain the momentum? he asked himself as he splashed on cologne in the bathroom. The answer that popped into his mind was surprising — take the plunge, marry Vikki, and embark on a normal, reformed life of domesticity and stability. Why not give himself a fresh start? Vikki had a lot of wonderful qualities. For openers there was her cooking, which was sensational. Maybe, the cynical part of himself protested, but if food preparation was the only criterion of a good wife there were any number of restaurants he could get involved with on a daily basis for a lot less trouble and less money than it would cost to marry Vikki.

Back and forth flew various ideas on the subject of marriage, but the fact that he could even contemplate the concept encouraged Sandy enormously. It meant that in his bottom-line thinking, he had turned the corner on despair.

Unfortunately, only a few hours later, in bed with Vikki, his fantasy crumbled into ruins. Sex with Vikki had never been sensational. In bed she plunged into the role of the performer, trying out every sexual trick the women's magazines promised would satisfy a lover. The problem was that, for all her efforts, it was obvious that Vikki felt little or nothing herself. Which for Sandy made the whole experience lonelier than masturbation. Certainly she was beautiful, with her long, slender legs, expressive hands finished with immaculately manicured nails, a highly defined neck and jaw framed by an enormous mane of glistening black hair, and a perfect body. But the reality of what Vikki experienced sexually mocked her efforts to pretend that Sandy's manhood drove her wild.

After the lasagna, Vikki had led Sandy to the bedroom, turned down the lights, lit incense, smoked a joint, and engaged in a little striptease before yanking down his trousers and going to work on his cock with the ferocity of a human Hoover vacuum cleaner. She tried to convince Sandy that she found him so arousing that she just couldn't keep her hands off him, but it was an obvious lie. Her frantic action lacked both intimacy and tenderness. The whole experience confirmed Sandy's belief that the real reason she thrashed around so violently was to disguise the fact that she never actually felt much of anything.

The entire situation exhausted and depressed Sandy, stimulating all of the feelings of alienation and despair he so desperately wanted to avoid. After a faked solo of orgasmic yelps from Vikki, he gave up and let himself come with a final dispassionate squirt. As much as he wanted to jettison the bleak side of his character, he found himself powerless to control the return of intense, disturbing feelings.

"Vikki?"

"Uhmm," she purred, attempting to sound contented.

"You asleep?" Sandy tried to adopt a neutral manner that would conceal his raging demons.

"No, just resting."

"I need your opinion about something. Can you handle being serious?"

Vikki sat up, fully alert, concerned by the anxiety in his voice. "Why? Are you mad at me? Did I do something wrong? I didn't please you?"

"Viks," Sandy told her, "it has absolutely nothing to do with you. *I* have a problem." At that moment he felt so desperate that almost any risk seemed worthwhile if it held the possibility of restoring a semblance of well-being. Despite everything, Vikki seemed to be his last link with normality; he had no choice but to trust her, and perhaps with one shocking admission deepen their relationship before it deteriorated to nothing. "If I tell you a secret will you promise never to repeat it to anyone, under any condition?"

"Sandford, what's wrong?"

"This isn't just a little secret, this is big and dangerous, something that could really get me hurt if it ever went public. I need to know that you'll never, ever repeat what I tell you, no matter what the circumstances. Do you agree to that?"

"Sandy," she sounded hurt, "don't you trust me?"

"Of course, but this is so important I need to hear you promise me."

"Okay, Sandford." Again she called him by his given name, which she knew he hated, to emphasize her commitment. "I promise to never tell anyone what you say to me tonight." Placing her right hand directly over her perfectly shaped, thirty-four, D-cup, left breast Vikki added, "On my word of honor."

Why, Sandy wondered, did he have doubts when he knew that her loyalty had always been uncompromising? Despite Vikki's dingbat manner and sexpot appearance, she was a complex person. Though she persisted on behaving in public like a seductive Betty Boop, in private and at work she was an entirely different person.

Since infancy, clothes and the clothing business had been Vikki's passion. Even at age five she had been obsessed with the garments she wore and fascinated by the stores in which they were purchased. Her consuming interest had led her to drop out of college and go to work for Shirley's, a small chain of expensive boutiques where she worked her way up from saleswoman to senior vice-president and chief buyer, second only to the owner and president, Shirley herself. In contrast to the way she acted with Sandy, at work Vicki was a killer, famous throughout a cutthroat industry for her ability to intimidate sales reps. To Sandy, who had once spent an afternoon just sitting in her office watching her in action, Vikki had a touch for buying and selling so highly developed that it could only have originated deep in her DNA. Observing the instinctive ease with which she negotiated and closed deals, Sandy had wished he were as effective at selling vitamins. The big difference between them, he knew, was that while she sincerely believed in and deeply loved her work, for him vitamins were only a job, a way to pay the bills. It had been very different for a time, when his work as a journalist had been all-consuming. But that was before his weekly alternative newspaper, *The Heart of L.A.,* had ended its short life with a dramatic public failure.

"You remember how I told you I did this?" Sandy lightly touched the three-inch gauze bandage taped on his left forearm over the tattoo.

Vikki nodded. "You burned yourself with boiling water when you knocked over your coffee maker. Serves you right for not calling me back."

"Remarks like that don't exactly inspire confidence."

"Forget what I said. Tell me about the burn."

"It's not a burn," Sandy admitted, "that was a lie. What's under this bandage is something else."

Sitting up in bed, Vikki propped her back against the wall and waited for him to continue.

"The night you called, when I didn't answer your message, Billy and I went to the Studio Bar and Grill and got really boozed. This is very painful to admit, but I put down so much scotch that when I woke up yesterday morning I didn't remember one thing I had done the night before. Nothing. If that isn't bad enough, besides the incredible hangover, I had one other much more frightening souvenir from the J&B."

"The thing under the bandage?" Vikki pointed to his arm.

Sandy nodded. "This is a little hard for me. If I show it to you, do you really promise you won't make fun of me?"

She bobbed her chin in agreement.

Slowly Sandy peeled back the dressing, painfully tearing out small patches of hair on his arm. Once the gauze was off, he held out the blue letter and numbers for Vikki to inspect. For the two long minutes she examined his arm, the expression on her face revealed nothing. Finally she looked up into his frightened eyes and smiled reassuringly.

"Sandy, I do love you. I hope you know that. But this is crazy."

"Crazy!" Sandy exploded in anger. "I open my heart to you and you tell me I'm crazy! Thank you very much and good-bye," he yelled as he tried to press the adhesive tape back into place.

"Sandy, relax," she continued in an affectionate tone. "I'm not using the word in a medical sense. You're not *crazy* crazy. I'm not calling for the guys with the straitjackets. I meant it as a figure of speech. What you've got on your arm is a concentration camp number like they tattooed on the people at Auschwitz. Am I right?"

Sandy just stared at her.

"Shirley has one. She was in Auschwitz. You and I have talked about it three or four times."

Sandy nodded, not certain where this was leading.

"So tell me what this is about. You get drunk one night and now you think you were once in a concentration camp?"

"Obviously I don't."

"Then what the hell is this thing doing on your arm? You see, it is crazy; it doesn't make any sense."

"Vikki," Sandy admitted, "if I knew why I did it, I'd tell you. But I don't; I haven't the faintest idea."

Smiling tenderly, as if talking to an injured child, she appeared to understand and accept his pain. "Sandy, you're taking this all way too seriously. One of your big problems in life is that you examine everything so closely. Life doesn't make near as much sense as you'd like to think. Dig deep enough anywhere and all you'll uncover is shit; that's my experience. You want to have a better time, ease up on your expectations, take things as they come and enjoy them. It works, I guarantee you."

"Vikki, that's not a philosophy, that's an excuse. With that kind of attitude you could happily marry Adolf Hitler! Think about this: I look at the tattoo, yes, a part of me is frightened and disgusted. But another part of me, a really sick, weird, dark part looks at these numbers and absolutely loves them. They're me and they're perfect. Not only do I want to keep them but I have an impulse to show them to people. For the first time in my life since my paper went under I feel connected to the pulse of history. You have your clothing business which you love. Me, I sell vitamins. That's it. *I have nothing else.* Zip. Zero. Everything that was important once is literally dead — Rachael, *The Heart of L.A.,* my marriage. I'm thirty-two years old and I can't start over again. Even my dreams are dead. You see, at least if I'd been through Auschwitz my pain, my loss, and my sufferings would be connected to something larger. Vikki, I had such hope for myself; I cared about history, people, the future; I wanted to do something wonderful and really contribute to the world. Look what's happened to me. I might as well have been through Auschwitz, don't you see? At least if I had, I could point to something important that I'd been part of."

"You know what you should do?" Vikki spoke after a minute of consideration.

Sandy shook his head.

"You need a commitment and a cause. Part of what I've always admired about you is your idealism. Why don't you let me make a few calls. I know people you'd like, lawyers who work for the ACLU — Democrats. With your brains and passion, you could make a real difference in politics. I mean, you could be instrumental in helping to re-elect the best senator in the United States, California's own Alan Cranston. What do you say you volunteer some time and be a part of U.S. history, for real? Wouldn't that be something you'd feel proud of?"

Sandy felt the black cloud descend again. He had presented her with a nightmare, and she was advising him to join the male equivalent of a society ladies' charity ball.

"Thank you, I appreciate the suggestion. Really. Let me think about it." Sandy tried to sound grateful in hope of ending the discussion. What was the sense of fighting with someone who recommended an aspirin to treat a life-threatening hemorrhage? Working for the Democratic Party was not even a remote possibility. Her advice was the final blow, absolute proof that the gulf between their sensibilities could never be bridged.

"Viks," Sandy said as he slid out of bed, "I've got a big breakfast meeting in the morning; I have to go home and get some sleep. Thanks for the wonderful dinner. And I'll think about your suggestions."

The finality in his voice deflected any possibility of argument. "I do love you, Sandy. I want you to remember that."

"I appreciate it, thanks." He gave her a polite kiss on the lips, then pulled on his shirt. Vikki's miniature Dachshund, Toady, waddled over, demanding to be petted. Sandy set down his trousers and gave the pooch a few friendly strokes.

"It's too bad you can't spend the night," Vikki teased, changing her approach. "Just looking at your cute little ass makes me horny again."

"There'll always be another night," he lied. "You know I can't stay away from you." Sandy stood up, fully dressed.

"Coming from anyone else I'd be offended. From you that's a signed and notarized commitment."

Sandy kissed her on the forehead. "Talk to you in the morning."

Vikki said nothing as she watched him walk out the door.

7

After leaving Vikki and driving home, Sandy spent the entire night wide awake, ruminating over the mystery of the Danish woman. In only a few hours, this person had seduced him into mutilating his own body. It was bizarre. He'd known Vikki for nearly eight months, and she could barely get him to show up for dinner. Somehow Erica had hooked into a central part of his character and been able to push every one of his buttons. How had she done it? Through the long night, troubling questions multiplied out of control. By the time he showed up at the Beth-Israel Hospital coffee shop for his seven-thirty breakfast meeting, Sandy was wired, exhausted, nervous, paranoid, yet surprisingly alert.

Waiting for him in a booth, drinking coffee and reading the *Wall Street Journal,* sat Stanley Furgstein, the director of development for Beth-Israel Hospital Corporation. Tall, skinny, and dapper in a charcoal pin-stripe banker's suit, the hyperenergetic fifty-year-old powerhouse of a fund raiser greeted Sandy with his sincerest super-salesman double handshake. It was a warm beginning to what quickly became a chilly, polarized interchange.

The problem began when Sandy pulled out the ten legal tablet pages of notes he had worked on the afternoon before, detailing his goals for the Florence Klein Cancer Research Center. As he began to discuss them point by point, Furgstein's eyes glazed over with boredom. The director of development was not a detail man, but a generalist and a promoter. Health care to him was an industry, a route to personal power. He wouldn't have known the difference between cardiac arrest and kidney failure except for the amount each was worth in insurance claims. His love was corporate and his concerns were cost-cutting and profits. Patients were a necessary evil, a pain in the ass. Furgstein's true god was illness itself, the never ending source of money in the bank.

Sandy could imagine Furgstein getting ready for bed, down on his knees praying, imploring the Almighty to ravage mankind with a pestilence serious enough to require long-term hospitalization for hundreds of thousands of people. If sophisticated technology was required to treat the disease, that was even better because it would result in larger government grants and increased insurance payments. Think polio. Or plague. Even a nice typhoid epidemic would do the trick. His career was pegged to the sickness and misfortune of others.

As Sandy discussed his objectives for the cancer center, Furgstein's boredom deteriorated into polite hostility. What the hospital administrators really wanted was to get the Kleins' money and then make all the decisions themselves. They planned to design, execute, and control the whole show. Furgstein's desire fixated on the presentation of a complete research center to the Kleins in exchange for their check. The fact that Sandy not only wanted to be actively involved, but intended to use every nickel effectively, caused the administrator considerable anxiety. Furgstein hated being pinned down to specifics, and his efforts to convince Sandy to simply "trust me" had no impact. Most appalling of all to Furgstein was the suggestion that the research facility actually accomplish something for the medical community and not just be an edifice honoring both the business success of the Klein family and the hospital's ability to attract donors. It was too much for Furgstein to take in. He cut the meeting short and excused himself, supposedly to mediate an emergency contract dispute with the nurses' union.

On the drive to Vita-Line, Sandy wondered what had actually been accomplished. Had he blown it? Had he acted crazy? Was his mental state so obvious that Furgstein had run in terror?

By nine A.M. Sandy was once again tied to his office chair, attempting to bury his demons under piles of work. But this morning he was able to accomplish little more than shuffling papers. No invoice seemed gripping enough to prevent him from ruminating over the long-gone glory years that had begun

in 1966 when he founded his weekly newspaper, *The Heart of L.A.*
"If it's news in L.A., we've got it wired," trumpeted the masthead.

Sandy had developed the concept behind *The Heart of L.A.* for
his master's thesis at the UCLA school of journalism, where he
had come to believe that Los Angeles needed a politically committed, intelligent alternative to the sloppily edited *L.A. Free
Press.* Sandy envisioned a Southern California weekly on the
order of the *Village Voice,* a serious newspaper determined to
cover the events of the day with a detached, real-world
perspective — beholden to no one, irreverent, opinionated, with a
definite sense of humor.

Everything about the project had quickly fallen into place
except for that universal problem: money. Sandy had found
himself in the classic small business dilemma: To succeed, the
paper required a capital base substantial enough to see it through
the inevitable lean start-up period. Compared with other week-
lies, *The Heart of L.A.* was inexpensive to produce. What made it
possible were the ethics of the time. In the middle sixties there
was no shortage of talented journalists, editors, printers, and even
accountants who believed in making a better world. United by
their opposition to the war in Vietnam, young people everywhere
were willing to make sacrifices. The individuals who went to
work for Sandy's paper shared a yearning for a life with meaning,
and were prepared to give up personal gain in order to promote
their idealistic principles. They had a deep and sincere skepticism of authority, coupled with a sense of humor. For a time it
had worked: *The Heart of L.A.* was a newspaper run by vision-
aries, filled with promise.

Those were heady years for Sandy, 1966 and 1967. He had
broken free from the cycle of paternal rejection and fraternal
scorn and jealousy. As an audience developed for the paper,
political figures began to seek him out. Big business tried to
influence him. The FBI even honored him with an occasional
visit to complain about charges against the agency. At the peak of
the paper's reputation Sandy was showered with invitations. He
seemed to be everywhere in the city at once. It was definitely an
exciting time.

Sandy's own carefully researched story on the defense industry's scandalous procurement procedures during the Vietnam
war received nation-wide publicity and became a minor classic
of investigative journalism. Although it never won a Pulitzer
prize, *The Heart of L.A.* received a huge circulation boost from a
four-part series about Los Angeles communes, written from the
inside by reporters who had lived with the groups. Other attention getters were the occasional pieces under the heading of
"Life on the Barricades," written by such figures as Timothy
Leary, Janis Joplin, and Eldridge Cleaver. And just to keep its
readers from becoming complacent, an ex-CIA bigwig wrote an
anonymous column offering a conservative but well-informed
analysis of the week's events.

Starting from a circulation of zero, an appreciative audience
grew at a rate almost, but not quite, sufficient to keep the paper
solvent. At the end of the first year, *The Heart of L.A.* was in the
red to the tune of $80,000, which was actually slightly better than
Sandy's original financial forecast. By the end of 1967 the annual
loss had been reduced to $43,000. In any normal business the
investors would have been ecstatic; break-even appeared no more
than two years away. But in Sandy's case, the financial backers,
who were his family, had mixed reactions.

Florence was delighted by her youngest son's success. But
Nat, Charlie, and Ed were enraged. It was one thing to fund
what they hoped would be a losing effort; the fact that the paper
was doing well by promoting a rebellious antiestablishment
sensibility infuriated them almost as much as Sandy's new-found
confidence, social status, and growing reputation.

Even marriage to his college girlfriend, Anne, in 1966 and the
birth of Rachael ten months later did nothing to reduce the
tension between Sandy and his father and brothers. The only
thing that changed was the effect of the conflict: With his life
progressing so wonderfully, his paper promising to be profitable,
and his wife and daughter so absolutely perfect, the difficulties
with Nat, Ed, and Charlie seemed to Sandy far away and unimportant. This state of grace lasted for nearly two years until that

horrible day in November, 1967, when Sandy's mother was diagnosed with cancer of the liver.

Florence's rapid decline and painful death devastated Sandy, who was stunned and outraged by the loss of the one person who had loved him unequivocally and supported him against all opposition. Her death was too sudden and shocking for Sandy to accept; despite Anne's attempts to comfort him, he went into an emotional tailspin.

Over time his grief worsened, expanding into a severe, chronic depression that crippled the imagination and enthusiasm his work demanded. Nothing mattered to Sandy but pain, death, and mourning. It didn't take long for the paper to reflect those preoccupations. Exercising his veto power as publisher, Sandy overruled his editors and commissioned lengthy headline articles on such topics as "Radiation Therapy Today—The Grim Truth." Despite the eccentric tenor of the times, such articles did not sell papers. People wanted to read trendy trash, such as the pseudoserious revelations of teenaged hookers, or to follow the investigations of sensational political or financial scandals. No one was interested in the "Fairfax Area Survivors of Auschwitz" and it didn't take long for the paper's circulation to go down the tubes, bringing with it a dramatic decrease in advertising revenues.

By May of 1968 Sandy's depression finally began to lift. But by then it was too late; the readership of *The Heart of L.A.* had plummeted to half of what it had been, and the staff was badly demoralized. The death blow came at the end of June when Nat reviewed the second-quarter financial statement and found the red ink up two hundred percent. The old man seized on this excuse to notify his son by registered letter that as of July first, *The Heart of L.A.* had lost its familial underwriter and was on its own to succeed or fail. All of Sandy's efforts to change his father's mind were useless; Nat claimed that it was a question of money, of not being able to afford the losses. To Sandy, that was a transparent lie. Even Florence's hospital-bed promise to support *The Heart of L.A.* for five more years meant nothing to his father, who claimed that as a result of probate he was in a cash-flow crisis. Nat's lies and betrayal sent Sandy back into the severe depression from which he had just begun to emerge. His self-confidence crippled, he wallowed in despair, unable to generate sufficient energy to hustle the $48,000 needed to keep the newspaper afloat. By September, *The Heart of L.A.* was as dead as Sandy's beloved mother.

Sitting in his office at the Vita-Line Corporation and looking back, 1968 seemed to Sandy like a grim hangover out of someone else's life. It was still difficult for him to understand how so many people and possibilities had been taken from him in such a short time. After two sensational years, his life had deteriorated over-night into a seemingly endless nightmare.

The death of the paper sent shock waves through his marriage, scaring Anne so badly that she lost faith in her husband and his dreams. A self-proclaimed realist, she urged him to forget what was lost and go to work as a well-paid executive with his father's vitamin business. Anne had no sympathy for Sandy's wish to move to New York, get a job with a legitimate newspaper, and start over, if necessary, at the bottom as a cub reporter. She had no interest in making further sacrifices in Los Angeles, and abso-lutely no desire to move to a strange city, fight the cold, the snow, and the humidity, and live in a fourth-floor walk-up while Sandy tried to make a life for them independent of his family.

Why had he listened to her? He had done what she wanted, turning down a reasonable, if low-level, offer from the *New York Times*. Now, years later, he lacerated himself for having sacrificed his dreams to her conventional, conservative, comfort-oriented needs.

From those two terrific years with *The Heart of L.A.,* the only good thing that remained was Sandy's friendship with Billy — and even that was questionable at this point. Against the advice of all his editors, on what amounted to instinct, Sandy had hired Billy, who was only five years out of Juilliard, to be the paper's music critic. To the surprise of everyone but Sandy, Billy's witty and knowledgeable weekly pop music column became an imme-diate hit, leading quickly to a lucrative career composing jingles for radio and television commercials. The irony was that Billy had only written the column as a way to earn money in order to support his real work as a composer of symphonies for classical orchestras. But early success in an easy, lucrative arena had changed the young composer. A year after beginning to write the music column, Billy was earning more money in one week writing jingles than he'd ever imagined he would earn in a year. It was as if he had been born with a magic touch. In fifteen minutes he wrote the TWA theme song, "Fly, fly away with TWA." The average jingle required only an hour's concentration. His hardest job, the Pontiac theme song, dragged on for two whole hours. Into his life came money and a peculiar kind of fame; out went the symphonies. Sandy was disappointed, but Anne pointed out that Billy was not only completely independent but extremely comfortable financially.

The rewards for going to work at Vita-Line were reaped almost entirely by Anne, who quickly altered their lifestyle until she was living in the manner to which she felt entitled. The new ranch house in Brentwood, the Ford station wagon in the driveway, and her first designer dresses went quite a way toward soothing the pain she felt for her husband's public failure with *The Heart of L.A.* Now cloaked in respectability, Anne's favorite evening activity became formal charity dinner dances, where she was admired for her beauty and felt the equal of prominent society ladies. Predictably, Sandy's reaction was discomfort, followed by dismay and then hatred. Except for the time he spent with Rachael, his life was torture.

In hindsight, Sandy had no doubt that even if his daughter hadn't been killed, the marriage would have failed — he and Anne simply had a conflict of values so dramatic that compromise was impossible. Four months to the day after the death of their daughter on August 18, 1970, Sandy and Anne separated forever.

In the three years since Rachael's death, Sandy had wallowed in his grief. In dramatic contrast, Anne had rebounded and remarried within a year of the divorce. This time she took no chances and found herself a socially prominent, successful older attorney with a thriving twenty-partner practice specializing in tax shelters and offshore investment schemes. Anne and her new husband were quite a public team; their appearance in the society pages of the *L.A. Times* was so frequent that Sandy had canceled his subscription to the paper.

The phone rang, jolting him out of his depressing reveries. The call was from Ed, reminding him of a family lunch date, scheduled to begin in fifteen minutes at Parcheesi's Italian restaurant. Sandy looked at his watch and was shocked to discover the time — a whole morning had vanished in his bitter daydreaming.

"I'm leaving now; you want to ride with me?"

"Ed, thanks, I would but I've got an appointment after lunch and won't be coming back to the office. So I'd better take my own car."

"Okay, see you there."

"Right."

Sandy hung up and within minutes was driving across Glendale, past the gas stations, the fast food joints, and the stucco apartment complexes toward a lunch he would have given almost anything to skip. He would be trapped not only with Ed, but with their older brother Charlie and Nat's new wife, Sylvia. The purpose of this meal was to finalize plans for the old man's surprise seventieth birthday party. Although no one was interested in his opinion, Sandy had to be invited to participate in the spirit of family democracy.

Across a round table, over Parcheesi's famous milk-fed veal scallopini, the lacquered, exercised, and beautifully dressed fifty-year-old Sylvia spelled out her plans to the three brothers and their two wives. Glamorous, sexy, and tough, Sylvia had been married to Nat for only two years. She specialized in lavish birthday parties that further inflated Nat's already zeppelin-sized ego. Sylvia's parties were quite a change from those modest and personal annual events hosted by Florence at home. Then, the old man had been a tightwad, spending little on anything other than charity. Since marrying Sylvia, he lapped up the lavish treatment she showered on him with his own money.

For his seventieth birthday bash, Sylvia planned to go all-out with a private room at Chasen's, the best in caviar and champagne, and Nat's favorite, steak diane. The problem she presented to the brothers was the "theme of the party." But even this, Sandy knew, she had decided in advance. Sylvia was a smart operator who tightly controlled every detail of her life. A lunch "for the purpose of discussing plans" was really a rubber-stamp confirmation of choices she had already made. She was a dictator who wanted her subjects to think she believed in democracy. Despite her solicitation of suggestions, the arrangements had already been finalized. It would be an event so lavish and spectacular that it stood the possibility of obliterating all past birthday parties from Nat's memory.

Sandy was only half-listening as Sylvia went into detail. The focus of his attention was the physical change in his brother Charlie, whom Sandy hadn't seen in almost three months. The formerly pudgy, pale, balding, shlumpy lawyer had been transformed into a reasonably athletic-looking, stylish individual. Diet, exercise, and an expensive Saville Row pinstripe suit took him part of the way, but the final touch was the small forest of hair that had been transplanted onto Charlie's once-bare forehead. The effect of this metamorphosis on his wife, Nora, who was normally thirty pounds overweight, was obvious — she had to compete. The bookworm and grind Nora had married long ago was no longer a sloppy, brilliant law student but an arrogant, wealthy, slick, ultraconfident man about town. To her credit, Nora had risen to the challenge by dieting and sweating her way down to an acceptable weight for the wife of such a socially prominent husband. They were an impressively well-matched couple, quite a contrast to Ed and his wife, Fran, who managed to get through the entire meal without saying one word.

Of course Fran *generally* didn't speak to anyone at family occasions, out of self-protection. She wasn't stupid, but her Las Vegas showgirl background hadn't equipped her to deal with the Kleins. Given the complexity of family politics, she had learned simply to keep her mouth shut. It was either that or have Sylvia, Nat, Charlie, and Nora put her down subtly but effectively.

Only one part of the lunch surprised Sandy: Ed and Charlie's lack of participation. Normally they would have fallen all over themselves with suggestions, hoping to win points in their lifelong struggle for their father's approval. Today, however, they contributed nothing but wholehearted approval of Sylvia's plans, and their manner suggested that they were preoccupied with some private matter that made the birthday dinner seem trivial by comparison.

At first Sandy speculated that his brothers were enjoying a good laugh over his reaction to their idea for a family birthday present. The chosen object satisfied all of Charlie and Ed's normal criteria — it was expensive, impressive to outsiders, not returnable, and created serious problems for their youngest brother. What they had in mind was commissioning Andy Warhol to paint one of his multiple canvas, silk-screen portraits — with Nat as the subject. To Sandy, it was formula art, one of an endless mechanical series — a gimmick. For cranking out this picture, Mister Warhol would charge $60,000. Split four ways, Sandy's share came to $15,000.

Not only did he not have that kind of money to throw around — even if he were as wealthy as a Beatle he wouldn't have gone for such a worthless rip-off of a birthday present. Didn't he want to make the old man happy? the brothers taunted Sandy. Hadn't Nat been good to him and shouldn't he return the generosity? For some reason that Sandy couldn't identify, Ed and Charlie continued with their sadistic routine far longer and with considerable more venom than usual. Like so many subtle interactions within a family, only an insider could have detected a shift in their abuse. Something was giving them permission to move beyond their normal limits of contempt. Who or what, Sandy had no idea. But something was going on. Some hidden agenda existed, he realized, that took precedence over everything else at lunch — a family secret that Sandy was certain everyone knew but him.

By the time coffee was served, Sandy's paranoia and anxiety had migrated into the physical world of abdominal cramps and gas pains, a minor-league version of what he'd experienced the morning he woke up with the tattoo. After a few sips of espresso, the pressure inside built to the point that he was forced to stand, say good-bye, and cover his exit with the explanation of an important meeting at Beth-Israel. A sudden jab of pain in his intestines rushed him through the farewell kisses and hand-shakes. Sylvia thanked him one final time for all his help, and Sandy made a beeline for the dining room exit and the men's room off the corridor by the entrance.

After he had locked himself in one of the four Carerra marble stalls, it took only minutes for him to empty his pain into the public sewer system. As he reached for the roll of toilet tissue, he heard the bathroom door open and the sound of familiar voices. Ed and Charlie were talking about Sandy, unaware of his presence in the bathroom.

"It looks to me like he still doesn't know," Charlie said. "But he is a clever son-of-a-bitch, and he may not want us to know that he knows. What do you think?"

Without making the slightest noise, Sandy picked his feet up off the floor and braced them against the marble door. Anyone looking at the row of self-closing stalls would have seen four apparently empty toilets.

Not five feet from where Sandy sat, his brothers stopped before the row of urinals and continued their conversation while Ed took care of business.

"There's no way he could know," Ed finally answered.

"What about Dad?"

"Nope. He told you himself—he has the same doubts about Sandy that we do."

"Yeah, but the old guy's getting sentimental. You know how he is; he gets some notion and, wham, he acts on it without thinking."

"Charlie, be serious. Dad's not going to blow five million bucks just because he's sentimental about Sandy. I mean, who the fuck do you think built the business to the point where it's worth that kind of dough?"

"Ed," Charlie whispered angrily, "we're in public, huh? Have a little discretion and leave out the numbers, will ya?"

"Don't be so paranoid, Charlie."

Not one to trust any situation, Charlie made a quick scan of the men's room. Inside the stall, Sandy held his uncomfortable position.

"You can't be too careful" — Charlie ended his search for eavesdroppers — "with these kinds of dollars at stake. Say, you going to flush it or what?"

"Does that have something to do with being overheard, too?" Ed responded sarcastically.

"It's called *hygiene,* schmuck. Give the handle a yank."

"You and your hygiene; how does Nora put up with you?"

"Listen asshole, just pull the handle."

Sandy heard the urinal flush.

"Happy now?" Ed asked over the roar of the water.

"No. And I won't be until those papers are signed. It's bad enough they're investing in a business six thousand miles from their home; what we don't need is for them to meet Sandy and suddenly start doubting the family's management."

"Listen, the cancer center has Sandy in way over his head already. He's so busy building the all-time great memorial for Mom, he'll never have time to learn about the investors. Trust me."

Charlie laughed. "I have to give you credit — that cancer clinic was one smart idea. What do you want to bet he fucks it up royally?"

"Maybe. But I don't like talking like that."

"Something's wrong with the truth, suddenly?"

"He's still our brother, Charlie."

"Does that mean you want him breathing down your neck the rest of your life, in on every decision, telling us how to run the business? You and I both know Dad's not going to be around forever. When he retires, then what's it going to be? You, me, and Mister Peace and Freedom? Is that what you want, forty more years of going to work with that wise guy and bullshit artist as our partner?"

"You already know what I think," Ed answered reluctantly.

"So why are you suddenly defending the guy?"

"I guess I wish things could have been different."

"Don't we all. But track records are track records. We have
families to look after. Children. We have to think of their futures.
This is one of those opportunities that only rolls around once in
a lifetime."

"Look, you don't have to convince me; I know you're right."

"You don't sound so sure. I mean, Ed, think of this as just
business. He's not being cheated out of anything he deserves.
The *whole* family owns Vita-Line. I've got a wife and two kids to
support. You've got a wife and two kids. Sandy's just got himself.
It's simple mathematics — Dad and Sylvia get half and each one
of us, our wives and kids, gets one-ninth of the other half. One
eighteenth of the whole thing is the share he deserves. I mean,
it's not as if he contributed to the business or this deal. Am I
wrong?"

"You know you're not." But Ed spoke without conviction.

"*If* he'd brought us something. *If* he'd been effective in the
negotiations. *If* he were acceptable to the new management, then
I could see him being entitled to a bigger share. But whatever we
gave him to do, he'd screw it up, you know that. Will he be happy
with the way things work out? No. But is he happy now? You
know the answer to that one, too. Think about this. Suppose he
got the same share our families get; what's he going to do with it?
I'll give you hundred-to-one odds he'd just piss it all away like he
did with his hippy newspaper. Whose money do you think he lost
on that thing? Those were bucks right out of Dad's estate. *We*
paid for that fucking pile of crap paper. Were you ever asked if
you wanted to underwrite a hippy newspaper? Yeah, well neither
was I. And in 1968 dollars. With this deal we get it back. Fair is
fair, you said so yourself."

After a long silence, Ed spoke quietly, acquiescing. "So when
are the investors going to make their decision?"

"My understanding is that it'll be a few weeks at most."

"Ohh, baby. Getting down to the short hairs." Ed sounded
excited.

"Momentum is finally moving our way, Eddie."

Sandy held his breath as the men's room door opened and his
brothers departed. Then he dropped his numb feet to the floor,

wiped himself, and stood up. Enraged to the point of murder, Sandy's mind raced over what he'd heard. His worst fears were confirmed. The family was selling the business for a ton of money and he was being deliberately screwed out of his rightful share. His first impulse involved buying a machine gun and splattering his father and brothers all over the antiseptic vitamin plant. Sure, those sons-of-bitches had their reasons. So did Hitler and Goebbels and Eichmann. And just like the fucking Germans, Sandy's brothers and father rationalized their behavior. Greed had transformed them into Jewish Nazis, cannibalizing the youngest son in their final solution to the family business. Survival of the fittest was their motto. Death to the weakest. The spoils to the victor. What they were attempting was a surgical eradication of Sandy from the family using tactics copied from the SS success in the Warsaw Ghetto. Step A called for isolation. Next came starvation. Step C was death. If it had worked in the Warsaw Ghetto, think of how well it would work in calm, unsuspecting, prosperous, little old West Los Angeles.

Worse than the money was the injustice of the situation. He had worked hard for the family. Selling vitamins wasn't his obsession, but he certainly made an effort, and if he wasn't inspired, so what? He was good at his job, earned profits for the company, and his Vita-Line responsibilities were an unqualified success. Nothing he did or didn't do warranted cutting him out of his rightful place as an equal in the family and its business. *One fucking eighteenth!*

Sandy flushed the toilet and left the stall. As he washed his hands, he noticed the time — if he didn't hurry he'd be late for his appointment with the Pasadena surgeon.

Fuck the doctor. Fuck the tattoo. Fuck the whole shitpile of a family, he raged in despair. Sandy was certain of only one thing: He had to get out of the restaurant without being seen. He needed time to calm down and think. He needed air. Slinking out of the men's room, Sandy peeked back into the dining room and was pleased to see that the Klein table was now empty. Pushing the front door open a crack, he surveyed the parking lot in time to see Ed's Jensen shoot out of the driveway, followed by Charlie in his Cadillac. The coast was clear.

Seconds later Sandy was out the door and striding down the side street to his Volvo, which he'd been lucky enough to park around the corner in a metered space. Finding that spot had been his one good move of the day. If he had left his car with the Parcheesi's attendant, Charlie and Ed would have seen it after their conversation in the men's room and Sandy would have lost his one remaining advantage.

As he accelerated away from the restaurant, Sandy tried to calm his rapid-fire stream of crazed, self-destructive thoughts. No matter how he interpreted this latest turn of events, the despair he had struggled against so recently closed in on him with a vengeance. All he knew was that the only possibility for survival was to get away from his family, his past, and the horrible losses that connected him to those vicious people. How could he do this? Where could he go? Whatever he did, one fact was obvious: Any course of action he chose required him to get the concentration camp tattoo removed from his arm immediately.

8

"Sandy Carroll to see Doctor McKeegan."

The reception nurse passed a masonite clipboard out through the sliding glass partition separating the inner office from the ultramodern chrome and glass waiting room.

"Fill this out. You're the next patient."

Sandy bent over the form, inventing lies to protect his anonymity. He would never have guessed that penciling in one crummy standardized form could be so draining. A phony name and address were easy enough, but occupation, close relatives, phone numbers — all the inventions and deceptions exhausted and further depressed him.

"Sandy Carroll," the receptionist called.

Doctor McKeegan received Sandy in a small, wholesome office decorated with impressively framed medical degrees alongside color photographs of a sturdy, wholesome wife and four pretty teenaged daughters. On the surface the set-up appeared reassuring. That's what the Jews in Auschwitz thought about the numbers above the clothes hooks in the changing room outside the "showers." "Remember your number," the guard kept calling, "so you can get your clothes after you're deloused."

The doctor was about sixty, and somewhat fleshier than fashionable. He had a barely tamed, Eastern European peasant look, as if his thick frame covered an earthy and gentle soul. McKeegan inspired confidence. Leading Sandy into a small examining room, the surgeon quickly got down to business. After flicking on the harsh light of a cantilevered lamp, the man carefully probed and inspected the swollen pink tissue surrounding the blue numbers on Sandy's arm. Problem number one was a mild infection which, in McKeegan's opinion, prevented any surgery for at least two weeks.

"I was hoping there was some way you could do it today. Couldn't you just give me some stronger antibiotics?" Sandy urged.

McKeegan shook his head. "There are enough problems in surgery without complicating the situation with a known infection. It just isn't done."

As the doctor continued to scrutinize the tattoo, Sandy sensed a change in the man's demeanor. McKeegan was not what he first appeared to be. His voice resonated with an eerie familiarity, as if hidden in the man's past was a foreign birth. Hungarian? Czechoslovakian? Polish? As he tried to get McKeegan to talk, in the hope of identifying his accent, Sandy grew more anxious. All he'd wanted was a competent, out of the way, *goyisha* surgeon with no emotional connection to the Nazis or to Auschwitz.

"If you don't mind my asking," the surgeon looked straight at Sandy, "how did this come to be?"

The man had gone right for the jugular, asking the unanswerable question. "It doesn't really matter, does it?" Sandy spoke in his most controlled, innocuous tone of voice.

McKeegan resumed his inspection of the infected flesh. "I've worked on a few of these in my time, but this is the freshest I've ever seen. Did you trace over the old tattoo, or is this a new one?"

"I didn't realize you needed that information to remove it." Sandy spoke defensively.

"The depth of pigmentation will make a difference. However, from what I can tell, this is a new one." He looked up at Sandy. "Why on earth would you have something like this put on your arm?"

"If you don't mind," Sandy spoke sharply, "I'm more interested in having it taken off. Can you do that or not?"

The doctor released Sandy's arm, then spoke softly. "With a name like McKeegan you may not believe this but I, myself, was for almost ten months a prisoner in Auschwitz. This is why I ask." The surgeon unbuttoned his own left shirt sleeve, rolled it up, and held out the arm for Sandy to examine. Faint but clearly legible on McKeegan's skin was a tattooed number of a size and style almost identical to Sandy's.

"In Slovakia, foolish youth that I was, I joined the Communists to oppose Hitler. When Germany invaded, I went underground and fought from the forests. They caught us the last year of the war and sent me to Auschwitz. At liberation I weighed ninety-two pounds."

A strange buzzing in Sandy's ears exploded in volume to rival the roar from Niagra Falls. McKeegan was the nightmare Sandy had traveled to Pasadena to avoid. Forcing himself to remain calm, Sandy felt time and space physically distorting. McKeegan, only two feet away, appeared to be sitting at the other end of a football field, as if seen through the wrong end of a telescope.

"Can you remove it or not?" Sandy finally was able to whisper.

"You're certain you want it removed?" McKeegan seemed to be bellowing through a bullhorn.

"There's no question about it."

The doctor hesitated for a moment as he rolled his shirt sleeve back down and refastened his cuff link. "If you did what I think you did and just recently had this tattoo put on your arm, I ask you very, very seriously to answer the question. *Why?* You must know this thing isn't a joke. People died, sometimes ten thousand a day, with these numbers on their arms. I saw friends shot for nothing but a camp guard's amusement. Alsatians, commanded by SS, tore my baby sister apart in front of my mother's eyes. The SS were looking for me. When my mother couldn't tell them where I was, what they did to her, well . . ." McKeegan stopped himself, momentarily looking away. "It doesn't matter," he resumed. "What I'm trying to say is that why you did this is serious, but it's your business. I'm a doctor and, yes, I can remove it but you must wait two weeks minimum for the infection to clear up." Abruptly McKeegan swung around, opened the maroon lacquered cabinet over the stainless steel sink, and handed Sandy a tube of medication.

"Apply this three times a day to the skin around the tattoo and come back in two weeks." McKeegan suddenly stared at Sandy with a piercing gaze. "Please think about what I told you of my family. You couldn't possibly have wanted to be at Auschwitz —

no one could wish to be part of that kind of horror. Such a thought is unimaginable. Ask yourself, *why. Why?*"

McKeegan opened the examining room door. "Tell Cheryl to make a one-hour appointment in two weeks. We should be able to do the work right here in the office. Good-bye, Mister Carroll." McKeegan gave Sandy's hand a fast, powerful shake, then vanished back into his office.

Quickly rolling down his shirt sleeve, Sandy paid the receptionist in cash for the visit and told her he'd call for an appointment as soon as he consulted his calendar, which he'd left at work.

Out in the hallway, Sandy stopped at the water fountain and took long swallows of chilled water in the hope of stopping the massive amount of nervous sweat his body had begun to generate. McKeegan had made him feel like primordial slime, subhuman ooze beneath the lowliest amoeba. Just his luck to have chosen through the phone book, at random, probably the only surgeon in Los Angeles County who'd been imprisoned at Auschwitz. It was almost as if some primal force of nature had it in for Sandy. Life couldn't content itself with simple humiliations; no, somehow he was targeted for heart-bursting levels of degradation and disaster. There was simply nothing else left in fate's arsenal to hit him with. His wife was gone, as was his daughter, career, and now his familial connections to the future. Everything that he'd loved and cared about had been taken from him. All that remained, he finally understood, was his own death. He had to end the pain: Now.

As Sandy drove back to the plant, he began to think how simple it would be to ease the steering wheel twenty degrees counterclockwise, smash through the chain-link divider, and finish the job in an embrace with the front bumper of an oncoming eighteen-wheel oil truck.

Only one thing stopped him from obliterating himself then and there: He needed to leave a note explaining the suicide. It wasn't enough just to end the suffering—the act itself also had to have meaning. A long, clear chronicle of the injustices he'd suffered at the hands of his family required being set down on paper. The whole community needed to hear about the injuries, lies, and betrayals in order to understand how Nat, Charlie, and Ed had pushed him over the brink. It would be his last and most personal legacy as a reporter. Only after the note was written, could he get back into his car and destroy himself against the chromed-steel bumper of the biggest, heaviest, and fastest semi barreling down the freeway.

9

All afternoon Sandy remained locked in his office working on the suicide note. As he refined each draft, paring the litany of grief down to the bone, he wondered how he could guarantee that the document would be read aloud at his funeral. Was such a thing ever done with suicides?

The funeral itself Sandy had no difficulty imagining. For the community's consumption, the Klein family would put on an Academy Award performance, grieving and lamenting a death they had worked long and hard to engineer. Hundreds of Nat's friends and business associates would show up to comfort the old man. Yes, the poor guy, they'd all agree, condemned by fate to endure so many tragedies, starting with the loss of his extended family in Germany, the death of his beloved wife, and now the worst blow a father could suffer—the suicide of his youngest son. Such a funeral would be an even more hypocritical circus than the one put on in honor of Sandy's daughter, Rachael.

How vividly Sandy remembered the sickening, theatrical breast beating so touchingly displayed by Anne and her friends at the graveside service of his darling daughter. One after another Anne and the mourners nailed the blame on reckless drivers, incompetent cops, lenient judges, and the ineffective criminal justice system. No one brought up the fact that Rachael's death lay solely and strictly in Anne's negligent hands. Had she been supervising her daughter instead of gossiping on the telephone, Rachael would never have pedaled her tricycle out of the drive-way, between those parked cars, directly into the path of that oncoming Buick.

As Sandy sat as his desk rereading his suicide note with grim satisfaction, his mind shifted to his current trauma and he couldn't help but wonder why Nat was cheating him, the youngest son, out of his rightful inheritance. It wasn't as if the old man hadn't many, many times promised Sandy an equal share in the company. And it also wasn't as if Sandy had done anything of real consequence to turn Nat against him. Obviously they had conflicts, even significant ones. But that wasn't new. The question was, what suddenly justified a knife in the back?

At that instant the telephone rang.

"Sandy Klein?" The German-accented voice startled him.

"Gunther, hello. What's up?" Sandy realized he had totally forgotten about the German.

"Today is the twenty-first; I wanted to confirm our meeting."

Sandy looked at his watch. Christ, he thought, it was already four o'clock and the god-damn banks are closed; where the hell am I going to get the cash? Suicide or not, he couldn't leave a loose end like Gunther hanging around. If the police ever got hold of that story, his death would take on distorted and confusing political overtones.

"Eight o'clock tonight at Ship's, right?"

"Correct."

"You have all the lists?"

"Everything you want."

"Then I'll see you there."

"Ya. Good-bye."

Hanging up, Sandy opened his wallet and counted forty-two dollars, far from the amount he needed. Picking up his private phone, he dialed a number.

"First National Bank," the operator answered.

"Walter Dirkson's office," Sandy said.

After a brief pause, a secretary's voice came on the line. "Mister Dirkson's office."

"Lena?"

"Yes."

"Lena, this is Sandy Klein. How are you?"

"Sandy, hi. Great. How you doing?"

"Lena, listen. I need a big favor."

As Sandy had expected, Lena was smart enough to authorize a little after-hours banking for a good customer like Vita-Line. In ten minutes he was out of the plant through the side door, down

the block, in and out of the bank, and back in his office without
anyone having noticed his absence.

On the pretext of finishing a backlog of work, Sandy stayed
late rewriting his suicide note. The final draft detailed a depressing situation that no one, he believed, could read without con-
demning Nat and his two remaining sons.

Hours after the other employees on his shift had left for home,
later even than the end of the freeway rush-hour traffic, at a time
when it seemed to Sandy that everyone in the world was back
home with their wives or husbands and children, eating dinner,
affectionately quarreling, doing homework, watching the tube —
all the usual after-work activities — only then did he finally leave
the Vita-Line plant for his last journey across town.

Twenty minutes later he shut off the Volvo's engine in Ship's
parking lot at the corner of Wilshire Boulevard, a block east of
Westwood. The stucco and glass coffee shop was packed, and it
took Sandy a couple of minutes to work his way past the people,
through the hot, fried-food smell of the main dining room to the
back. There, alone at a booth, sat Gunther, looking nervous and
uncomfortable. Beside him on the banquette seat lay a suitcase-
sized cardboard box of computer printouts.

10

The association with Gunther had begun six months earlier with an article Sandy had read in the "View" section of the *Los Angeles Times*. The piece described a reunion held every year on June fifteenth in a little village not far from Bonn in West Germany. It was a "strictly private affair," a "sentimental weekend" in which the survivors of Nazi Germany's infamous and brutal SS units took over an entire hotel, excluding all press and family, and celebrated in a "nonpolitical way, drinking beer, singing, and sharing memories of the war." Like how much fun it was to rape and murder innocent Jews, Sandy had reacted, outraged that such an event could be tolerated in the modern world. Over the next few weeks, his rage festered. If he had still been the editor of *The Heart of L.A.*, he could have assigned his best reporter to the story. But now all he could do was chew over the facts and implications in isolation.

To tolerate the SS as a sentimental organization reflected a public still willing to embrace the World War II German vision of the world. Nazism wasn't a relic of history, but on the upswing, a legitimate political position.

For a few years back in the late forties, things had appeared to be different. At Nuremberg a handful of war criminals had ended their careers swinging from Allied gallows. But they were the exception. In the nearly three decades since those trials, only a few grandiose exhibitionists like Adolf Eichmann, who practically begged to be caught, ever met justice. The bulk of the men who did the actual torturing and killing, the SS, were let off the hook, in effect given permission to live freely, in peace — which they did not only in Germany, but in the United States and most other non-Communist democracies as well. The article in the *L.A. Times* made it clear to Sandy that if an SS reunion could be celebrated like a Boy Scout Jamboree, then the world had forgotten one of the basic lessons of the war. Not only were Nazism and the SS alive and flourishing, but the actual killers and war criminals themselves were everywhere, apparently normal citizens of communities throughout the United States and the world.

It was a matter of public record that, after the war, Wernher Von Braun and hundreds of other Nazi scientists were given blanket immunity to come to the U.S. and work on the fledgling ICBM missile program. Also invited were hundreds of German military and security officers who were "staunch anti-Communists" and could contribute to cold war national security. This was known; what wasn't known was the fact that these people, the legitimate technicians, were a drop in the bucket compared with the thousands of immigrants brought in under the category of displaced persons, individuals "forced from their homes by Soviet postwar occupation." With the lax immigration controls, only the clumsiest of liars would have had trouble obtaining legal residency in the United States. And that being the case, Sandy made the mental leap, the odds were a hundred percent that somewhere in Southern California, hidden away in at least one little neighborhood, was an unpunished Nazi, propelled from the old country by those years of mass murder.

The image of all those SS veterans openly and proudly flying to Germany for their annual reunion had nauseated Sandy. For weeks he hadn't been able to stop thinking about it. As an ex-reporter, nothing would have pleased him more than to track down such a person.

That's when the idea had occurred to him: The discovery of a Nazi war criminal living safely in Southern California would be an accomplishment of historical proportions, something that would really force the community to take notice of their complacency. Sandy knew that such a project wasn't in the category of a Weizmann trying to found the state of Israel, but it was certainly a big step above haggling with salesmen over wholesale vitamin prices. And since Rachael's death, the possibility of hunting down a Nazi was the first and only idea, outside of grieving, that had aroused passion in Sandy. It would be one hell of a weird hobby, but come hell or high water he, Sandy Klein, was going to find and expose a Nazi living in his community.

Sandy had begun his research with the idea that an SS officer traveling to Germany for the annual reunion would choose to fly Lufthansa, the airline of the fatherland. Such a man probably wasn't rich, which meant he'd have only a limited time away from work for a vacation — three weeks at the most. So a good place to start was with the Lufthansa flight lists from Los Angeles to Germany beginning two weeks before the SS reunion. Out of the thousands of individuals flying to Germany during those fourteen days, Sandy was betting that at least one of them was a Nazi war criminal.

After spending almost a week of evenings at the L.A. airport studying the Lufthansa ticket agents, Sandy focused on the man called Gunther. This particular airline employee regularly wore the same white cotton shirt for two consecutive nights. In six days the man had worn only three shirts. Sandy assumed that such a habit meant the young German was financially strapped and cutting corners to save money — the perfect person to approach for help.

Late one evening, after Lufthansa flight number 212 departed for Frankfurt, Sandy followed Gunther into the airport lounge where the German took his nightly coffee break. After Gunther sat down alone and had comfortably begun to sip his paper cup of coffee and read the latest issue of *Soaring* magazine, Sandy joined him at the table, introducing himself as a private detective hoping to buy some information. At first Gunther had been wary. But a hundred dollar bill passed across the table in a paper napkin convinced the ticket agent to listen. Sandy claimed to be trying to locate a missing ex-husband in a divorce case. The story involved a wealthy man who was supposedly six months behind with his child support payments. The only information on the man's whereabouts was the fact, admitted by one of the ex-husband's present girlfriends, that he was flying to Germany some time during the first two weeks of June. If Gunther could supply copies of the passenger lists for every Lufthansa flight out of LAX in that period, Sandy promised to pay the German five hundred dollars in cash. After a moment's thought, Gunther agreed. It was almost too simple, Sandy had worried at the time.

This explained his highly inconvenient meeting in the back room of Ship's at eight o'clock on Thursday, June twenty-first. Instead of the whole myriad of complications that Sandy had feared, the only unusual feature of the meeting was a strange awareness of his tattoo: As he shook Gunther's hand, *A7549653* began to itch and burn as if it were a Jewish divining rod reacting to the presence of a German.

A nervous but practical man, Gunther simply took the envelope of cash, counted the contents in his lap out of sight of the crowded dining room, thanked Sandy, looked around to make sure no one was watching, then stood up and strolled out of the restaurant. The entire transaction had taken no more than three minutes.

Surprised that anything so questionable could have gone so smoothly, Sandy left a two dollar tip on the table, picked up the container of computer paper, carried it out of the restaurant, slid it in the back of his Volvo, and drove out of the parking lot. As much as he wanted to toss the incriminating contents of the box into a roadside dumpster, something about the printout's value stopped him. Perhaps there was some way he could write an addendum to his suicide note and leave his few assets as payment to a reporter to follow through with the investigation. It was an interesting idea, and it appealed to the newspaperman in Sandy, who hated the idea of a sensational story going to waste. As depressed as he felt and as much as he loathed sitting down at his desk and revising that note one more time, he realized that he had no choice. He also knew that the wonderful smells of grilling hamburgers, fried onions, and coffee in Ship's had made him hungry; if he expected to work for another few hours, he had to eat.

Instead of hurrying home via Sunset, Sandy detoured two blocks, heading south on Westwood Boulevard, where he drove into the parking lot of the local Westward Ho supermarket. After locking all the doors of his Volvo, Sandy hurried into the store to buy a bottle of scotch and the ingredients for a tasty, filling, easy-to-eat last meal.

11

"The Ho," as the miniature supermarket was affectionately known to its loyal patrons, was a throwback to another era, a time when the community surrounding the UCLA campus was a sleepy world of university professors, state-subsidized college students, and Spanish-style shops. The charm of the little Westward Ho was nostalgia. It had remained unchanged while everything else in the area succumbed to the microvisionaries euphemistically called developers. *Recidivists* would have been a more apt description. Old apartment buildings with spacious rooms, high ceilings, and custom tile work surrendered to the wrecker's ball, to be replaced by stucco and plastic rabbit hutches given the pretentious identity of *condominiums*. Mom and Pop stores with actual, on-the-premise owners were bought up and converted into bland, anonymous boutiques. Coffee shops vanished; in their places appeared ethnic restaurants—Thai, Indian, Mexican, Italian, up, down, in fashion and out, like urban culinary weeds. It was a forerunner of a phenomenon sweeping America, the transformation of cities from stable communities into minimum-wage, service-oriented, identityless sprawls, the beginning of the USA as a nation of coast-to-coast shopping malls. Westwood Boulevard met corporate America and found itself transformed into K-Mart. Only the Ho had bucked this trend, and that is what accounted for its popularity.

Sandy pushed open the big glass door and entered the refrigerated store. On some nights the place was empty, but this evening it was as jammed as a Saturday morning department store sale—dozens of basket-wielding women fought aggressively for territory in the gridlocked aisles.

Given his mood, Sandy did not relish any further aggravation; he hoped for a simple in and out. But as he reached for the one remaining shopping cart, a bony old woman yanked it away from him. He wanted to argue with her, to insist that he was there first.

Instead, he told himself he didn't need a cart. Smiling politely, he slipped around the angry lady, headed for the meat counter, and shoved his way through the crowd, grabbing the last hot chicken from the infrared take-out display. Then it was on to the dairy section, where he searched in vain for his favorite, blueberry yogurt. Settling for raspberry, he also picked up a carton of strawberry, just in case. The thought of all these flavors made him even hungrier and drove him to the deli section, where he reached through the crowd to grab a particularly good-looking hunk of aged New York cheddar. From the bakery section he obtained a baguette of French bread, plucked an apple from the fruit counter and a fifth of J&B from the liquor locker. Juggling this substantial armload, he headed down the soft-drink aisle for a big bottle of soda water.

Locked in combat for customers, Coke, 7-Up, and Pepsi were all on sale at huge discounts. It would have taken a machete to clear this particular section of the store for a quick purchase. Thanks to the fact that he didn't have a shopping cart, Sandy was able to weave around portions of the pushy mob with a certain ungainly freedom. Because of all the food he was carrying, as Sandy spun to avoid stalled shopping carts, he more than once whacked people inadvertently with the heel of his French bread. But this was war and, a good foot soldier, he finally made it to the soft-drink section. Unfortunately the quart bottle of Schweppes he needed was located exactly where it was most difficult for him to reach — on the bottom shelf. Nearing the end of his patience, Sandy shifted the long baguette from his hand to his armpit and transferred the yogurts to his right arm, which now also clutched the apple, the chicken, and the cheese. Balancing himself like Rudolf Nureyev, Sandy reached down with his left hand and maneuvered the neck of the J&B bottle against the glass top of the Schweppes soda water. Just as he tightened his grip and prepared to hoist, the unexpected occurred.

A passing shopper (perhaps one he'd whacked with the French bread) slammed her shopping cart into his precariously balanced body, knocking him off balance, causing him to topple, crash against another lady's cart, bounce off the soda display, and splash to the ground in a heap of yogurt, cheese, French bread, and thousands of shards of broken glass from cases of shattered soda bottles.

For almost a minute, Sandy lay on the floor, stunned. When he finally sat up, what he saw horrified him. From his left elbow to his hand, his arm was bright red, drenched with blood. *Whose blood?* He didn't wonder long; it was obviously his own. The question then became, where was it coming from? And, why was there so much of it?

Rotating his hand, Sandy found the answer. Jammed deep into his wrist was an enormous shard of jagged glass that had accomplished as effective a job of slashing his artery as any single-edged razor blade could have. As he watched, blood trickled out of his flesh like water from a leaking spigot, already soaking his sports coat and flooding the yellow linoleum floor with a pool of deep red liquid.

The reaction in the aisle was paralysis. Instead of helping, the nearby customers drew back in fear. Sandy, losing his strength to shock, knew he had to do something. Gathering his courage, he yanked the piece of glass from his wrist in one quick motion. Instead of stopping the bleeding, the unplugged artery spurted blood like a miniature fountain, soaking everything with red, sticky liquid. While the shoppers screamed, Sandy felt his strength ebb and, despite his best efforts, found himself unable to stand. An aisle that only moments before had been a calamitous jam-up was suddenly empty. No one was willing to assume the slightest responsibility for the injured stranger. Finally one brave soul, behaving in a manner she believed to be heroic, yelled at the top of her lungs, "Call the paramedics." Even Sandy, who remained propped up against the soda display, knew this would take too long. It was all over, he feared — and so unexpectedly. He needed time, he wanted to protest, he hadn't finished his note. It wasn't fair. Bleeding to death on the floor of the Westward Ho made no more sense than the Coke sign facing him across the aisle. A six-pack was on sale for thirty-nine cents. What a good deal. Why not buy some? According to the ads, Coke had something for everybody; maybe it would stop his bleeding.

"Let me see your wrist," a voice commanded.

Floating above his head, Sandy saw a white, hazy shape that appeared to be female. Why not? he asked himself, and weakly held up his arm.

A hand, which somehow seemed to be connected to the woman's face, hurriedly pushed up the sleeve of his saturated sports jacket, then tore open the cuff of his shirt, exposing Sandy's flesh all the way to his elbow.

"Someone get me a towel, quick," the woman yelled.

Seconds later the hand began to mop the blood on Sandy's arm with paper napkins. As she moved up from his elbow, searching for the source of the bleeding, the dinner napkins scraped the crimson bandage covering his tattoo. With the last of its adhesive dissolved by the blood, the protective dressing slid off, revealing a forearm heavily coated with sticky red fluid. Locating the site of the injury, the woman pressed a thick pile of the absorbent paper firmly against the slashed flesh of Sandy's wrist. In seconds the flow of blood dribbled to almost nothing. As she maintained pressure on the laceration, the woman used another pile of napkins to mop up his forearm in a search for secondary injuries. As the skin emerged from the coating of blood, she saw the tattoo imprinted on his flesh. *A7549653.*

Momentarily stunned by the blue numbers, the woman dropped his wrist, allowing the blood to resume pumping from the artery. As an onlooker screamed, Sandy plummeted toward a blackout. But firm pressure on his wrist quickly stopped the bleeding and kept him conscious. Then, in what seemed only a few moments, someone helped him to his feet and supported him as he walked in a daze out of the store. Seconds later he was sitting in the low-slung passenger seat of a dark blue Datsun 240Z.

"If I let go, are you strong enough to keep the pressure on your wrist?" the woman's voice floated in from the parking lot.

"I think so," he answered, squeezing the pad of dinner napkins.

The next hour or so was a little vague for Sandy. He retained a faint memory of a high-speed drive up Westwood Boulevard into the emergency room entrance of the UCLA hospital. From there a man dressed in white (an orderly?) lifted him from the Datsun, placed him in a wheelchair, and rushed him through the double sliding doors into the emergency room. Then came another man in white, some hushed words, a nurse, an injection into his wrist, the smell of alcohol, a bright light shining overhead, and a numb sensation in his arm as sutures closed his wound. After bandaging his arm, someone injected him with a tetanus vaccine. Then he was wheeled into a small examining room where he was stretched out on a firm, padded table and told to rest. Everything around him was white, clean, and comforting. He felt safe and protected, free from worry. There was only one thing for him to do and that was rest. For the first time in years he had absolutely no trouble closing his eyes, obeying orders, and drifting off to sleep.

12

"Take a few sips of this; it should help you feel better."

Sandy opened his eyes. A paper cup filled with steaming tea hovered a foot from his face. What the hell am I doing here? he asked himself. In a single second the entire episode at the Ho reappeared in his memory. He was alive in UCLA hospital with a terrible, dry, drugged taste in his mouth. Sitting up slowly, feeling dizzy and groggy, Sandy grasped the cup of tea.

"Got it?"

Sandy nodded, lifted the cardboard vessel to his lips, and sipped the hot, sweetened drink. Good old Lipton's.

"I was worried about you in the market; it really looked like you'd lost a lot of blood. But they ran a red cell count, and your hemoglobin was thirteen-four—at the most you're down a pint, the same as if you'd given blood to the Red Cross."

Sandy looked up from his tea. Talking to him in a friendly, deep, gravelly voice—obviously a New Yorker—was a black-haired, tall young woman with a thin, faintly masculine body. Dressed as a stylish professional, she wore tan trousers, a chocolate-brown silk blouse, and an eggshell Italian linen sports jacket. Her face was free of makeup, intelligent, attractive, but certainly not a world class beauty—in another era she would have been described as handsome. No question about it, she was an impressive, self-confident individual who was obviously intolerant of nonsense, a woman of substance. The only incongruity in her otherwise immaculate appearance were the reddish-brown stains dried on her coat sleeves, trousers, and shirtcuffs.

"I guess you probably don't believe me, with all the blood you saw on the linoleum. I was surprised myself. But as any doctor will tell you, almost everyone visually overestimates the quantity of blood lost in a trauma case like yours. So you have no reason to worry; you're going to be fine."

Sandy recognized the woman's hands; she was the one who had pressed the napkins against his pumping artery.

"The big problem was shock. You came this close to passing out." She held her thumb and forefinger a half inch apart. "Your skin went gray and your eyes started to roll up into your head. That's what really pissed me off. I mean, not you—the rest of those clowns in that market. There were probably two hundred people in that store. Not a mile from UCLA hospital. I bet there were five doctors not fifty feet away and not one god-damn one of them, or anyone else for that matter, so much as lifted a pinkie to help. It's some time to be alive, isn't it? Half the people in the Ho were UCLA students and half of those, I'd bet again, had marched in the streets protesting Vietnam, the bombing of Cambodia, or the draft—a real liberal group, this Westwood crowd. But will they help a fellow human in trouble? Those bastards thought they were heroes because they yelled for someone to call the paramedics. If that's all anyone had done, you'd have bled to death. It's some time we're living in—everyone claims to care, screaming and marching for social justice—but no one lifts a finger to help one needy individual. Sometimes our society is a real disappointment." Suddenly she stopped talking and blushed, as if she were embarrassed. Then she spoke softly, with a tinge of shame in her voice. "I'm sorry. You of all people don't need me to tell you this. How are you feeling?"

Sandy looked at her curiously. She's sorry? Me of all people? What the hell was she talking about? Was she so grandiose as to believe that the nature of the real world was her responsibility? "I take it you're the one I thank for being alive?"

"Ple-eeze," she dismissed the whole idea. "I only did what every one of those bastards in the store should have done."

Sandy set down his empty cup and, with some difficulty, slowly raised himself to a sitting position.

"Dizzy?"

Sandy nodded. "Take it slow and relax; there's no reason to rush."

"I'd like to get out of here."

"Who wouldn't? But you made a big enough mess at the store; I wouldn't want you falling and ripping open your stitches."

Sandy nodded, pleased that his head was beginning to clear. "There must be a bill for all of this; who do I pay?"

"It's already been taken care of," she answered.

"What are you talking about?" he asked, genuinely perplexed.

"This is a university teaching hospital. A couple of stitches, a tetanus shot, and some gauze don't amount to much."

"You're not charging me?" Sandy was astounded.

"Why would *I* charge you?" she asked, equally surprised.

"In my experience doctors normally charge for their services. I'm not a charity case, you know."

"I'm not a doctor."

Sandy stared at her. "But they let you stitch me up?" he asked.

She shook her head. "All I did was stop the bleeding and drive; a resident did all the work."

Sandy pointed to his jacket hanging on the door. "In the inside pocket is my wallet. If you'll hand it to me and lend me a pen, I'll write a check to whoever it is I owe for all this and another one to you, to replace those clothes."

She didn't move. Instead, she smiled. "Sandy, forget it. The bill was nothing and these clothes are old rags. The important thing is that you're feeling better."

"How do you know my name?" he asked with suspicion.

"Oh, I'm sorry. The hospital needed your ID so I fished out your American Express card. You know how bureaucracies operate."

Did he ever. He also knew something about clothes, thanks to his ex-wife's expensive habits. Not only were the woman's garments not "old rags"; they were new, stylish, and imported.

"Why won't you let me pay for anything?" Sandy asked.

"Don't make a big deal out of nothing. When you get a chance, help a stranger who needs it. This may be hard for you to accept, but the world really isn't *all* bad. There are actually people in our society who like doing things for others. Just because you've had more than the normal run of terrible experiences doesn't mean life's always like that."

The certainty with which she delivered this opinion unnerved Sandy. How did she know about his life? What was she referring to? It didn't make any sense.

"I don't know what you're talking about."

"I think you do. But we don't have to discuss it now."

"Who are you?"

"Oh, I'm sorry. Paula Gottlieb." She extended her hand.

"You're really not a doctor?" Sandy asked, as he grasped her soft, warm, and inviting palm.

"No way," she said, releasing his grip.

"Then why do you sound like one?"

"My father's a doctor. I guess I've absorbed the terminology."

Sandy nodded. "Well, I'm sure he'd be proud of you tonight." He smiled warmly, then examined his left arm. Clean white bandages covered his flesh from his wrist half way down the arm to his elbow, concealing the stitches and the tattoo. "Since everything's been taken care of, I can just walk out of here, right?"

Paula nodded.

"I'm not a great fan of hospitals," Sandy said, slipping his feet off the cot and onto the floor. "There's a lot of sick people in these places; who knows what a person could catch." He stood up, supporting himself on the examining table. "You've been great. Unbelievable, in fact. But I'm embarrassed by how much you've put yourself out. If you know where there's a pay phone around here, I'll call a cab to take me back to my car. I really don't know how to thank you, Paula." Sandy extended his hand, as if to say good-bye.

"You truly are a case." She shook her head in amusement, ignoring his gesture. "Would it injure your sense of reality if I drove you back myself? I mean I'm going that way because I live right around the corner. Honestly, you're not going to be incurring any further obligation."

For a moment Sandy stared at her. She seemed sincere, yet it made no sense to him. "Why are you doing all this?"

"If I told you I find you interesting, would that satisfy you?"

"How can I be interesting when you don't even know me?"

"I sense it."

"Like you sense my run of terrible experiences?" he probed.

"Of that I have no doubt," she smiled.

It was no surprise to Sandy that he was in bad shape, but he couldn't fathom how it was so obvious to a perfect stranger. Apparently grief was spilling from him completely out of his control. Before he deteriorated further and became incapable of action, he had to get moving, get back on track, finish his suicide letter, and do away with his torment forever.

"A ride to my car would be great. But only if it's not out of your way."

After the first couple of wobbly steps, the walk through the emergency room was uneventful. Outside in the parking lot, the unusually chilly June night air energized him to the point where the dried blood on the bucket seat of Paula's 240Z was suddenly amusing, one further reminder of a life soon to be finished.

"If you're not in a big rush," Paula suggested, "we could stop for a quick bite to eat. I think something in your stomach would help you feel a whole lot better."

What was with this woman? "Thanks, but I'm not exactly dressed for a restaurant. Another time," he lied.

"I really think you should eat before you drive. What if we stopped at my apartment and I made you an omelette?"

"You've done enough for one night, thank you."

"You said you wanted to pay me back for the hospital. Do it by letting me cook something for you."

For a moment Sandy was too unnerved to respond. After the world's worst day, he had been saved by a lunatic. It figured, he told himself. Why not see it through? She seemed harmless, and he did need to eat. What was another hour compared with eternity?

"Sure. An omelette sounds great."

13

Given the political tone of her statements at the hospital, Sandy wouldn't have been surprised to find Paula living with an assortment of left-wing activists in a ramshackle commune. However, her home turned out to be a rented upstairs/downstairs apartment, one of six units in a beautiful white Mexican-colonial apartment building.

To make the walk shorter for Sandy, Paula ignored her back-alley garage and parked on the street in front of the walled courtyard entrance. After shutting off the 240Z and locking the doors, she headed for the open wooden gateway, her high heels clicking against the terra cotta tiles, and led him across the entryway into apartment number one. After flipping on the lights and directing Sandy to the couch, Paula disappeared into the small kitchen and began preparing the food.

Sandy's first impression of the apartment was one of *order*. Each object in the room, every piece of wicker furniture, occupied a carefully chosen place in the all-white decor. From the antique New England quilt over the fireplace to the Shaker pine sideboard, the living room radiated not just professional accomplishment but a life consisting entirely of work and career.

For a few minutes Sandy was comfortable simply lying on the couch and enjoying the feeling of a total stranger taking care of him. It was an unreal sensation, like a dream — the modern Los Angeles version of the Good Samaritan. Such generosity was not something he had ever known or believed possible. The more he thought about it, the more he wondered what was really happening.

In the hope of finding a clue, Sandy got up and crossed the room to the staircase. Mounting the first steps, he examined a few titles of the hundreds of hard-back books filling the floor-to-ceiling shelves adjacent to the stairs.

What he found explained everything, and infuriated him. From bottom to top, all the way up to the second floor, the shelves were filled with law books! Once again, he berated himself, he'd been a sap and fallen for a line of bull. Paula wasn't an altruist but a predator, money-grubbing attorney who viewed Sandy not as a person but as a case. He was business and, thanks to her intervention, a partner in a fat lawsuit against the Westward Ho. No wonder she had driven him to the hospital. No wonder she hadn't cared about her clothes or his medical bill. No wonder she'd spent so much time with him. She was a woman who, while shopping for dinner, found herself unexpectedly in possession of the goose that laid the golden egg. It was poetic justice, the cheap and deceptive ambulance chaser attempting to pacify her find with an ordinary double grade A omelette.

"You do good work," he spoke with quiet sarcasm from the kitchen doorway.

"Thank you," Paula answered, missing his critical inflection as she skillfully broke two eggs into a copper mixing bowl.

"I wasn't referring to cooking."

Puzzled, she looked up.

"Your entrepreneurial ability is impressive," Sandy said coldly.

"I'm not following you." Paula stopped what she was doing and waited for an explanation.

"As far as your acting skills go, well, I'd say you're up there with the best. Why not start a career in the movies?"

"What are you trying to tell me?"

"Think about it for a moment. What am I doing here?"

"I'm making you an omelette."

"Why?"

"Since you think you know something, why don't you just tell me directly?"

"Okay. I'll get right to the point. Which I wish *you* had done."

She waited and said nothing.

"I was sitting out there on the couch thinking how lucky I was to find the one selfless person, the only Good Samaritan I've ever met. I actually believed what you told me in the hospital; isn't that a testament to your abilities?"

Paula didn't respond.

"Then I went over to your bookshelf and what do I find? You're a lawyer! All I can say is that with your kind of talent, look out Schweppes and Westward Ho; lawsuits are on their way. En garde and prepare to defend yourselves!" Sandy spoke feverishly, near hysteria.

Paula smiled as if at a secret joke, turned away from him, flopped a tablespoon of butter into her sizzling hot iron pan, swirled it around, quickly whipped the eggs with a whisk, and poured the frothy liquid into the pan.

"Just out of curiosity," he asked, "how much are you going to charge the insurance company for my omelette?"

After shaking the pan and waiting for the eggs to set, Paula sprinkled a small handful of grated Gruyère cheese over the top. "You tell me." She spoke with an almost perverse innocence as she jerked the pan back and forth, folding the eggs up into a perfect French-style omelette.

Without waiting for a response, Paula slid the omelette onto a plate along with a quarter of a baguette, carried the snack into the adjacent dining room, and set it down on an Indian cotton place mat just across the narrow butcher-block dining table from her own empty table mat.

"Eat before it gets cold," she suggested.

"Fuck you and fuck your eggs."

Paula simply smiled, amused, as if she had heard a joke instead of an insult. "Sandy, I can understand your anger. But I still wish you would eat before the eggs get cold. If your accusations are right, do you think I'll charge any less for an uneaten omelette? In a restaurant if you order food and don't touch it, they still give you a bill, don't they? C'mon. Sit down and eat. You need the protein. Please. Whatever my motives, I did just possibly save your life in the market. So pay me back by eating. Okay?"

Sandy glared at her, stuck. Even if her interest had only been money, she was right — she had saved his life. Surrendering to his hunger, he took a bite of the omelette, which was not just good but superb, absolutely the best he had ever eaten. Concealing his pleasure, Sandy swallowed a second bite.

"I know it's not *that* bad."

Sandy cut another forkful and ate it with no apparent enjoyment.

"It wouldn't be the end of the world if you told me you like it."

"You wanted me to eat it; I'm eating it. Compliments weren't part of the bargain."

"God," Paula grinned, shaking her head in disbelief, "you are truly impossible."

"Yeah," Sandy spoke between mouthfuls, "well, you should take a little look in the mirror yourself. That was some speech you made to me in the hospital about your reasons for helping me. All the doctors that must have been in the Westward Ho. Your disappointment in the liberals and society in general. You were impressive. Real first-class BS."

"Meanwhile," she continued, unfazed, "I see you're not doing too badly with my cooking. Would you like another one?"

"Not at . . . What? A hundred dollars a pop? No thank you."

"Wait a minute. You saw my law books, assumed correctly that I was an attorney, then jumped to the conclusion that I want to make money off of you. Sandy, I'm curious. Is it conceivable that a smart and experienced cynic like yourself could come to a conclusion that's simply not correct? I know you've gone through some really terrible things in your life, but it's just possible that I'm not one of them. Has that occurred to you?"

There she goes again, Sandy reflected, alluding to something in his past that she had no way of knowing about. What the hell did she mean?

"Tell me something," she continued, "just what sort of law do you think I practice?"

"You'll have to forgive me, but I forget the technical term for ambulance chasing."

Paula narrowed her eyes; his probe angered her. She paused, then continued in a calm tone of voice. "Look, I know you've had a hard life, but the whole world really isn't as bad as you think. That's what I'm trying to get you to understand. Believe me, I'm sympathetic to what you've been through; I understand how you could develop such attitudes. You needed to survive. In a dangerous jungle, paranoia is essential. And it worked: You stayed alive while most others died. But that was in the past; now things are very different. Yes, I am an attorney. But I have absolutely no interest in representing you or your case, should you choose to make one. I work for an organization called the Democratic Legal Clinic where I do public interest law. I represent the have-nots, Sandy. My clients are welfare mothers, skid row alcoholics, native Americans, farm workers, and so forth. Not only have I never chased an ambulance, I don't intend to start with you, okay?"

"That surprises me," he muttered, still wary.

Paula smiled. "Just for the record, if 'that surprises me' is your idea of an apology, I think you can do better."

"The money really doesn't interest you?" Sandy was floundering, his bearings lost.

She shook her head. "I'm still waiting for that apology."

"Okay, I'm sorry," he admitted reluctantly.

"Thank you. You're human after all. Now would you like some coffee?"

"Why not?"

She walked behind his chair, reached for his dinner plate, and in the process brushed the side of her breast against his face, startling him with an unexpected sexual electricity.

"Espresso okay?"

"Absolutely," he said, unable to take his eyes off her as she carried the dish back into the kitchen, set it and the pan in the sink, and went to work on the coffee. Had she meant to touch him? What the hell was going on? Was she testing him? Was she playing with him? A situation that had seemed so clear only minutes before had turned into something very different. But what?

It must be the eggs, he told himself. The protein and fat had hit his depleted bloodstream and revived his energy, allowing him to appreciate viscerally what he had hardly noticed earlier. Paula's appeal wasn't obvious like Vikki's — the classic California blond. No, Paula's sensuality arose from her compelling character, a sense of self-possession, competence, intelligence, and mystery. Watching her as she moved efficiently about the kitchen, grinding coffee beans, assembling her small Italian espresso machine, Sandy wondered if she had any idea of her effect on him. What had started with a single brush of her silk blouse expanded into a deepening warmth, stirring the nerve endings in his thighs and crotch. After so much hemorrhaging in the Westward Ho, Sandy found it amazing that there was enough blood left in his system to so completely pump up his erection. How could he feel so terrible one minute and the next radiate with life? Who was this woman?

"Paula," he called to her, "tell me something. Do you help out everybody you see who's in trouble? Or did you single me out for a reason?"

"One second," she told him as she poured coffee into two china cups. "Do you take milk or sugar?"

"Black's fine."

Paula set one cup in front of Sandy, the other across from him, then sat down and took a sip.

"Are you going to answer my question?" he asked.

"I thought I already did."

Uncomprehending, Sandy could only stare at her.

"It's because of your past," she explained. "Initially, I helped you in Westward Ho just the way I would have helped anyone in your situation. I took a first aid course in college, so I knew what to do. I would have stopped the bleeding and then left you to the paramedics — what any decent person should have done. But when I realized who you were, I had no choice but to go the extra mile." She turned away, blushing, as if she were embarrassed by having her feelings for him exposed prematurely.

Was she crazy? he asked himself, unable even to guess at the circumstances to which she was referring.

"Sandy, honestly, I know that you're reticent. And you should be. If I'd been through what you've been through, I'm sure I'd be that way myself."

"I see." Sandy stalled, unsure of what to say next. As attractive as she appeared, it was becoming obvious Paula was a nut case.

"Do you remember, once the bleeding stopped, that I cleaned off your arm to see if there were any more shards of glass jammed in the skin? You had a bandage taped to your forearm. It was soaked with blood and when I touched it, the adhesive let go. Do you recall me dropping your wrist?"

Sandy shook his head.

"You must've already gone into shock. When I wiped the bandage it just fell off. I couldn't help seeing your tattoo. It was so unexpected that for a moment I let go of your arm. Believe me, I can understand you covering up the numbers. Most people don't have the faintest idea how to deal with them. What your tattoo represents isn't foreign to me. I grew up with them — both my parents have tattoos just like yours. My mother and father are survivors of Auschwitz. Out of a huge family — we had hundreds of relatives — only my parents lived through the war. That's why, when I saw the tattoo on your arm, I couldn't let you be taken away by some paramedic just doing his job. For me that would be like abandoning a cousin.

"That's why I keep saying that I understand what you've been through. I feel so strongly about this whole issue that I teach a class on the Holocaust with another lawyer friend. I'd love you to come sometime. Sandy, you've suffered for the rest of us. Without what you endured, Israel wouldn't exist. You lived through the most horrible and important event of the twentieth century. You were a participant in history, one of humanity's true heroes. But the world doesn't want to recognize you. Even the people who attend my Holocaust class find it frightening to know how close we all are to the monstrous human impulses, political decisions, and economic crises that could lead to a repetition of the Nazi horrors."

Speechless, Sandy nodded. Paula wasn't the lunatic he'd imagined. No wonder she had jumped to an incorrect conclusion; she was obsessed with Auschwitz and the death camps just like he was. That explained why he felt so comfortable with her. Her appeal was far more than simply his erection speaking; she was a kindred spirit of the concentration camps, a philosophical soul mate.

The long moment of silence was magical for Sandy. He had never felt this sort of sudden, deep-rooted, passionate connection to a woman before. Sipping coffee, basking in her affection, enjoying the electricity emanating from this attractive, articulate, courageous, fascinating woman, Sandy allowed himself to surrender to the remarkable aura of peace and contentment. He felt like a space traveler returning to a hero's welcome on earth after decades of interstellar travel without a single human companion. His soaring joy overwhelmed the tiny amount of guilt he felt over her obvious misunderstanding. As much as he wanted to tell her the truth about the tattoo, he was afraid of destroying the extraordinary moment. Sandy needed her to like him. He needed her to want him. He needed the magic to continue. Why jeopardize what was beginning by revealing a confusing fact? Better, he told himself, to get to know her. Then the minor jolt over the truth would be easier for her to accept. Timing was the key to understanding.

"You're not angry with me for bringing all this up, I hope?" She purred in the sweetest tone of voice.

Sandy shook his head. "You only told me what I asked for."

"I know this isn't something you want to discuss. I mean, what you went through is very personal; no one I've ever known likes discussing the camps. Obviously if you did, you wouldn't have hidden your tattoo under that bandage. You may not believe this, but I think that instead of being ashamed of that tattoo, you should walk around in short-sleeve shirts, showing it off for everyone to see."

"I really would rather not talk about it."

"Of course. And I respect your telling me that. I understand. But also know that if you ever *do* want to talk about it, I'll always be here for you. Just call me, day or night. Will you do that?" Her eyes were pleading, underscoring the depth of her passion for him.

Sandy felt like a starvation victim who'd suddenly been offered a feast. After years of self-loathing he was facing a woman who not only approved of him but had a burning need to help, nurture, and understand him. For the first time since his *Heart of*

L.A. days he felt someone looking at him as if he mattered. Through Paula's eyes he saw himself as a hero, a figure out of history, a person of extraordinary importance. What bliss! What a long-forgotten sensation of joy! The feelings she aroused revived dormant reservoirs of a survivor's hunger for more. He was a man again — desired, respected, appreciated. Could he do anything but act to sustain and heighten this promising situation?

"Yes," he answered simply. "Thank you."

Paula smiled with gratitude, then slid her hand across the table to squeeze Sandy's. It was a gesture of support, a simple movement of friendship. But as their palms touched, a surge of energy blasted between them. For Sandy, it was as if his entire existence dovetailed into the highly charged, erotic surface of Paula's soft hand. What for years had been only a drudgelike tool at the end of his arm was suddenly so hypersensitive that it felt as if it might explode from overload. This wasn't a handshake, but a profoundly sexual union.

Completely certain of himself — also for the first time in recent memory — Sandy stood up, momentarily released her hand, slipped around the dining table behind her seat, and wrapped his arms around her. When she swiveled her neck he leaned down and very delicately, very slowly, kissed her. For what seemed an eternity of pleasure, their mouths barely touched. Lips rubbed one another with the unique erotic energy that only a first kiss can generate. Eagerly, Paula took the initiative and thrust her talented tongue into his mouth, running it over his gums, darting it back and forth like the flip of a muscled whip. Remaining seated, she rotated her body on her chair and began to caress his legs and inner thighs with her finger tips, arousing him to a fever pitch of excitement.

Without speaking Paula unzipped his fly, unbuttoned his trouser waistband, slid his blood-stained slacks down around his ankles, and began fondling, squeezing, and languidly stroking his tightening balls and bulging erection through his jockey shorts. When the soft cotton material seemed incapable of stretching further without disintegrating, Paula slipped the underpants over his pulsating hard-on, dropped them to his knees, took her mouth from his lips, and hungrily slipped his cock down her throat. Using her teeth and varying pressure of her jaws, she drew his erection back and forth, dragging her incisors on the pulsing flesh. As his arousal built she squeezed his balls, maintaining that fine edge of pleasure over pain. Just as he thought he couldn't take it any more Paula lathered her middle finger in saliva and suddenly slid it into his relaxed open ass, burying it up to the third knuckle in the wet, ultrasensitive tissue of his long-untouched rectum.

Almost unable to believe what was happening, Sandy simply stood there in a joyous erotic stupor nearly as paralyzing as the physical shock from the broken bottle in Westward Ho while Paula's touch reverberated through every cell of his body. Whatever self-control he'd been able to manage until now was rapidly vanishing. His needs were urgent, too urgent. Pulling himself from her mouth, his erection quivered in the air.

"I want you now," he commanded her.

Without the slightest hesitation she stood, pulled off her trousers, slid down her lacy bikini underwear, and lay chest down on the dining table with her feet, still in high heels, flat on the floor.

Sliding his fingers between her thighs, Sandy felt paradise on earth—Paula's vulva and clitoris were engorged to extremes, so soft, so open, so unbelievably wet. Kneeling on the floor, he thrust his mouth between the cheeks of her remarkable ass and ran his tongue and lips over her luscious, fragrant sex. As Sandy took her hard clitoris in his mouth Paula began to undulate her hips, while clutching tightly to the edge of the dining table with tensed white knuckles.

"Oh, Sandy, I want your cock. Sandy, fuck me. Please Sandy, I need you."

The command was too much for him to refuse. Pulling his tongue from her he stood and, for a brief moment, admired the spectacularly arousing view: Paula lay chest down on the dining table dressed only in her silk blouse and linen sports coat. From her waist to her ankles, she was stark naked. Her upper body appeared bizarrely quiet and businesslike while her lower half was hot. Those gorgeous hips rocked back and forth, urging him to penetrate her. Out of a perverse joy, Sandy paused for a moment longer, cherishing her long, thin legs, which tapered perfectly into exquisitely defined achilles tendons, hidden but obvious beneath the scarlet socks that disappeared inside of black patent leather high heels.

"Sandy," she cried, "I need you. I need you now. Please Sandy, fuck me."

In one smooth motion, Sandy slipped between her thighs and slowly eased his rock-hard erection deep into her slippery vagina.

"Oh my god. Jesus," she moaned. "Sandy, that is so wonderful. Oh Sandy, you're so big, you fill all of me. Yes Sandy, that's it. Fuck me. Ohh, Sandy, do it."

Barely controlling himself, Sandy stood on the floor with one hand on each cheek of her ass, slowing her motions as he rhythmically undulated his cock back and forth, in and out, around in circles. Paula's voice mellowed to a bass, purring moan that slowly accelerated in tempo. Soon his attempts to keep the movements languid were opposed by her more urgent appetite as she thrust herself forcefully against him, using the dining table as leverage.

"I don't believe it; I've never, ever felt anything so wonderful," she cried.

Pounding against him, Paula wiggled, bounced, and twisted her ass with an animation Sandy had never known before. As her excitement heightened, Paula's movements became larger, wilder, even less controlled. As her yelps and cries grew louder and more frequent, she suddenly lifted her upper body off the dining table, bent her knees into a kind of balanced power squat, forcing him backwards, then spread her legs as wide as possible and began to grind, urgently whipping Sandy's pelvis and cock with unbelievable power and speed. Her orgasm was approaching and she went for it, uninhibited, at full tilt.

"Oh Sandy, you fucker," she screamed. "Fuck me harder. Oh, Sandy, please fuck me harder."

The effect this had on him was considerable. He had never experienced anything like Paula, and he was finding it increasingly difficult to hold himself back. He tried to divert his attention by thinking of anything but sex. Death perhaps. UCLA hospital. Westward Ho. The SS research. But it was impossible. Nothing was as compelling as the image and feeling of Paula pounding away over him, sweating, swearing, humping—a jungle creature in heat. As he felt his prostate swell to what seemed the size of a basketball, his self-control disappeared. He was an erection with only one purpose — to bury himself as deep as possible within the inflamed tissues of Paula's vagina. Past the point of no return, Sandy grabbed her hips and began to ram and grind himself against her. On the edge of coming, he stopped himself and slowly withdrew his cock until only its head made contact with the swollen lips of her vulva. For an instant this drove Paula crazy. Moaning, she fought him, pushing against him until he finally surrendered to her need and buried himself deep within her luscious pussy.

"Oh Sandy, that's it. Fuck me! Oh Sandy, I'm coming. Sandy, don't stop! Screw me. Fuck me. Oh Sandy, yes! Yes! Yes! Ohh! Ohh! Ohh! Fuck me. Fuck meeeee! Ahhhhhh!" she screamed as she came.

Unable to hold back any longer, Sandy slammed himself in and out of her without restraint. It felt like a tidal wave was forming inside of him. From his toenails to his scalp, his orgasm was beginning. Never in his life had he known such deep erotic suction; it was as if every cell in his body twisted inside out, demanding to be blasted at cyclotron velocity through the barrel of his erection into the pulsing, receptive softness of Paula's quivering vagina. With a life of its own, Sandy's orgasm finally exploded, filling Paula with what felt like gallon after gallon of spasm-powered sperm.

"Sandy. Yes. Yes. Sandy, that's it," she urged as she reached with her left hand and squeezed his balls until every drop of his orgasmic juices had emptied into her.

Never had Sandy known such a feeling. Nor would he have guessed he would find it under such bizarre circumstances. But apparently sex, like god, moved in mysterious ways. Who is this woman? he asked himself as he curled over her back, kissing her earlobe. Talk about arousing; talk about sexual. Paula was passion itself.

"Sandy," she purred, "that was wonderful. Amazing. I've never felt anything like that. What did you do to me?"

Afraid to say even one word for fear of breaking the spell, Sandy lifted the hair covering the nape of her neck and ran his lips over the soft, damp flesh. After so many years of moment-to-moment pain, he wasn't about to question the reasons for remission. As if in agreement, Paula began another assault on his libido by subtly, rhythmically squeezing and unsqueezing the talented muscles of her vagina. The tightening, loosening, gripping, and releasing quickly achieved the effect she desired, and Sandy once again felt his cock stiffen into an impressive erection.

After a few small bumps and grinds to get him going, Paula stood up, forcing Sandy to bend over backwards in order to stay inside of her.

"Let's go upstairs," she murmured.

Sandy nodded and slid himself out of her. Heading for the staircase, Paula took his hand. Following eagerly, Sandy forgot about his trousers, which were still down around his ankles. After one step, his hobble tripped him and he fell to the floor. Unhurt and laughing, he pulled his pants off over his shoes, stood up, and walked behind her up the stairs. Although he knew they were an amusing sight—fully dressed from neck to waist and naked on the bottom half—Sandy was no longer laughing; he was focused on the compelling sight of Paula's glistening inner thighs and the surrounding taut muscles of her tight, delectable ass.

Overcome by desire, Sandy lunged forward, buried his face between her legs and slid his tongue into the swollen crevice of her vulva. Instantly Paula stopped walking, kneeled over to expose herself more fully and, as the pleasure flooded through her body, began thrusting against his face, twisting, turning, seeking more and more sensation. As his tongue probed the inside of her pussy Sandy became aware of Paula's hand, which slid across her flat belly and began to stroke the inflated, fleshy hood of her clitoris. This erotic scene inflamed his already amazing erection, giving him the sense that he was hard and strong enough to be the main girder in a New York skyscraper.

"Let's go to the bedroom," he said.

Without a second's hesitation Paula stood up, pulling off her sweat-soaked sports coat and silk blouse and tossing them on the floor, and led Sandy down the short hallway into her bedroom. In the time it took him to extract himself from his own jacket and shirt, she had removed the antique quilt comforter covering the king-size bed, and folded down the plum-colored top sheet. Then she sat down on the edge of the mattress and bent over to remove the last vestige of her clothing, her socks and shoes.

"Leave them on," he said gently, aroused by the image of this tall, naked beauty in red socks and spike heels.

Surprised but amused, Paula sat up and smiled. Listening only to the erotic orders issued by his erection, Sandy approached and wrapped Paula in his arms, kissing her on the mouth while easing her down backward on the bed. He lifted her legs up in the air until her spike heels pointed to the ceiling, and slowly slipped his cock into her astoundingly wet vagina. The hunger that he satisfied in her with this action was so tremendous that she moaned with audible relief.

Slowly Sandy began rotating his pelvis, rubbing her clitoris while flexing his erection within her vagina. Paula responded by bending her knees over his shoulders, arching her ass up into his lap, and pressing her heels against his back to drive him deeper into her. Slowing her down was a challenge. Pinning her in a bear hug so that she was unable to move, Sandy centered all of her attention on his erection, which he inched, as slowly as possible, out of her pussy. At the last moment before separating from her, he stopped and, with the head of his penis, made little circles in the opening of her vagina. Then, very delicately, he slid his seemingly endless erection all the way back in. Pressing hard for only a moment, he withdrew once again, only to repeat and repeat the same languid sequence.

For Paula this was sweet torment—frustration, then momentary satisfaction that magnified her cravings. But because his hold prevented her moving with the violent, pile-driver motion her appetite demanded, she had no choice but to submit to his torturously slow rhythms. Paula was on the precipice, quivering with arousal. But as desperately as she wanted to come, Sandy wouldn't allow it; the more palpable her excitement, the slower and more subtle his movements became, forcing her to such a peak of pent-up passion that her sole outlet lay in throwing the only part of her body that she could move — her head — back and forth, as if somehow the centrifugal force in her brain would force out the climax she craved.

Vividly aware of the nearness of Paula's orgasm, Sandy stopped virtually all movement. Limiting himself to a slow, delicate caressing of his pelvis against her clitoris, he undulated his erection inside of her, torquing his member as if it were a compressed spring seeking to expand. For Paula the pleasure was almost too intense. As the cascade of orgasmic feelings over-whelmed her, the edges of her mouth strained as if in torture and the tendons in her throat bulged, mimicking an Olympic weight lifter bench-pressing three hundred pounds. All expression left her eyes and Paula's skin flushed pink.

"Sandy, do it to me. I want you to come. Do it, Sandy." Glancing up at him, she saw that her urgings were having a definite effect. "That's it Sandy, harder. Jam it into me. Oh, Sandy, that's it. Oh Sandy. Oh my god. Ohh Sandy. Ohhh. Ohhh. Ohhh. Aahhh!" Paula screamed as she threw her head from side to side, freed her arms from his grip, grabbed his ass with both of her hands, and forcefully rammed him into her as she came and came and came.

Overwhelmed by excitement, Sandy took up where she left off, driving himself, as she demanded, deeper and harder into her, once again transformed by his passions into one enormous cock whose only function was to fuck and to come.

"Sandy, that's it. Let it go," Paula commanded as she squeezed his balls.

Sandy's sperm burst into her with such force that it felt as if he himself had been stretched inside out and launched through his erection into her vagina.

After the last throbs and spasms subsided, he relaxed his hold on Paula. Easing out, he lay down on the sheet beside her. Never in his life had he known sex to be so purely carnal. Just a few hours earlier he had been closing in on suicide; now, he was having the unquestioned peak erotic experience of his thirty-two years. The contradictions, ironies, and conflicts were too much for his exhausted mind to sort out; life had finally surprised him in a miraculous, joyful way. After being so far down, in only a few hours he was now riding higher than he'd ever imagined possible. How could this be?

Wrapping his arms around Paula, Sandy pulled her tight against him. In awe of the connection they had made, he was afraid to speak, certain that words would only diminish the magic. Paula also remained quiet, and he interpreted this to mean that her reaction was similar to his. Was he suddenly the luckiest man in the world? Or was he simply in the presence of a highly sexual woman—just another male in a long line of anonymous conquests? Pushing this paranoid fantasy from his mind, Sandy trusted his gut; for Paula to have acted the way she did, she must have felt the same rare and wonderful sense of being connected that he had just experienced. A moment of peace had entered both of their lives. Paradise had been achieved; could anything improve on the contentment he felt? Such joy tapped into feelings and needs absent from his life since the day Rachael had been killed. Paula had turned everything about Sandy's life upside down, becoming essential to him—his minister to the future, for whom he'd fight the world, even risking his life if that were required to retain her passion for him.

Drugged by exhaustion, immersed in a mental utopia more euphoric than anything induced by booze, Valium, or psychedelics, Sandy wanted only to cuddle and cling to the lifesaver called Paula. Nat, Ed, and Charlie, the family's betrayal, the death of his mother, Rachael's obliteration, his divorce, the failure of *The Heart of L.A.,* even the surgeon and his contempt for Sandy's tattoo—everything painful, all humiliations simply vanished from Sandy's consciousness as his mind floated, embracing the peace of sleep. As he relaxed, giving himself up to the idyllic sensation, something interrupted. It was a physical feeling; a hand — Paula's hand. At first it caressed his belly, then quickly crawled down toward his groin. Too tired to move, he let her continue. Soon Paula's long, thin fingers had wrapped themselves around his balls and went to work stroking and squeezing his very tired penis.

"Paula," Sandy moaned quietly, "have pity. I'm short of blood, remember?"

Ignoring him, she continued until Sandy's limpness expanded into the rigid erection she was seeking.

"I'm impressed," she purred. "If this is what you're like when you're anemic, I can't wait to see you with a full tank."

"Please," he protested weakly, "you're going to kill me."

"That's not what your friend here in my hand tells me."

"Don't listen to him; listen to me. I'm beat. Honestly."

"You mean you don't want me?" She actually sounded hurt.

"Of course I do. But the body has limits."

"Am I not attractive to you?" Her voice wavered, betraying an edge of timidity. Meanwhile, lower down, she continued her success with his erection.

"Paula, without a doubt you're the most attractive woman I've ever met."

"Do I please you?"

Sandy was confused by her serious manner. Was she kidding? Could she imagine any other answer than *yes?* But something in her voice told him she had doubts. "Paula, feel what's in your hand. Doesn't that tell you anything?"

"I want to hear it from your lips."

Sandy, marveling at the effect sexual excitement had on his exhaustion, found himself caressing and fondling Paula's nipples, while at the same time wondering how she could have any question about his response to her. Although she seemed sincere, perhaps it was all a skilled act, maybe even part of some erotic game he didn't understand.

"Look," he told her, "I've had more pleasure with you tonight than I've ever known was possible. Aren't you able to feel that? Isn't this something wonderful for you, too? Four hours ago I was close to death. Now my cock aches for you. And for a third time! Do you think this could happen if I wasn't wildly excited by you?"

She smiled. "I like hearing that. It's really me that's making your cock hard? I mean, you're not fantasizing about screwing Linda Lovelace or some other woman?"

Instead of answering, he rolled Paula onto her back, lifted her right leg up off the bed, and slipped his erection into her. After a few slow movements he wrapped his arms around her and rolled onto his back, carrying her with him. Paula now lay on top of him, her back on his chest while he remained inside her from behind. Delicately, Sandy caressed the hood of her clitoris while rhythmically undulating his hips. It was a position that took little physical energy and, to an exhausted man, was a godsend.

"Oh Sandy, that feels wonderful."

"Yes?"

"Is it good for you?"

"Fantastic."

"How fantastic?"

"Paula, if they could package you as a drug you'd put heroin and the entire Mafia out of business."

She began to move urgently, rotating and thrusting her ass, grinding over him, seeking more and more of his hard-on.

"I want to be heroin for you. I want to addict you. I want you to need me. I want you to crave fucking me."

"I already crave fucking you."

"How much do you need to fuck me? Tell me. I have to hear it from you. Please Sandy."

Very excited himself, Sandy enjoyed the verbal as well as the physical connection. "I ache for you. My cock is huge for you, only. I have to be in your cunt, live in your cunt. I need you, Paula. I have to have you fuck me. Spread your legs over me. Take my cock deep into you. Take my balls. Take all of me into you and fuck me. Screw me. Come all over me."

"Sandy, oh Sandy. God, you excite me so much." In a frenzy of passion, Paula began pounding herself up and down on his cock.

As difficult as it was for Sandy to believe, her exertions fully revived every bit of his flagging energy. For the third time that night the animal in both Sandy and Paula took over, connecting them on the most primitive, carnal level. Place, time, and identity vanished; all normal markers of daily life were erased by their overwhelming eroticism. It was a coupling so vividly sexual that its memory would sustain Sandy through the difficult and dangerous months to come.

14

At six-fifteen the next morning Paula's clock-radio blared, as programmed, ending the night's sleep after all of three hours. Without a word, she dragged herself from the bed and disappeared into the bathroom. Sandy, however, remained motionless, basking in an aura of contentment he had forgotten was possible. Life in Paula's bed was a paradise so completely free of grief and pain that he was worried about moving even his little finger for fear of puncturing his astonishing mood. Within the short span of eighteen hours, his life had flip-flopped from the horrible to the marvelous; nothing could have prepared him for such a miracle.

After what seemed like only moments, Paula came out of the bathroom wrapped in a terry-cloth robe, blasting her wet hair with a noisy, high-powered portable dryer. Avoiding eye contact, she handed Sandy a clean bath towel and gestured to the shower. Obediently he entered the white-tiled bathroom and climbed under the powerful stream of hot water.

In minutes her hair was dry, Sandy was clean, and both were dressed, out of the apartment, driving the few blocks to the Westward Ho. Paula's explanation for the rush was her need to be downtown for an early court appearance. Her schedule was so tight, she claimed, that she didn't have time for her usual cup of morning coffee.

Sitting in silence as Paula negotiated the half-mile of twisting shortcuts, Sandy began to worry. The tension radiating from her was infectious. Was she just trying to get rid of him? Was she one of those women who could only enjoy themselves sexually with strangers? Why was she so remote, when only hours before she had been connected to him with such spectacular vividness? Was he so needy, he asked himself, that her feelings for him had only been his imagination? As they approached the Westward Ho parking lot and Paula downshifted her 240Z, Sandy's mind began to race. The five-minute drive had turned into a crisis, and he had to find a way to defuse their sudden estrangement. He could not let Paula go; without her he had nothing.

She pulled in beside his Volvo, leaving her engine running.

"I don't know if you planned it this way, but I don't even have your phone number," he probed.

She nodded stiffly, reached into her leather briefcase, pulled out a legal pad, scribbled her number, and handed the paper to him.

"Is there a way to get in touch with you?" She spoke professionally, without affect.

"Sure," he responded, unable to read her intentions. Taking the pad and pencil from her, he wrote down two numbers. "This one is my home number. And this one is my private line at work."

Without speaking, she slipped the pad back into her briefcase. Something was obviously bothering her. Was she thinking about how to get rid of him?

"I want to thank you for the incredible evening." He spoke nervously, formally, out of fear.

She looked down at the speedometer and asked shyly, like a little kid afraid of being refused, "Will I see you again?"

"You *are* kidding!" Sandy blurted, overjoyed with relief that she was just as anxious as he was about the possibility of rejection.

"It was just a question, for god's sake; I'm not asking for a commitment." Paula's voice was stressed, aggressive, and defensive. She had totally misunderstood his answer.

"How about dinner tonight?" he spoke gently.

"Tonight?" She was obviously surprised.

"Yes. You know, like after work. Today is Friday. Let's say seven-thirty? I pick you up at your apartment, we go to a restaurant. That's what *dinner tonight* means."

Exhaling deeply, obviously relieved, she looked him in the eyes for the first time that morning. "I'd love to. More than you know. But I have a meeting that I can't get out of. Would you be offended if we got together another night?" She seemed to hold her breath as she waited for his response.

"What's your situation tomorrow night?"

"My time is yours."

"Okay. If you'll do me one favor now, I'll take you out to dinner tomorrow."

"What's the favor?" Once again her voice sounded anxious.

"I don't know about you, but I had a pretty amazing experience last night. I owe you a lot."

She shook her head, uncertain where he was leading. "It wasn't so bad for me either, Sandy."

"Make it perfect by giving me one more kiss before I get out of the car."

For the first time that morning her warmth came back and she smiled. Without hesitation she leaned across the shift lever and hungrily embraced him.

"Okay," he finally spoke after a long, passionate kiss. "I'll see you tomorrow at seven-thirty?"

"You'll be able to find my apartment?"

"In my sleep," he teased as he opened the passenger door.

Paula nodded affectionately as he climbed out of her car and shut the door. Then she waved, accelerated out of the parking lot, down Westwood Boulevard, and out of sight.

Feeling as if he didn't have a care in the world, Sandy unlocked the door of his Volvo, sat down, and started the engine. In the back, where he'd left them, were the Lufthansa computer printouts in the big cardboard box. Nothing had been disturbed. After so many muggings, fate had finally handed him a few extraordinary breaks. Slipping the transmission into gear, he followed Paula out of the parking lot.

Speeding north, Sandy headed home to change from his bloody clothes into something clean; showing up at work looking like the victim of a massacre would cause major problems. Once inside his canyon home, Sandy found three messages on his answering machine. The first, from Vikki, simply asked for a call. The second was Billy, checking in. And the third was from Vikki again, this time at "two-thirty in the morning." Furious, she read him the riot act for not calling back and for not having the decency to thank her for the lasagna dinner she had gone to such effort to prepare. She called him "a bastard," sarcastically told him she hoped he was having a wonderful time with whatever "bimbo he was fucking," and ordered him never, ever to call her again for any reason. "And fuck you" was her final comment before hanging up. It was just like Vikki to grandstand, Sandy reflected, in far too good a mood to succumb to her manipulations. To avoid further grief he decided to take her literally, not phone, and let things end without further complication.

After changing clothes he locked the box of Lufthansa printouts in the closet, along with the now unnecessary final draft of his suicide note. Then he reset his answering machine and headed down the canyon toward work.

For the first time that Sandy could remember, the early-morning traffic actually seemed exhilarating. Instead of living in a world that existed only to enrage and frustrate him, Sandy felt an uncharacteristic sense of exuberance, as if he were suddenly an integral part of life's big picture, embraced by humanity, part of the eternal flow. Everything around him, from the idling brown Mercedes behind his Volvo, to the overheating 1968 Oldsmobile belching steam and smoke in front of him, to that perpetually sneaky cop on the Harley hidden behind a hedge of bright pink oleanders—all of it radiated a unique, glittering, joyous newness.

As he thought back over the events of the last twenty-four hours, Sandy lingered on the fantastic emotional and physical connection that he and Paula had made. The tide had turned. Order had once more been restored to his universe. One night—one wonderful night—and it was a whole new world.

15

At work, Sandy's first order of business was to calculate in dollars and cents exactly where he now stood with his family. Aside from his heavily mortgaged house, he had virtually no assets; all that would be available for him to start a new life, free of his father and brothers, was the token share he would receive from the sale of Vita-Line. *As far as my family's concerned, they're dealing with me like the German government treated the Auschwitz survivors, doling out pathetic crumbs of reparation payments as if that meager distribution somehow made up for all the pain,* Sandy lamented as he turned on his adding machine and began to nail down his financial situation.

Calculating from five million dollars — the sales price discussed between Ed and Charlie — Sandy's rightful share of the business would come to $833,000 before taxes and $667,000 after paying capital gains to Uncle Sam. This amount was figured on the basis of fifty percent of the business going to Nat and the other fifty percent being divided evenly — three ways — among the brothers. Compared with what Sandy had been promised, the new financial arrangement would give him only one-ninth of the fifty percent: $277,000 before taxes and $222,000 after taxes. Under this formula Ed and Charlie would each receive $1,108,000 before paying the IRS. The difference between the two figures was staggering. *Ed and Charlie were each getting $831,000 more than their youngest brother!*

On paper, in black and white, the meaning of those numbers revived Sandy's despair. The message from his father was clear and brutal. A man who saw life only in terms of money, Nat was telling Sandy that his value was only one-quarter that of his older brothers. Nat's love and affection, Nat's appreciation for both Ed and Charlie, was four times — four hundred percent — greater than his regard for Sandy!

As painful as this insight was, Sandy began to wonder if perhaps the conversation he'd overheard wasn't actually the best thing that could have happened to him. Now he could no longer deceive himself about the family's intentions. All pretense was gone. He had no choice but to cut himself loose and start a new life, completely free of guilt. What he'd been handed in the toilet of Parcheesi's was not the death sentence he'd feared but the reverse: his own personal emancipation proclamation. If his father and brothers wanted to behave like criminals and Nazis, so be it. To get involved in a blood-feud over his own legitimate share of the business would be a long, grim, and ultimately losing battle that would drag on for years and destroy his ability to make a new life for himself. Much better to take the $222,000 and use it to buy himself a new start, clear of the family.

From his locked file cabinet, Sandy removed a plain manila envelope with a typed label identifying its contents simply as "forms." This anonymous paper container held the key to Sandy's future. If he did his homework, played his cards right, and his luck held, it was just possible that he could achieve everything he desired.

The brown envelope contained two undated pages of apparently legitimate business correspondence. At the top of each sheet a letterhead, printed in a Gothic-Bavarian type style, identified the sender as "The German-American Travel Agency." The company, the stationery, and the text of both pages were as phony as the letterhead; all were part of Sandy's plan to locate and expose the SS war criminals living in Southern California.

The first paper was a promotional letter supposedly written by the president of the German-American Travel Agency offering high-quality discounted travel packages to the Deutschland with special rates for Americans of German descent. In an effort to increase its clientele, the German-American Travel Agency (according to the letter) was staging a spectacular drawing. The grand prize was a Mercedes 450 SEL delivered at the factory, first-class round-trip air fare on Lufthansa, and two weeks of hotel accommodations anywhere in Germany. The contest rules were simple; the entrant only had to fill out the accompanying questionnaire. Even this (page two of Sandy's creation) was easy. All the form asked was the entrant's name, birthplace, occupation, birth date, and future travel plans. Who could fail to return something so promising and yet so effortless?

Now that he had possession of the Lufthansa mailing list, Sandy scrolled the cover letter into his IBM Selectric and typed the date — June 22, 1973 — in the upper left-hand corner. Moments later he was out the back door of the plant, driving across Glendale to an instant printer where he was sure he would not be recognized. Although the franchise turned out to be hot, crowded, and noisy, it was efficient. The Guatemalan owner guaranteed that five thousand copies of both pages, as well as envelopes imprinted with Sandy's rented post office box number, would be ready for pick-up by five-thirty.

The phony contest had only one goal: obtaining the birth dates of the five thousand people listed on the Lufthansa flight records. Anyone over seventeen years old in 1945 met the basic criterion to be a potential war criminal. These individuals would all have been born before 1927, making them at least forty-seven years old in 1973. Sandy's plan rested on two assumptions. First, that any German under seventy-five would still be vigorous enough to get excited by the idea of a free Mercedes and an all-expense paid trip home. And second, that even someone as guilty as Adolf Eichmann would have no fears about answering the innocuous questions on the contest form.

Once the questionnaires had been returned, the real work would begin. This involved taking advantage of the Freedom of Information Act passed in 1966 and effectively put to use by Sandy on countless occasions in his *Heart of L.A.* days. Once the Lufthansa flight lists had been culled down to those individuals matching the correct age profile, Sandy planned to make written requests under the FOIA asking for each individual's files from the FBI, the CIA, Immigration and Naturalization, and the Justice Department. Then it was only a question of waiting ten to twenty days for the agencies to respond.

Driving back to the plant, Sandy congratulated himself. *It was one damn clever piece of work*. Obviously he didn't expect that the

FOIA forms would be returned with a definitive statement proving an individual to be a war criminal. No, the whole process was more subtle than that. What he was seeking was an omission, inconsistency, or error that would point to something ultimately incriminating after further investigation. Sandy hoped that his plan would ultimately lead not just to an old Nazi but to a true war criminal. The idea of tracking down such a fugitive excited his long-dormant journalistic juices. Nothing was more energizing than the hunt. And this one promised to lead to a big-time quarry.

Should he succeed (and at that moment Sandy had no doubt that he would), all kinds of changes in his life would be possible. The accomplishment itself would be something to be proud of. To write up his success as a magazine article would be a great start toward resuming his life as a journalist. Not only would it be proof to himself of his capabilities, but it could launch his life in all kinds of wonderful directions, maybe even reviving the possibility of a job writing for the *New York Times*. And what would happen, he fantasized with a confidence he hadn't felt since the heyday of *The Heart of L.A.*, if the *Times* actually wanted to publish his article in their Sunday magazine section? Wouldn't that get his life up to a meaningful speed in a hurry? Yes, he told himself, if it all fell into place, this war criminal research could turn everything around and give him a second chance at a future of substance.

Back in his office, such thoughts inflamed Sandy's enthusiasm, propelling him into his work with energy and enduring concentration. No disaster seemed insurmountable. He felt capable of taking on the world single-handedly. Victory in life was inevitable.

As if fate had been listening to his thoughts and wanted to test him, Sandy's office door swung open and his brother Ed strutted in, looking pleased with himself.

"Dad would like to talk with you, if you're not too busy," he said.

Sandy wondered if they were going to tell him about the sale of the business and his own paltry share.

"What's up?" he asked innocently.

Ed shrugged as if he had no idea, and changed the subject. "I meant to tell you, I think we solved your problem about Dad's birthday present. After you left Parcheesi's, Charlie, Sylvia, and I came to an agreement. We all love the idea of the Warhol painting, and we want to give it to the old man. I know your share — fifteen thousand bucks — is a burden, given your divorce and all the losses you took paying back the creditors of your newspaper. What we talked about was that we want Dad to have the picture, and we want you to be part of it. So what we've agreed to do is loan you the fifteen thousand, interest free. Don't pay it back until it's comfortable for you."

Sandy smiled, amused at this new form of humiliation. "It's still a rip-off, Ed." He spoke with equanimity and conviction.

"Thank you very much," his brother flared in anger. "I thought we were making a very generous offer; you tell me where else you can get an interest-free loan with no limitation on when you pay it back."

"You're missing the point. It's what you call *the painting* that's a rip-off: Sixty thousand bucks for a production-line silk-screen is a joke. Warhol doesn't even make them himself; all he does is sign them. In twenty years it isn't going to be worth the canvas it's printed on. It's not art, it's not enduring, it's not insightful — it's toilet paper."

"Yeah, well, I suppose your opinion as an art expert is worth about as much as your reputation as a publisher. The world admires Warhol; more important, so does Dad, and it's *his* birthday. The fact is, Sandy, we're getting him the portrait and your problem boils down to, do you want to be part of it, yes or no?"

Sandy had no doubt that his opposition made the Warhol even more attractive to Ed, despite the flagrant waste of money.

"I'm going to have to think about it," Sandy said, knowing that he wouldn't participate in the gift. Whose money was paying for Ed's and Charlie's shares? Fifteen thousand dollars was nothing compared with the bonus they were getting from depriving Sandy of his rightful portion of the vitamin business. Interest-free loan or not, Sandy had no doubt he was paying for the whole painting ten times over.

"Well, think about it hard; you don't *always* have to be the one member of the family to disappoint Dad." Smiling with self-satisfaction, Ed swung around and opened the door. "The old man wants to see you *now;* I suggest you get moving."

The big thing to remember, Sandy told himself as he slipped on his sports coat and headed down the hall, was not to rise to his father's bait. Whatever it was Nat wanted, Sandy couldn't let himself react in anger. The long view was all that mattered.

After knocking once, Sandy entered Nat's office and took a seat not far from Ed, facing the giant illuminated Yosemite scene and the old man himself, who finished his conversation and hung up the phone.

"I want to congratulate you."

Nat's opening took Sandy aback.

"You did a hell of a job on Furgstein yesterday. You know what he told us this morning?" Nat included Ed in his gesture.

Sandy said nothing, trying to fathom what his father was getting at.

"He was hoping I'd replace you and put Ed in charge of the cancer center. You know why?"

Sandy shook his head.

"You scared him with all your questions. As good a man as Stanley is as a fund raiser and administrator, he's not so hot with the details. And you hit him right where it hurts. I told him if he couldn't give you answers, you weren't going to give him money. Furgstein was so surprised he choked on his lox."

"You had breakfast with him?" Sandy asked calmly, controlling the rage he felt building inside.

"Yeah. This morning. He called me right after your meeting yesterday. I think you're off to one hell of a start; I just wanted you to know that."

"Uh, Dad, how is it you happened to have breakfast with him without telling me? I mean if the cancer center's *my* responsibility, *I'm* the one who should be dealing with Furgstein, not you."

"That's what I told him."

"But you met with him behind my back. And he knows it. You just undercut my authority."

"You're wrong, Sandy. Next time he has no choice but to deal with you."

"Not true. Because I'm turning the whole thing over to you unless you promise right now that you won't interfere again, period. Is that agreed?"

"I think you're forgetting whose money this is."

"Yeah, well, if that's the case then you supervise the cancer center. I'm not going to get put in the middle and have that jerkball calling you every time he doesn't like the way I polish my shoes. Either you trust me or you don't. Either I have the authority or I don't. It's a yes or no proposition, Dad, and there's no middle ground."

"You don't think that because it's my money I have a right to say something?"

"Of course you do. But to me, not to Furgstein."

Nat exchanged glances with Ed, then smiled.

"You're getting tough in your old age."

"I had a good teacher."

Nat maintained his smile, pleased by the flattery.

"Okay, you got a deal."

Sandy nodded without pleasure. The meeting was over and nothing had been said about the sale of the business. Would they lie to him forever? He decided to press the issue.

"I was talking to one of the jobbers yesterday who asked me, in confidence, if the rumor he heard was true that we were putting Vita-Line up for sale. Of course I denied it. But it did make me wonder; is there any basis to the story?" Sandy watched his father and Ed exchange a subtle, revealing glance.

"Not that I know of." Nat pulled on his earlobe with his thumb and forefinger, pretending to be perplexed. "But people approach me all the time with wild schemes. Who knows what kind of bullshit someone was slinging to make himself look important? If I had a contract to sell Vita-Line, Sandy, believe me, you'd be the first to know."

If only I had a machine gun, Sandy raged silently, would I have a wonderful time blasting away these two liars grinning at me now with that see-no-evil-hear-no-evil look the Germans perfected at the Nuremberg trials. Throw them in the gas chamber, slap them in the ovens and incinerate the hypocrites!

Despite his intense reaction, Sandy's face revealed nothing. He simply stood up, told his father he was returning to work, and hurried out.

Back at his desk, trying to plan his next move, Sandy alternated between despair and euphoria. On the one hand, his father's lie was the final blow in a lifelong history of rejection and contempt. Yet at the same time the purity of the act—such a vivid and undeniable family crime, the emotional equivalent of murder—was somehow freeing. With this grotesque lie, Nat had finally severed Sandy's last fantasy of winning his father's approval. So much for blood ties. Nat's lie was an official declaration of war.

The only thing that mattered now, Sandy told himself, was his Nazi research and writing the article that, in his mind, would extricate him from the family concentration camp. The major problem he now faced was time: It would take at least three months to complete the investigation, and he needed his salary to subsidize his research. He couldn't afford to walk out on the family immediately. The best course of action was to pretend to work, do the minimum, collect his paycheck, get whatever money he could from the business, and at the same time bust his ass, take risks, follow every lead, and write the best damn article in the history of investigative reporting!

Once again, the telephone jolted Sandy out of his ruminations.

"Hey, what's the matter; you don't return calls anymore?" Billy opened the conversation.

"I'm sorry," Sandy told him, "but the last twenty-four hours have been real mind blowers."

"You didn't run into that Danish woman again, did you?"

"I can't talk about it now. How about coming over tonight?"

"After what she did to you, you saw her again? Are you crazy?" Billy shrieked, misunderstanding the meaning of Sandy's request.

"This has nothing to do with her. This is far worse. And far better."

"What are you talking about? What could be worse than tattooing a concentration camp number on your arm?"

"If you don't mind," Sandy said angrily, "this is not something I want to discuss right now. I should be home by seven. I'll see you then, okay?"

"Just tell me, does this *mind blowing twenty-four hours* have anything to do with Auschwitz or the Nazis?"

"In a way."

"Oh, Jesus."

"That's not the bad part."

"Like that Erica wasn't the bad part?" Billy asked.

"When I tell you the whole story you'll understand."

"I'll bet."

"See you at seven?"

"For sure."

After hanging up, Sandy felt his despair returning and had a sudden, passionate yearning to hear Paula's voice. He dialed the number she had given him.

"Democratic Legal Clinic," the receptionist answered.

"Paula Gottlieb, please."

"One moment."

Relieved that the name and number written down were real and not a trick, Sandy relaxed, leaned back in his chair, and waited for the line to be connected.

"Ms. Gottlieb's office," another secretary's voice announced.

"This is Sandy Klein, calling for Ms. Gottlieb."

"Ms. Gottlieb's not in, may I take a message?"

"Is there a number where I can reach her?"

"I'm sorry, she's in court. Is this an emergency?"

A good question. Would an attack of despair be considered an emergency?

"Hello, Mister Klein, are you there?"

"Yes. I mean, no, it's not an emergency. But it's important, and I'd like to talk to her."

"Does she have your number?"

"Yes."

"I'll make sure she gets the message."

"Thank you."

The phone went dead, and he returned to his paperwork.

At five o'clock, Sandy drove to the printer, where his contest forms were boxed and ready. After paying in cash, he loaded the reams of paper into his Volvo and headed home, flushed with a steady surge of long-forgotten energy.

16

"She actually believes you were in Auschwitz?" Billy was incredulous.

"Hey, it was her assumption; I never told her one way or the other."

"Sandy, give me a break. I mean, she saw your tattoo; what else could she think?"

"There're hundreds of possibilities; it's just a little ink on my arm. Is it my fault she jumped to conclusions?"

"No, of course not," Billy said sarcastically. "Just because you've got numbers tattooed on your arm and just because they happen to be perfect forgeries of the real thing, and just because she's seen the real thing every day of her life on her own parents' arms, that's no reason for her to assume you went through Auschwitz. No, as you say, there are any number of other explanations. My question to you, Sandy, is, tell me *one*."

After some reflection, Sandy admitted, "I can't bullshit you. You're right and I know it. The question is, what do I do now?"

"I don't think you should do anything. Consider what you've accomplished. Using the most astounding line in the history of the pick-up business, you met a terrific woman in a supermarket, got her to pay your hospital bill, *and* make you dinner. Then you humped the shit out of her. I'd get a tattoo tonight," Billy pointed to his left forearm, "if it meant I could do the same thing."

"I guess I deserve that for asking you," Sandy complained. "If you can't be serious at least get back to work." He gestured to the stacks of German-American Travel Agency forms and envelopes piled up in front of them on the large oak dining table.

Billy took a long swallow from his glass of chilled vodka. "Sandy, I'm a composer, not a secretary. This is ridiculous. Hire someone. This is a week's work for the two of us."

"It's no more than three nights if you don't talk so much and just keep writing."

"Listen, I'm not a white-collar ditch digger. If you want to be cheap, fine — that's your business. But I have better things to do with my time. Why don't you let *me* hire a secretary? Hell, I'll hire two secretaries. We'll call it an early Christmas present. What do you say?"

Sandy shook his head. "The more people who know about this, the less likely it is that the scheme will work. Surprise is everything."

"I think you're overestimating how much people care. I know a couple of back-up singers who have day jobs as secretaries at the ASCAP offices. All they know is rock'n'roll, Sunset Strip, and singing on key. Auschwitz to them is probably some weird variety of German pork sausage. What do you say I phone them?"

"I'd rather you kept working." Sandy pushed the pile of Lufthansa passenger lists closer to Billy.

"Can I tell you what I think?" Billy asked.

"Only if I see your fingers moving."

Billy nodded, addressed an envelope, then filled it with the two forms, the stamped, self-addressed return envelope, and a color travel brochure of Germany, obtained in bulk at no cost from the German Tourist Bureau. After wetting the adhesive with a damp sponge and stamping the envelope, he waved it in the air for Sandy to see and appreciate.

"It's a good beginning; now see if you can keep up with me." Sandy addressed, folded, and stuffed with impressive speed.

Billy took a sip of vodka, copied another address, and looked across the table. "How long have we been friends?"

"I'm only going to answer you if you keep folding."

Reluctantly, Billy stuffed the envelope. "Sandy, I don't want you to mail out these letters. There are consequences here I don't think you've fully considered."

"Anything else you want to get off your chest while you're working?"

"Look, I'm not emotionally involved in this like you are; I'm a step back where I can still see the big picture — and believe me, it's not reassuring. This is an absolutely fucking brilliant plan, but it's also totally, off-the-wall crazy. *Meshugina.* The kind of thing people go to jail for. Or get shot over. This is felony city here. I'm not even a lawyer and I could name a list of federal offenses you're committing. Sandy, this plan isn't just high risk, it's straight-out nuts."

"That's what you wanted me to hear?"

Billy nodded.

"Okay, I've heard you, but I don't happen to agree with you. We have a difference of opinion. It's no reason not to keep working." Sandy sealed a completed envelope and tossed it into the box with the others.

"You think I'm some kind of fucking retard?" Billy shouted. "I'm trying to keep your ass out of trouble."

"You haven't figured it out yet?" Sandy spoke calmly.

"Figured what out?"

"You're a witness to my life. Can't you see that sending these forms out doesn't matter because I'm already way over my head, not just in trouble but in deep shit. Taking this risk is my only alternative to getting buried."

Before Billy could respond, the telephone rang. Sandy barreled into the privacy of the kitchen and picked up the extension.

"Hello?"

"Sandy?"

"Paula!" Deliriously happy, his voice resonated with energy. "I was starting to worry."

"You wouldn't believe the day I've had. And it's not over yet— this is a coffee break in a meeting that's going to last god knows how many more hours. My secretary did tell you I was in court, I hope."

"She did, yes. Listen, part of the reason I called was to thank you for what you did for me at the hospital. You know I'm mad at you," he teased. "You never did tell me how much money I owe you."

She laughed, then lowered her voice to a whisper, as if she were afraid of being overheard. "Sandy, forget it, will you? Last night you more than paid me back."

"No," he spoke firmly. "I won't allow it. One thing isn't related to the other. I insist you let me reimburse you."

"Try to make me," she murmured seductively.

"Paula," Sandy heard a man's voice call to her, "if you don't mind, I'd like to get this over with."

"I'll be right there, Larry," she hollered back. "Sandy, I guess you heard; I've got to get back to work. Am I still seeing you tomorrow?"

"Yep. Seven-thirty, I'll pick you up at your apartment. Like it or not."

"What's not to like? Are you feeling better today?"

"At the moment."

"How's your wrist?"

"Thanks to you, the least of my problems."

"Paula, darling, I haven't got all night!" Larry's voice called once again.

"I gotta go, Sandy. See you tomorrow. 'Bye."

"Good night, Paula."

Sandy strolled back into the dining room, where he poured himself a fresh glass of scotch, took a long swallow, and let his mind drift back over his extraordinary connection with Paula. Only that name *Larry* interrupted his fantasies of a new life with her. Was Larry a lawyer? Were they really working? Was he a rival? Why did he call her *darling*?

"I take it," Billy probed, "that was the well-known female Resistance hero twenty-hours hours after rescuing her Auschwitz survivor."

Sandy glared at his friend and sat back down at the dining table.

"You've got to tell her the truth, Sandy."

"Yeah. And you've got to get back to work."

Billy nodded and followed Sandy's lead, addressing, folding, and stamping another bogus contest form.

Larry is definitely a lawyer, Sandy told himself without much confidence. Yes, they're only working. And "darling" was nothing but a sarcastic prod to get her attention.

17

Chicken Kung Pau. Green beans with garlic sauce. Peking duck. Szechwan fish. Beef marrow, Hunan-style. Pressing on Paula's door-bell, Sandy rehearsed his pitch for a Chinese restaurant an hour away. Eating locally seemed like a bad idea; all he needed was to run into some acquaintance from high school, Paula would learn the truth about his past, and in a microsecond they would be history. It wasn't that he didn't want to tell her the real story; but given the delicate state of their budding relationship, timing was critical. To rush Paula with outrageous complications would virtually force her to abandon him. It would all come out soon enough; he hoped it would even be that night. But more impor-tant than clearing up the false impression was the expansion and deepening of the passion and trust that would make it easy for her to excuse that misunderstanding.

The mental roulette wheel of Chinese delicacies stopped at *mushi pork* when the front door opened. Immediately, Sandy saw that something was wrong. Instead of being dressed for a casual dinner, Paula was still wearing her work clothes — black slacks, pumps, black blouse, a single strand of pearls around her neck, pearl ear studs, and an almost masculine charcoal Italian summer-weight sports coat.

"Sandy. Uh, listen, I know we made plans — I've been looking forward to seeing you all day — but I have a problem. Two problems, in fact."

Paula didn't even have to finish for Sandy to be convinced he was lost, abandoned and forgotten already.

"You can see I'm still dressed for work. The meetings on my police brutality case didn't end until half an hour ago, and I'm exhausted. I need a bath and I need to sit down. Plus, I have to get up tomorrow — Sunday — for an off-the-record breakfast meeting with the district attorney. Eight-thirty. Can you believe it?"

Sandy shrugged casually, attempting to cover his hurt.

"The other item, which both of us forgot, is the Watergate hearings. I don't know about you, but I haven't had one second to watch them all week. Thursday was my only free evening and you know that I didn't watch TV that night." She consulted her watch. "In twenty-two minutes on PBS there's going to be a three-hour summary of this week's hearings. It's something no American should miss."

"What about dinner? You don't think a little food would give you some energy?"

"I picked up a couple of salmon steaks on the way home. I'll cook them fast and we can eat watching the hearings."

Even though he was relieved that he wasn't being cut out of her life, Sandy shrugged noncommitally. "I don't know, TV I can watch on my own. I was looking forward to some quiet conversation and getting to know you better." He spoke warmly, in an attempt to draw her closer.

"It's not *just* TV, Sandy, this is history in the making. The presidency is unraveling in front of our eyes. This is a national crisis on prime time. Don't you want to see it happen?"

"Yeah, but I've been watching it all week," he lied. "Why don't we drive downtown to this great Chinese place I know on Broadway and I'll tell you everything that's gone on?"

She shook her head. "I want to see it with my own eyes. I think it's important that I tell my children that *I*, Paula Gottlieb, witnessed the impeachment of the president." She paused, then spoke carefully. "I'm sorry, I forgot for a moment—Watergate's not much compared with what you've been through."

"You have children?" Sandy asked without affect.

"No. Why, do you?"

Sandy averted his eyes and shook his head as a bolt of despair racked his body at the thought of Rachael. If she were alive, his daughter would be seven. What would Rachael have looked like at seven? Her devilish, manipulative smile flowed through his memory. If only he could see her again, even for a minute. One hug. One kiss.

"Is something wrong?" Paula asked, concerned by what she saw pass across his face.

"No, not a thing." He smiled, covering his feelings. "Why not? I mean, what the hell; who cares about Chinese food. I'd love to watch the hearings with you."

Paula took his hand, led him inside her apartment, and shut the door. Then, like a painter stroking paper with a sable watercolor brush, she delicately and almost imperceptibly caressed his mouth with her soft, familiar, welcoming lips. A quick dart of her tongue plunged him into complete surrender; he'd follow her anywhere if it meant she would continue.

"Now sit down and relax," she broke off. "I've got to cook the fish or we're going to miss the hearings."

Willing to agree to almost anything, Sandy nodded. After one more promising kiss, during which she ran her fingers through the hair on the long-neglected back of his head, she left him for the kitchen, where she readied the salmon steaks for broiling.

Sandy followed her to the dining room and stood in the doorway, watching her work. As in everything he'd seen Paula do, she was organized, efficient, and competent to the point of appearing professional. In seconds, she whipped up a teriyaki marinade from Mirren saki, soy sauce, and chicken stock and quickly dipped the salmon into it. After slipping the fish under the broiler, she stir-fried thinly sliced Japanese eggplant with garlic in a wok. As the salmon neared completion, Paula concocted a glaze made from the marinade, cornstarch, and sugar. And in what seemed to Sandy like only seconds, the dinner was on plates, ready to eat.

"What'd you do, put yourself through college working as a chef?" Sandy asked as they carried the food and a bottle of Chardonney upstairs.

In the bedroom she set the plates down on the king-sized bed. "I used to be ashamed to admit this, but for a summer I went full time — twelve hours a day — to cooking school. The Cordon Bleu on Forty-Fifth Street. It was the summer between high school and college. My parents are European, remember. They thought a girl should know how to cook in the classic manner. I spent three months in an un-air-conditioned kitchen that was so hot in August we called it Cordon Hell. I learned to gut salmon and bake puff pastry in a sweat bath. It was the worst experience you could imagine."

Sandy nodded blankly, sat down on the bed, and poured them each a glass of wine.

Paula turned pale, embarrassed by her statement. "I mean in New York, in 1964," she apologized. "Obviously, compared with what you went through, it was nothing. But everyone else I went to school with was doing interesting things like going to Europe. Or the Caribbean. I didn't mean to diminish you. God, I'm stupid. You'd think I'd learn, wouldn't you? You have to understand that at the time, being forced to go to cooking school was absolutely the last thing I wanted to do. Just talking abut it brings up all those feelings again and makes me angry. But I am sorry, Sandy. I didn't mean it the way it sounded."

Sandy handed her a glass of wine and clinked his against hers. "To forgiveness," he said with amusement.

"Thank you," she gushed, relieved, missing the irony in his voice. After a sip of wine Paula glanced at her watch. "Oh my god, it's starting." With a click of the remote control box in her hand, the TV flickered on, revealing the familiar figures of Sam Erwin, Howard Baker, Elliot Richardson, Sam Dash, and the rest of the Watergate Investigating Committee. The weekly summary of the national prime-time scandal had begun.

Sandy and Paula sat back on the bed, cradling their plates, resting their wine glasses on the bedside table.

"This is delicious," Sandy commented after his first bite.

Paula smiled, only momentarily distracted from the mesmerizing event on the television.

Had it not been for that exquisite kiss at the front door, the idea of just sitting in front of the TV would have been agony for Sandy. He needed to feel connected, to be wanted; fortunately Paula's presence filled that aching void. Just the simple act of lying on the bed next to her made him feel that he belonged. Their chit-chat about the events they were watching, the wonderful food, and the cool bottle of wine washed over Sandy and nearly drowned him in serenity. Once again life offered possibilities. Without a doubt Paula was the locomotive pulling up his self-esteem. With the slow but steady progress of the Watergate hearings, it even seemed possible that the national consciousness was shifting course and moving toward a fair and just society. If the president could be indicted, no one was beyond reach, Sandy reflected, excited by the possibility that this cultural phenomena would also embrace his Nazi war criminal research.

Turning to Paula, he studied her as she concentrated on the television. Here was a person he hardly knew and yet on whom he was suddenly, inexplicably dependent for his very life. Intense yet warm, capable, competent, brilliant, and sensual, she was the kind of woman he'd always longed for. Her one weakness — her minimal sense of humor — wasn't that important. The big picture was close to perfect, and he was in love.

"Paula," he interrupted her concentration, "you want to set your plate down, snuggle up, and get comfortable?" Sandy extended his arm, inviting her to curl up against him.

Turning, she vacillated at first. Then she seemed to make a decision, set down her empty plate, and gestured to the bathroom. "Let me change out of these," she indicated her work clothes, "before I ruin them. I won't be long, but I want you to tell me *everything* that happens."

For the fifth time that night, Sam Erwin pounded his gavel. The old Southern curmudgeon was closing in on something. Justice was at hand.

Paula returned and lay back down on the bed beside him. She was now wearing a white silk robe, casually closed with a loosely knotted sash. The motion of climbing onto the bed drew the sheer fabric across her skin, exposing nipple, stomach, and the creamy flesh of her inner thigh.

Captivated by desire, Sandy's swelling erection obliterated all thoughts of Sam Erwin, Howard Baker, and Richard Nixon. Nothing could have been more vivid or compelling than the magnificent woman beside him. Without thought or hesitation, he slipped his hand over her breasts and began caressing her right nipple. Rolling up against his body, she kissed him. As she brushed his crotch with her fingers, the last memories of Watergate vanished from Sandy's consciousness.

Paula seemed even more passionate than she had been the night before last. Something about changing into the silk robe freed her from her businesslike, cerebral, self-controlled attorney sensibility. Carried away by pleasure, over the next few hours she experienced more orgasms than Sandy would have believed possible. Her uninhibited passion was a revelation, driving the recent grim bedroom activities with Vikki even further from his mind than his distant sexual memories of Anne. As a man, he once again felt desired, connected, and vividly alive.

At three o'clock, too exhausted for conversation, Sandy passed out with his arms wrapped tightly around Paula's soft, warm, relaxed body. They lay on their sides with Sandy's chest and stomach perfectly conformed to the luscious curve of Paula's back and rump. As in everything else they had done that night, the fit was superb, better than anything he could have imagined.

Four hours later, at seven A.M., Paula's alarm went off as programmed. Sandy drifted back to sleep but Paula was quickly up, out of bed, showered, and dressed for her business breakfast. The last thing he remembered was a kiss good-bye and a request that he lock the door as he left.

When Sandy next glanced at the clock, it was nearly ten o'clock. Awake in a flash, due at a family Sunday brunch at his father's house, he ran to the bathroom and showered. But as much as his brain told him to get dressed and get going, his senses called on him to linger. As he dried his body on her bath towel, the smells of Paula brought back the wonders of their night in bed. Her silk bathrobe, hanging from the bathroom door, radiated her powerful scent. How he wanted her again! And how lonely he felt thinking of her without him, out somewhere to breakfast, so prim and proper, negotiating with the district attorney. Nevertheless, Sandy forced himself to focus on Paula in a less sensual mode as the lawyer, the activist, the agent of social change. It was either that or face the impossible task of sliding his trousers on over an erection of painful proportions.

Once dressed, Sandy descended the stairs to the front door. On that quiet Sunday, he noticed for the first time the strange contradiction between the neat, clean, and tidy decor of Paula's carefully decorated apartment and her wild, uncontrolled, passionate nature. The apartment was like her surface appearance — formal, cold, even intimidating. But behind that proper front was a reservoir of eroticism he would never have dreamed possible.

Even more difficult than getting out of bed was the act of closing the front door of her apartment and locking himself out. In the instant it took for the spring-loaded bolt to do its job and make reentry impossible, Sandy's mood descended from euphoria to depression, back to the war zone of his unhappy world. Starting the Volvo, he drove toward his father's house.

18

"After you leave the plant, what do you do with yourself at night?" Nat asked.

"What do you mean?" Sandy stalled, wary.

They were sitting alone in the walnut-paneled den of Nat's one-year-old Bel Air Tudor home — a "present for his new bride." Sylvia was on the phone. Charlie, Ed, and their wives and children had already departed after eating a huge, noisy brunch of lox, bagels, cream cheese, pickled herring, eggs — the works — during which Sandy sat silently, the outsider required by familial decorum to be present. While his brothers and Nat talked business, Sandy slipped into his usual role of the silent observer. But that Sunday morning, for a change, he knew exactly why he was there — to maintain his normal profile as cover while he secretly executed his plan for escaping the family. Everything went as expected, except for his father's last-minute request to have a private chat after everyone else had gone. Such an unusual thing couldn't be good, Sandy thought.

"What I mean is exactly what I mean; it's a simple question, Sandy." The old man sounded annoyed. "After you leave work, what do you do with yourself? I know what I do. I go home, say hello to Sylvia. We have dinner, sometimes at the house, more often out. At least once a week we attend charity affairs. If we stay in, we usually watch TV. If there's anything good playing — which isn't often — we go to the movies. That's what I do after work. What I'm asking you is what *you* do. Since you and Anne split up I have no sense of your life. Charlie, him I know about. Ed, I could tell you what he did. But you, you're the million dollar mystery man. Last night Sylvia and I were talking; she pointed out to me that I have absolutely no idea what you do with your private life. I thought about it and she's right. She's a very perceptive woman. Your own father doesn't have the slightest notion of what you do after work. Amazing. Why is that?"

"Maybe you never asked," Sandy stonewalled.

"Maybe you don't want me to know."

"Dad, isn't it enough that I spend ten or eleven hours a day at the plant? Other than sleep, there's not much time for anything else."

"You're trying to tell me that you leave the plant, go home, make dinner, and go to sleep, every night?" Nat asked skeptically.

"No."

"Then what the hell do you do with yourself?"

"I read."

"What do you read?" Nat wasn't going to let him off easily.

"Books. Fiction. Some history. Not the kind of thing you'd get excited about. But it interests me. Sometimes I see friends. Every once in a while go to a movie. A date now and then. It's a normal life, nothing to get worked up about. No big deal." Sandy lied with ease.

Nat nodded that he understood. "A date now and then, huh?"

"From time to time."

"Anyone serious?"

"I should be so lucky." Sandy certainly wasn't about to mention Paula.

"You looking for anyone serious?"

"It's not easy, Dad. You were fortunate finding Sylvia so quickly. There're a lot of loony women out there."

"But you're keeping your eyes open?"

Sandy nodded, hoping for an end to the conversation.

"You do any exercise?"

"Dad, what's with you this morning? This is like twenty questions."

"Listen, I'm your father. I care about you. Like I told you the other day, I'm concerned about you. You don't look happy and I've been trying to figure it out. I'd like to help you, if you'll let me."

"Dad," Sandy tried to cover his impatience with an affectionate manner, "I've known you my whole life. Why don't you just skip the preliminaries here and tell me what you've got on your mind, hm?"

"Why do you have to be so jumpy? What's wrong with a father wanting to have a personal, meaningful talk with his son?"

"Not a thing."

"So are you going to let me have a talk with you?"

"Dad, you are talking to me. What is it you want?"

"Sandy," Nat seemed genuinely perplexed, "you have a real gift for making simple conversation impossible. I'm not a complicated man. I see something wrong; I like it to be corrected. I know we spoke about this the other day, but it still concerns me. Since you split up with Anne your life seems to have gone into a tailspin. You come to work, put in your time, do your job, then you leave. You know, Son, in this world there are basically two kinds of people: those few who really live life, and the rest of the herd who only exist. Years ago, when you and Anne were married, yes, I admit I didn't care for your crazy newspaper but at least you seemed alive then. Now you worry me; all the fire is gone. You've got to get it back, Sandy. You need to vary your interests. Enlarge the scope of your activities. Maybe what you need is an exercise program. I think you should take a good look at yourself. How old are you?"

"You don't remember the year your son was born?" Sandy rebuked his father.

"Of course I do, I'm just trying to make a point. You were born in 1941. That makes you thirty-two. My point, Son, is that you've let yourself go. You're only thirty-two but you look forty-five. Ed and Charlie could introduce themselves as your younger brothers and not one person in a million would doubt them."

Sandy remained silent.

"You got to start doing what they both do — exercise. Charlie and Ed play golf three times a week, minimum. Sandy, why don't you take up the sport? That two mile walk, out in the fresh air, away from all of life's problems; it would do you a world of good, believe me."

"You know I hate golf," he said.

"How can anyone hate golf?"

"How can anyone spend half a day smacking a white ball, then chasing after it? It's a perfect sport — if you're a dog."

"There are millions of people who think differently, Sandy." His father spoke with surprising restraint.

"Maybe. But I don't see *you* out on the course."

"What about tennis?"

"There, two guys chase the *same* ball; it's even stupider than golf."

"Isn't there any sport that interests you?"

The quickness with which Nat posed this question cleared up the mystery of the conversation. It was another one of the old man's programs. Nat was big on programs; they were a natural outgrowth of his desire to control everything around him. Sandy suddenly realized that his father had hooked into the idea of reforming him through a program. But was that *all* it was about?

"The only sport that interests me is sailboat racing, like in Star boats, the dinghies I raced on San Francisco Bay the two years I went to Berkeley."

"So why don't you do that here?" Nat inquired.

Sandy shrugged as if the answer were obvious. "There're a lot of things I'd like to do that I can't. Racing sailboats — even dinghies — costs money."

"But if you had one, would you use it?"

"Dad, the point is that I don't have one. I've got to be realistic; I don't fantasize about things that are impossible."

"Well, I'm asking for a reason. It obviously still interests you; why don't you get a boat and do it?"

"You may not remember this," Sandy spoke patiently, as if he were talking to a child, "but I had one hell of an expensive divorce settlement. Combine that with what it cost me to pay off the debts from my newspaper and you come to the fact that both now and in the foreseeable future, a little indulgence like a sailboat isn't possible. Unless of course you want to give me that big raise I deserve," he added with a wicked smile.

"What kind of money would such a boat cost?"

"Dad, don't get me started. I don't like thinking about things I can't have. It makes me depressed."

"I'm curious. How much would a boat like you want really cost?"

Sandy thought for a moment. "I don't know exactly. It's not as if I've been following the market. But my guess is that a used, competitive Star with good sails and a trailer would probably run close to ten thousand dollars. That's for a boat capable of winning, which is what you have to have to make it any fun. Plus of course maintenance."

"What would you say if I loaned you the money to buy a boat like that? Such a loan would come under one condition — that you used the thing. Sandy, I want you to do it, take a couple of afternoons off work each week and sail. Have some fun. Get healthy. Pay me back whenever you can — take years if you want. The important thing is that you get out and enjoy yourself. What do you think?"

"I'm shocked. I mean, it's very generous, Dad. I appreciate it."

"Does that mean you'll do it?"

"Do you mind if I think about it?"

"What's to think about? The money's there. You've got no obligation. What can you lose?"

"It's not simply buying a boat — racing a Star is a commitment. I have to find a crew. Then we'll need months of practice. I can't just decide in one second if I can do it."

"If it's time you're worried about, you've got a promise from me to let you off work for whatever afternoons you need."

"What about my responsibilities? How am I going to get my work done if I'm not there?"

"We'll figure something out. What good is work if it's killing you? Who knows; maybe with a little time off each week you'll function better when you're there. Such a thing is not unheard of."

On the surface Nat's offer appeared wonderful. A stranger observing the conversation through a one-way mirror, Sandy thought, would have the highest praise for the old man's sensitivity and generosity. But in Sandy's mind, Nat's plan meshed perfectly with the secret scheme to sell the company behind his back. Nat's offer could only be another world-class manipulation. The man wanted Sandy away from the center of the action, where he wouldn't see what was happening and cause trouble.

Okay, Sandy thought, if that's the way he wants it, fine. But the question remained, how to respond? To turn down the sailboat would arouse Nat's suspicion. Why would Sandy reject such a wonderful offer? No, he had no choice but to accept the thing. Not only would saying yes cost nothing, but there would be secondary benefits. Having the boat would give Sandy an excuse to leave the office, pursue his war criminal research, and speed up the process of extricating himself from the family business.

"Okay, Dad," Sandy smiled. "How can I say no to such a generous offer? Thank you."

Nat grinned, pleased. "The point here is that if it gives you a little enjoyment, you've made your father a happy man. I only want what's good for you, Son, you know that."

Sandy nodded.

"Tomorrow morning, first thing, the check will be on your desk. You can start looking for the boat today, if you like."

"I really appreciate it, Dad. This is very unexpected. Thank you."

The way Nat appeared to bask in the pleasure of his gift amused Sandy, who marveled at the difference between the appearance of their interchange and what had really transpired. It was almost as if they were cryptologists, talking in code. Each had a secret message, and each thought the other only understood the obvious. The big difference between them, Sandy believed, was that he knew something his father didn't want known — the truth. That fact, Sandy hoped, gave him the advantage.

"By the way," Nat added, "that bandage I see on your arm. What happened?"

Sandy glanced down at his shirt sleeve and saw the white gauze visible through the long slit of the cuff. "Oh nothing; something stupid."

"What'd you do?"

"It's not even worth talking about."

"I'm interested. You know why?"

Sandy shook his head.

"Remember Ray Beasy who came in Friday — Mister Health Products Inc.?"

"Who can forget Ray?"

"He's kind of paranoid about lots of things, as I don't have to tell you. After he spotted your bandage he confided in me that such a dressing is the classic sign of a drug addict. He wanted to know how long you'd been 'shooting up,' as he put it."

Sandy smiled, genuinely amused. "You think I do that?"

"All I know is what I hear from my friends. You just wouldn't believe the number of kids in trouble with drugs these days."

"Dad, let me get this straight. A nut case like Ray — this is a man who lives on yogurt, brown rice, alfalfa sprouts, and distilled water — tells you something like that about me, and you believe him?"

"No, of course not," Nat said evasively, "but we're in the health business and we've got to look purer than snow."

"What did you tell fruitcake Ray?"

"I said you hurt your arm."

"Well congratulations; you told him the truth. A couple mornings ago I knocked over one of those funnels of drip coffee and spilled boiling water on my forearm. I went to the UCLA emergency room, where they treated me for third degree burns. Three times a day I put medication on. It's going to take weeks to heal. That's why I was late the other morning. Okay? So now you know. A stupid kitchen accident. Happy?"

Nat nodded in apparent sympathy. "I figured it was something like that. But you know how it is; I had to ask."

"Sure." Sandy stood up, happy to finally end the conversation and get out before his rage made him say something stupid.

"You do know I want the best for you," Nat extended his hand.

"I know, Dad, thanks." He shook his father's hand.

"My son, the yachtsman." Nat smiled. "I just wish my father could have lived to see this. In his day only the Kaiser raced yachts."

"This isn't a yacht, Dad; this is a dinghy. Like a big rowboat."

"In my book, any rowboat that costs ten thousand dollars is a yacht, thank you very much."

"They're only expensive because they're handmade."

"Look, to an immigrant from Germany, a Jew in a sailboat is a remarkable thing. You should only enjoy yourself."

"Thanks, Dad. I'll try."

Minutes later, after formally thanking Sylvia for the brunch, Sandy was in his Volvo, on his way home, trying to make sense out of the morning. New variables were coming in faster than he could handle them. Life was getting too complex; he needed to slow time down and think things out. So much was happening and all of it was so critical that he was afraid the slightest error on his part would cause everything to explode and destroy him.

How strange that the sailboat, which should be something enjoyable, was in reality another aspect of his familial death sentence. They wanted him off the premises and inconspicuous while they sold the business out from under him. To his father and brothers, the Star boat was a ten thousand dollar insurance policy designed to keep the multimillion dollar negotiations far from Sandy's awareness. Despite his desires, and regardless of his sensational night with Paula, the facts of the betrayal hit hard, reactivating his despair.

At home, he picked up the phone and dialed.

"Hello?"

"Billy, it's Sandy."

"The stranger," Billy said glumly.

"What are you talking about?"

"Last night I left two messages on your machine. I told you I needed an answer this morning. My watch says it's now two-thirty in the afternoon."

"I'm sorry, I didn't come home last night and haven't listened to my machine. What was it you wanted?"

"Hey, well, that's great. Sounds like you had a wonderful time. No more tattoos, I hope."

"That's the least of my problems."

"You went out with Miss Concentration Camp again?"

"Her name is Paula."

"Did you tell her?"

"She isn't the problem."

"You *didn't* tell her?"

"Billy, we had a wonderful time."

"Why do you sound like you died?"

"It's my family again."

"So what's new?"

"A lot."

"Why don't you explain it all to me tonight at dinner? The reason I called was that I got tickets to a screening of *Hollywood Werewolf*. It's directed by Kit Flynn, the guy I told you about who's promised to hire me to score his next film. In this picture a man changes into a wolf right in front of the audience's eyes. With no cuts. The special effects are supposed to be unreal."

"Sounds like a documentary on my father."

"That's why I wanted you to see it," Billy kidded.

"Thanks," Sandy said bitterly, "but I'm not in the mood. I'd rather address envelopes."

"Look, would it be so terrible to come with me and have a little fun? What's one evening? The envelopes aren't going anywhere."

"Another time."

"Sandy, come with me. Please. It'll be good for you to get out. Do it for me, will you?"

"I don't know . . . "

"What's the big deal? Just say yes."

"I want to think about it. Can I call you back in an hour?"

"You're really making me feel important. Why can't you just come?"

"Because I want to think about it."

"It's just a movie and dinner, for Christ's sakes. I mean, I'm not asking you to sign up for the Marine Corps."

"Yeah, I understand. I'm sorry, but I'm going to have to call you back in an hour."

"Okay, you talk to Paula," Billy said sarcastically, "and if Miss Auschwitz will give you a night off from the gas chambers I'd really like to see you." The phone line went dead; Billy had hung up. Sandy dialed Paula's number.

"Hello?"

"Paula, what are you doing home? I expected to get your machine."

"I just walked in. God, am I tired."

"How'd your breakfast go?"

"Spare me from right-wing district attorneys," she answered.

"That good, hm?"

"Worse."

"What do you say we have dinner tonight?" He felt suddenly upbeat, amazed that simply talking to Paula inspired such happy feelings.

"Oh Sandy, you're very sweet. I'd love to. But I'm so exhausted from last night I can't even think straight. Let me get some sleep and we can get together tomorrow."

"Great. I know just the restaurant."

"You don't remember about tomorrow?"

"I'm not following you."

"John Dean's testifying tomorrow."

"Oh my god, you're right; I totally forgot." At that moment Sandy didn't care about Watergate, but he tried to sound as if he did. "How about if I bring over some Chinese food?"

"Sounds perfect."

"I'll see you at seven-thirty. And get some sleep," he teased, "I don't want to stay up late watching TV with a zombie."

"Worry about yourself, big talker. I didn't see you getting up this morning at the crack of dawn."

"Look, when it counted, I did okay. Wouldn't you agree?"

"I don't recall complaining," she murmured affectionately.

"You *had* to leave this morning; I missed you, Paula."

"Me, too," she spoke barely audibly. "Now hang up and let me get some sleep," her voice rose. "I don't want to be a zombie tomorrow either."

"Okay. Seven-thirty. 'Bye."

"'Bye."

For several minutes Sandy sat without moving, basking in the afterglow of her affection. Just talking to Paula made him feel better. And the fact that he would actually be seeing her again in slightly more than twenty-four hours gave him another shot of self-confidence. Energized, he once again picked up his phone and dialed Billy.

"Yo, Sandy here!"

"And?" Billy asked suspiciously, confused by his friend's mood shift.

"If you still want me, I'm yours."

"Just for a movie and dinner. Save the rest for Miss Auschwitz."

"What time's the film?"

"Eight."

"Shall we meet at Musso and Frank's at six?"

"That's lunchtime for me, Sandy, let's eat afterwards."

"You're talking to a man who has to get up for work at six-thirty."

"Since when?"

"You want dinner with me or not?"

"Okay. Six o'clock, Musso's. And tell your mother I'll have you home before eleven. Okay?"

"Sounds sensational."

19

The six o'clock dinner at Musso's was perfect, but Sandy thought the movie was an hour and a half of stupidity. He just didn't understand how anyone could get excited by the sight of men transmogrified into wolves. Who actually believed that the real monsters in life could be recognized by their appearance? Did anyone really think that the good guys always wore chinos, tennis shoes, and La Coste shirts while the bad guys had hair all over their faces and drooled like snarling dogs? What about the horrors committed by the clean-shaven, blond-haired Germans during World War II? Six million dead Jews. Twenty million vaporized Russians. Hundreds of thousands of slaughtered Gypsies. How anyone could take seriously all that emotion and melodrama over a couple of phony werewolves was beyond Sandy's comprehension.

Applause rippled through the dark of the Director's Guild Theatre. The film was over and the packed house clapped fiercely, whistling and howling its approval. On screen the werewolf was dead, evil had been conquered, and peace was restored throughout the world.

Immediately after the credits, the house lights came up and Billy led Sandy straight to the director for the ritual post-screening flattery.

"So, William, what do you think of my little epic?" Kit Flynn grinned innocently. "I want your honest opinion."

Flynn looked the part of the hip young Hollywood director. He was tall, blond, bone-thin, and possessed such a handsome face that could he have passed for Robert Redford's brother except for the neatly trimmed full beard he sported. To this fellow, horror movies were high art, on the cutting edge of culture. To Sandy, the man was all surface and no substance, the essence of Hollywood, a fraud — in the vernacular: full of shit.

"I was surprised and impressed," Billy complimented the director. "The texture, the wit, the timing, the richness of the images and sound—Hitchcock in his prime couldn't have done better."

"You really think so?" Kit pretended humility.

"No question about it," Billy replied. "If this were France and not the United States, instead of being referred to as a 'box office bonanza,' you'd be right up there as an officially recognized, signed and sealed artist—a national treasure."

"I'm glad you appreciate what I do. What did you think of the music?"

"It's different from the way I would have handled it, but I could see what you were after and it works brilliantly. You have what few directors possess—a real ear. I can't wait for us to work together; it's gonna be a real exciting creative process."

"Good work, Kit." An older executive in blue jeans, gold chains, and fresh transplants thrust his hand past Billy, pushing the composer out of the way.

"Thanks, Morty," Kit shook the studio boss's hand. "Billy," he spoke quickly in mid-handshake, "call me mañana and I'll tell you about my next film. I want your input from the beginning." Without waiting for an answer the director turned his back on the composer and pulled the high-powered executive close to him so they could share a laugh over some private observation.

"Can you believe it? He's going to give me the job!" Billy was ecstatic as they walked out onto Sunset Boulevard.

"Congratulations," Sandy responded without enthusiasm.

"Is that all you can say? This is a big break for me."

Sandy nodded. "I'm happy for you, I really am. If that's what you want. Just don't deceive yourself into thinking that the movie we just saw was anything other than horrible. Even you have to admit that."

"What do you mean, *even I*? Who do you think you're talking to?"

"I heard your pile of BS to that director. Puke city."

"Sandy, you're taking things too seriously again. What I said about Hitchcock was the Hollywood equivalent of *Hi, how are you*? You think he's going to give me a job if I tell him I hate his work? Plee-eeze! This isn't Dostoevski here; this is Saturday night entertainment."

Sandy knew that Billy was right. In Hollywood nothing any-one said really mattered. Everything was fashion; only press coverage and money had any real meaning. Where they were standing was a perfect example. Eight years earlier, not a block away on Sunset Boulevard, there had been a nightclub called Pandora's Box that became a hot political issue one summer. A popular place with teenagers, the club angered local residents, who objected to the weird-looking kids hanging around late at night. In response the city condemned the place, causing a mass confrontation between the police and the teenagers. For weeks the kids defied the cops and tried to remain on the property. But finally, inevitably, after a little tear gas and a few arrests the nightclub was bulldozed and the confrontations ended. Any-where else in the world this would have been an embarrassing community joke. But in Hollywood those few weeks took on the quality of a medieval legend, immortalized by the opening line of Buffalo Springfield's hit song *For what it's worth:* "Something's happening here."

The ominous melody and apocalyptic lyrics gave the impres-sion to the world that evil incarnate had been inflicted on the teenaged patrons of Pandora's Box. All across the United States kids took up the tune as the theme song of their revolution — at least for as long as it remained on the *Billboard* charts. More teens knew and cared about the injustices inflicted on a crummy nightclub called Pandora's Box than they did about what hap-pened at a real historical horror like Dachau or Treblinka. Where else but Hollywood could such a thing have happened? No wonder Billy wanted to work on horror films.

"Yeah, you're probably right," Sandy relented.

Billy grinned. "It's only a movie, remember?"

Sandy nodded and was about to respond to that Hollywood cliché when a woman's voice interrupted.

"So, Sandy, this is the work that keeps you out of the house and far from your phone."

Standing not ten feet away was Vikki, dressed to the nines in handmade suede trousers and blouse, lavishly finished off with turquoise Indian jewelry. Beside Vikki, clutching her hand, was a tall, dark-haired man in his thirties wearing a tailored blue jeans suit.

"Vikki. Hey. How are you?"

"Sandy. Billy. This is Allen Strachen."

Sandy and Billy nodded politely and shook the man's hand. Allen's reaction to the introduction was impossible for Sandy to assess because the man's eyes were hidden behind dark sunglasses. Had he been to the ophthalmologist, Sandy wondered, or were his retinas just too sensitive for the cruel glare of the Hollywood street lights? Talk about pretentious; who was this asshole?

"Great movie, wasn't it?" Vikki chirped with genuine enthusiasm.

"Landmark effects," Billy agreed.

"I thought it rivaled Hitchcock at his peak, as good as *North By Northwest*," Allen pitched in without irony.

"That's almost word-for-word what I told Kit," Billy said.

"You know Kit Flynn?" Vikki was obviously impressed.

Billy nodded. "I'm going to score his next film."

"You know what I thought?" Sandy addressed Vikki. "It's the biggest piece of over-rated garbage I've ever seen. I can't believe we all saw the same movie. Mine was about werewolves; what was yours about?"

For a moment an embarrassed silence reigned. Then Vikki broke the ice. "Goodnight, Billy. 'Night, Sandy. Like I told you on your machine, there's no need to call back." Without waiting for an answer she clutched Allen's arm tightly and led him away.

"Well, looks like old Viks finally found herself a boyfriend," Billy volunteered.

"Yeah. You think he's related to Stevie Wonder, or is he just a junkie?" Sandy spoke with bravado to cover his hurt. It wasn't that he wanted anything more from Vikki; in fact, he was happy that it had ended so cleanly. He just didn't enjoy feeling such contempt from someone with whom he'd so recently been intimate.

"You know, you just proved everything I've been trying to get you to see about yourself," Billy said. "Think about this. You, me, Vikki, and that creature Allen all saw the same movie. Three of us enjoyed it. That doesn't make it Chekov, but it's something. Yet you hated it. Maybe, it's just possible that you reacted to whatever really went on in the bathroom of Parcheesi's in the same kind of way. Maybe you got it all wrong, and they're *not* trying to fuck you over. Maybe there's even a way to make things work with your family that you're not considering."

"Right. Thank you." Sandy spoke formally, controlling his anger. "That was a fascinating, helpful insight. I'll definitely try to keep it in mind. Goodnight. And thanks for the entertainment." Without shaking hands, Sandy turned and walked down the dark residential block to his Volvo.

Once home, Sandy went back to work on his Lufthansa questionnaires. Only the Nazi investigation and his upcoming Monday night date with Paula gave him a sense of being connected to the future.

20

"Did you hear the news?" Breathless with excitement, Paula stood in the doorway of her apartment talking to Sandy, who was crossing the courtyard at precisely seven-thirty. Precariously balanced in his arms were half a dozen white cardboard cartons of fragrant Chinese food.

"What news?"

"John Dean's testimony. He implicated Nixon in the cover-up! Isn't that incredible?"

Sandy shrugged, unimpressed. "It's not as if we didn't know it all along."

"Yeah, but now there's proof. The smoking gun. You really didn't hear about it? Where were you all day? What could you have been doing that you didn't hear? *Everyone* knows about it; that's all anyone's been talking about today."

"Paula, please, spare me. I had a really terrible day and I didn't have a chance to listen to the radio. If you don't mind, I'd rather skip the cross-examination and relax."

"You're right, I'm sorry." She smiled warmly. "You're here; we can watch it all on TV. Let me try this again. Maybe I can get it right." For a second she turned her back on him, then swung around, pretending to see him for the first time. "Sandy, how wonderful to see you. And look at this dinner. God, it smells wonderful. Come in and let's eat."

But Sandy didn't budge.

"What is it? Did I do something wrong?" Paula appeared worried.

"You forgot the kiss. Isn't that part of a normal hello?"

Paula stepped up to Sandy, maneuvered around the carton containing Hunan beef with garlic sauce, and kissed him eagerly on the lips. The combination of her perfume with the ginger, garlic, peppers, and sesame sent a reassuring warmth down Sandy's belly and between his legs.

"Now do I pass?" she whispered, withdrawing her lips from his.

"Depends," he answered as he slipped past her and set the cartons of Chinese food down on the dining table.

"On what?"

"On whether you have chopsticks," he teased.

She nodded, searched her kitchen drawers, then called out, "How hungry are you?"

"Starving."

"Okay," she spoke gravely, "I'll bring the chopsticks. But on one condition."

"Why can't you just bring me the chopsticks and tell me your conditions while we eat? Does everything have to be high-pressure negotiations? I mean, start off easy; we hardly know each other," he kidded.

"That's exactly my question."

"I'm not following you."

"That's obvious. Listen, how long *have* we known each other?"

"Five days."

"And in that time, what have you learned about me? You know where I live. You know where I work, what I do, what I think and feel, my opinions on all kinds of issues. You know a lot about me."

Sandy said nothing.

"But you, you're something else. I understand that what you went through makes you a very private person and I respect that. But Sandy, I know nothing about you and your life. Zero. I need more information. Tell me a little about yourself—what you think, what you feel, where you're from, who you are, what you do with yourself every day. Is that too much to ask?"

"All that, you expect me to trade for two sticks of wood?" he teased, with exaggerated incredulity.

Paula nodded, then handed Sandy the chopsticks, which he used to dole out the contents of the six cardboard cartons, splitting the food onto two large plates.

"Sandy," she squealed in delighted protest, "there's enough here for six people."

"Well, you never know," he smiled seductively, "with John Dean and everything, it's going to be a long night; we're going to need all the energy we can muster."

"What's this?" Paula held up a coral-colored tube covered with a translucent sauce.

"Beef marrow, Hunan-style."

Cautiously, Paula took a bite. "This is incredible."

Sandy nodded that he agreed.

After a second bite she took a sip of beer, set down her chopsticks, and leveled a serious gaze at Sandy. "So, now are you going to tell me about yourself?"

"What is it exactly you want to know?" He spoke without affect as he chewed.

"Start with where you live."

"I have a house. Off Beverly Glen."

"Is it on a street that has a name?" she asked.

"Rising Glen Drive."

"Is that on the Valley side?"

"The L.A. side."

"I've been up the Glen but I don't know the street."

"It's a cul-de-sac; it doesn't connect to anything."

"Do you rent or own?"

"Jeez," he acted surprised. "That's one hell of a question. Yes, I do own. But don't you think that's a little personal? I mean, we're not in court here."

"I shouldn't be personal, is that what you're trying to tell me?"

"Paula, I've known you less than a week. Money isn't something you just blab about. I don't see you telling me how you afford this apartment on the salary of a public interest lawyer."

"I was just curious." She avoided his question.

"Some things take time; relax, you'll find out everything. Just let it evolve."

"Sandy, if things hadn't happened as fast as they have, I'd say fine. But I don't think the normal rules apply here, do they? I mean, for example, the usual rules between men and women stipulate you don't go to bed on the first date — you're supposed to let it, as they say, *evolve*. But that's not the way we started out, is it?"

"Paula, you're making me feel like I'm in court again. What exactly are you doing? You went to bed with me the day you met me. I'd hardly call it a date. I thought we both had an inspired, spontaneous, wonderful time, but now you seem to be holding it against me. Is this your normal routine with men?"

"Is *what* my normal routine?"

"Going to bed with them on the first date, then crucifying them for it."

"You really want to know?" she threatened.

"No, in fact, I don't," he spoke tenderly after a long moment of thought. "I like you far too much to have our few nights together ruined. Maybe you don't want to see me tonight? Maybe you'd like me to go home? I had a bad day today, and I don't want it to spoil what's good between us. Shall I see you another time when we're both in a better mood?"

"No." She spoke without hesitation.

"No go or no stay?"

"Stay." She reached across the table and tenderly squeezed his hand. "Please."

"Paula, what the hell is going on here?"

"I want to know something else." She avoided his eyes.

"Okay."

"Do you think less of me for going to bed with you so soon after meeting you?"

"Why do you imagine I'd think less of you?"

"Sandy, god damn it, I'm asking *you* a question; don't answer my question with another question!"

"You think *I* think less of you?" He was genuinely surprised.

"If you're trying to make me angry, you're sure succeeding."

"Paula, consider this fact: Since the night we met on the floor of the Ho, I've been trying to see you every minute I've been off work. What does that tell you?"

"I don't know. What *should* it tell me?"

"That I think you're wonderful. Exciting. The best thing that's ever happened to me."

"You're not just seeing me because you like my omelettes?"

Sandy shook his head. "I adore you. In every possible way."

She nodded, moved by his statement of affection, and once again tenderly squeezed his hand. "You feel like we've made a real connection?"

"I think it's obvious."

"We're not talking here just about sex?"

"Paula, I will tell you once more: We connect in every area I can think of. It's magic. Scary. And in my limited experience, not something you want to analyze to death or you'll kill it, okay?"

"You're probably going to laugh at me — I'm laughing at myself just saying this — but for the first time in my life I don't know whether to agree or disagree. Since we met — and you are the only man I've ever gone to bed with the day we met — I've been nothing but confused. I've known you only a few days yet I feel so familiar and comfortable with you. You're the first man I've ever known who doesn't fade in my mind when I'm not physically with you. The days I haven't seen you, you're with me, alive, as much a part of me as you are right now. I feel you. I smell you. I hear your voice. It's eerie. But here, with you, except for that tattoo on your arm, I don't really know anything about you. I mean, of course, the tattoo does tell me a lot but I need to know more."

"I wouldn't read too much into the tattoo," Sandy said quietly, hoping to diminish the inevitable future embarrassment.

"Right," Paula snapped back. Obviously she had expected more of an answer. "How should I look at it? Like a stylish suit or a new hairstyle? C'mon, Sandy, who are you trying to kid? I know the price my parents paid for their numbers. And believe me, I respect it. So don't try to diminish me and my experience by pretending that what you went through was nothing."

"Paula, I am not exaggerating when I tell you that my life today has absolutely nothing to do with this tattoo." He gestured to his forearm. "Accept me for who I am, here, now, in front of you, in 1973. Don't diminish me by romanticizing my past because of a crummy bit of ink embedded in my skin."

"Can I get you to tell me anything about your life in the camps?"

"You don't seem to hear me at all."

"Will you at least tell me where you were born?"

"Paula, do your parents like talking about their experiences in the camps?"

"Not to strangers. But to me they don't mind."

"Well, I don't talk about my past with anyone. I'm sorry, but if you want to know me you're going to have to respect that fact. My early past is history. My life is now. Period." As soon as Sandy had improvised this rule, he hated himself. Here was his opportunity to tell her the truth and what did he do but wiggle deeper into his lie. The excuse he gave himself for this was weakness; he needed Paula too much to risk anything that might scare her away. That look in her eyes when she talked about her feelings for him was so poignant, so adoring and passionate that even the possibility of severing such a high voltage connection frightened him into abandoning the promise he had made to himself to clear the air, tell her the truth, and seek her acceptance of his real self.

To rationalize his cowardice, he labeled the deception "a little white lie." Some understatement, he knew. Withholding this information was not a trivial matter, but a hydrogen bomb of an omission capable of destroying everything it touched. But in Sandy's mind, the overriding concern was preserving this wonderful and still fragile relationship. He simply couldn't allow himself even to think of jeopardizing his future with Paula until they were clearly interdependent, in love and, as a couple, rock solid.

"You know," she said affectionately, "you claim to adore me; why can't you trust me?"

"What does trust have to do with dredging up my past and torturing myself?"

"How else can I get to know you?"

"Use your imagination."

"Thanks a hell of a lot. Isn't it important to you that you feel connected to me?"

"I don't understand the mystery here. Who is sitting across the table from you? Who brought you this beef with garlic sauce? It's me, Sandy Klein. I'm right here. If you don't believe it, touch me." Sandy reached across the narrow dining table and delicately caressed Paula's cheek with his fingertips. "See, it's me. Right here. Sandy. Remember?"

Both frustrated and reassured, Paula didn't know what to say. While she considered the situation, she let herself enjoy his touch.

"Hey, look what time it is." Sandy held up his watch. "We better go upstairs and turn on the TV."

Paula nodded but didn't move.

"You don't want to see John Dean?"

"Of course I do. But I also want you to talk to me."

"These things take time, Paula; they can't be rushed."

"I know you're right. You're not mad at me, are you, for being curious and pushing?"

He smiled seductively. "The only *mad* I am is *mad about you.*"

Amused and touched, she stood, walked around the table to stand behind him, and leaned over to lick his ear. "I know I can be a pain sometimes with my questions," she purred, "but don't let it drive you away. It's just me. I want to know everything about you."

"Keep doing that with your tongue and I'll forgive anything."

"I'll keep that in mind for the future." After a final kiss on his neck she straightened up. "Shall we go watch John Dean?"

"Wouldn't miss it for the world."

But Paula never did see John Dean implicate Richard Nixon that night. After changing into her silk robe and crawling onto the bed with Sandy, her interest in the presidential scandal was subverted by her carnal appetites. Instead of watching the TV, Paula unzipped Sandy's trousers and began running her tongue over his instantly swollen erection.

"I, uh, thought you wanted to see John Dean," Sandy murmured, his eyes closed.

"Is that what you'd prefer?" Paula only removed her lips

from his stiffened penis for as long as it took to speak the words.

"It was only an observation, not a complaint." Sandy's voice was barely audible.

Paula went back to work, licking, sucking, fondling his cock and balls, bringing Sandy right to the edge of orgasm, then backing off, cooling him down, only to repeat the sequence.

"You're driving me crazy," he moaned over the pounding gavel of Sam Erwin. "Paula, I need to fuck you."

"Not yet," she purred as she delicately stroked his swollen cock.

Sandy opened his eyes to observe Paula bent over, on her knees, masturbating herself while sucking on his erection.

Conscious of his gaze and highly aroused, Paula spoke between mouthfuls. "Did you think of me today?"

"Every minute," Sandy moaned, yearning for her to finish him off.

"What did you think about?" Her intonation was obviously sexual.

"Your pussy. How wet it is. How much I wanted you to wrap your thighs around my cock and take me deep inside of you. I wanted to run my tongue on your clit, rub my face on your pussy. I needed to feel you dangling your tits in my face while you thrust my cock back and forth with your hot cunt, humping me hour after hour."

"Uhmm. And did thinking about me give you a hard-on?" she asked as she continued to fondle both his cock and her own pussy.

"Paula, fantasizing about you made me so big I could hardly walk around at work. It was very embarrassing."

"Did you masturbate thinking about me?"

"I thought about it," he answered. "What about you? Did you think about me today?"

"Why didn't you masturbate?"

"Would it excite you to know I masturbated thinking about you?"

"Uhmm," she moaned.

Unable to figure out what that meant, he pushed further. "You didn't answer my question; did you think about me?"

"I couldn't get you out of my mind."

"What did you think about?"

"Your cock."

"What about my cock?"

"How big it is. How much it excites me. How I like to feel it inside of me. How I like it to slide between my legs and bury itself deep in my pussy. How I like to feel it ache for me. How I missed it when you were gone."

"You thought about this in court today?"

Paula only nodded.

"You must have had a hard time concentrating on your arguments," he teased.

To Sandy's surprise she nodded again.

"You're going to laugh, but it was terrible. It's not the kind of problem they teach you how to handle in law school."

"What did you do?"

Avoiding his eyes, she continued to stroke both her clit and his balls. "I'm embarrassed to say."

"Why don't you try me?" Sandy spoke affectionately. "Paula, you've seen me half-dead, you've seen my number, you've fucked me over and over. Besides," he teased, "when you have your hand on my balls, do you think I'd be self-destructive enough to say anything to make you angry?"

Continuing to stroke him, she avoided his eyes. "That vividness I feel about you — a lot of it is sexual. I've never felt that before. To be honest, one of the reasons I moved out here is that it seemed there wasn't one man in New York I could connect to. With you it's a whole new world, and it terrifies me. I can be sitting at work — in the courtroom — and start thinking about you and suddenly, before I realize what's happening, I can feel myself getting wet. Then, no matter what's going on, images of us start running through my brain, out of my control. I picture you and me together, naked. In bed. I'm straddling you or sucking on your cock, or you're humping me from behind. We're not making love. It's not something gentle and sweet, all that roman-

tic stuff. What we're doing is fucking. I'm spreading my legs and
you're shoving yourself deep into me. I want to scream; I want to
screw like an animal, coming and coming. I thought about that
in court all day." She glanced up to observe his reaction. "I've
never felt anything like this before. What happened today was that
right in the middle of my summation to the jury I lost track of
my argument. I had to ask the judge for a recess." Shifting her
eyes, Paula spoke rapidly. "I went to the ladies' room, locked
myself in a stall, fantasized taking your cock all the way up my
pussy, and masturbated until I came. It cleared you out of my
head so I could go back and concentrate on my closing arguments. It must have worked because we won." Paula sat staring
down at the carpet almost as if she expected to be punished.

"That's a very sweet and sexy story. Thank you for telling me,"
Sandy said gently.

"You don't think that what I did was disgusting?"

"Come up here. I want to kiss you."

They embraced with great tenderness.

"Tell you what I'll do," he whispered. "Tomorrow I'll go to
the courthouse men's room and masturbate. Would that make
you feel better?"

Amused at the idea, she smiled, then shook her head. "I'd
rather have you for myself." Without another word she squatted
on the bed, spread her legs, grasped his cock and slipped him
deep into herself. "Oh my god, how wonderful," she groaned
with relief.

John and Maureen Dean, Senator Howard Baker, and all the
other characters in the Watergate circus disappeared for the
night, filtered into the background by passion. For President
Richard Milhous Nixon, the night of June twenty-fifth must
have been long and painful. But in Los Angeles, Sandy and Paula
had one of the great erotic experiences of their lives.

Near dawn, after only two hours of deep, peaceful sleep, Sandy
was awakened by the primal, frightening feeling that someone
was watching him. Without moving his head on the pillow,
Sandy listened, concentrating on the almost inaudible sounds in
the hope of locating the intruder's exact position. In the dim

glow of the night-light, he imagined a murderer standing over him with a gigantic, razor-sharp butcher knife, a Charles Manson clone—a modern visitation of the Hitler youth—here to slaughter two more Jews.

Tensing his muscles, Sandy took a deep breath, then sprang up from the bed, landing on his feet, crouched like a boxer with fists clenched.

A scream of terror echoed through the room. At first Sandy thought it was himself. But almost instantly he realized that the noise originated from Paula. Nothing was out of place. There was no intruder. They were alone.

"Sandy, what is it?" Paula was sitting up, staring at him as she apparently had been for some time before he awakened. *She* was the presence he had sensed.

"I thought I heard something. I felt someone was watching me; I was sure there was a burglar in the room."

"You had a nightmare, Sandy. But, boy, did you scare me when you jumped."

As Sandy's heart rate cooled down from triple time, he sat back down on the bed. "How long have you been up?"

She shrugged. "Not long," Paula lied.

"I'd bet my life savings you haven't slept at all. What's wrong?"

"It's so late it's almost time for me to get up; I couldn't stop thinking about work." Another lie.

"That was you I felt watching me?"

She nodded.

"I know something that might help you sleep," he said seductively.

"Thanks. But I'm so tired I don't think I could feel anything. If it weren't so close to the time I have to leave for work I'd take a sleeping pill."

"Take the day off."

"I can't."

"You know what sometimes works for me?"

She shook her head.

"A hot bath. I mean a really hot bath. Something about all that heat is very relaxing. And the worst that can happen is that if you still can't sleep, at least you're clean."

Paula laughed.

"Try it, it works. I'm not kidding." Sandy studied her without success; whatever she was thinking was impossible to read.

"Sure, what the hell." She slid out of bed. "What do I have to lose?"

"That's the attitude. But make it as hot as you can stand; the temperature is what wipes you out."

She nodded, disappearing into the bathroom.

Sandy lay without moving, too tired even to wonder why she had been watching him.

After what seemed like only seconds, a gentle touch on his shoulder awakened Sandy. When he opened his eyes he was surprised to see that the room was light. He had fallen back to sleep, and now it was morning. Paula was up and dressed in black slacks and a silk shirt, ready for work. As Sandy squinted against the morning sun streaming through the open window, Paula handed him a mug of steaming French roast coffee.

"What time is it?"

"Eight. I shut off the alarm so I could wake you myself."

"Thank you." He took a sip of the coffee. "Woo, is this strong. And wonderful."

She nodded. Despite her makeup she looked tired.

"I take it you weren't able to go back to sleep."

"No, that's not true," she claimed. "The bath worked wonders."

"You want to reconsider, call in sick, and spend the day here with me?" He patted the bed.

She grinned. "You know there's nothing I'd like better. But I'm late as it is. Don't you have to go to work?"

Sandy nodded. "But just give me the word and I'll call my office. You wouldn't believe how fast a case of stomach flu can develop."

"Another time."

"I'm going to hold you to that."

As she nodded, her expression became serious. "I would have let you sleep, but I wanted to ask you something. Will you do me a favor and listen to what I have to say without interrupting me?"

"Am I going to like what I hear?" he probed, alarmed by her detached, almost businesslike tone of voice.

"I hope so," she said seriously.

"Hey, Paula, slow down. Nothing important should be decided this early in the morning. Let's talk about it tonight at dinner."

"You don't even know what I'm going to say," she protested.

"I sense enough to know it doesn't sound good to me."

"I look that serious?"

Sandy nodded.

"It's just because I'm tired. All I wanted to do . . ."

"I thought we were going to discuss this at dinner," he interrupted.

"I wanted to invite you somewhere tonight. The reason I look so serious is that I'm concerned about your reaction; I don't want you to be angry with me."

"Why should I be angry about an invitation?"

"Because it involves Germany and the concentration camps."

"What about them?" His inflection was immediately hostile.

"See, that's why I wanted you to let me speak without interruption."

Sandy gestured for her to continue.

"A colleague and I have been conducting one-night, three-hour seminars on anti-Semitism, the rise of the Third Reich, Nazism, Hitler, and the final solution. It's a kind of slide show and lecture that we got into as a result of a legal case. A couple of Valley kids were caught defacing a synagogue in Sherman Oaks. You know, the usual spray-painted swastikas and slurs. We were asked to defend them. You can imagine my reaction. Larry Carton — my colleague — comes from a family background similar to mine so he wasn't too excited either. But when we looked into it, we found out that these kids had no idea of the meaning of what they were doing. They were just young, angry, uneducated troublemakers being provocative. The concentration camps were ancient history, as unreal as Greek mythology. The problem, we realized, was making the Holocaust current. So we put together our little show. And we've been amazingly successful.

"Already we've given it for more than a thousand people. The United Jewish Appeal's been booking us at schools, churches, and temples all over town. Tonight Larry and I are going to do our spiel at Valley State College in Northridge. Sometimes we get those maniacs who argue that the whole thing is Zionist propaganda, that the camps never happened. But it's usually interesting, people's reactions. I thought you might come and listen, maybe afterwards give us a few tips on where the presentation needs improvement. What do you say?"

"I'm sure it's fascinating." His lack of enthusiasm was an obvious refusal.

"Then why don't you check it out?"

"If you were speaking on any other subject I would. But I've already had more than enough experience with the camps, thank you very much."

"Sandy, have you heard of Elie Weisel?"

"It's hard to miss his self-promotion in the bookstores. He's turned his experiences in the camps into a world-wide cottage industry. The man should be ashamed of himself."

"You don't think he's doing the right thing? I mean, thousands of people are aware of what went on only because of that man."

Sandy shook his head. "Preaching to the converted is not my idea of effectiveness."

"What is?" she asked angrily.

"I'm not sure anything is. Books describing the horrors of war have been published for centuries. Yet in the last forty years the killing has only gotten worse."

"You know, you've got a real depressing view of things."

Sandy shrugged as if to say, What do you expect?

"I don't think everything has to be so terrible."

"I wish I could believe you're right."

"Then come with me tonight and hear our talk. I know we've changed people's minds. Come. See. For me, Sandy. I'd really like to hear what you think about our presentation. Please."

"Last night I thought we came to some agreement about not talking about my past."

"Who's asking you to talk? All I want you to do is listen. Will you at least consider coming?"

"That I can do."

For a moment she studied him. "You know, something's bothered me about you that I just figured out. You grew up speaking German. English isn't your first language. So how come you don't have any accent?"

He was prepared for this question. "German was my father's language." This was true. "But given what the Germans did to my family I learned to hate everything about them, including their language." This aspect of his story was also true. But the next part was such an all-encompassing lie that it seemed to cut off the possibility of ever telling her the truth. "That hate was so powerful that when I arrived in this country as a teenager I swore to myself never to have anything to do with Germany ever again. Never to buy German. Never to do business with Germany. And most of all, never to speak German. I watched American television. I took speech lessons. I learned all the idioms — you know how obsessed kids can get. I made myself obliterate every trace of German from my speech."

"It's remarkable."

"That's what my speech teacher thought. She said I had the best ear for dialect she had ever heard. It also helped that I was young."

Paula nodded, impressed. "You really haven't spoken German since?"

Sandy nodded.

"What about food; do you order sauerkraut?"

"No."

"Wiener schnitzel?"

"I wouldn't touch the stuff."

"You *are* a fanatic, aren't you?"

Sandy shrugged. "Having your family killed has a strange way of hardening you." Again, this was the truth.

"I can accept that."

"Then you can understand why I won't attend your lecture."

She nodded, unable to counter his argument. In her confusion, she noticed the clock by the bed. "Oh my god, look what time it is. Sandy, I gotta go."

"Since I can't see you tonight, can we have dinner tomorrow?"

"For sure." She gave him a quick kiss. "Just make sure the door's locked when you leave." Instantly she was out of the bedroom, down the stairs.

"I'll call you later," he hollered.

The front door slammed. She was gone.

Late for work himself, Sandy slipped out of bed and headed for the shower. What an extraordinary woman, he told himself. I'm a lucky, lucky man.

21

Arriving at work two hours late, Sandy was startled to find neither his father nor brother on the premises. According to Nat's secretary, they were both out at a meeting. As the hours passed, Sandy had no doubt what sort of a meeting Nat and Ed were attending—a *screw you* meeting, working out the details of the sale of the family business. Why else would they be gone together for the entire day? That kind of absence was unprecedented.

After spending the entire work day refining the details of his investigation, at six Sandy headed for home, where he substituted a big glass of scotch for dinner and continued his slow progress on the German-American Travel Agency contest forms. But he had addressed and stuffed only twenty-six envelopes when the doorbell rang.

Visible through the peephole in the front door was Billy, flanked by two flashy teenaged women: a peroxide blonde and a brunette. Both wore skin-tight jeans, turquoise jewelry, and extremely unsubtle makeup. Were they hookers? Was Billy suddenly into paying for sex? If so, what did he want with Sandy? Was he trying to initiate some sort of orgy? Whatever was going on in Billy's mind, Sandy told himself, he wanted none of it. Time was flying and envelopes needed addressing.

"Sandy," Billy greeted him, "I brought a little surprise for you. This is Beth," he indicated the dark haired woman, "and this is Alicia."

"Hi Sandy," cooed Beth.

"Hello Sandy," echoed Alicia.

"Hi." Sandy nodded politely to them but addressed himself to his friend. "Billy, this is, uh, very nice. Except I don't have time to play tonight; *as you know*, I have work to do." He gestured to the pile of envelopes, forms, and Lufthansa computer printouts stacked on the dining table.

"Would I interfere with a project of genius?" he grinned. "Beth, Alicia, and I are here to help. Aren't we girls?"

Both women smiled and nodded. Were they all stoned and drunk?

"Beth and Alicia are the ones I told you about who do backup vocals for me," Billy reminded his friend. "During the day they work for ASCAP as secretaries. And they're the best, believe me. In every department."

The girls giggled at the innuendo.

"Tonight they're here only to work. You watch, Sandy. We're going to sit down and go to town on those envelopes of yours. However many hours it takes, we're going to get them addressed and mailed, tonight, so that you and I can start doing something fun with our evenings. Remember when that used to be the case, way back, ages ago? When was it? Last week?"

Billy, here to help and selfless, Sandy thought. Unbelievable.

"So what's it going to be; you going to let us in or what?" Taking control, Billy gestured for the girls to enter.

Fueled by vodka and an occasional line of cocaine, Billy and the girls worked beside Sandy for seven straight hours. Functioning assembly-line fashion, the four of them churned out contest forms at a phenomenal rate. It was all business; the only conversation involved brief interruptions to refill glasses or change records on the stereo. By mutual agreement it was decided that the Rolling Stones provided the most enjoyable accompaniment to the boring task. Nothing like Charlie Watts, Keith Richards, Bill Wyman, and Mick Jagger with their wailing rhythm section to pump up a dull activity. By three o'clock in the morning everyone was exhausted, but the job was finished. All the contest forms were ready for the mail.

"You owe me an evening next week—dinner at the restaurant of my choice. Just you and me. I've got some funny stories to tell you." Billy grinned, proud of himself, as he escorted Alicia and Beth toward the front door of Sandy's house. On the floor, ready to be taken to the post office, were two large cardboard cartons containing five thousand stamped and addressed envelopes.

Holy Jesus, Sandy suddenly thought, what happened to Paula? During the day he'd called her office three times and left messages. Why hadn't she phoned back? Maybe she had, he told himself — it was possible he'd missed the call because of the ear-shattering volume of the Rolling Stones on the stereo. Possible, yes; likely, no. Perhaps the lecture had run late and when she got home all she wanted to do was sleep. But he didn't believe it. The lawyer, Larry Carton; who the hell was he? What was Paula's relationship to him? At eight in the morning, the thought of Larry Carton hadn't meant much; but at three A.M. he suddenly assumed an astounding importance. Maybe the reason she hadn't called was that she was in the sack with Carton. Paula was an extremely attractive woman. Why wouldn't she have more than one man hot for her? Carton was perfect. A Jew. Concentration camp preoccupations. Some of his family killed by Germans, perhaps. And a lawyer to boot.

"Pick any night, Billy," Sandy forced himself to behave graciously. "And thank you. You know how much you've helped me. All of you. Alicia, Beth. I'm truly grateful."

"Thanks for the vodka," Alicia responded.

"Good luck with your travel agency." Beth spoke with a straight face, obviously not understanding the true purpose of the contest.

Sandy nodded, opening the door for them.

"I'll call you tomorrow. 'Night." Billy winked, wrapped his arms around both women, and escorted them out to his car.

Sandy watched as the three of them piled in Billy's 1965 Mustang GT350. The engine roared to life and the powerful white car rocketed out of sight down the canyon.

After slamming the door and charging back into his living room, Sandy dialed Paula's apartment. The phone rang and rang; just as he had feared, no one answered. *Three fucking o'clock in the morning and she wasn't even home!* It didn't take a genius to realize that the woman was in bed with that son-of-a-bitch Larry Carton, fucking her brains out, obliterating all memories of Sandy.

This thought made Sandy feel diminished, minuscule — as if he no longer existed. Why hadn't he gone to that god-damn concentration camp lecture? Paula had asked him and asked him; if he'd only listened more closely he'd have understood her request for what it was — a plea to stop her from fucking Larry Carton. She had been crying out for help and he, Sandy, had turned her down. The fact that the man was a lawyer somehow made everything worse. It was too reminiscent of Anne and her betrayal, culminating in her marriage to that older, conventional, socially prominent tax lawyer. What was it, Sandy moaned, about Jewish women and lawyers? Didn't the women realize that being an attorney was not one iota of protection from the real issues of life? Look what happened in Germany in the thirties: All those German-Jewish lawyers went to the gas chambers with their wives and were killed just as permanently as everyone else.

His reaction to her imagined betrayal terrified Sandy, who was afraid he'd lost all perspective on what was happening. Nevertheless, his situation was suddenly far too clear. Instead of being special to her, as he had wanted to believe, he was only one of many interchangeable men, with no value beyond the moment. She must view him simply as the stud with the number on his arm, of no more significance than the stud with the law degree or the stud with the medical degree. Take a number, get in line, and wait to be called.

Again Sandy dialed her number. Again there was no answer. He tried to reassure himself that, as usual, he was jumping to the most pessimistic conclusion. Probably she had come home exhausted from her lecture, gotten into bed, and shut off the phone.

After no response from a third try at Paula's number, Sandy quit speculating and went into action. He quickly loaded the two cardboard boxes of contest forms into the back of his Volvo and drove off down the canyon.

First stop was the giant central post office in the Westwood Federal Building. At three-thirty in the morning, the place was deserted. Nevertheless, carrying the awkward, heavy boxes of envelopes into the building and stuffing the five thousand forms through the stainless steel bulk-mail door took nearly half an hour. It was four o'clock by the time Sandy was back in his car, driving toward Paula's apartment.

After parking the Volvo equidistant from two widely spaced street lights — the darkest spot on the block — Sandy scuttled through the Spanish Colonial courtyard, barely managing to avoid tripping on the thick above-ground roots of a giant elm. Pressing his face against Paula's multipaned living room window, he could see virtually nothing: a bit of the stairs, the oak coffee table, the edge of the quilt hanging on the wall leading to the kitchen. At least, he told himself, there were no clothes strewn across the floor. That was a good sign. Then he heard a noise. Was it a moan? Sandy held his breath and listened carefully. So faint as to be barely audible, another low-decibel sound floated across the courtyard. Irrational or not, Sandy knew he had to find out if Paula was alone.

Silently sneaking out of the courtyard around back to the alley, Sandy studied the thick, unpruned wisteria vines growing up the side of the building around and above Paula's second-story bedroom window. Placing his left foot in a crotch of fiber three feet off the ground, Sandy grabbed the plant with his hands and pulled himself up. The wisteria held. He found another step and levered further. Slowly, with great effort, Sandy found higher footholds and worked his way toward Paula's window.

Fourteen feet above the alley, the wisteria began to thin out; in only two more steps he'd be able to see clearly into her bedroom. Shimmying a foot to his right, Sandy hauled himself up on the thin, stiff fiber, balanced precariously, and pressed his face against the glass.

The room was dark. Obviously someone was in the bed — one person or two, it was impossible to tell. Shifting his weight slightly for a better angle, Sandy misjudged the strength of his new perch, which broke without warning, and down he plunged to the accompaniment of loud, collapsing explosions of wisteria fiber.

Sandy grabbed frantically at adjacent tendrils, but it was no use: The wisteria plant itself was peeling away from the brick wall. Five feet from the ground, his descent stopped abruptly in a tangle of particularly tough vines. For a moment, the plant remained attached to the building. But before he could catch his breath, the branch gave way again, dropping him the last couple of feet onto the metal trash cans below. As Sandy and the six galvanized forty-gallon containers bounced across the asphalt, he knew that the incredible noise reverberating down the alley would awaken not only Paula but the entire block.

As lights went on in the apartment buildings all around him, Sandy jumped to his feet, stunned but uninjured. In what seemed like hours but was actually only a few seconds, he was around the block, back in his Volvo, and accelerating down the street. From every direction, police sirens converged on Paula's building.

Waiting until he reached the relative safety of Wilshire Boulevard before turning on his headlights, Sandy finally slowed the car and studied the streets around him. No one was on the road, not even a late night drunk. At Beverly Glen he turned left; no car followed. Was he safe? Had he made it? Only when he was back inside his own house was he sure he had escaped. What a horror, he told himself as he locked the front door.

At that moment his phone rang, reactivating all of his terror.

"Hello?" he muttered into the mouthpiece, pretending to be half-asleep.

"Sandy, this is Paula."

At first he felt great relief; then his anxiety and paranoia returned full blown. She must have seen him at her window. "Paula, what time is it?" he asked innocently. "What's wrong?"

"It's ten after five. Sandy, listen, I'm sorry to wake you but I had to talk to you. The police just left and I'm alone. There was an intruder. They don't know if it was a burglar, a rapist, a Peeping Tom, or what. Sandy, I'm scared. I feel so vulnerable. He climbed up my wall and looked into the bedroom. I could see him hanging there, staring at me. It was horrible. I was afraid to move. And I was afraid *not* to move. I didn't know if he had a gun. He might have shot me."

"That's horrible."

"Oh Sandy, I wish you had been here."

"Me too," he lied. "Did you get a look at him?"

"It was too dark."

"What about the neighbors?" Sandy tried to control his anxiety. "Could any of them identify him?"

"It happened too fast."

"Someone must have seen him."

"The police are still taking statements. But when he fell off the wisteria vine outside my window, he ran away before anyone knew what was happening. Sandy, do you realize that if the vine hadn't broken, I might have been raped and murdered? You know what I'm going to do?"

"What?"

"I'm buying a gun. Today. That's what the cop recommended. Either that or a guard dog. But you can't exactly live in my apartment and work the kind of hours I do and own a big dog. So it's a gun. Can you believe I'm saying this? Me, with a pistol? That old joke must be true. You know, What's the definition of a conservative? A liberal that's been mugged. That's me. The cop gave me a name, a friend of his who's a gun dealer. I'm buying a pistol. Will you go with me and help me learn how to shoot?"

"If that's what you want, sure. Listen, you don't sound like you want to be alone. Shall I come over?"

"Would you?" She seemed surprised.

"Give me the word and I'm out the door."

She laughed. "Did I say something funny?" Sandy was confused.

"No, but I just remembered. Something about the way the rapist tilted his head reminded me of you."

"Thanks a lot." Sandy tried to sound calm, despite the sudden shot of adrenalin blasting through his stomach.

"You're not moonlighting as a rapist, are you?"

"Paula, I have certain what I think are healthy sexual fantasies, as you know better than anyone. But rape isn't one of them. Now, how about if I drive over?"

"No, it's okay." She spoke after a long moment's consideration. "Just talking to you has made me feel better. I'm sure the rapist isn't coming back, at least tonight."

There was a shading to her voice that Sandy didn't understand. Was she just frightened, or was she hiding something? Perhaps she suspected him. Or maybe she wasn't actually alone and the reason she didn't want him to show up was that Carton was still there.

"I'm honestly happy to drive over. I mean, I'm up now anyway. At this hour I'm only fifteen minutes away. Just relax. I'll be there before you know it."

"Thanks, Sandy, but no. I'll see you tonight." Her firm voice left no room for argument.

"I want you to call me if you get scared again. Promise?"

"I promise. See you tonight." Paula hung up.

As Sandy put down the phone, he thought not only about how lucky he had just been, but how his stupid obsession had almost blown the relationship. To learn more about Carton, Sandy knew he would have to be more circumspect. This meant attending Paula's next lecture and seeing Carton interact with her. Being a spectator would be a risk, but if he kept his tattoo hidden behind the triple protection of a bandage, a buttoned shirt sleeve, and a sports coat, no one could expose him for the fake he was.

Back in bed, Sandy stretched out, closed his eyes, and tried to relax. Despite the fact that he hadn't slept in two nights, some good had been accomplished: The contest envelopes were in the mail and his Nazi investigation was finally under way. *I'm going to get you, you fucking war criminal*, Sandy repeated over and over in an unsuccessful effort to lull himself to sleep.

22

For the second morning in a row, Nat and Ed didn't show up at the plant. But instead of letting his conclusions paralyze him, Sandy concentrated on his own interests.

Openly taking the afternoon off, he drove to Marina Del Rey, where he had made an appointment with a yacht broker who took him on a whirlwind tour of all the Star boats for sale in the area. It was a nostalgic afternoon for Sandy. Inspecting the boats, he was flooded with college memories of perfect days on the water. Such past pleasures were so tempting that he momentarily considered buying the most hi-tech, tricked-out racing machine available and organizing a true National Championship campaign. But reason prevailed and he realigned his purchase with his priorities — the boat was only a decoy, giving him an excuse to get out of the office. State of the art wasn't necessary; what Sandy needed and found was a Star in reasonable condition that would look to his father like a racing boat but wouldn't cost a fortune.

By five-thirty that afternoon Sandy was the owner of an $8,000 Star, which came complete with a spare mast, two sets of sails, and a trailer. All he needed was a bumper hitch on his Volvo and theoretically he was ready to compete in regattas all over California. As a cover for his activities, the Star was flawless. His plan was moving forward faster than he'd imagined.

23

"I know what you're thinking, and you're wrong." Paula spoke angrily. "You *and* my parents," she added sarcastically. "Well, I'm not going to let that son-of-a-bitch do to me what the Nazis did to your family and mine. I absolutely will not live as a victim."

"Like me, you mean." Sandy glanced at her as he drove the Volvo northbound on the San Diego Freeway.

"I believe I made myself perfectly clear," she said, lightening the statement only slightly with her parody of Nixon.

Sandy nodded that he understood. "Listen, I know you'll probably be angry at me for disagreeing with you, but the situations really have nothing to do with one another. In the thirties and forties Jews in Europe were being persecuted for their religious beliefs. That's not what happened last night at your apartment."

"Right." Again she spoke angrily. "That's the classic, subtle distinction of a victim. Sandy, can't you see — dead is dead whether you're a Jew in Germany or a woman in Westwood. Persecution is persecution. That bastard last night saw me as a defenseless woman. Well, I'm going to show him exactly how helpless I am. Just let that dumbshit rapist try to break into my apartment again and you'll see how long he lives to victimize this particular Jew."

Sandy nodded, feigning agreement, as they passed Mulholland Drive and began descending the steep grade leading through the sprawling suburbs of the San Fernando Valley.

"You think what I'm doing is crazy, don't you?" Paula asked with hostility.

"No, it's totally understandable."

"Sandy," she said calmly, coldly, "you really don't have to lie to me, you know. I understand how you think. You want to be a victim, you want to remain a victim. Be my guest."

Sandy glanced over at Paula, unsure how to respond to her rage.

"I mean," she continued, "you went through the whole god-damn Holocaust, and what do you do about it now? Just like my parents, you hide. You know what you *should* be doing—telling the world, making them see what happened, forcing everyone to remember. That's the only way to keep it from happening again. But you won't even come to my lecture. You want to be an ostrich and I want to fight the oppressor. There's a bigger difference between us than I thought."

"I deserve all this abuse only because I didn't go to hear you talk?" Sandy was astonished. "Who's with you in the car right now? Where am I going with you? Who offered to drive over at five in the morning?"

"You learn early on as an attorney that in life if you don't fight back with everything you have, your enemy regards you as a worm."

"Paula, you're saying that to fight the Nazis I have to use Gestapo tactics myself? Or die?"

"In the real world, yes."

"Can you understand that it's just possible I'd rather be dead than live my life as a Nazi?"

"That sounds just like the kind of thing my father would say."

"For some people there are worse things than death."

"In my book, being a victim is just about the worst thing there is."

"Paula," he spoke angrily, "just because I didn't attend your god-damn lecture does not put me in the category of being a victim."

She shrugged, obviously not agreeing. Then she pointed out the window to the freeway sign announcing "Chatsworth 3."

"Paula, you're making this into a much bigger deal than it is, and you're wrong about me. You know how I'm going to prove it to you? The next time you and that guy—is it Carton?"

She nodded.

"Your next lecture; invite me and I'll go. Now does that take me out of your wormlike, subhuman, victim category?"

"Friday night," she smiled.

"What do you mean?"

"That's our next lecture. It's at Orange Coast College in Huntington Beach. Eight o'clock."

"I'll be there."

"Really?"

"You're making a big mistake, underestimating me."

After a moment's thought she conceded. "You're right, I'm sorry." She pointed to the upcoming off-ramp. "That's our turnoff."

24

"Take a deep breath. Exhale. Now hold it and squeeze the trigger slowly."

Standing at firing station number three of the Chatsworth Gun Club, Paula followed the instructions to the letter, pumping one .38 caliber slug after another into the life-sized human silhouette printed on the white paper target twenty yards down the firing range. After a sixth and final shot she flicked open the empty cylinder, set the pistol down on the station counter, removed her hearing protectors, and faced her instructor, Richard Peters.

"That was excellent, you're really getting the hang of it," Peters grinned. "Let's have a look." He pushed the retrieve switch, causing the target to zoom up to the firing station. The forty-year-old weight lifter and off-duty cop examined the holes in the paper. Three bullets had penetrated the vital chest area. Another had hit the shoulder. The fifth had gone through the abdomen just above the balls. And the last had barely missed the head.

"I'd say," Peters commented enthusiastically, "that we have one very dead rapist."

Sandy, standing behind them, smiled. It probably appeared that he was impressed by her extraordinary ability with the pistol, but that wasn't the reason for his grin. No, he was genuinely happy — grateful, in fact — that Paula hadn't owned that Smith and Wesson when he had climbed up the wisteria to her bedroom.

Peters turned to Sandy. "Think you can top that?"

"No sweat." Sandy he picked up the revolver, loaded all six chambers, shut the cylinder, flicked off the safety, assumed the spread-eagle firing position, and waited for the fresh target to stop in position at the end of the range. Sandy knew how to shoot; in the late sixties he had taken lessons so that he could blend in at various firing ranges in order to research a gun control article for *The Heart of L.A.*

With the imposing black target in place, Sandy aimed, exhaled, and fired six shots into what he imagined to be an SS war criminal.

"I'd bet money on another dead rapist," Peters joked as he brought the target up the range.

Sandy smiled again, pretending to be amused. Guns held little interest for him.

"Six out of six," Peters pointed to the target. "I'd say you're both ready for assignment to the Watts Division."

Both Paula and Sandy grinned pleasantly, pretending to be amused by the cop's racist wit.

"I understand," Paula said, "that you know how to avoid the ridiculous wait the state imposes on handgun sales. Is that true?"

Peters nodded. "The way the law works is this. I'm a gun collector, not a gun dealer. If I sell you something from my collection it's considered a private transaction and not subject to the gun control laws. Of course, you still have to register the weapon with the state, but there's no waiting period before you take possession."

"Both of us," Paula indicated Sandy, "are interested in .38s like this." She gestured to the Smith and Wesson on the counter. "Is it possible you could sell us two new ones from your personal collection?"

"Stranger things have been known to happen," he agreed.

"How much?" Paula opened her purse.

"Four hundred each. Nonnegotiable."

"There's no break for two?"

Peters shook his head.

"Who should I make the check out to?" she asked, pen poised, ready to write.

"My business name is spelled CASH. Two, right?"

Sandy and Paula nodded.

"I'll be right back." Peters turned and disappeared out the door.

"Good DBA for a cop." Sandy rolled his eyes in sarcasm.

Paula shrugged as she wrote out the check. "You know, you don't have to buy this. I mean, don't do it to please me, because I don't care."

"No, I think it's smart. What happened to you last night could happen to me. And if it does, I want to be able to protect myself." Sandy removed a check from his wallet and filled it out.

Gunfire on the range ate up the few moments of silence until Peters returned carrying two identical cardboard boxes. "Here you are, you lucky devils," he told them enthusiastically. "I just happened to have exactly what you wanted in my car; what a coincidence. And I'll tell you what; I'll throw in fifty rounds of ammo, gratis. What do you think of that?"

"You're a rare bird, Peters. Thank you." Paula poured on the charm.

Peters read the two checks, which he then folded and inserted into his wallet before handing over the two pistols and the fifty rounds of .38 caliber ammunition.

Later that night, lying in bed beside a sleeping Paula, Sandy thought, Never has four hundred dollars bought so much. The simple act of writing that check had purchased not just the Smith and Wesson but a future with the woman he so badly needed. Paula's contempt for him had dissolved in the face of the obvious: Individuals committed to being victims didn't own handguns.

The drive home from Chatsworth had been an entirely different experience from the ugly journey out to the firing range; affection was back, as well as romance, sensuality, and joy. The rage was still there, of course, but no longer was it directed at Sandy. The rapist was the problem and now, thanks to the revolver which she had loaded and placed in the drawer of her bedside table, even that nightmare had been taken care of. One could almost say that life was back to normal.

Too wound up to sleep, Sandy reflected on the miraculous transformation his life had undergone thanks to that aberration on his arm: *A7549653*. What had first appeared to be an abomination had in fact given him the promise of a wonderful future. Yes, he told himself, he was living a lie. Yes, he had two separate, conflicting identities, one with Paula and one with his family. But in his present euphoric state, Sandy saw the situation as easily manageable, hardly warranting serious concern. So far, he hadn't experienced the slightest difficulty maintaining the two unconnected lives; in fact, everything had been evolving with a mysterious and pleasurable perfection. Look at life as an adventure, he challenged himself; take pleasure where you find it and stop trying to control the uncontrollable. Dare the impossible and let yourself enjoy what comes.

25

By Friday afternoon, reality had reasserted itself. The drive down
to Orange Coast College was bumper-to-bumper misery. But
that was the least of the problems worrying Sandy. What if Paula
really was having an affair with Carton? What if one of the Jews
in the audience spotted his tattoo? Even worse, what would
happen if someone recognized him and exposed his true identity? The three-hour drive of gradually escalating paranoia ended
in his arrival at the college only twenty-five minutes before
Paula's lecture was scheduled to begin—a full hour later than
he'd promised to meet her.

After parking in the public lot, Sandy sprinted across the
campus, still hoping to rendezvous with Paula and Larry Carton
in the cafeteria as they had arranged.

Orange Coast College was a two-year junior college located
on the edge of Huntington Beach in Orange County, the most
politically conservative area (except for Pasadena) in the entire
state. This was right-wing paradise, home of the John Birch
Society, the Fluor Corporation, and the kingpin and hero of the
zealots, Mister John Wayne himself. The values taught at the
two-year junior college conformed closely to those of the surrounding voters. Vietnam was a noble cause, lost only through
liberal cowardice and Communist influences in government.
Gun control was a Russian plot to disarm America, easing the
way for an invasion. Richard Nixon, even in deep trouble, represented everything wonderful about presidential leadership. And
Watergate was a Democratic conspiracy designed to bring down
the government and set the stage for an eventual pinko takeover.

Finally arriving at the stucco and glass, shopping-center-style
student union, Sandy found Paula sitting at a white plastic table,
sipping coffee with a man who appeared to be about thirty years
old. Before stepping into the cafeteria and revealing himself,

Sandy studied the two of them; but he found it impossible to draw any conclusion about the true nature of their relationship.

Hurrying across the crowded cafeteria, Sandy approached Paula from behind. "Sorry I'm late. The traffic was just unbeliev- able." He put his hand on her shoulder and watched his rival's reaction as he leaned over and kissed Paula on the lips. Carton showed no emotion, but Paula responded to the passionate kiss by pulling away in apparent surprise.

"Sandy, Jesus, you scared me." Her ambivalence further con- fused the situation. "Yes, we got caught by rush hour too. In fact, we didn't get here until a few minutes ago ourselves. Great way to start a lecture, huh? I'm already exhausted. That's why we're chugging coffee; want some?"

Sandy shook his head, then extended his hand across the table. "I'm Sandy Klein."

"Oh, I'm sorry. Larry, this is Sandy. Larry Carton."

The two men shook hands over the carousel slide trays stacked in the middle of the table. Carton's limp grip added to Sandy's instant hatred of the lawyer. It certainly didn't take a genius to see that Carton was a pretentious, soulless, ivy-league impersonator. Sandy guessed correctly (he was later able to confirm this) that his rival tried to give the impression that he was a Harvard man, but was really a graduate of the adult-education program of the take-anyone-who-can-pay West Valley Law School in North- ridge. The Harris tweeds, khaki trousers, button-down collar, bow tie, and tortoise shell glasses might have fooled some people, but not Sandy. What he saw sitting across from Paula was a man of limited experience and shallow sensibilities — the sort of quasi-adult/adolescent still trying to be taken seriously by the standards of 1950s high-school politics.

"Nice to meet you," Carton spoke flatly. "I've heard a lot about you from Paula."

"As have I," Sandy answered as he continued to appraise the lawyer.

Paula broke the ensuing silence. "Well, shall we get going?"

"Why not?" Sandy answered.

"Okay, you carry these." She handed Sandy the boxes of slides, then picked up her heavy briefcase and led both men out of the cafeteria, down the corridor to the adjacent building.

"Sandy, just so you'll be prepared," she said quietly, "it's possible we could have a little trouble tonight. The local Hillel that's sponsoring this lecture series received a couple of threatening calls. Whether they're cranks or what, no one knows. But this is Orange County, the bigot capitol of California, so I wouldn't be surprised at anything that happens."

"Supposedly," Carton added, "this community is so anti-Semitic they have ordinances forbidding delicatessens. Possession of chicken soup is a misdemeanor; chicken soup with a matzo ball is a serious felony."

Paula smiled, obviously amused. Her reaction angered Sandy; only lovers laughed at such stupidity. However, before he could say anything, Paula swung open the door labeled 106 and entered the lecture room.

It was a rectangular space that seated a hundred people on ten rows of orange plastic chairs. Facing the empty seats was a four-foot-high oak lectern positioned directly in front of a large green chalkboard hanging on the wall. Suspended from the low ceiling, ready for use, was a screen in alignment with the Kodak slide projector padlocked to a formica stand in the back of the classroom.

As Sandy took a seat in the rear corner closest to the door, Paula and Carton quickly set up for the lecture, which was scheduled to start in fifteen minutes.

"Can you hit the lights?" Carton asked Sandy, who walked to the nearby switch and plunged the room into darkness.

At the lectern, Paula clicked the remote control switch and the first slide dropped into place. As Carton's clumsy lens manipulations slowly brought the image into focus, Sandy found himself emotionally gripped by a photo he had come across many times in his readings. On the screen was a black and white scene from the Warsaw Ghetto. It was winter. Outdoors, on a crowded, snow-covered street, a German soldier was using a wooden club larger and heavier than anything allowed in professional baseball to beat to death a ten-year-old Jewish child. Blood was every-where, pooling in the street, splattering the trousers and jack-boots of the Nazi killer. Cowering passively, terrified and grief stricken, were emaciated Jewish men and women wearing clothes so threadbare that no one in the U.S. would have used them even as rags. Were the onlookers members of the child's family? Why were the Germans killing this child? It was obvious that, surrounded by German soldiers holding machine guns, none of the adults could do anything to stop the horror. As many times as Sandy had seen this picture, he never ceased to become enraged.

Always the same questions rolled through his mind. How could the world have allowed such cruelty? Why didn't the Allies try to slow down the mass murder by bombing the cre-matoriums at Auschwitz as they were asked to do so many times during the war? And why were only a small number of war criminals actually punished?

Suddenly the lights in the classroom came on, obliterating the image on the screen. Paula, at the door, had flipped the switch before opening the lecture hall to the surprisingly large crowd that had gathered outside. Pouring in, the horde of strangers quickly filled not just the seats but every nook and cranny of standing room. Sandy could see that Paula and Carton were as unprepared as he was for such the avalanche of people.

At first glance the audience appeared to be mainly college students. A few wore *yarmulkes*. Figuring that for every *yarmulke* there were perhaps five times that number who weren't religious but were still Jews, Sandy came to the conclusion that the majority of the people were what his father would have called *goyim*. This puzzled Sandy. Since when were Orange County Christians fascinated by the Holocaust? Examining the noisy crowd more closely, he observed that most of the non-Jews were men, many of whom looked to be considerably older than the typical undergraduate. More worrisome was their behavior. They acted like arrogant kids in a gang, grinning at one another, making loud noises and laughing too hard at private jokes. The conclusion was obvious: These *goyim* were organized and attending the lecture for a hostile purpose. They were trouble, present not to listen but to intimidate.

Sandy's paranoia went to work and in no time he began to feel personally threatened, almost as if he were a Jew wearing a yellow armband in Nazi Germany. As the bulk of the crowd took on the character and aura of the SS, Sandy began to perspire heavily. The more closely he observed the faces in the mob, the more clearly he could feel their hatred. These men had come to the lecture with only one intention and that was to finish the job started by the Fuehrer. *Kill the Jews.* Would he live through the evening? He kicked himself for not having brought his Smith and Wesson. How could he have been so stupid — a Jew venturing into Orange County, unarmed, to attend a lecture on the Holocaust? Could the situation end in anything but violence? On the lectern, Sandy noticed Paula's briefcase. Had she been smart enough to bring her gun?

The audience quieted quickly when the local Hillel representative, a bearded student with a *yarmulke*, introduced Paula and Carton as experts on the Holocaust era, "excellent scholars whose knowledge of the period should be one of the highlights of our twenty-week lecture series on the history of the Jewish people." At the conclusion of his brief talk only a few people applauded. The rest of the audience sat in stony silence and waited.

Paula stepped behind the lectern, introduced herself, and launched into her well-practiced talk. She began with such uncharacteristic restraint that she appeared nervous. But to Sandy's relief, her experience before hostile juries prevailed and as the lecture gathered momentum, old habits fell into place, her enunciation improved, her volume and projection increased, and the facts began to emerge with authority.

After concluding a brief summary of the political, economic, and cultural history of Europe after World War I, Paula shut off the lights and used slides to illustrate the rise of Nazism and its impact on Jewish community life in Germany, Poland, Slovakia, Rumania, France, Holland, Belgium, Italy, Greece, and Yugoslavia. To Sandy, the presentation was a decent, unprovocative, well-organized encapsulation of the period.

At the beginning, the audience was quiet and attentive; but when the first picture of the gas chambers at Auschwitz flashed on the screen, the atmosphere began to crackle with tension.

"I can't believe you're showing us these lies," a voice spoke from the darkness of the audience.

Ignoring the comment, Paula pressed on with her factual description of the German production line that ultimately incinerated up to fourteen thousand Jews a day.

"Who are you trying to kid, lady?" the same male voice called out from the darkness. "No one believes the fantasies you're telling and you know it."

"If you don't mind," Paula said calmly, "I'd appreciate it if you'd save your comments for the question and answer period at the end of the lecture. Now at Auschwitz," she returned to her prepared talk, "the Nazis also had a hospital. This they used for two purposes: They killed sick people by injection, and they also performed, under Dr. Josef Mengele, what they called 'medical experiments.' Virtually all identical twin children that entered the concentration camp were sent to the hospital for use as guinea pigs, to be injected with chemicals just the way we inject laboratory rats. After the war, on review by legitimate doctors, every single one of the Nazis' experiments was discredited as scientifically useless and morally criminal—just another form of torture."

"Lady," the same voice interrupted, "instead of this old Zionist propaganda, why don't you show us some proof? You can't and you know it because your proof doesn't exist."

At this comment, at least half the audience broke into applause, almost drowning out Paula's attempts to refute the attack.

"Mister," Paula spoke with anger, "there's evidence everywhere. More than one hundred thousand people were rescued from the concentration camps by the American and Russian armies. Look at the archives. Read the accounts of the first soldiers into Auschwitz. There's endless, overwhelming documentation that proves without the slightest doubt that more than six million Jews were killed by the Nazis. There's simply no question about that fact. Now the next slide is . . . "

"That's a nicely stated lie, but it's a lie nevertheless," the heckler again interrupted. "You're quoting directly from Zionist propaganda. It looks great on paper, but just show me one person who can prove it."

On cue, the applause, whistles, and jeering erupted, obliterating Paula's efforts to continue her speech. In desperation she signaled to Carton to turn on the lights. Able to see and identify the hecklers, Paula stood in front of the hundred and fifty people and waited. She was like a school teacher using eye contact to quiet an unruly room. Slowly her tactic succeeded, and she resumed.

"If you don't believe me, read the testimony of the Nuremberg Trials or the transcripts of Eichmann's trial. The facts are all there, in black and white. They're simply indisputable."

A man seated in the middle of the audience suddenly stood up. "May I ask you something?" He was manicured, well-tailored, about forty, with a scholarly beard. His voice identified him as the heckler.

"There will be a question and answer period when I finish. Now I'd like to continue please, without interruption." Paula glanced at Carton, who stood by the light switch.

"My question is," the man continued to stand, "why is it people like you come to university campuses and try to sell us these tired Zionist lies? Truth is supposed to be a part of the Jewish tradition, but you expect us to believe this nonsense when you can't prove that the Germans killed even one Jew in those camps. Now I'm not saying that no Jews died in the work camps — that would be absurd. It was war and in war, when thousands of families are moved from one place to another, people do die. Some, like in every population, have heart attacks or cancer. Some are just old. But these gas chamber stories and those crematoriums: They were just invented by Jewish propagandists. Sure the camps had showers. So does every local high school. As for the crematoriums, they were for those who died, just like the crematoriums at Forest Lawn.

"Of course, next you'll show us photographs of all those supposedly emaciated bodies. You and I both know those were staged by the Jews and the British just to make the world accept the concept of Zionism so that Palestine could be stolen from the Arabs, who'd lived there for thousands of years, and given to a few rich Jews. My question to you is, why persist in insulting our intelligence with these transparent Zionist lies?"

For the third time the audience burst into applause, cheering the heckler's remarks. The man tugged at the razor-sharp creases of his trousers, raising them precisely one inch, then resumed his seat.

Paula remained frozen in her authoritative teacher pose, attempting to wait out the ruckus. But as the situation grew more uncontrollable, she began to appear desperate. What should she do? Her eyes pleaded with Sandy in a momentary exchange across the room. All he could manage was a sympathetic shrug. Finally, as the audience grew bored with their victory, the clapping and whistling diminished.

"If you won't believe pictures," Paula spoke, "or the court testimony of eyewitnesses, then what *would* convince you?"

The leader of the hecklers smiled. "Show me one honest man who saw it, one man the Germans tortured only because he was of the Jewish faith, and I'll believe you. But you can't—because your stories are no more real than Hollywood science fiction movies."

Again, the bulk of the audience pounded the room with applause.

To Sandy, Paula's next glance wasn't just an appeal for support, but a panicked plea for something more.

"What if . . . " Paula spoke over the diminishing hubbub, "what if I could produce such a person for you? In fact, what if that person were in this audience right now? If he spoke to you about his own experiences at Auschwitz, would you believe him?" Paula's eyes locked with Sandy's—*help me, rescue me*, her expression pleaded.

Overwhelmed by his terror and enraged at her betrayal, Sandy turned away. It wasn't enough that she wanted him to reveal himself to *her*; now she demanded that he expose himself to an entire audience of Jew haters! If he actually did such a thing and they found out he was a phony, they'd kill him on the spot. Hadn't he made it clear that he was attending the lecture only to listen? Hadn't he come to Orange Coast College under explicit ground rules, the first of which was *no speaking?* To humiliate him for the sake of the already disastrous lecture was unforgivable and outrageous. To publicly embarrass him into a suicidal exhibition was complete betrayal.

"I'd be delighted to believe a person like that, if you could show him to me," the anti-Semite was saying. "But you know you can't because he doesn't exist." Paula, in a last-ditch appeal, stared at Sandy with such intensity that many members of the audience swiveled in their seats, scanning the room to ferret out the object of her attention.

Terrified, on the verge of exposure, Sandy took the only action he could to save himself. Without a word he slid out of his seat, turned his back on Paula, and slunk out of the lecture room.

26

Outside in the corridor, as he headed for the exit, Sandy's relief at escaping immediately changed into despair. In the process of saving himself he had abandoned Paula, an action he knew she would never forgive. Already he could hear her accusations, attacking him as a spineless victim, just like the Jews in Germany, totally ineffective at standing up to fascism, even in its most petty form. No matter what course he chose, he was damned. The overwhelming, inescapable truth was that by running out he had lost her forever.

Sandy suddenly felt unable to breathe. Faint, he had to stop walking and prop himself against the wall while frantically hyperventilating. What he was experiencing, he realized, was an anxiety attack. It was exactly the sensation he'd fought once before, moments after he'd been informed that his daughter had been killed. What terrible symmetry, he told himself: first Rachael's death and now the end of his relationship with Paula. If only he'd had the balls to stand up in front of a room full of right-wing, anti-Semitic psychopaths and lie about his past, Sandy berated himself. What difference would it have made? Could he have been any worse off than he was at this moment? What could have been so terrible about telling that group of neo-Nazis a fictitious but convincing story about his past? The god-damn concentration camps were real, and he certainly knew enough to be convincing. So what if he distorted his personal history; didn't the fanatics in the audience do far worse with the actual facts?

Sandy ran the situation over and over in his mind as he stood, hunched over in the hallway, forcing himself to take slow breaths and exhale fully. In life, everyone lied, he reminded himself. Everyone tells stories about themselves that are shadows of reality. What was disgusting about his action was his incredible cowardice; he could have easily lied to the Nazis. Instead, he had lost everything. How could he have been such a miserable, worthless worm?

"Sandy, wait, please. I need to talk to you."

Down the hall, from the direction of the classroom, Paula was running toward him. "Sandy, please," she pleaded, "forgive me. I had no right to ask you to talk. I was desperate. You saw what happened — the bastards got to me and I wanted to show them; you were the only thing I had. I'm sorry. Forgive me, please, Sandy; I don't want to lose you over this."

With his hands in his pants pockets and his shoulders hunched up tight against his skull, Sandy appeared to be the model of such withdrawn, chilling rage that Paula was actually afraid of standing too close and provoking him.

"You invited me to your lecture. I told you I only wanted to listen. You knew exactly why. And I was stupid enough to think I could trust you. You did a job on me, Paula."

"You're right, I made a mistake. What I did was stupid. Is there any way you can forgive me?"

"What did you even think would happen? I mean, do you really believe that showing those fascists my number would have made one iota of difference? Those people have already made up their minds."

"I'm not convinced of that. The leader, maybe. But there are a lot of others here too. Something as real as your tattoo would be very hard to dismiss."

"Please," Sandy said. "They'd have called me a liar and rationalized the whole story as fiction. You heard that bastard on the subject of the crematoriums. Just like Forest Lawn, remember?"

She shook her head, disagreeing. "That's abstract, from books. You're real. Only a truly disturbed person — a lunatic — would tattoo a fake Auschwitz ID number on his arm. I'm telling you, if you showed your number to them they'd have to believe you."

"I'm sorry, but if they can't accept the Nuremberg Trials, my evidence would be a joke." A lunatic, he thought. How the hell was he now ever going to tell her the truth?

"You're wrong and you don't realize it." Paula spoke gravely, changing the tone of her apology. Then she smiled, softening what she feared was another provocation. "And I'll tell you how I'll prove it to you. Let's go back into the lecture. You show them your tattoo, tell them how you got it, and I'll bet you *anything* they believe you."

"Paula," he spoke angrily, "am I wrong, or do I remember you coming after me to apologize?"

"Just so I understand," she asked quietly, "what exactly do you have to lose by trying?"

"You don't quit, do you? Can't you understand that if I don't even want to talk to you about what I went through, why would I stand up and expose myself to a bunch of neo-Nazis?"

"Because I love you and I'm asking you to. Whether I know the details or not, I have a real sense of what you survived. Your story, to me, is not really going to make a big difference one way or the other." She gestured to room 106. "But those animals, they need real, live humans to stand up to them and say 'you might have got away with killing Jews once but it's never going to happen again. I'm not going to run; I'm going to fight. You try to hurt one of us and you and your families are going to die.' That's how you deal with bullies. Sandy, you can make a difference here; that's what I'm trying to get you to see."

"You really do believe," he shook his head in amazement, "that showing my number to those scumbags is the first step in preventing another Holocaust?"

"Absolutely."

"I wish I could. But you know I can't."

"You mean you *won't*."

Sandy shrugged. "It's a pity you can't grasp the fact that my feelings are just as real to me as yours are to you."

"I'm sorry, but that's a cop-out." Paula spoke with sudden anger. "When it comes to the crunch, you're just like my father; once a victim, always a victim. You know what I think about all of you supposed survivors? You're not survivors; you're already dead. If the Nazis took over again you'd go right along with them, all the way to Auschwitz, without even raising your voice to protest. And I thought you were different!" Spinning on her heel, Paula charged back toward the lecture room.

If his running out on her talk hadn't finished things off, this last argument certainly had done the trick. Each step she traveled toward that room full of neo-Nazis put him that much closer to the end of their relationship. *Run away,* a part of himself commanded; *get out while you can.* But another, deeper, more desperate aspect of Sandy's psyche took over.

"Paula!" he yelled down the hall, "Wait a minute!"

27

A7549653. Sandy held up his left forearm so that the number was visible to everyone in the lecture hall. Without a sound, like an attentive church congregation, the audience strained forward to get a better look. What they saw on his arm was strange and shocking. They were like swimmers frolicking in the Pacific surf, suddenly confronted with the open jaws of a twenty-foot great white shark. No one knew what to do, how to think about it, whether to run, to attack, or to curl up in a ball and disappear.

"This was done to me on September tenth, 1943, at four in the morning on the day I arrived at Auschwitz," Sandy lied in a soft, humble, convincing voice.

"A tattoo doesn't prove anything," the leader of the neo-Nazi challenged, "except that the Germans tattooed you for identification, like a hospital wristband. How else could they keep track of thousands of workers?" The logic of his statement prompted a mumbled chorus of agreement.

Having gone this far in his impersonation, Sandy glanced at Paula, who smiled at him with the kind of adoration that encouraged risk-taking. "Let me tell you what it was like to arrive at Auschwitz," he continued. "The cattle cars came in at night, in the darkness. In my case we had been traveling for five days without food or water. There were no toilets. It was so crowded you had to sleep standing up. Six people died; one was a woman in labor who bled to death. When the transport stopped and they finally opened the door, it was a scene from hell; we had no idea where we were. They pulled us from the trains and shouted orders; searchlights blinded us. Guards with clubs and whips herded us to the selection lines. In front of our eyes, men, women, and children were beaten to the ground if they didn't obey immediately. One man who tried to run was brought down by a dog. Husbands were separated from wives, parents from children. In one instant, families were split up and destroyed forever."

"We've heard all that before," the neo-Nazi interrupted. "When I was in the U.S. Army boot camp, that's basically the way they treated us. You were in a war, remember? Did you expect the Germans to put you up in five-star hotels when they couldn't feed and clothe their own troops at the front lines?"

"That's right. That's a good point," the crowd grumbled.

"What happened then," Sandy continued as if there had been no interruption, "was an SS officer, an elegant man wearing a beautifully pressed uniform, complete with immaculate white gloves, stood in the front of the selection lines, examining every Jew. I was twelve years old and big for my age. On the transport, thanks to my parents who had brought cheese and bread, my sister and I had both managed to eat and keep up our strength. My parents had taken nothing for five days and were weak. The selection officer, Dr. Josef Mengele, must have seen that I was fit for work because he indicated I should pass through the gate on the right. My father, mother, and sister were sent to the left. At the time, I didn't know what that meant. Separated from my family for the first time in my life, as they took us to the barracks I started to cry. But a man walking next to me tapped me on the shoulder and whispered, 'If you ever expect to get out of here, never let anyone see you cry.' And he was right. Because if the Nazis sensed that kind of weakness, they would have sent me to the left immediately. I never saw my mother, father, or sister alive again. Everyone sent left went directly to the underground gas chambers where they were murdered within one hour of arriving at Auschwitz." Sandy glared directly at the neo-Nazi leader as if to say, *Deny what I've seen with my own eyes.*

"That's a pack of lies," the man rose to the challenge. "Your parents and sister were deloused in the showers, then put to work. If they died in one of the typhus epidemics — remember, this was before penicillin — they were some of the unfortunate ones. The Germans needed labor; the last thing they wanted was for their workers to die." The man smiled, defying Sandy to dispute his version of the facts.

"The truth is that I know without a doubt that my parents and sister were dead within an hour of arrival at the camp," Sandy went on. "And it wasn't from typhus but from Cyklon B gas. In your so-called delousing showers. To save the cost of having to feed them a meal, the SS killed them immediately. How do I know this fact about my parents and sister? Because the next day I saw, with my own eyes, their bodies, stiff as boards. How many of you have seen your father, mother, and sister lying outside in the dirt like firewood?"

No one in the room moved.

"On the night we arrived, there had been a fire that damaged the crematorium. The next day — my first day — I was assigned to a work detail of prisoners ordered to dig the hard ground and bury those who had been gassed the night before. An hour after I started shoveling, I saw my mother, naked, stacked under two other corpses. On her face, I can't describe it: her eyes wide open with the most terrible expression of fear I've ever seen. I threw up. Even now, every night, I see that face in my dreams. But there was nothing I could do. If a *kapo* or one of the SS had even seen me get sick they would have shot me on the spot. I pretended to shovel while two other prisoners tossed my mother's naked body into that mass grave. To the Germans she was just another piece of Jewish garbage. My own mother. And you," Sandy addressed the neo-Nazi leader, "tell me such a thing never happened. You should be ashamed."

Again, no one in the room made a sound.

"Later that day I saw my father in another pile of corpses. Under him was my sister — five years old. Her name was Rachael." Sandy stopped himself; mixing the real with the imaginary brought forth memories of pain and rage that required a moment to control. "Little children were of no use to the Germans so they killed all of them. After we stacked their bodies in the huge pit, the *kapos* soaked the corpses in gasoline, then set them on fire. So mister," Sandy again addressed the leader, "don't you tell me they didn't murder Jews in the concentration camps. I saw thousands die every day. They were human beings just like myself who the Nazis shot, gassed, clubbed, electrocuted, hung, burned — you name it; they did it and I witnessed it. We all did. They wanted us to; the Germans were proud of their savagery. I'm here to tell you, I saw it all with my own eyes." Slowly, dramatically, Sandy rolled down his left shirt sleeve, once again covering his tattoo. As he buttoned the cuff, the only sound in the lecture room was the uncomfortable squirming of the audience looking to their leader for direction.

Paula, radiant with admiration, caught Sandy's eye. He had pulled it off.

"If you're so German," the neo-Nazi leader spoke with hostility, "why is it your English has no accent? Maybe what we're hearing here is one more good propaganda story. Isn't that the truth?"

Sandy froze, rigid with anger, staring the man straight in the face with the most severe expression possible. "I speak without an accent because I hate the Germans and I hate their language. For three hundred years my family lived in Germany — more years I'm sure than your ancestors have lived in America. I was as German as any German. A German first, I thought, and a Jew second. Then those Germans, my countrymen, killed every member of my family. After Liberation, when I got to the United States, I swore not only to never speak one word of German again but also to learn to speak American English without a trace of an accent. I was young, and had a fanatic's determination to obliterate my past. And you're witness to the fact that I accomplished what I promised myself. This is America; if you put your mind to it you can overcome anything, even ignorance and prejudice, as you now know first-hand."

This time the neo-Nazi said nothing. Nor did anyone else. Sandy slipped on his sports coat and returned to his seat in the back of the room.

Taking advantage of the momentum, Paula immediately returned to the lectern, gestured for Carton to kill the lights, and plunged back into her lecture/slide show. This time, to Sandy's delight, there was not a word of interference from the audience. He had been convincing. Certainly what he had said had felt convincing. In fact, it was more than a little shocking to realize how easy and natural his improvisation had been. Standing in front of that audience and inventing his past had been an instinctive process, not an intellectual one. His mind seemed to shift into automatic as it tapped into the thousands of concentration camp experiences he'd read about over the years, and the story spilled out with the seamless continuity of truth. Finally, he told himself, his obsession with the camps had paid off.

As he sat in the darkened room pretending to watch the slides, Sandy was euphoric. The creation of his family history at Auschwitz had been the most exciting moment of public *chuztpah* he could ever remember. What an incontestable success! It was as if historical Auschwitz had merged with his own overwhelming grief into a creation of fiction more real than everyday life. *A7549653* was a clear, understandable man — the ultimate victim with a definite place in history, larger than life, beyond the ambiguities and petty pain of everyday existence.

Sandy was enveloped by an all-encompassing sense of well-being. As survivor *A7549653* he was more real to himself than was Sandy Klein, vitamin executive, son of Nat Klein, brother of Charlie and Ed Klein. *A7549653* was a red-blooded, Jewish-American hero who only moments before had defeated a room full of Orange County anti-Semites. *A7549653* had struck back on behalf of six million victims. This *A7549653* was a new breed of righteous Jew; a one-man verbal Israeli Defense Force. It was a repeat of David and Goliath, with one Jew demolishing not only a roomful of neo-Nazis but also his rival, Larry Carton. Sandy actually felt happy; for the first time in recent memory he had achieved an outstanding victory with no visible downside.

28

The hour and a half trip home from Orange Coast College was like no automobile journey Sandy could remember. He understood how Caesar must have felt, returning to Rome in triumph; or Churchill in Parliament, announcing the surrender of Germany to England. With Carton left behind to drive back by himself, Paula rode in the Volvo. She couldn't seem to get close enough to Sandy or stop touching him. His fictitious speech had apparently aroused her to new heights of erotic desire. He was Paula's warrior-hero, conqueror of the world, worthy of the most lavish tribute.

As soon as the deadbolt of Paula's front door sealed them from the outside world, she dispensed with all foreplay and immediately yanked off her clothes. Dipping her finger into her pussy, she rubbed Sandy's lips, coating them with her sweet vaginal fluids. Without a word she led him across the living room, where she turned her back, grasped the edge of the couch, spread her legs and, wearing only her high heels, thrust her tight, naked butt up against his rock-hard erection.

"Take off your clothes, Sandy. I want you now."

29

For Sandy the month of July flowed by on an endless wave of excitement. After his success at Orange Coast College, it was inevitable that he would speak out again in public. Sandy had no doubt that it was risky, even physically dangerous, but after years of emotional starvation, turning away from the exhilarating embrace of acclaim was simply impossible. What an astoundingly satisfying adventure to stand alone in front of an attentive audience and bare his soul! Who wouldn't enjoy the immediate rewards, the adoration and applause? Almost overnight, it seemed to Sandy, he had become a star of the first magnitude on the Jewish lecture circuit, a kind of Sandy Koufax/Sholom Aleichem of the death camps.

His new avocation as a public speaker began only twelve hours after the confrontation at Orange Coast College, when Paula received a call at work requesting "that concentration camp survivor" for her talk two days later at UC Santa Barbara. Apparently word spread fast about any speaker whose presence promised to excite the sort of deep emotional response so dear to the hearts of professional fund raisers.

Sandy accepted the invitation to speak with only one condition: complete anonymity. He wanted no one ever to identify him as Sandy Klein. At first Paula resisted. But on this issue, Sandy wouldn't budge; it was a take-it-or-leave-it proposition.

So at UC Santa Barbara, when Paula introduced her speaker as "Uri," the man who walked out onto the small stage was an unrecognizable Sandy, transformed by his disguise. In addition to the full dark beard and mustache he had purchased from Western Costume on Melrose Avenue, he also wore a pair of glasses with quarter-inch-thick lenses set in heavy, black-rimmed frames. At a thrift shop, Sandy had found a shapeless, over-sized black suit, old-fashioned white shirt, and dark blue tie. A subtle application of charcoal makeup under his eyes added to his look of torment. Normally Sandy appeared a good ten years older than his thirty-two years. Now he resembled a fifty-year-old rabbi — a man with a complex past, half in and half out of his Eastern European *shtetel* birthplace. From twenty feet, he was sure that he was not recognizable to anyone outside his own family. *A7549653* had found form in the impressively authentic creation applauded as *Uri*.

The speech at Santa Barbara was an even bigger success than his improvisation in front of the Orange County neo-Nazis. Something about the disguise freed Sandy from the last of his inhibitions and allowed him not just to recite the concentration camp experiences, but actually to feel and project them most convincingly. Uri wasn't simply a character actor in a one man show; he was truly *A7549653*, the articulate victim and survivor. What had been a twenty-minute talk at Orange Coast College became at Santa Barbara a fast-moving sixty minutes of captivating confessions.

The audience adored Uri and hung on every word he uttered. Throughout the talk no one left the room, squirmed in their seat, or whispered to their neighbor. They were responding to a cry from the depths of their cultural and religious past, a connection to the soul of Judaism itself, as related through the personal account of a twelve-year-old boy and his struggle to survive a year and a half of Nazi sadism at Auschwitz. The bond between speaker and audience was magical. Uri joined them all in an ageless union, the chronicler of history, creating in his listeners an instant, authentic community.

For an hour, the hundred and fifty people in that audience relived the darkest moment in their thousands of years of collective persecution. Uri's torments were the stuff of every Jew's nightmares. *He* had suffered for *them*. His story was heartbreaking, that of a true saint or Messiah.

Most of the young Jewish undergraduates in the audience led lives that were materially fat and spiritually vacant, while Uri seemed just the opposite: a living channel into the dark side of their Hebrew identity. Unlike the history books, Uri wasn't abstract. His enemies were their enemies; his survival was their victory. There was no question that night that Uri was a remarkable man, an authentic hero, a living cultural icon. Their five-minute standing ovation at the conclusion of his speech reflected that assessment.

For Sandy, the applause was a miracle, a startling contrast to his own family's view of him as a parasitic bullshit-leftist *schlepper*. At Santa Barbara (and everywhere else he spoke that July) Sandy was idolized and celebrated. *If only they could see me now,* he thought, knowing that this could never come to pass without disaster and death for Uri, *A7549653,* and just possibly Sandy himself.

The next four weeks were like something in a dream. Accepting speaking engagements — sometimes five nights running — Sandy, in his disguise as Uri, traveled to high schools, colleges, and synagogues from San Luis Obispo to Mission Bay. With each speech, his audiences grew larger and his reputation swelled. As always with speakers at fund raisers, the test of Uri's success lay in the bottom line, and those numbers were incontestable. When Uri spoke, the money flowed, in some cases quadrupling all previous records. Something about the moving and horrifying account of his experiences reached deep into the wallets of his listeners and commanded them to give generously. By the end of the month, Hillels, congregations, and Jewish organizations throughout the state were bombarding Paula with requests for Uri. Had Sandy been able to clone himself, he could have spoken simultaneously three or four times a night and still not have kept up with the demand.

Sandy's family problems, his boredom with the vitamin business, his rage over the financial shellacking he was about to receive, all vanished in the excitement. His speaking engagements overshadowed all problems, generating a wild ride through stardom, with one success following another.

If that phenomenon weren't amazing enough, the power of his public acclaim funneled down into his relationship with Paula, heightening their passion. Something about his moving accounts acted as an aphrodisiac on the women in his audiences, forcing Paula into the role of intermediary, turning down, on

Sandy's behalf, blatant sexual invitations from what could only be called concentration camp groupies. Whether the other women's erotic desires excited her competitiveness, or only made Sandy's appeal more apparent, the effect was to intensify Paula's need for him. In addition to their regular late-night marathon humping, a new variation entered into their lovemaking.

After his first successful lecture as Uri, Paula had relayed to Sandy four explicit sexual propositions from audience members. Aroused, Paula and Sandy had fucked right there in the UC Santa Barbara parking lot on the front seat of his Volvo. This experience was so thrilling that it became part of their nightly lecture ritual.

The run of astounding experiences continued unabated until Saturday, July 28, when Sandy was forced into his first direct confrontation with the monster he had created. The occasion was the long-planned surprise seventieth birthday party for Nat. Sandy, both older brothers, and their wives and children all gathered at Chasen's before six forty-five to wait in the clublike atmosphere of the oak-paneled private dining room.

Chasen's was Nat's favorite restaurant, not because of the food but because of the extraordinary service. What the restaurant sold wasn't fine cuisine but status. For Nat and Sylvia, to be seated automatically in the exclusive front room was society-page heaven. Even better was that the old man could order from Martin, the haughty maître d', by simply asking for "my usual." Just two little words and the kitchen automatically disgorged steak diane, french fries, baby carrots, a side order of Chasen's famous chili, and cheese toast. This level of recognition was, for Nat, the pinnacle of success.

At exactly seven o'clock the door of the private room swung open.

"What do you want to sit here for; what's wrong with our regular booth out front?" Nat growled at Sylvia as he backed in through the open door.

"Surprise! Surprise!" screamed Nat's sons, their wives, and their children. As the old man swung around, Ed's flash camera snapped photos while the entire family warbled the traditional off-key *Happy Birthday*.

Dinner went somewhat differently from what Sandy had expected. The form, of course, was like every family gathering he could remember. At one end of the table sat the men, talking business. The other seats were occupied by the women and children, whose opinions on the essence of life — money — were generally ignored. As always, Sandy was in the middle, the family hermaphrodite, half on the men's side, half on the women's, trusted and respected by neither group. He was an observer, licensed only to listen.

Tonight what he heard was a subtle but undeniable alteration in the Klein family's internal rhythms. Instead of a spontaneous conversation, he realized that he was listening to a partially rehearsed performance, done solely for his benefit. The family was going through the motions of normalcy to keep him from knowing about the sale of the business.

After the main course had been cleared, out came Chasen's famous banana creme birthday cake, accompanied by another round of *Happy Birthday*. As the old man sliced the first piece of cake, Charlie and Ed slipped out of the room for a few moments and returned carrying a package four feet wide, six feet high, and three inches thick, wrapped in heavy brown butcher paper, tied with a yellow ribbon. Nat tore off the wrapping to find himself staring at four Andy Warhol paintings hung together, two above and two below, backed by a thin piece of masonite. Warhol's subject was Nat Klein, whose photographic image stared back from each of the four silk-screen portraits. The only difference from painting to painting was the colors: One was day-glo green, the next orange, the third yellow, and the last frosted blue. To Sandy's mind the series should have been called "Portrait of a Psychedelic Businessman" — a strange image for a German immigrant, now lodged so successfully in the heart of the vitamin establishment. But Nat was thrilled: To be painted by a famous artist was, in his mind, to be made immortal. Now he saw himself not just as a successful Jew but as a man whose image would hang on the wall of a museum for eternity, the contemporary version of a burgher by Rembrandt. Formally the old man walked around the table and thanked each signatory of the card, including his youngest son. This last fact was a particular surprise to Sandy, who had never made a contribution to what he still considered to be a rip-off of a gift. Apparently his brothers had signed for him.

The real crunch came after coffee. The problem began when Sylvia questioned Sandy about his recently announced plans for a black-tie charity dinner, the purpose of which was to honor Nat and simultaneously to raise a significant portion of the additional two and a half million dollars required by the Florence Klein Cancer Research Center. The specific amount of money needed, Sandy explained, was not an arbitrary figure, but had been arrived at after extensive talks with medical researchers, architects, hospital experts, and, of course, Mister Fundraiser himself, Stanley Furgstein. Sylvia's concern was not the cancer center, but the arrangement of the September eighth gala dinner. With the family's reputation at stake, she wanted to make sure that the evening would be up to the proper standards. What she wanted to hear from Sandy were not generalities but specific details. After an eternity of discussion, the last questions were resolved and Sandy was beginning to think he was home free when Charlie entered the conversation and dropped the bombshell.

"Ever hear of this guy?" Charlie reached into the inner pocket of his cream-colored Italian silk and linen jacket and flashed Sandy the front page of the latest *B'nai Brith Messenger*. "We've got to get this man to speak at Dad's dinner."

Staring at the picture on the front page, Sandy's body went rigid and his mind numb. The article was about the German-Israeli-American known only as "Uri."

"It says here," Charlie told the group around the table, "that this Uri's lectures have not only been attracting huge audiences but that his, and I quote, 'stirring and uplifting descriptions of his experiences in Germany and Poland under the Nazis have not only moved audiences to tears but have resulted in a fourfold increase in donations wherever he has spoken.'"

"Interesting," Sandy mumbled. "Can I see that?"

Charlie passed him the article. "Except for the beard and glasses, he looks a little like you."

The grainy photo, Sandy realized, had been taken when he had spoken at Cal Poly in San Luis Obispo. As the adrenalin raced through his system, Sandy's mind began to boil over with questions. Who had taken the picture? And how had the son-of-a-bitch done it? One of the requirements he'd insisted on at every speaking engagement was *no photographs*. Without exception. Yet some asshole had snapped one anyway. Fortunately, the light in the room had been dim enough to render the picture unrecognizable.

"The reason I bring this up, Sandy," Charlie continued, "is that I think you should go listen to this Uri. He sounds like our kind of guy, doesn't he, Dad? I mean, any speaker who can quadruple donations is the sort of man the cancer center could use for its keynote speech."

"It's remarkable," Nat agreed.

"I'll put him on my list," Sandy nodded.

"Do more than that," the old man insisted. "Go hear him talk. That's the only way."

"Dad, I do have a question." Sandy pointed to the article. "Do you really think a man whose subject is concentration camps and the Nazi exterminations is the appropriate person to speak at a black-tie dinner on behalf of mother's cancer research center? Gas chambers and the ovens have to do with killing people, not saving lives, if you see what I mean."

"The object, Sandy," Ed intoned, "is money. Let's not be naive. If this Uri talks about death camps or men from Mars it doesn't matter, as long as it makes people dig deeper into their pockets. That's what they're there for, isn't it? Or do you think it's for the food?"

Sandy glared at his brother. The worst thing he could do now would be to refuse the idea of Uri. That tactic would guarantee Ed's unrelenting demands to hire Uri as a speaker. "Okay, your point is a good one," Sandy agreed. "I'll go hear the guy."

Everyone seemed satisfied, and the conversation shifted to other aspects of the charity dinner. This allowed one part of

Sandy's mind to slip into automatic, searching for a way to avoid having Uri speak at the fund raiser.

By the time dinner ended, it was after eleven. Still shocked by the horror presented to him at Chasen's, Sandy drove to Paula's with only one thing on his mind: escape. He craved holding, touching, kissing, caressing, and fucking Paula, ached to bury himself deep within her and obliterate all the evening's pain. Paula was his key to a sense of hope. On the short drive between Chasen's and Westwood, Sandy knew he needed her as he had never needed anyone before.

But from the moment she opened the door, Sandy sensed that something was dreadfully wrong.

"So how was your dinner?" she asked as they sat in the dining room sipping Earl Grey tea from china cups. On the table were stacks of legal briefs concerning the case Paula was preparing for trial.

"All I got out of the evening was indigestion. You don't happen to have any Tums, do you?"

She shook her head. Something was definitely awry; despite the sheer, seductive silk robe she wore, Paula was highly focused and gravely serious — all business.

"Where'd you eat?" she asked.

"Chasen's," he answered with disgust. "Did you get anything done on your case?"

Paula nodded but said nothing, obviously considering her next move. Was it her work? He knew she was under severe stress, putting in an absurd number of hours on a major case against the City of Los Angeles.

"Who exactly did you have dinner with?" she asked lightly.

"A couple of business guys, why?"

"What sort of business guys?"

"Boring," he evaded her question. "You going to be ready in time for the trial?" Sandy gestured to the stacks of paper.

"You don't want to tell me who you had dinner with?"

"Paula, my time with you is too precious to trash it talking about dull business types and a wasted evening. The deal I was hoping to do with them isn't going to work, and it pisses me off. I'd rather forget about it and not give myself an ulcer."

"What was the deal about?"

"Money."

"For what?"

"For nothing, as it turns out. Can we change the subject, please? Just thinking about it makes me sick."

She stared at him as if trying to reach a decision. "Sandy," she asked spoke softly, "do you love me?"

"You know I do."

"Then why won't you tell me what business you're in? Don't you think after knowing me for six weeks that I might be interested?"

"Sure. But this isn't the right time; I'm too angry at those assholes."

"Will you tell me tomorrow?"

"Okay."

Paula smiled sweetly. "That's a lie and you know it; you've been avoiding my questions for weeks."

"What are you talking about?"

"How many times have I asked you about your house? Do you realize that I've never seen where you live? I have no idea what sort of work you do. I've never met any of your friends. I don't have the faintest idea where you go when you leave here in the morning. All I have is the phone number of a private line only you answer. Sandy, can't you understand that I know virtually nothing about you? You could be married with ten kids and I wouldn't be the wiser."

"Paula, that's just not true."

"You're telling me," she burst out angrily, "that I know what I don't know?"

Sandy stood up, slipped around the dining table, put his arms around her from behind, and nibbled her ear while caressing her taut nipples through the film of silk. "Paula," he whispered affectionately, "this is Sandy you're talking to. I swear to you that you know me like no other woman has ever known me. Can't you see that?"

"It's not enough." She slithered out of his embrace and stood up to face him. "I need to know who the hell you are."

"Paula, what's happened to you tonight? Yesterday everything was great. Last night was one of our best times together. Don't you remember last night?" He spoke seductively.

"All the more reason for me to know."

Sandy stared at her, his instincts urging him to probe further. "What happened today?" he asked.

"Nothing."

"Something happened, I know it. Tell me."

Her subtle hesitation convinced him that he had hit on the truth.

"Don't change the subject," she persisted.

Sandy returned to his side of the table, sat down, took another sip of tea, and thought it over. "Is it another man? Are you seeing someone else? You're bored with me, aren't you; that's what you're trying to say. Be honest; I can take it." The expression of pain and grief on his face contradicted the hardness of his words.

"Sandy, give me a break!" she screamed. "I'm not seeing anyone else and you god-damn well know it. What I'm asking you now is important. Who the hell are you, really? What is your life when you're not with me? Why are you so ridiculously secretive about everything? Sandy, I don't even know what, in God's name, you want from me."

"For starters, I want the truth. What happened today that's got you so upset?"

After a long moment of apparently painful reflection, staring at the floor, she blurted out her secret. "I talked to my parents tonight. I told them about you. About us. They could hear how happy I was. And then they started asking me questions, basic things, like what kind of work you do." She looked up at Sandy. "I didn't have the answers. You know how I handled it?"

Sandy said nothing.

"I lied. I invented things. To my own parents. Do you understand how humiliating that is? Talking to them made me realize how little I know you. Yes, I love you. Yes, we're incredible in bed together; I've never felt anything like it. And, yes, I've heard your

history as Uri. But that was thirty years ago. Something's very
wrong when the 1940s are more real than the 1970s."

Sandy let her continue.

"So I'm going to ask you one more time. Who are you? What
was your business tonight? It's not a difficult question, Sandy. If
you love me, you'll answer it. Otherwise, I don't know . . ." she
broke off sadly.

"Do I hear you threatening me?" He bristled with anger.

She shook her head. "I don't care what you do for a living. I
just need to know; it's that simple."

"That's *all* that's bothering you?" he tried to minimize her
concern.

"If you think this whole thing is so trivial, what's stopping you
from telling me?"

"That's really all it'll take for you to be happy?"

"Absolutely."

"And we can get back to enjoying one another?"

"Yes."

"I have one question, first. Why did you involve your parents
in this? You've told me over and over how they've never approved
of any man you ever knew, and how they undermine all your
relationships. It looks to me like you're letting them do it to you
again. Think about it. We were doing just fine until you mentioned me to them."

"I'm waiting, Sandy."

"Okay, I'm in the import-export business. Happy now?" He
smiled, hoping to end the subject.

"What sort of import-export business?"

"All kinds of things. But mainly pharmaceuticals."

"Who buys these *pharmaceuticals*," she asked with disbelief.

"Every country needs pharmaceuticals," he stated.

"I don't believe you."

"You don't think every country needs pharmaceuticals?" he
asked, incredulous.

"Of course. But that's not what you do."

"Well, that's news to me. That's what I thought I did. I mean,
that's what I do at the office every day."

"What's the name of your company?"

"What's the point of telling you? No matter what I say you're not going to believe me."

"If you started with the truth, it might save us a lot of time."

She wasn't budging an inch. How could he satisfy her? Sandy wracked his brain. "Look, there are some things people aren't able to discuss, you know what I mean?"

"No, in fact, I don't."

"Paula, I was going to have to tell you about this sooner or later but I didn't want to burden you with something you couldn't handle."

"I'm a big girl, Sandy. Or haven't you figured that out yet?"

"If I told everyone I met what I did, I'd be in serious trouble. And so would they, by the way."

"You do something illegal?"

Sandy shook his head.

"Then why would they be in trouble?"

"Because it's *classified information*, okay? Now you know. *Only* you. Now will you give it a rest, please, before you get both of us in deep shit?"

"You think I'm going to let you off the hook that easily?" Her curiosity had been aroused.

Sandy shrugged. "You don't have much choice. There's nothing else I'm allowed to tell you."

"I'm sorry, mister, but you're going to have to. Or tell me why you can't."

"I'm not being cavalier, Paula. If anything went wrong with what I'm involved in and certain people found out you knew something you shouldn't, life could get very dangerous for both of us. Your little Smith and Wesson wouldn't do much good against these people. Honestly, coming from someone who truly loves you, you'd be one hell of a lot better off not knowing about me, okay?"

"*Not* okay," she shot back. "I can't go on loving and fucking a mystery. I don't care how satisfying it is at the moment. I want to know what it is you do."

Sandy stood up and began to pace. "Okay," he finally turned to her, "but remember that I did warn you. And you have to promise you'll never, ever, repeat what I tell you." He spoke with a chilling gravity.

"Of course," she answered immediately.

"Okay, this is all I can say. I work for some people. They're not American. But here in Los Angeles I'm their, uh, representative. The dinner I had tonight was with my boss, who flew in to hear how a project of ours was progressing."

"Which is . . . ?"

"Believe it or not, the project has to do with World War II and the Displaced Persons Act. We have research proving that in the five years after the war ended, the United States opened its borders not only to legitimate refugees but to German war criminals — perhaps ten thousand of them. We're not talking here about rocket scientists like Wernher Von Braun, but Gestapo officers, death camp personnel, and SS collaborators. No one seemed to care then, and no one cares now. As a group they've stayed out of the public eye. But they're war criminals nonetheless, going free and unpunished. The goal of our project is to expose these sons-of-bitches. My job is to focus on Southern California. That's what the dinner meeting was about."

"Who exactly do you work for?" she asked.

"I can't tell you."

"I take it this is not the U.S. government?"

Sandy's smile was opaque. "My official work is the import-export of pharmaceuticals. That's as much as I can tell you."

"You must work for Israel, then?"

Sandy shrugged, refusing to confirm or deny her guess. "This also has something to do with why I didn't want to speak out in public about the concentration camps. You know what my boss showed me tonight?"

Paula didn't answer.

"This." Sandy handed over the *B'nai Brith Messenger* with the picture of Uri on the front page. "He and I had a big argument. He was very angry and accused me of jeopardizing the project. If someone identifies me it could ruin years of work. He wants me to quit speaking in public."

Paula set down the article. "Do you agree with him?"

"No. But he makes a very persuasive argument. I mean, he did recognize me, disguise and all."

"Doesn't he appreciate how much good you're doing as Uri?"

"I tried to convince him. The problem is, there are a lot of people involved in our work. A lot of time has been put in. Money has been spent. I don't want to be the one who screws it all up."

"How exactly do you fit into this whole thing?"

The question couldn't have made Sandy happier. Her uncensored curiosity meant that she believed the story. Another big hurdle had been cleared. To complete the alibi, Sandy described the supposed mechanics of the project by detailing his own progress with the "German-American Travel Agency" and the bogus contest plans.

Paula was clearly impressed by the cleverness of the scheme. "Of the five thousand forms you sent out, how many have been mailed back?"

"Four hundred. But the deadline is still five days away. We expect a last-minute flood."

"How many more?"

"Maybe three or four hundred. That's as much as a sixteen percent return. Which, for a direct mail advertisement, is a terrific response."

"How many of the questionnaires fit your potential war criminal profile?"

"So far we have sixteen." This fact was indeed true.

Paula smiled. "It's a brilliant plan. I'm impressed."

"Thank you." He shrugged modestly.

"This really was all your idea?"

Sandy nodded.

"I can't tell you how knocked out I am. Honestly. You're suddenly a whole, complex person. And it explains everything." She stretched her arm across the table and squeezed his hand. "I know it was difficult for you to trust me, but it does make things all a whole lot easier. Thank you."

Without responding, Sandy allowed his palm to be caressed.

"Don't you think so?" She was alarmed by his lack of reaction. "I mean, don't you feel better sharing yourself with me, knowing that I understand and accept you?"

"Look Paula, by the standards of my work I just fucked up by telling you all this. Instead of protecting you, I've made you vulnerable. These guys we're after aren't going to be happy about their sudden public exposure, and they're liable to go to considerable lengths to protect themselves. They're Gestapo killers. And now I've exposed you to them. I love you, and that frightens me. Paula, now you're involved."

She spoke quietly in that voice that was so connected with her urgent erotic appetites. "I was already involved, wasn't I?"

Her manner aroused in him all kinds of lascivious reactions, but at that moment Sandy hated himself for the mountain of lies he had just put forth so skillfully. If he truly, selflessly loved her, he would risk losing her by admitting the truth. But, being as needy as he was, he couldn't afford to take the chance. What he *had* done, he rationalized, was give her not just more lies, but also a few pieces of his real—albeit disguised—story. This last fact could actually be a good thing, he argued with his conscience, because it dovetailed into what was now the most obvious way of obtaining forgiveness and understanding for the stories he'd invented about the tattoo. If he could make his war criminal investigation a success, write a great article, and actually convince the *New York Times* to publish the piece, such a stupendous accomplishment would overwhelm and defuse her anger at the deception. Who could hold a grudge against a publicly acclaimed hero?

"Those sixteen contest forms you received that match the war criminal profile," she asked, "what are you going to do with them now?"

"I've got Immigration, the FBI, and the Justice Department working on them."

"They're cooperating with you?" She sounded surprised.

"Under the Freedom of Information Act." Sandy clearly enjoyed her reaction to his cleverness.

"When should you hear back?"

"By law, something could be in the mail next week." Sandy assumed that, as a lawyer, Paula knew that the Freedom of Information Act required the government to respond in no more than twenty days to a proper request.

"If you find something promising, what will you do?"

"I'll investigate it."

"How?"

"That's something I'd rather not discuss." He used his gravest tone of voice to hide the fact that he wasn't sure himself how he'd handle such a breakthrough; it depended on the person and the information available in the file.

"Sandy," she spoke with an almost girlish excitement, "you know I'm very good at investigations; it's what I do every day. If there's anything I can do for you, *use me*. I mean it."

"Thank you, I just might." What would she think, Sandy wondered, if she knew he was already using her for a purpose far different from the one for which she had just volunteered? He needed her, all right, but not for anything so trivial as a criminal investigation. Her importance, her service, went to the core of his existence, preserving life itself; without Paula, there was nothing in his future but grief, despair, and probably suicide.

30

By the third week of August the euphoria of the preceding
month had become ancient history, as relevant to Sandy's state of
mind as his long-ago success with *The Heart of L.A.* Like Richard
Nixon, Sandy was under siege. But Sandy's nightmare had far
worse personal consequences. At the worst, Nixon faced
impeachment. *Big fucking deal,* thought Sandy. After thirty years at
the top, the president had the goods on friends and rivals alike.
No senator or congressman would consider allowing a font of
compromising information like Richard Nixon to get near a jail,
where he might tell everything he knew in exchange for a lenient
sentence. In contrast, Sandy felt himself unprotected, out of
control, heading for the ground in an uncontrolled spin. Of the
Freedom of Information Act requests he had sent out, ninety
percent had been returned and not one contained a shred of
evidence. There were no omissions, not one inconsistency, not
even a blacked out section that would warrant further investigation. His inspired plan was apparently ending up a humiliating
failure, like everything else in his life.

"We've got a fucking nightmare of an anti-Semitic government
of assholes; look at this bullshit." At home, sitting at his dining
table, Sandy held up an FOIA form for Billy to examine. "On
Shleigheim we get what the FBI says is a *No File.* Now look at
this Stoltz." Sandy passed Billy the top sheet from one of the
stacks of official documents piled all over the table. "Immigration and Naturalization gives us a couple of completely untraceable affidavits proving this slimebag spent the entire war farming
in Bavaria."

Billy took another sip of his vodka and continued to examine
the evidence.

"Heinrich Becker. Guess what? Another *No File.* Then we
have Wilhelm Maltousen, whose immigration file is clean as a
fucking whistle. Just like all of these German dickheads." He

shook a pile of documents in Billy's face. "We've got here," Sandy ranted, "FBI, Justice, and Immigration. And look what they've come up with. Our tax dollars at work, the incompetent sons-of-bitches. 'Nothing on Record,' 'Nothing on File,' 'Nothing on Record,' 'No Record,' 'No File,' 'No Such Individual on Record.' Nothing, nothing, nothing! What are they hiding, these bastards? Why won't they give me what I need? My god-damn life is at stake here. What the fuck am I going to do?"

"You might consider telling her the truth." Billy spoke quietly but deliberately.

"Yeah, and then I'll go slit my wrists. C'mon, I need to find a way to make this work. Help me."

"Sandy, you can't hide forever; eventually she's going to find out."

"That's why I have to root out a Nazi. Once I expose the son-of-a-bitch, my little deception will be irrelevant. That's when I'll tell her."

Billy nodded skeptically. "I think that's a wonderful dream, Sandy. But my advice to you is to give up this whole crazy scheme, scale your life down, and live for the here and now. Do what is possible. You're thirty-two years old, you've got maybe fifty years left. And then after that there's nothing; it's eternity talking. History just doesn't care. Be practical and enjoy life while you can. This woman, Paula, I guess is really terrific. But Jesus Christ, I mean, if she can't accept you as Sandy Klein, you gotta forget her. You can't spend your life jumping off cliffs just to keep her interested. Look at you; I've never seen you this nuts. Is this the way you want to live your life?"

"I've got to figure out a way to find this Nazi." Sandy gestured at the FOIA papers.

"Will you at least do one thing for me? And don't get angry."

Without agreeing, Sandy nodded.

"Quit this business of speaking in public. It's one thing for this woman to think you went through the concentration camps. But bullshitting the world! Sandy, I read about Uri in the *L.A. Times*. I know *you* know how deadly serious people take the concentration camps. And they should. If those people find out you're a fake and that you've tricked them, they're not going to be amused. You're treading in deep water here and I think you should back out fast before they make you into one very unhappy martyr."

"It's worse than that," Sandy said morosely.

"Worse than what?" Billy was confused.

"My family's involved now."

"With Uri?"

Sandy nodded, then proceeded to explain the latest wrinkle in his darkening story.

"So did you ever go hear Uri talk like you promised?" the old man had asked at the one appointment Nat and Ed had kept with Sandy during the first three weeks of August. If that break in their routine weren't strange enough — for five years the three of them had met together almost every day — their excuse for their absence was even less credible. Vita-Line, Nat and Ed explained, was being sued by a wealthy old Pasadena health nut who claimed that a bad batch of Vitamin C had poisoned her, causing a paralyzing stroke. Did they actually expect him to believe that such BS was the real reason for all those lawyers trooping in and out of Nat's office the few hours a day he actually showed up at the plant?

"Of course I went to hear him," Sandy had answered. "But I'm waiting for a final response from a much better speaker: General Yitzak Alon." In an attempt to avoid the whole problem with Uri, Sandy had, through Stanley Furgstein, contacted the ex-Defense Minister of Israel and asked him to speak at the dinner. The general, who was an old friend of Nat's and who was known to love all-expenses-paid, first-class trips to the United States, had expressed his wish to accept the invitation, but couldn't make a commitment until the political situation in the Mideast became less dangerous. With Egypt openly preparing for war, Israel had first claim on his time.

"Given what Sadat's been saying, I wouldn't hold my breath on that one," Nat dismissed the idea. "Tell me how this Uri sounded."

Sandy shrugged. "After the big build-up you gave me I wish I could say I was impressed. Yes, the guy lived through Auschwitz;

but so what? A hundred thousand other people did too. Uri's real impressed with himself. Talk about an arrogant guy: This is one *nothing* who thinks he's some big shot. I drove up to Bakersfield to see him. The audience hated him so much a third of them walked out before the speech was even over. I don't know how the guy got his reputation, but believe me, this is not the kind of speaker you want at your dinner."

"Sandy," Ed challenged, "the issue for Dad's dinner is not how much *you* liked Uri as a person — no one cares about that — but how much money the man can raise."

Nodding in agreement, Nat looked to Sandy for an answer.

Controlling his rage, Sandy only smiled. What was important here, he told himself, was not the momentary satisfaction of a clever, cutting response, but a longer term victory. "You're absolutely right, and I checked on that. The Bakersfield Hillel collected only half of their normal take. The only thing Uri seems to do well is hiring the right publicist — someone who can turn his failures into media-hyped success stories." Sandy reached into his inner coat pocket, withdrew a small address book, and copied out a name and number onto a piece of note paper. "Here's the number of the Bakersfield Hillel." He tore the sheet from the pad and handed it to Nat. "If you don't believe me, call them and see how enthusiastic they are."

Such bravado actually involved no risk for Sandy, who as Uri had deliberately enraged his Bakersfield audience with an offensive, inflammatory speech. Instead of being his usual gentle but heroic victim self, he had lashed out at the local Jewish community, accusing them of gross complacency in the face of danger. "While other Jews are still fighting for freedom," he had told them, "the U.S. Jews wallow in neurotic luxury, worrying only about driving the right cars, buying the correct and fashionable clothes, and anguishing over their careers. Meanwhile, throughout the Mideast, Jews are dying because Arabs want to drive us into the sea. What Israel needs is not lip service or charity but people to live there and make the place a home for Jews the world over." Sandy's final statement compared the American Jews to their counterparts in the 1930s who had turned their backs on their relatives in Germany, Poland, Hungary, and the rest of Europe. "Accomplices to murder" was his final characterization of their behavior.

This speech easily achieved its objective — the audience had hated him, and only a few local Jewish masochists had come forward with minimal donations. When Nat called to verify Sandy's allegations, Sid Halprin, president of the Bakersfield Hillel, confirmed the disaster.

"That's exactly what I told you," Sandy said self-righteously. "Now maybe we can talk seriously about some alternative speakers in case Yitzak Alon falls through."

"Yes and no," Nat said. "Halprin dug just a little bit deeper than you did. According to Uri's lawyer and booking agent, Uri was sick that night, with a high fever. Which was why he was so off his normal form. Halprin advised me to give the man another chance. And you know why?"

Stunned, Sandy shook his head.

"Because Halprin had seen Uri speak in Santa Barbara. 'The single most moving hour of my life,' was how he described the Santa Barbara speech. He said that Uri wasn't simply a good speaker but a great one. The reason I'm bringing all this up is that Charlie just called. He's heard the same thing from all sorts of different people. He's personally intrigued and wants to see Uri himself. I told him the two of you should go together."

"Dad," Sandy finally spoke with a forced calm, "the Hillel guy has his facts ass-backwards. After the speech I spent fifteen minutes talking to Uri. If that son-of-a-bitch was sick, I'm Catholic."

Nat shrugged, unimpressed. "I wasn't there, so who am I to judge. Do me this favor. Give Uri a second chance. You and Charlie, go together and hear the man. Two hours one evening isn't going to kill you."

"Dad, I don't understand why you're so fixated on this jerk. Forget him; you don't want the embarrassment. Who's to say he won't do to you what he did in Bakersfield?"

"Look, if you don't want to hear the man, Charlie's going to go without you. Am I wrong, or do I remember you telling me you wanted to be in charge of this dinner?"

Trapped, Sandy could only nod his agreement. Back behind the locked door of his own office his mind had begun to race out of control, and had remained in that panicked state up through the moment that Billy walked in and their conversation began. From the walls, the floor, the air, all Sandy heard was *Uri, Uri, Uri.* The three-letter chant bellowed from Paula, from the *B'nai Brith Messenger,* from the *L.A. Times,* and now from his father and brothers. Why had Uri become so successful so fast? Now that everyone had heard of the son-of-a-bitch, Sandy couldn't just have him vanish by announcing that he was moving to Israel. That would cause a further investigation. No, the man would have to die. What was needed was a suicide or a car accident. Something definitive.

Sandy's mind whirled. How could Uri die? And even if such a thing could be accomplished, he would need a death certificate and a funeral. Too many people would have to be involved. The truth would come out and his family as well as the community would go apeshit. If it weren't for Paula, Uri could just disappear. But Paula would never let him out of it. Without an explanation of his refusal to appear as Uri, her contempt for him would end their relationship. Yet he knew that if he did tell her the whole truth she would also abandon him.

Something had to be done. At the present rate, Sandy lamented, Uri was becoming so popular that it wouldn't be long until he was offered two weeks headlining in Las Vegas. Sandy could hear the advertisement: "Come to the Tropicana and be entertained by the sentimental charms of Uri, Star of the Death Camps." He seemed to have only two choices. Either stop Charlie from going to Uri's talk, or quit speaking in public — period. The dilemma was, both alternatives were impossible. Was there a third possibility, as yet unclear? This was what he had hoped to get from Billy.

"Introduce me to Paula," his friend said simply.

"No way."

"Sandy, it's very hard to me to advise you how to handle this situation when I don't have a good sense of the person involved."

"I can't."

"Why not?"

"Billy, c'mon on, think." Sandy was on the edge of hysteria. "This is a very smart woman we're talking about here. Ten seconds after meeting you she'd sense something was wrong. And then where would I be?"

"Where are you now?"

Sandy glared at his friend. "I'm so glad I turned to you for help."

"Look, if there's something you want me to tell you, let me know what it is because my ideas obviously don't interest you."

"You think this is funny, don't you?"

"Listen, I don't think this is funny at all. I think it's crazy. Suicidal. I want you to stop it today. Can I make it any clearer?"

Sandy considered this plea, then rejected it. "You could tell me not to panic, that I've still got ten or fifteen FOIA requests the government hasn't responded to. And it would make sense that someone with something compromising in their past would require more time for the FBI, CIA, or Department of Justice to analyze and present, wouldn't you think?"

"If I told you that, would you believe me?"

"It's not unrealistic."

"Suddenly you're concerned with reality?" Billy sounded genuinely surprised.

"Look, I'm trying. That's why I need your help."

"You have to tell her."

"The day I find a Nazi."

"Why do I feel we're not getting anywhere?"

"Big problems rarely have simple solutions."

Unable to formulate anything innovative, Billy just nodded his head.

Later that night, alone in bed, Sandy was unable to sleep. Counting sheep accomplished nothing. A hot bath had been useless. Even trying to lose himself in sexual fantasies of Paula had resulted in nothing, not even an erection. Life was closing in on him. What few options he had left were fast disappearing.

Somehow he had to get out of this mess in a legitimate way. *But how?* he asked his sleep-deprived, malfunctioning brain. *Tell me how!*

31

The next morning, August 20, a ray of hope arrived at Sandy's post office box in the form of an oversized envelope from the Department of Justice in Washington, D.C. Fearing yet another disappointment, he yanked out two folded sheets of paper.

The first page was the routine cover letter, a form indicating that the request concerning Heinz Hoffmann of Oxnard, California had been processed, investigated, and returned within the legal time limit. But the second page was a different story.

Sandy could hardly believe what he held in his hand. The second sheet was a xerox of his original FOIA request with one alteration: Stamped across the black type was a bright red imprint that read, "Exemption from FOIA, Personal and Medical and Similar Files, the disclosure of which would constitute a clearly unwarranted invasion of privacy." For an investigative reporter, this stamp was pure gold! The red letters telegraphed the possibility that the Justice Department was protecting Mister Hoffmann. This was exactly the kind of bureaucratic evasiveness Sandy had been looking for. His plan had borne fruit. Finally, his man appeared to be not just a theoretical possibility but a living human being.

The emotional rush was overwhelming, more powerful than drugs or even sex; Sandy took several deep breaths to dampen his excitement. His first impulse was to jump in his car and highball it the thirty miles to Oxnard. But to do what? To move rashly might tip off his quarry, who would simply disappear. Any Nazi confident enough to fly openly to Germany for the annual SS reunion was certain to be involved with ODESSA, the worldwide fraternity of SS veterans so effective at protecting its own. One hint of a problem, and Hoffmann would be on his way to Argentina, Paraguay, or Brazil. He'd be one more German with perfectly forged identity papers ready for employment with one of the South American dictatorships, training death squads in the SS techniques.

At work Sandy locked himself in his cubicle and concentrated on his next move. His first order of business was to confirm Hoffmann's address. Oxnard information came through with two listings for Heinz Hoffmann. The first was the address on Sea View Drive that the German had given to Lufthansa Airlines. The second was a business address: Captain Heinz Hoffmann of Channel Islands Harbor. Could they be the same person? Sandy dialed the harbor number. On the second ring it was answered by a woman who spoke in a receptionist's tones.

"Neptune of Oxnard, good morning."

"Uh, yes," Sandy managed, his mouth dry, "is, ah, Captain Hoffmann in?"

"I'm sorry, he's out with the Neptune on a half-day trip. Can I help you?"

A half day trip! The man ran a sport fishing boat. "Will he be in tomorrow?"

"No, sir, the captain is working every day now. I can leave him a message if you'd like."

"Can you tell me what time Captain Hoffmann leaves the dock?"

"That depends on the day, sir. Were you interested in a half-day, full-day, or one of our three-day Albacore Weekenders?"

"I'm not sure," Sandy lied. "I had good luck the last time with the captain. Which trip does he skipper now?"

"All three. Half-days are Monday, Wednesday, and Friday, leaving the dock at six A.M. sharp and returning to the dock at one. Tuesday and Thursday he runs the all-days; same six A.M. departure, with a return at eight P.M. And the Albacore Weekender leaves Friday at nine P.M. and is back in on Sunday around midnight. If you have a credit card, I can take your reservation now."

"What does each trip cost?" Sandy inquired.

"Half-days are twelve. All-days run twenty-two. The Albacore Weekender is eighty-eight fifty, bait included but no food or beverages."

"I'd like to think about it and call you back. How late are you open?"

"Five in the morning until eight-thirty at night. Fridays, until the boat leaves."

"Thank you."

"Sir, the Albacore Weekenders have been selling out on Wednesday, so I'd recommend you call me back just as soon as you make your decision."

"I will. Thank you for your help."

The woman hung up.

Ecstatic, Sandy dialed Paula at her office. To his surprise, he was put through instantly.

"How're you at deep sea fishing?" he asked.

Since she'd never been, she had no idea.

Could she take Wednesday off for a matter of life and death importance?

Paula agreed readily; how could she refuse such a request?

On Tuesday morning, the two letters in Sandy's post office box contained even more promising information about Heinz Hoffmann. One from the Immigration Department held a copy of the German's application for admission to the United States under the Displaced Persons Act. Dated 1952, the contents of the form revealed nothing incriminating. Obviously the man wouldn't have put in writing that he'd once been an SS killer; but this information, combined with the second letter, made the situation ever more interesting.

Response number two was from the FBI. Very much like Monday's form from the Department of Justice, the FBI had returned a xerox of Sandy's request modified only by a rubber stamp that read, "Exemption from the FOIA, specifically authorized under criteria established by an Executive Order to be kept secret in the interest of national defense or foreign policy (because unauthorized disclosure reasonably could be expected to cause at least identifiable damage to the national security)." Together, the returns from the FBI, Immigration, and Department of Justice spelled out a pattern that Sandy interpreted as *Bingo, Bingo, Bingo!*

32

On Wednesday morning at five-thirty, Sandy stood with Paula on a floating concrete pier in the Channel Islands Harbor. The two of them, along with forty-five other fishermen, were waiting to board the ninety-foot fishing boat *Neptune of Oxnard*. Although the sun wasn't yet above the horizon, there was enough light to see the breakwater and harbor entrance. Departure time was near, and the tanned young deckhand unclipped the line blocking the boarding ramp and began collecting tickets from the eager fishermen.

For Sandy, this was a terrifying moment. On one level, he was stepping into a well-maintained party boat — that was easy enough. But his mind and heart reverberated with the paranoia of a Jew who was risking his life, paying to trap himself on a floating boxcar captained by a Nazi war criminal. Endless scenarios of disaster and death reverberated through his imagination; for this very reason, Sandy had hidden his Smith and Wesson .38 in the bottom of his tackle box — not that it would do him much good against a boatload of storm troopers. But it was a psychological assist, a sort of blued-steel insurance policy. Despite his fears, he forced himself to appear calm, both for his own sake and to reassure Paula, who was even more anxious.

"There's nothing to worry about," Sandy whispered in her ear. "He has absolutely no idea who we are. He's the one with the problem, not us."

She smiled and moved forward as Sandy passed their tickets to the seaman. Carrying fishing poles and tackle boxes, they moved with the small crowd onto the aft deck of the *Neptune*.

Following the example of the first fishermen to board, Sandy led Paula to a seat sheltered by the flying bridge. As they sat clutching their fishing gear, Sandy studied the other people around them. Most were men, and most were outfitted in clothes and tackle very similar to his own. Sandy's $436 had been well spent on fishing gear and clothing, allowing the two of them to blend right in. But appearances were one thing, and reality was quite different. Sandy hadn't gone fishing since he was ten or twelve years old; the closest Paula had been to the sport had been the one time she'd been forced to eat sushi in a Japanese restaurant on Sawtelle Boulevard.

Adding to Sandy's anxiety was the marine weather forecast: eight to ten foot seas. These rolling swells, the height of a one-story building, could make fishing an uncomfortable and possibly nauseating nightmare.

A whirring electrical noise deep in the bilge interrupted Sandy's thoughts. Seconds later, the boat's enormous Caterpillar diesel engines roared to life, enveloping the aft deck in a cloud of white smoke. As the huge iron straight-sixes settled down to idle, their low rumble mixed with the gurgled pumping of heat-exchanged salt water, ocean air, traces of fish, seagulls, diesel fuel, and other marine odors to remind Sandy of his few childhood memories of deep-sea fishing from the Redondo barge with his mother.

With a sudden surge, the *Neptune's* transmission locked into gear and the big displacement hull moved slowly away from the dock. At six in the morning they were on their way, passengers of a Nazi, paying to be on his fishing boat heading to god-knows-where. In an effort to reassure both of them, Sandy squeezed Paula's hand. Now that they were under power, it was time to quit ruminating and get to work.

"I'm going to walk around and check things out; you want to come?" Sandy asked Paula.

"No, no. I'll just sit here and stay warm, thank you."

"Well, I'm going to go forward for a few minutes. If you change your mind, head for the bow. And keep an eye on my pole, okay?"

Short on enthusiasm, Paula nodded.

Sandy strolled around the perimeter of the pilothouse, past the fisherman who were chatting, smoking, and drinking coffee. No Heinz Hoffmann. Moving forward onto the bow, Sandy saw no one. The view, however, was so spectacular that for a moment he forgot his reason for the trip.

As the Neptune cleared the Channel Islands breakwater, the big diesels accelerated the boat to fifteen knots, leaving Oxnard in its wake. The city itself, which was normally a dull conglomeration of dilapidated stucco structures, took on an almost ethereal beauty as the enormous August sun rose over the skyline. Such intense light transformed the forbidding, dead gray sea into a rich, friendly, nourishing ocean of dark blue water teaming with life. Seagulls shrieking for a handout chased the *Neptune*. The early morning damp chill evaporated into the clear, warm, oxygen-laden atmosphere of Southern California at its healthiest. *It's the perfect day to be on a boat,* Sandy thought, only an instant before the Neptune rose and fell over the first of an endless series of offshore swells. Grabbing the rail to keep from being thrown to the deck, he studied the ocean. It was just as the National Weather Service had predicted: *big fucking seas*. A surge of green water smashed the bow, raining down on the deck, convincing him that lingering forward was not the smartest course of action. But before returning to the comfort of his aft deck seat, Sandy had a mission to accomplish.

Bracing himself between a three-foot stainless steel capstan and the above-deck windlass, Sandy faced the stern and tried to see through the smoked lexan windows of the raised pilothouse. After considerable maneuvering to escape the direct rays of the sun, he found a vantage point that allowed him a limited view of the boat's command post. Behind the big wheel, steering the craft, was a man Sandy knew instantly could only be Heinz Hoffmann. Who else but a German and a Nazi would stand so rigidly, like a force of nature with a stick up his ass, guiding the ship through the pounding, rolling swells? The skipper was everything a mid-fifties SS murderer should be: perhaps five-ten in height, muscular but not fat, a strong, tanned, human fireplug. He still lived by the book, wearing the traditional dark blue peaked captain's cap over his military-style haircut. Most impressive were the man's determined eyes, scanning the horizon, and his short, meaty fingers clamped around the destroyer-type wheel. In a fight, this would be a formidable and dangerous opponent.

"Excuse me," Sandy spoke to the blond deckhand who had come forward to remove the fenders from the bow. "Is that Captain Hoffmann at the wheel?"

After a quick glance into the pilothouse the deckhand responded, "That's your man," before returning to his chore.

Startled by the young seaman's comment, Sandy wondered for a moment if the Nazi wasn't already on to his and Paula's mission. That's impossible, he told himself, just another paranoid fantasy. A sudden lurch from the boat nearly threw Sandy across the bow. The seas were getting worse; it was time to move aft, where the motion of the *Neptune* would be less exaggerated.

Working his way back across the pitching teak deck, Sandy was surprised at how easily the boat was thrown around by the rolling water. Every step of the way, he had to grip the handrail to keep from being knocked off his feet. Thank god it was at least warm and clear; if the weather had been cold and overcast, this kind of sea would have made the day miserable.

For Sandy, the motion was an inconvenience, a discomfort. For Paula, however, it was infinitely worse. As he rounded the aft end of the pilothouse, one look at her told him everything. Paula's skin had turned the color of moldy white bread, and the expression on her face was that of a living corpse. All of her energy was channeled into staring out past the stern of the boat toward the stable horizon of Oxnard.

"Did you bring any Dramamine?" Sandy asked as he sat down beside her.

Her answer was a curt shake of her head, the implication being that to say even one word would result in total loss of stomach control.

"Keep staring at the land and take deep breaths. I'm going to find something for you to take."

Barely nodding, Paula didn't even turn toward him.

Descending the stairs to the lower deck, Sandy found the snack bar closed. The motion of the boat was too violent for anyone to remain inside the closed quarters permeated by the smells of fish, fried food, and diesel fuel.

Quickly climbing back up to the outside deck, Sandy stood by the rail, taking deep breaths and watching the horizon until his stomach had calmed down. Then he sought out the crewman who had earlier identified Captain Hoffmann.

"Excuse me, my wife is incredibly seasick. Is there anywhere I can get some Dramamine?"

"Try the captain." The blond deckhand pointed up to the pilothouse.

"Can't I just get someone to sell me some from the snack bar?"

"Talk to Captain Hoffmann." The crewman spun around and hurried toward the bow.

Jesus Christ, Sandy cursed to himself. For a lousy Dramamine I have to go to a scumbag Nazi murderer. It wasn't as if he had a choice. He couldn't very well leave Paula to heave her guts out on the aft deck. SS killer or no SS killer, his first priority was taking care of Paula.

Climbing the stainless steel ladder to the bridge was terrifying, not because of the ship's motion but in anticipation of what he would find in the pilothouse: A face-to-face meeting was not what Sandy had planned for this trip. The idea had been to use the half-day excursion as a scouting mission. Stay anonymous. Gather information. Don't let the son-of-a-bitch get an inkling he was being observed. And now look what was happening. What if the German sensed Sandy's suspicions? A person like that would definitely have heightened perceptions.

At the top of the stairs Sandy double-checked his shirt sleeve, fearful that despite his precautions Hoffmann would spot the tattoo. If that happened, Sandy couldn't imagine making it out of the pilothouse alive. In the flick of an eye, the Nazi would kill, chop him into pieces, and use the gory mess as chum for sharks. Chalk up another victim of the Third Reich and raise the total to six million and one.

"Ya?" the deep voice responded to the knock on the wheelhouse door.

Sandy swung open the wooden door and entered the captain's domain. There, behind the wheel, was the muscular figure of

Heinz Hoffmann, as the newspapers might label him in the future, "the alleged German mass murderer and war criminal."

"Captain Hoffmann?"

The man nodded, returning his gaze to the confused seas confronting his vessel.

"The deckhand sent me up. My wife is seasick and the snack bar's closed. I need to buy some Dramamine."

Hoffmann nodded. "One moment, please." After a final scan of the water in front of him, the captain flipped a breaker switch and punched a button, turning the helm over to his Neco autopilot. Another few seconds passed while he studied the boat's course to ascertain that the autopilot had actually cut in and was doing its job properly. Then, Hoffmann opened a drawer beside the wheel and extracted a small bottle of blue pills. The German poured out two Dramamine tablets and handed them to Sandy.

"Give her both of these. Don't let her lie down, and make her watch the horizon. It steadies the brain. We'll be at Anacapa in an hour, where it should be calmer. I hope." Hoffmann smiled benignly, dropped the bottle of pills back into the drawer, disengaged the autopilot and returned to the wheel.

Sandy slipped the pills into his shirt pocket, his brain racing. There he was, not two feet from a vicious war criminal. Yet only he, Sandy, knew that terrible secret. Or thought he knew, anyway. To anyone else, Hoffmann would have seemed nice enough, certainly not evil. But Sandy was vividly aware that in life, one saw only the shadow of evil, seldom the evil itself. The German appeared to be simply a physically hardy, foreign-born fishing boat captain. No traces of the sadist were visible. The craft he piloted wasn't a killer U boat. Nor were they heading toward a secret Channel Islands concentration camp. Reality was quite the reverse. The man had just dispensed, in the most humane manner, a couple of seasickness pills for a passenger who was a total stranger. Who would have guessed this to be the behavior of a war criminal?

"Thank you very much," Sandy said as he opened the door to the stairs.

"Good luck to your wife," Hoffmann remarked without taking his eyes off the ocean.

As Sandy made his way down the ladder, he told himself that it was just possible that Hoffmann already knew that both he and Paula were Jews. In coloring and general appearance, the two of them had some physical characteristics that could be stereotyped as Jewish. For a Nazi, Paula's seasickness could be a real opportunity. Perhaps the war criminal kept a bottle of pills for just such an occasion; what appeared to be Dramamine might actually be a fatal dose of cyanide. A crazy idea? Only maybe. In Sandy's mind, there were no such things as ex-Jews or ex-Nazis. A Jew was a Jew and a Nazi was a Nazi forever. Just because the war had ended didn't mean that Hoffmann had stopped killing Jews. Wasn't it possible that the man was still carrying on the work of the Third Reich? Hitler lives! Death to the Jews! Viva the SS!

The only hitch in Sandy's hypothesis was Hoffmann's need to keep himself out of the public eye. Killing Jews hardly fostered anonymity. But then fanatics, Sandy reminded himself, often had highly illogical priorities. Life itself didn't necessarily matter to these people; what counted was *the cause*. In Hoffmann's mind, the death of another Jew might buy him a good spot in heaven for all eternity. Thus it was possible that the blue pills weren't Dramamine or cyanide, but some highly sophisticated, ODESSA-created poison. Detection could be evaded if the tablets did their fatal work over a long period of time through the introduction of, for example, an uncurable fatal liver disease. Or heart damage. Who but Hoffmann knew what the blue pills would accomplish?

Fortunately, the whole paranoid argument was moot. By the time Sandy returned to the aft deck, Paula was clinging to the stern rail, hanging her head over the leeward side, vomiting up her bacon, egg, and whole wheat toast breakfast. In that state, no stomach could even begin to digest medication. The Nazi's work was foiled, Sandy rejoiced, resolving to send the tablets off to a lab for chemical analysis. Meanwhile poor Paula retched with such fury that the rail was clear of fishermen for ten feet on either side of her.

"Sorry it took so long, but the snack bar was closed and I had to go up to the bridge for Dramamine." He stroked her head in the hope of providing some comfort, but the words *snack bar* stimulated another round of vomiting.

"You're doing great," Sandy lied. "Once it's all out of you, you'll feel a lot better."

Paula nodded, took a deep breath, and threw up again.

As Sandy continued to caress Paula's hair, he pondered how to prove his suspicions about Hoffmann. It was one thing to suspect the man of war crimes; it was quite another to make an iron-clad case against him. Sandy couldn't exactly climb the ladder back up into the pilothouse and ask the captain how many Jews he had killed during the war.

Hoffmann's weak point, which had been established by his response to the travel contest, was his sentimental attachment both to Germany and to his war time adventures. Why else would the man fly home for an SS reunion? In Sandy's experience, sentimental men were collectors. The nature of sentimental men let them live in the present only by sustaining themselves with mementoes from the past. Any old soldier who flew to Germany in order to spend a week with his Gestapo buddies had to be a man who cherished souvenirs along with his war stories. Germans were notorious about medals. Perhaps Hoffmann had a secret stash of war booty. Maybe he even kept something truly horrendous, like a wallet fashioned from Jewish skin. Whatever it was that reminded Hoffmann of his glory years would be kept well hidden and only brought out during those sad times when the German was alone, depressed, and wanted to feel close to the memories of his youth. Sandy could just imagine, using his own bitter experiences, how Hoffmann might come home late at night from a fishing trip, open a bottle of German beer, put Wagner on the record player, pull from his secret hiding place a few souvenirs of his triumphant days, and let his mind drift back, momentarily escaping his identity as an outsider and expatriate in Oxnard, California. Wasn't this the same sort of behavior that he, Sandy, had allowed himself in recent years?

Thinking about their similar natures made him feel a little closer to the Nazi. They both shared, Sandy imagined, a common sense of alienation from the society around them. Each, in very different ways, lived and fed off the emotional richness of the past. They were Nazi and Jew, more deeply connected than Sandy had ever guessed. This fact inspired him to accept his leap of speculation: Somewhere, most likely at Hoffmann's house, was the hidden proof of his war criminal past that Sandy so desperately sought.

A sudden drop in the noise level of the big diesel engines signaled a decrease in speed as they arrived at the extensive kelp beds surrounding the west end of the narrow, mile-long, arched ocean rock known as Anacapa Island. In a well-rehearsed move, the large Danforth anchor on the bow was lowered, the chain let out as the Neptune backed down, and the anchor was set. Just as Captain Hoffmann had predicted, the island blocked the Pacific swells, transforming the motion of the boat to a comfortable, peaceful bobbing. Seconds later, the fishermen went to work baiting hooks, casting lines, and praying for strikes.

The absence of rolling had an almost immediate effect on Paula's stomach, and the color returned to her face along with her normal vitality. To maintain their cover, they had to fish. Following the other passenger's examples, Sandy baited both his and Paula's hooks with live anchovies, showed her how to work the reel, and demonstrated casting.

The next three hours were truly remarkable; almost, Sandy thought, as if the ocean itself wanted to repay Paula for the misery of her ride across the Santa Barbara Channel. Virtually every time she plopped her bait into the water, she caught something. Paula landed eight rock fish, five kelp bass, a small yellowtail, and one of the great all-time lunkers of sheepshead. This last fish was the heaviest catch of the day, and won the ship's pool — $45, collected from the other fishermen on the way to the island. The whole thing was such a thrill for Paula that she almost forgot the misery of the trip over.

A call from the bridge and all lines were pulled out of the water; it was time to go home. Paula looked up and saw Captain

Hoffmann approaching, accompanied by a deckhand with a Polaroid. The German held up her fish while the crew member snapped a picture of the two of them. After a brief presentation of the prize money and a little applause from the other fishermen, the captain went back about his business of weighing anchor.

What surprised Sandy was Paula's reaction to the captain. She was paralyzed with fear. In the Polaroid photograph, it appeared that she was terrified of holding the fish, as if it were a live grenade. Paula had panicked, and only the confusion of the situation prevented Captain Hoffmann from sensing what lay behind her behavior.

Once the anchor was up, Captain Hoffmann gunned the engines and headed the boat away from the island back to Oxnard. With the wind up, the seas were even worse than on the way over. Before Paula even had time to consider taking the Dramamine, the seasickness returned and she resumed her old spot, hanging over the rail, vomiting.

For the entire ninety-minute ride, Sandy stood beside her, again trying to provide comfort. Finally, the *Neptune* entered the calm waters of the Channel Islands Harbor. In the few minutes it took for the boat to reach its slip, Paula's nausea diminished and she positioned herself to be the first off the boat. Once the docklines were locked down and the boarding ramp extended, Paula lunged forward onto the concrete pier, heading for solid ground.

Moving more slowly, Sandy got caught in the log jam of heavily burdened fisherman carrying tackle boxes, poles, reels, and coolers. As the crowd of tired anglers, smelling of sweat, fish guts, and beer, pushed toward the narrow ramp, Sandy looked around for a last sight of Captain Hoffmann. But the man was nowhere to be seen. This surprised Sandy, who thought that the German, as a businessman, would be out by the exit saying good-bye to his customers. The fact that he was apparently hiding in the pilothouse worried Sandy. Was the Nazi staying out of sight because he realized he'd been identified? Trapped by the crowd, it was just possible that he, Sandy, was being set up for some preemptive tactic designed to preserve the German's freedom.

Maybe Hoffman and the crew had worked out a plan to murder him. Be calm, he told himself. The worst thing you can do is to let them know you're afraid.

"Hey mister," a voice yelled to Sandy just as he began the descent from boat to dock.

Swinging around, terrified, Sandy thought, *this is it*. He expected the last sound he would ever hear to be a gunshot fired from the vantage point of the pilothouse into the center of his head.

"You forgot your fish," the deckhand called out, pointing to the large plastic bag containing Paula's cleaned and filleted catch.

Sandy set down his pole and indicated one minute. Don't blow it now, when you've done so well, he told himself, waiting for the last of the fishermen to depart so that he could reboard the boat.

"How much do I owe you?" Sandy gestured to the bag of fish.

"A buck a fish comes to fifteen dollars."

After Sandy counted out the money, the deckhand immediately pocketed it and returned to his task, cutting up a green and yellow torpedo-shaped kelp bass.

"Can I ask you something?"

"Yeah?" the man answered without stopping his work with the razor-sharp knife.

"I wanted to thank Captain Hoffmann for being so nice when my wife was sick. I thought I'd send him something — scotch or bourbon maybe. Would you happen to know what he or his wife likes to drink?"

"The captain don't have no wife."

"He lives alone, huh?"

"When he ain't on the boat."

"Do you know what he drinks?"

"Wild Turkey." The deckhand flipped over the fish carcass and began filleting the second side.

"Great, thank you."

"If you want to thank *me*," he looked up from his work with an arrogant grin, "I like Coors."

"So do I." Sandy smiled, picked up the bag of fish, and quickly descended the ramp toward the dock.

33

"I *really* don't think this is a good idea." Paula struggled unsuccessfully to conceal her anxiety.

"There's not much choice," Sandy said flatly, studying every detail of the beige stucco ranchhouse at 1810 Sea View Drive.

"Sandy, it's stupid; what if he comes home?"

"What if he does?"

"He might see us."

"He won't."

"C'mon. We're strangers in his neighborhood. Look at the houses. They're all the same. Look at the cars. *They're* all the same too. This is a tract, Sandy, and we're parked on the street in a Swedish sports car. How can he *not* notice us?"

"I thought you wanted to help me."

"I do."

"Then be quiet."

"This *isn't* what we should be doing," she whispered in obvious fear.

"Um." Sandy ignored her and continued to study the details of Heinz Hoffmann's house.

"You know, what you should really do now is call Simon Wiesenthal."

"Oh, please." Sandy dismissed the idea.

"Don't *oh, please* me. He's an expert on this kind of person. I bet he's got a file on Hoffmann two inches thick."

"Paula, calm down for a minute and think. If our captain is really the war criminal we believe him to be, do you imagine the name he gave immigration is the name he was born with in Germany?"

"Maybe," she hedged.

"It's not something I would bet on. You see those windows over there on the side of his house?" Sandy pointed, changing the subject.

"What about them?"

"They're louvered windows."

"So?"

"They're about as secure as an unlocked door. I can slip them out and be inside that house in less than a minute."

"No." The thought terrified Paula.

"How else are we going to find out who this Hoffmann really is?"

"You're planning to break into the man's house?"

Sandy nodded. "And you're going to help me."

"Absolutely not. Going on that boat was bad enough; this is insane."

"You want to let a war criminal go unpunished?"

"I'm telling you, call Simon Wiesenthal."

"And say what?"

"That you've discovered a war criminal. Send him your Freedom of Information Act evidence."

"Paula, that stuff isn't proof."

"Yeah, well, have him look in Hoffmann's eyes like I did on the boat. If that man wasn't a Nazi, I'm not a Jew."

"Look, I agree with you. But Wiesenthal needs something real. That's why I have to go inside."

"You're serious."

"I'm waiting to hear a better alternative."

"Sandy, you're talking about committing a crime. Breaking and entering. Burglary. People go to jail for that. If I was caught with you, I'd be disbarred for life. You're not doing this; I'm not even listening to you talk about it, much less willing to help. And that's final. Period. Now let's get out of here."

"You're really scared."

"God-damn right."

"In 1973, a tough New York Jew's scared of an old Nazi?" he asked with sarcastic incredulity.

"I'm starting to be scared of you, too. Did something happen out there on the ocean? I mean, are you taking some kind of drug? Have you lost your mind?"

"I can't believe that someone as angry as you are, someone whose family was destroyed by the Nazis, whose parents were tortured in concentration camps, who speaks out in public against the Nazis at every opportunity, is intimidated by one old German charter-boat captain."

"I'm an attorney, Sandy; we have to do this legally."

"Even if it means he gets away?"

"There's got to be a legal way to obtain evidence."

"I'm all ears."

"I wish you'd drive."

"You think we can go to jail for sitting at this curb?"

"I don't want him to see us."

"Paula, for a tough trial lawyer, you are behaving like an irrational, hysterical person. I thought you told me you were good at investigations."

"I am."

"Then come up with something helpful."

"I did."

"The Wiesenthal business?" Sandy asked skeptically.

Paula nodded.

"He doesn't know anything about any Hoffmann. I already checked," Sandy lied.

"*You* did?"

"*We* did. Wiesenthal's a man, not a god. He knows a lot but not everything. That's why we have to take a more strenuous approach when it comes to methods of investigation."

"*He* told you that?"

"You know what the man's accomplished; he's not opposed to such tactics."

Paula thought it over. "There must be some other way; there has to be. What do the people you work for say you should do?"

"When you're interested in results you have to take an unorthodox approach to problems. This is one of those times."

"You don't think that's what Gordon Liddy told his men at the Watergate break-in?"

"Probably. But in our case it's true."

"Okay, fine. Let's say I agree with you. Just for the sake of discussion, what *would* happen if things went wrong and they caught us?"

"Who's *they?*"

"The police. If it was Hoffmann I don't think there'd be any question of what he'd do, do you?"

"Paula, there's a concept here much larger than the trivial issues of local legal decorum. The man is a war criminal. This is exactly what we've been speaking about in public. I'm asking you to take a stand and help me get this son-of-a-bitch. Will you do that with me?"

"And if we get caught, everything I've worked for in my life is down the drain in two seconds."

"You really don't trust me, do you?"

"Sandy," she pleaded, "we're human. We're not perfect. Things go wrong all the time. What do we do then?"

"I thought you prided yourself on your courage?"

"Sandy, get this straight. Courage means *bupkus* if you're behind bars. Out in the world as a lawyer I can—I am—accomplishing important things. And I intend to continue."

What to do? Nailing Hoffmann was without question the key to his own future. To fulfill his mission, Sandy knew he needed help; he couldn't do it on his own. He hated himself for lying to Paula about Simon Wiesenthal. But facts were facts; the great Nazi hunter would only have shrugged his shoulders at the paucity of evidence Sandy had gathered. Why waste the weeks and months flying to Austria and showing the data to Wiesenthal when the conclusion was obvious: More proof was required.

"Look," Sandy finally spoke, "I want you to consider very carefully before you answer. You asked me to help you with your Hillel slide shows. Just observe, you told me, and give constructive suggestions. I did. Then you humiliated me in front of those Orange Coast College neo-Nazis and made me exhibit my number to them. Be courageous, take a chance, do something for the memory of those six million, you bullied me. And I did. And am still doing. Now I'm asking you to help me with this. My arguments to you are the same as yours were to me. Except that this situation is infinitely more important. This is a real war criminal we can expose. Think about the number of opportunities you're going to have in your life that will be more important than bringing to justice a Nazi mass murderer." Sandy waited for his argument to sink in, then turned from her, shifted the Volvo into gear, and slowly drove away from Sea View Drive.

"I have to think about this for a couple of days." She spoke uncertainly.

"I need an answer tomorrow; with you or without you, this weekend I'm going in there."

Paula stiffened. "Not Friday. Uri's speaking in Anaheim, remember?"

"*For you,* he's speaking. And now, finally, he's asking for something for himself. You're really not in a strong moral position to refuse him."

"I told you I want to think about it."

Sandy nodded and drove the rest of the way to Paula's apartment in silence.

34

"Okay, I'll do it. But on two conditions."

Barely awake, Sandy propped himself up on his elbow. The time was six o'clock, Thursday morning. Paula had been up for half an hour and was already showered and dressed, about to leave for her office, where she hoped to make up some of the time she'd lost because of the fishing trip.

"First, I'm not having anything to do with going into that house. I'll drive you. I'll drop you off. But from then on you're on your own."

"I'm going to have to get someone else to pick me up afterwards and take me home?" Sandy asked.

"That's not what I meant. I'll do that too. Happy?"

"What's the second condition?"

"I can't tell you yet."

"You expect me to agree to something when I don't know what it is?"

"Why not; don't *you* trust *me*?"

"Paula, it's six in the fucking morning. I'm still half asleep. Can we dispense with the linguistic exercises, please, and talk straight here. What is it you want me to do?"

"It's something I don't want to discuss until after Saturday. It's not horrible. It's not dangerous. And it's not humiliating. But it's important to me and I want you to promise that you'll do it."

"Why can't you tell me now what you want?"

"Because if I'm going to put myself in your hands Saturday, I need to know you'll do the same for me."

"Haven't I already done that as Uri?"

"Just promise me you'll do what I ask."

As she waited for an answer, Sandy was aware both of how serious this conversation was, and of how exhausted Paula looked. Despite makeup and lipstick, her eyes appeared to be sunk deep in her head, surrounded by barely concealed dark circles. Obviously she hadn't slept.

"Okay. I'll bite. I herewith pronounce your blank contract, signed. Whatever you want, I'll do it. Now are you happy?"

Paula shrugged, kissed him quickly, and headed for the door. "Don't forget to lock up when you leave. 'Bye."

Puzzled, Sandy got out of bed. Another mystery was not what he needed. But at least he now had some help, he told himself.

Sandy was the first to arrive at the plant that morning. However, he wasn't there to sell vitamins but to work out the details of his Nazi investigation. Behind his locked office door, he spent the day going over and over his plan to search Hoffmann's house. Illegal, yes. Crazy, yes. But a bold choice, he told himself. The world responded to courageous risks, and he was going to utilize every means at his command, legal or illegal, to root out that Gestapo war criminal.

Thursday night Sandy stayed home, alone, refining the details of his plan. What kept his adrenalin flowing long past midnight were his fantasies of the future. Once he was able to expose Hoffmann, write that article, present his findings to the public, and tell the whole truth to Paula, Sandy had no doubt his life would change quickly and dramatically. Finally he would be able to discard his long-suffering identity as the depressed *schlepper*. After so many years of grief he would truly have achieved something worthy of world attention! Like a butterfly from a cocoon, Sandy would emerge from his Glendale cubicle to be recognized and honored as a man of courage and integrity, a citizen of the world, to be remembered forever in the annals of historical, heroic figures.

At work on Friday, however, Sandy's father dropped another bombshell.

"You going into the rectal exam business or what?" Nat surprised his youngest son in the hallway outside the chemist's lab.

"Oh, uh, I've got to do a little repair on my boat with fiberglass resin and I needed something to protect my hands." Sandy held up the half-dozen pairs of translucent latex surgical gloves he had just filched from the lab. The story was a lie; but Sandy could hardly explain to his father that the gloves were required for a burglary.

Nat grinned. "I have to tell you how pleased I am you're having such a good time with that boat. I really think it's great. And let me tell you something else: It shows. Since you've been going out sailing you look two hundred times better. This is not just my opinion; I hear it from everyone. You look years younger."

Sandy shrugged. "Shows you what a suntan will do."

"Well, it makes a hell of a difference. Keep looking so healthy and I might even slap a *before* and *after* picture of you on our new vitamin E brochure."

"Except that I don't take the stuff."

"Who's to know? Listen, the reason I came looking for you was about something else more important. What are you doing tonight?"

Sandy's blood seemed to congeal. That evening he was due in Anaheim for a speaking engagement.

"I just talked to Charlie," Nat continued. "Today's Fredricka's eighth birthday and he's taking the afternoon off and *schlepping* the family around Disneyland. Nice, huh?"

Absolute fucking no, Sandy thought. Old Walt Disney had built his damn amusement park in the dead center of Anaheim, not two blocks from the temple at which Uri was to speak.

"By the way," the old man digressed, "did you send your niece something terrific for her birthday?"

"Is there a point to this, Dad? I have work to do."

"Sandy, I just asked you a simple question; there's no reason to get upset. Family is important; it's all there is. That's why you have to give your nieces and nephews presents; they're the only things children understand."

"Dad, it really is none of your business whether I sent her a present. But just this once, I'll tell you. Yes, I did. So now what is it you want?"

Scrunching up his face as if he were totally confused, Nat tried another approach. "I really wish I could understand you. I do try, you know. Here I ask a simple question and you turn the whole thing into an argument. Why do you make it so hard for me to talk to you?"

"Am I to assume you came running down the hall to discuss Fredricka's birthday present?"

"No, I wanted to tell you that Charlie just called to say that around the corner from Disneyland is a temple, Beth-Torah."

The exact nightmare Sandy had feared!

"That Uri fellow is scheduled to speak there around nine tonight, as part of the sermon. Since Charlie was already going to be nearby, he figured that Nora could take the kids home and he'd go listen to Uri. I suggested you join him. Doesn't that sound like a good idea?"

A great idea. Death would be preferable. It wasn't just the humiliation of being publicly exposed by Charlie; if Uri were revealed as a fake, the publicity would destroy Sandy's chances of being taken seriously as an investigative journalist. Who would accept the reportage of a proven fraud and con artist? No matter what it took, Sandy had to stop Charlie from visiting the temple in Anaheim.

"Where's Charlie now?" Sandy demanded.

"At his office, I think. Why?"

"If I'm going to meet him in Anaheim, I have to talk to him and make the arrangements before he leaves. Excuse me."

Without waiting for a response, Sandy swung around and sprinted down the hall to his own windowless cubicle, where he locked the door, looked up Charlie's number in the Rolodex, and dialed his brother.

"Altman, Polsky, and Klein," the receptionist answered.

"Charlie Klein, please."

"One moment, sir."

On hold, Sandy became acutely conscious that his pulse had suddenly accelerated to supersonic velocity. In his ears, cymbals crashed in rhythm to the kettle drum pounding through his arteries. *God damn it Charlie,* Sandy yelled in his mind, *answer the fucking phone before I have a heart attack!*

"Mister Klein's office," a calm secretary's voice answered.

"Hello," Sandy forced himself to speak slowly. "This is Sandy Klein, Charlie's brother. Can I talk to him please; it's very important."

"I'm sorry, but Mister Klein isn't in. Would you like to leave a message?"

Ahhhhhh! Sandy wanted to scream at her, *Shit! Fuck! Dammitall!* "Did he go home or did he already leave with his family for Disneyland?"

"I don't know, Mister Klein."

"You don't know?" Sandy lost control and screamed. "You're his secretary, aren't you? I need my brother; now where is he?"

After a long moment of silence, the woman spoke quietly. "Uh, Mister Klein, like I told you, I don't know. He didn't tell me. All I know is that he left with his wife."

"Shit. That means I missed him." *What to do? What to do?* Sandy repeated to himself mechanically.

"Shall I give him your message?" the secretary finally asked.

"Yes, please. Tell him to call me immediately. At the plant. What time did he leave?"

"About an hour ago."

"Will he call in for messages?"

"I don't know, Mister Klein, but if he does I'll tell him you need to speak to him immediately." She hung up without waiting for Sandy to say more.

On automatic, Sandy phoned information, obtained the number of the Magic Kingdom, and dialed.

"Disneyland information, good morning," a recorded voice explained so slowly and patiently that a retarded monkey could have understood. In what seemed to take weeks, Sandy heard about ticket information, "A" rides, "B" rides, "C" rides, "D" rides, and "E" rides, as well as ticket book prices, admission policy, the dress code, park hours, parking information, and even route planning. As the taped message went on and on in frustrating detail, Sandy's anxiety and rage grew to outrageous proportions. Another nightmare — this time a machine, out to drive him crazy. Finally, as his patience reached the breaking point, the tranquilized voice ended its monologue with a "phone number for further information": the park switchboard.

Sandy hung up immediately and dialed what he hoped was the park itself.

"Good morning, Disneyland," a human voice answered cheerfully.

"Hi," Sandy told the woman. "My name is Sandy Klein and I'm trying to reach my brother, who's inside the park. There's an emergency in the family; can you page him?"

"One moment please."

On hold, Sandy's imagination again went wild. They couldn't be paging Charlie because they didn't know his name; had the receptionist dismissed the call as a crank and cut him off? Would he, Sandy, have to go through that horrible message again to get the number, which he hadn't written down and now had forgotten?

"Mister Klein?" A man's voice came on the line.

"Yes."

"This is Disneyland security, Rogers speaking. What can we do for you?"

"I'm trying to reach my brother. There's an emergency in the family. I need you to page him for me." The desperation in Sandy's voice would have sounded convincing to anyone.

"You're sure he's in the park?"

"He should be. If he isn't he'll be there any minute."

"Okay, give me your name and number and we'll page him every fifteen minutes for the next two hours."

"That'd be great. Thank you. I'll be sitting here right by the phone."

"I must warn you, there's a lot of noise in the park. Fridays during the summer, we're very crowded and many times people never hear themselves called."

"I appreciate you trying."

"We just don't want you to get your hopes up and be disappointed. Now what's your brother's name?"

After giving him the information and receiving, in return, a direct number to security, Sandy hung up. *Hear the page. Please hear the page,* Sandy pleaded.

After three hours and five more conversations with Rogers, Charlie still hadn't responded to the pages. "That's par for the course," Rogers finally admitted, adding that more paging was impossible: The park's loudspeaker system was shut down while the engineers traced a short.

Flat-out crazed, Sandy hung up. What had started as a hopeful morning with Paula had deteriorated into a day of terror. More direct action was required; he dialed another number.

"Hello," Paula answered her own newly acquired private line on the second ring.

"Listen, don't ask me to explain because I can't, but I have to cancel the speech tonight in Anaheim."

"Why?" She spoke coldly.

"Just do as I ask, please. Call, tell them what you want, but get me out of it."

"Sandy," she spoke in her most patient tone of voice, "if this was a normal talk, I'd do it for you. But this is special, remember? This is Temple Beth-Torah. They sent out printed invitations to their entire congregation. Your speech tonight is the centerpiece for the 'retire the mortgage' fund-raising effort. If you don't show you'll set their Hebrew school construction fund back a year. The mayor of Anaheim's even going to be there; that's how important this is. Any place else I'd be happy to make the call. But this event you can't cancel."

"I have to."

"Why," she asked, "do you *have to*?"

"Paula, you're just going to have to accept the fact that it's something that has to be. If you like, view it as an act of God."

Instead of more anger, she spoke intimately, affectionately. "Sandy, this is me, Paula. You can tell me the reason. Not only will I understand, but I'll help you with it."

"Good, then call the temple and cancel."

"And tell them what?"

"It doesn't matter. Pick what you think sounds best. Say I'm sick. Try stomach flu; it's contagious. They'll be happy to reschedule. No one wants the stomach flu."

"Sandy, you have to understand something. I happen to know Rabbi Birnbaum at Beth-Torah. He's from New York and he's a nice man. I'm not going to lie to him and cancel unless you tell me why it's so important that you not speak tonight."

Sandy's mind was on fire. How, he asked himself, could he satisfy Paula without bringing down his whole house of cards? There had to be a way. There was always a solution. But what?

"It has to do with tomorrow night and Hoffmann," Sandy attempted to sound ominously convincing. "There are some things I have to do tonight that I don't want to discuss over the phone. You'll just have to take my word for the fact that this is serious."

"What is serious?"

"Paula, this isn't the time or place to discuss it."

"No, I guess it isn't," she responded angrily. "But unless you explain it to me now, I'm not going to call the rabbi. So either tell me, or show up like *you* promised and *they* advertised."

"Paula, please, don't do this to me. I'm under an unbearable amount of pressure as it is; you know how much is riding on tomorrow night. Give me a break and help me out here, please."

"Not unless you tell me why."

"Just phone the rabbi and get me out of it."

"You're a son-of-a-bitch, Sandy. These are real people with real problems. They need you and I won't disappoint them by canceling. It's three hours out of your night — nothing. So stop being so selfish, think about what I've just said, and call me back in an hour with your answer." The phone slammed down, cutting the line.

Sandy tried to calm himself by moving slowly. As he gently replaced the receiver, the idea came to him in an inspired flash. This brilliant solution would embarrass no one, hurt no one, and everyone's interests would be protected. After all, Sandy reflected with renewed confidence, how much good would it do Paula or the temple if, in the middle of the speech, Charlie exposed Uri as a fake?

In seconds, Sandy was out the side door of the plant, in his Volvo, driving east, in search of the perfect gas station. Fifteen minutes later he found exactly what he was looking for in a run-down old Texaco station on the fringes of the East L.A. barrio. He parked, locked his car beside the isolated phone booth, entered the glass and metal compartment, shut the folding door, deposited a dime, and dialed.

"Information," the operator's voice announced.

"I'd like the number of the *Anaheim Daily News,* please."

"One moment."

As he waited, Sandy checked out the surrounding area; no one, not even the gas station attendant, was looking in the direction of the phone booth.

When the operator came back on the line with the number, Sandy hardly hesitated before redepositing the dime and dialing the newspaper.

"*Anaheim Daily News.*"

"The editorial page editor, please."

"Would you like Mister Thomas or Mister Gruen?"

"Mister Thomas is fine," Sandy guessed.

"One moment."

While Sandy waited, he rehearsed his short but pointed speech.

"Editorial page, Thomas speaking."

"Listen carefully because I'm not going to repeat this." Sandy spoke rapidly. "Send a reporter over to Temple Beth-Torah to cover that Jew's speech tonight. And tell your man to stay outside the building and listen through a window because I wouldn't want an honest reporter to get hurt by the bomb that's going to blow up that pinko Jew troublemaker and his followers. Remember this, Thomas, there're a lot of us out here who won't stand for the lies this Jew, Uri, and others have been spreading about the Third Reich."

Before the man could respond, Sandy slammed down the phone, slipped out of the booth, and drove back to his office.

At five-ten, his private phone line rang. Please, he pleaded, let it be Charlie from Disneyland.

"Hello?" he spoke cautiously into the receiver.

"You bastard!" Paula screamed. "How could you? And to think that I loved you, respected you, and believed in you! What kind of slimebag are you?"

"Paula?" Sandy sounded baffled, feigning innocence. "What the hell is going on?"

"You know exactly why I'm calling, Mister Klein; don't you play stupid with me."

Sandy paused a moment, as if he were trying to make sense of the situation. "Look, I understand you're upset," he said at last, "but would you at least have the courtesy to calm down and tell me why you're swearing. You can't still be mad at me for trying to get out of the speech in Anaheim?"

"I can't, can't I? You vicious lowlife. You're a real asshole, you know that? So you wanted to cancel, and you couldn't give me your reason — that doesn't give you the right to do what you did. How could you stoop so low? Who the hell do you think you are?"

After another long moment of silence, Sandy sounded sincerely incredulous. "Paula, who the hell do you think *you* are? I don't understand one word of what you're telling me. I'm a lowlife, vicious, asshole? Why? Just because I didn't want to talk tonight? Okay, I mean, I understand Anaheim's important to you. I'm sorry. I was anxious about tomorrow; I have a lot to do. But I thought about what you said and you're right; I should honor this commitment and I shouldn't have tried to get out of it. *I* was wrong. But that doesn't justify you yelling at me."

This time the silence on the phone came from Paula.

"Hello?" Sandy inquired. "Paula, are you there? Hello?"

"It wasn't you that phoned the *Anaheim Daily News*?" Paula asked.

"Why would I call them?"

"You don't know?"

"Paula," Sandy sounded annoyed, "I really don't know what's gotten you so crazy, but I've got more than a few things on my own mind and I don't have time for all this hysterical nonsense. Do you hear yourself?"

"You really don't have any idea?"

"No. And I don't have the patience to run this around with you again, either. You want to tell me what's going on now, or save it for after the speech in Anaheim?"

"There's not going to be any speech."

"Why not? I told you I was wrong and would honor my commitment. You're not canceling on me out of spite, are you?"

"Jesus, Sandy, I'm sorry. I thought it was you." Her voice dropped, pained by remorse. "Will you forgive me? I mean, I'm so sorry about what I just said. You must think I'm awful. I want to make it up to you. Will you let me? Say something to me, Sandy, please. I'm wrong, I'm stupid and I jumped to conclusions. No one's perfect. Please give me another chance."

"Why were you swearing at me?"

"Right after we talked someone phoned the *Anaheim Daily News*. A neo-Nazi, the editor thought. The guy threatened to blow up Uri and the entire congregation. I just got a call from Rabbi Birnbaum. They've got the bomb squad out there, searching the temple. But the police need a couple more hours to do the job properly, so the temple has to cancel your appearance. They want to reschedule in October. Sandy, I thought the caller was you."

"Oh, I see. Now I understand. That's what the opening attack was about."

"I told you I was sorry." She spoke meekly.

"You obviously have a high opinion of me, don't you?"

"We all make mistakes, Sandy."

"Yeah, but look at the first conclusion you jumped to. Look what you accused me of."

"Can't you understand how I made that mistake?"

"I'm very disappointed in you, Paula. I trusted you. I thought I could count on you." He sounded defeated.

"You can, Sandy, I swear to you I'll never doubt you again."

"Why should I believe you?"

"I'm giving you my word. In the future, whatever the circumstances, no matter what the evidence, I'll believe the story *you* tell me."

"And defend me to the world?"

"With my life."

After another long moment of thought, Sandy spoke affectionately. "Okay. Then I'll forgive you."

35

At the Oxnard Boulevard off-ramp Paula flicked on the turn signal of the mud green 1966 Pontiac Bonneville and eased the big automobile off the Ventura Freeway. So far, everything about the trip was going perfectly. The Pontiac, hired from Bundy Rent-A-Wreck, was the perfect vehicle for the mission — big, comfortable, in good mechanical condition, and so nondescript as to be virtually invisible. No one in Hoffmann's neighborhood would give it a second thought. As a further precaution, Sandy had removed the front license plate and covered the rear plate with a mixture of ninety-weight gear lubricant and dirt from his yard. At night, even with the lights on, the license number was indecipherable from five feet away. For only ten dollars a day and ten cents a mile, the massive Bonneville was perfect transportation for a burglary.

Their first stop, which they made on schedule at eleven-thirty that Saturday night, was the parking lot at the Channel Islands Harbor. As Sandy had anticipated, the *Neptune* was gone and the office closed. The boat and Captain Hoffmann weren't due to return until midnight on Sunday.

From the harbor, Paula drove back toward Sea View Estates while Sandy took a final inventory of his equipment. He was wearing a black turtleneck shirt, dark blue jeans, black socks, and black tennis shoes. On his head was a midnight blue, U.S. Navy issue, wool watch cap. Clipped to his belt were a couple of small flashlights and two canvas sacks. One contained a selection of hand tools — pliers, screwdrivers, a Swiss Army knife, and a pry bar. The other satchel held his folded Polaroid camera, three packs of flashbulbs and film, the loaded Smith and Wesson .38, and a dozen extra rounds of ammo.

"We're getting close," Paula whispered, as if she were afraid someone might overhear.

Sandy nodded, retrieved a small jar of grease paint from the glove compartment, and coated both his face and hands with the sticky black substance. After pulling on a pair of surgical gloves, he turned to Paula for a final inspection.

"How do I look?" He spoke softly, disguising his fear.

Alternating her gaze between Sandy and the road, Paula meticulously reviewed his appearance, not speaking until she was satisfied she'd seen him from head to toe. Finally she grinned bravely. "You could pass for Al Jolson in the *Jazz Singer*."

"Very funny. Does any of the skin on my face show?"

She shook her head. "Only the whites of your eyes."

Sandy nodded and slipped on a pair of sunglasses, blocking out the last possible source of reflected light. To Paula he looked like a professional burglar who had done this sort of thing before. In truth, the closest he had ever come was researching a story for *The Heart of L.A.* about a thief who billed himself as the Beverly Hills Cat Burglar. Sandy recalled grimly that eight months after the article had appeared, the man had been caught and sentenced to ten years in prison.

Paula made her first pass down Sea View Drive a few minutes after midnight. Hoffmann's house was dark, as were his neighbors'.

"You scared?" Paula whispered.

"Let's just say I'm getting a nice, steady flow of adrenalin. How are you doing?" Sandy spoke with bravado, attempting to cover the fact that he was terrified. And why not, when his entire life rode on the outcome of the next few hours?

"I'm actually better now than I was this morning at work. You know what I noticed about myself?"

Sandy shook his head.

"I kept having to pee," she spoke with disbelief. "It seemed like every hour, on the hour. I think it's the waiting that kills you. Now I feel calm and even a little excited. I keep telling myself that tonight we're making history, like when the Israelis captured Eichmann."

Sandy nodded. "You remember the signal to pick me up?"

"One blink of your flashlight."

"And if you see cops around the house or in the neighborhood, what do you do?"

"Drive straight home and wait for your call from jail."

Sandy's plan required her to drop him off, drive away, and return one hour later. After that, she was to cruise past Hoffmann's house every fifteen minutes and wait for his signal. Should the police find him, he had reassured Paula, they wouldn't be able to connect her to his activities. Despite having involved her in so many lies, Sandy promised himself that nothing would jeopardize her life or career; he loved her too much to drag her down with him if something went wrong.

"Okay, let's get this over with," he said quietly.

Paula turned the corner and once again drove down Sea View Drive toward Hoffmann's home. As the Pontiac approached the unlit tract house, Sandy's awareness of his heart and pulse momentarily distracted him from the job at hand. The tom-toms in his body were beating again, the savage instincts unleashed, the warrior inside preparing for battle. He rolled down the window, in an effort to cool himself off. But the August breeze accomplished nothing and Sandy's overheated core continued to pump sweat like of a marathon runner passing mile twenty. By the time Paula turned the Bonneville into the driveway of 1810 Sea View Drive, his black cotton turtleneck was soaked through. As the car rolled to a stop, Sandy reached for the door handle.

"Good luck," Paula's voice was barely audible. "I love you."

Sandy nodded, saying nothing. He slipped out of the car, silently closed the heavy passenger door, ducked low, and ran to the side of the house, where he dropped to the ground behind the corner of the garage.

Paula backed out of the driveway and cruised off down the street. To an outside observer, it would have appeared that she'd gotten lost and had used Hoffmann's driveway as a turn-around.

Restraining his impulse to head immediately for the louvered window, Sandy checked his watch. The time was nine minutes after midnight. Instead of moving, he forced himself to sit motionless for five long and lonely minutes to make certain that no one was watching. Squatting on the concrete, protected from

the moonlight by the shadow of the garage, he found himself
missing Paula. What the hell was he doing in Oxnard, risking his
life on a crazy venture, when he could be home in bed with her,
wrapped in her arms?

Checking his watch, Sandy found that instead of five minutes,
he'd been sitting for eight; all around him the street was quiet. It
was time to get to work.

Slipping his sunglasses into the satchel holding his pistol,
Sandy crouched low and tiptoed down the side of the house
toward the back yard, stopping at each window to check for signs
of life inside. Foot by foot he circled the perimeter of the stucco
structure. Every exterior window was not only closed but
locked — a sure sign on a summer night that no one was home.

Working his way back around to the side of the house, Sandy
began the simple task of gaining access through the louvered
glass window. One quick torque on the aluminum frame with
his pry bar bent the catch, and the venetian-blind-like mecha-
nism rotated every rectangle of glass horizontal and open. All
Sandy had to do then was push forcefully on the edge of each
pane and one by one slide them out of their frames. Within two
minutes he had created an opening large enough to crawl
through. Pulling himself up over the window ledge, he slipped
silently inside the dark house.

The moonlight now became his ally. Standing up, he could see
that he was in the dining room. As much as it would have
delighted him to find the walls covered with guns, swastikas, and
Nazi memorabilia, what he actually saw was just the opposite. In
the center of the room sat a heavy mahogany trestle dining table
surrounded by six solid matching chairs, none of which
appeared to have endured much use. Against one long windowless wall stood a dark-stained walnut breakfront. This looked like
a good place to start his search. Inch by inch he slid the massive
bottom drawer out far enough to reveal its contents. Using his
flashlight sparingly, he sifted through a meaningless set of ivory-
handled fish knives and forks and a stack of German bone china
dinner plates.

Next Sandy moved to the more accessible middle drawer, which was filled with neatly folded tablecloths and matching napkins. The top drawer was equally disappointing, containing only stainless steel cutlery. Opening the tall cabinet doors on the upper part of the breakfront, Sandy found shelf after shelf of wine glasses, beer steins, and ordinary tumblers of various dimensions.

Moving to the kitchen, Sandy viewed an area which, in contrast to the dining room, actually looked like it was put to use occasionally. Hoffmann might not be a man who threw dinner parties, but he obviously cooked regular meals. The place wasn't set up for gourmet extravaganzas, but it was neat, clean, and well-equipped with the basic appliances. Other than a Bavarian calendar advertising BMWs, and a few Teutonic knickknacks in porcelain, this was simply another mass-produced tract house kitchen, indistinguishable from millions of others.

The cabinets contained a mixture of German foods — cans of Black Forest ham, Mueslix multiple grain cereal, and boxes of strangely shaped noodles — along with all the usual American cooking staples. But after examining every drawer and cupboard and even emptying the contents of the freezer onto the counter top, Sandy found nothing incriminating. The white freezer bags contained filets of fish, the only indication so far that the owner of the house had anything to do with the *Neptune*. After replacing everything in its original spot, Sandy stopped for a moment to evaluate the situation.

The time was twelve-forty; already he'd been in the house more than twenty minutes. He knew he had to move faster. Creeping back through the dining room, Sandy stopped in the small entry hall by the coat closet. *Where to go next?* The rest of the house consisted of two bedrooms, two bathrooms, a living room, and the garage. After a quick glance at each he started in on the narrow hallway closet, which contained only an overcoat and a couple of umbrellas.

Entering the first bedroom, Sandy again found a room that appeared never to have been used. Two single beds stood at right angles to one another in the corner. Both were covered with dark, fringed woolen bedspreads protecting mattresses without sheets, blankets, or pillows. Under the beds themselves was only the carpeted floor. In the closet linens were stored in unopened plastic packaging. This place is so god-damn barren, Sandy told himself, it looks like a motel.

The adjoining bathroom didn't contain so much as a toothbrush. Hoffmann not only didn't entertain, he apparently never used his house for anything other than eating and sleeping. A jolt of terror passed through Sandy as he considered the possibility that Hoffmann kept his World War II mementos at the real center of his life: his boat. But he immediately discarded that idea; no mariner would jeopardize his valuables by storing them on a boat where they could be soaked in salt water, attacked by corrosion, or infected with moisture-induced fungus. No, Sandy concluded, Hoffmann would definitely keep his irreplaceable secrets ashore, out of reach of both the destructive environment of the sea and the equally damaging curiosity of his crew members.

The more he thought about it, the more Sandy was encouraged by the fact that Hoffmann's house was so obviously the habitat of a loner. The German, like so many men with hidden criminal pasts, couldn't afford the risk of opening his life to strangers. The question was, where would a meticulous, well-organized Nazi hide something dangerous and yet still have easy access to it?

Heinz Hoffmann's bedroom was as Teutonic and sterile as the rest of the house. On the single bed lay a German eiderdown comforter, the only personal touch other than the six-foot mahogany chest of drawers against the wall opposite the bed. As Sandy opened each of the six sticky drawers and sorted through the neatly folded socks, underwear, shirts, belts, pants, and sweaters, he couldn't help but wonder why the Germans, as a group, were drawn to such massive, heavy, and oppressive furniture. Give the same piece of raw wood to a Swede a hundred miles north of the German border and you'd end up possessing a light, cheerful, modern cabinet with twice the storage space of Hoffmann's heirloom. German furniture all seemed to convey the same message: I'm here, I'm strong, you can't hurt me, I'm indestructible and will live forever. That's what the Germans must admire, Sandy reflected. In contrast, he thought the same furniture reeked of a doomed, primitive, and brutal culture drawn to blood sacrifice, dark rituals, and apocalyptic fantasies.

By one-thirty Sandy had still found nothing even remotely promising. He completed his search with the living room, where a careful examination of couch, coffee table, leather chair, fireplace, and flue revealed nothing.

Now Sandy was really beginning to sweat. To walk out of that house empty-handed would be as real a suicide as putting the .38 into his mouth and pulling the trigger. Choking down panic, he made himself stop, sit down, and rethink the situation. If I were a Nazi, Sandy asked himself, where would I hide life-threatening information?

Two possibilities came to mind: the attic, or a crawl space under the floorboards. Moving from room to room, Sandy began examining every square inch of carpet. On his hands and knees he scrutinized the perimeter of each wall, tugging on the beige nylon shag in search of an unfastened edge. Nothing in the guest room appeared out of place. The hallway carpet checked out impeccably. In the living room, even the oak floorboards under the couch revealed not one loose plank. It was the same story in the dining room — sliding the breakfront across the slick waxed wooden floor revealed nothing but tightly nailed tongue-and-groove oak strips. And throughout Hoffmann's bedroom the thick shag seemed equally untouched. The only area of the house impossible to reach was the three-by-six-foot strip of carpet under the huge chest of drawers holding the Nazi's clothes. The god-damn thing was so heavy, Sandy grimaced, it would take the entire German army to move it. Maybe he should first try the attic and come back to this mountain of wood as a last resort.

But a close inspection of the shag fibers around the base of the dresser drawers revealed something exciting: For about three-quarters of an inch around the mahogany monstrosity the nylon shag carpet was crushed and distorted, as if the massive hunk of furniture had been moved on more than one occasion. No one, Sandy was certain, would slide such an enormous assemblage of wood for something trivial like vacuuming; the reason for the movement had to be more profound.

In the stance of a Dallas Cowboy guard blocking his opposition in the Super Bowl, Sandy lined up against the side of the cabinet. But no matter how hard he pushed, it wouldn't budge. Instead of being discouraged, he was elated and could feel a sudden rush of chemically induced excitement explode through his nervous system. One at a time, Sandy struggled to remove all six drawers of clothes until only the mahogany carcass was left. Resuming his football stance, Sandy bore down, focusing every bit of strength in his body. Very slowly, half an inch at a time, the mahogany clothes mausoleum moved away from its resting place and the carpet underneath was revealed.

Dripping with sweat, Sandy knelt down and experienced his second thrill of the evening. Not only was the carpet loose, a two-foot-wide flap had been slit from the main body of the shag fiber. Without a moment's deliberation, Sandy folded back the fabric, extracted a two-by-two square of felt carpet padding, and examined the plywood subfloor. What he saw was unmistakable; a hand-cut door, complete with finger hold — the lid of a hidden compartment. After a quick inspection for wires, strings, or other booby traps, he stuck his index finger into the one-inch hole and lifted the plywood.

On a simple wooden shelf nailed to the floor joists lay a clear plastic bag containing a thick photo album. Before touching it, Sandy again checked for trip wires, finding nothing. After fixing the position of the book in his mind, he hoisted it out of its hiding place, untwisted the tie seal and extracted the old leather album from its polyethylene pouch. For a moment Sandy was too overcome with fear of disappointment to open the binder. His whole life seemed to hang in the balance; either the bonds chaining him both to his family and to his years of despair were about to be cut forever, or else his future would be permanently demolished. Focusing his flashlight on the leather cover, he gently opened it.

For a moment Sandy knew what Moses must have felt like standing on shore, watching the Red Sea part. God had intervened, saving the Israelites just as fate had now blessed Sandy with more than he could have hoped for. In his hands were the documents of his dreams, a photographic history arranged in chronological order, cataloging the life of Heinz Hoffmann from birth certificate to a final photo of the German at the wheel of the *Neptune*. In between were pictures from the Nazi years, incriminating beyond belief.

Sandy's first impulse was to grab the album and run. But he controlled himself, knowing that if the captain came home on Sunday and discovered the album missing, he would make a beeline for Paraguay, never to be seen again. Sandy needed Hoffmann alive, in the United States.

The birth certificate mounted on the fly leaf revealed that Heinz Hoffmann's real name was Klaus Hagen, born in 1923. Following the birth certificate were pages of black and white photographs. Klaus Hagen had apparently been born in the summertime on a German farm. His parents were a thick, sturdy young couple, obviously proud of their son. The one-year-old Klaus was photographed with a baby sister, who herself was joined by a second sister perhaps a year later. Photo after photo showed the young Klaus working on the farm, helping his father. In the spring their horse pulled a plow across a field. In the winter, Klaus was seen in the barn, milking the cow. A series of photographs of the teenaged Klaus featured his hunting skills: In one hand he gripped a shotgun, and in the other a string of pheasants. A winter scene showed him wearing snowshoes, holding up a pair of dead white rabbits. Had the album stopped there, it would have been charming and romantic — the German version of the conventional, idyllic scenes Sandy's own family tried so hard to display to the world.

The meat of the album began when Klaus' Tyrolian outfits and blousy farm attire suddenly changed to the starched and pressed dark uniform of the Brownshirts. Klaus had joined the National Socialist Party. Now he was photographed as part of a large group of older teenagers marching down a cobblestone city street.

There were pictures of Klaus training with weapons. Another scene showed him in a beer hall crowded with Brownshirts toasting the photographer with huge steins of lager. The following page revealed another transformation. Klaus had changed units. Standing in front of a brick building decorated with enormous swastika flags, Klaus stood formally, proudly, as he was captured on film from a low, heroic angle, making the most impressive use of his new image as an officer dressed in an SS uniform, complete with jackboots, black leather jacket, and the death's head insignia on his cap.

The next picture showed a harder, less manicured Klaus, in a winter scene on some small-town train depot. Strapped to his hip was an automatic pistol over which he rested a leather-gloved hand. Above the German's head, Sandy could barely make out the sign identifying the train station: Rava Ruska. The Ukraine! There was only one reason for an SS officer to be in a Russian city, and that was for the purpose of killing Jews. Sandy had read all about the SS and their activities in Russia. In the Ukraine, the SS had formed a group called the *Einsatzgruppen,* which ran the mobile killing squads. Their job was to organize, train, and direct the local militias in what the Nazis referred to as "actions," a euphemism for identifying, assembling, and slaughtering all the Jews in the community. In the Ukraine the SS hadn't yet perfected the efficient techniques later utilized at Auschwitz, but what they did accomplish was horrifying and impressive enough. The entire *Einsatzgruppen* consisted of only three thousand men. Yet within one year of the German invasion of the Russian territories, the *Einsatzgruppen* — as obsessively detailed in their own meticulous records — had killed 481,877 Jewish men, women, and children. Under SS command, the local communities rounded up their Jewish neighbors, many of whose families had lived there for hundreds of years, herded them outside the town, machine-gunned them, and buried them in mass graves. Could Hoffmann have been a member of the *Einsatzgruppen?* The following page provided the shocking answer.

On an overcast winter day, Klaus, looking very much in command and wearing his full SS uniform, stood aiming his automatic pistol at the terrifying and bizarre scene taking place in a barren field bordered by fir trees. Below the Nazi, in a pit the size of an Olympic swimming pool, lay hundreds of bloody, naked corpses. Piled to the side of this pit were stacks of black garments like those typically worn by Hassidic Jews. On top of the dead stood perhaps fifty shivering, naked Jews with their arms up over their heads. German soldiers and local militia pointed machine guns at them. Obviously, the living Jews were about to be shot and buried in the mass grave they had most probably helped to dig. Particularly remarkable about this photo was the moment that the photographer had chosen to snap his shutter. Everyone in the scene — Jews, Germans, and militia — was looking up at the ridge to their commander, SS Officer Klaus Hagen, whose raised pistol was obviously the signal to start firing. Most terrible of all was the lack of expression on Klaus Hagen's face. The man showed no reaction to the inhumanity he was committing; it was as if the Jews in the pit were metal targets in a fairground shooting gallery. He was a man consoled with the idea that he was *only doing his job.*

From the sack tied to his belt, Sandy extracted his Polaroid camera, slipped in a flashcube, and took aim at the hideous photograph. But as he was about to snap the shutter, he stopped himself and set down the camera; if one of Hoffmann's neighbors saw the flash, the police would be there within minutes.

Resuming his page-by-page examination of the album, Sandy searched without success for other incriminating photographs. Except for Rava Ruska, the rest of the pictures were conventional German tourist shots of Klaus Hagen, dressed in his SS garb, in front of such famous places as the Arc de Triomphe in Paris, the palace at Versailles, and the Spanish Steps and Trevi Fountain in Rome. After the dissolution of the *Einsatzgruppen,* the man had apparently been sent on assignments all over Europe. At least he had the one picture, Sandy consoled himself. And that one was truly extraordinary. One good one was all that was required to hang the Nazi.

Flipping back through the album, Sandy found the incriminating photo, removed it from the little angled slits holding it to the thick paper, then rearranged the six other photographs until it appeared that the seventh black and white print had never been attached to the page. Stealing the picture was a great risk, but Sandy really had no choice. Even if he *had* tried to copy it with the Polaroid, the crude lens would never have been able to capture all the significant details. He could only hope that with a little luck, Hoffmann wouldn't figure out what happened to the missing picture.

As he turned the photo over to slide it into his wallet, Sandy noticed handwriting on the back of the double-weight Agfa paper. The faded ink spelled out the familiar words *Rava Ruska*. More evidence, he told himself as he slipped his wallet, now containing the picture, into his pocket.

Following up on his discovery, Sandy once again plowed through the photo album, this time examining the back of each picture. A third of the way through he struck gold for a second time. Hidden behind the snapshot of the young Klaus in his first SS uniform was the Nazi's SS identification card, faded but still legible. On one side of this priceless bit of evidence was a small photo of Klaus Hagen, as well as his ID number, date of birth, and the unit to which he had been assigned, the SS *Einsatzgruppen*.

Tempted to remove that card too, Sandy controlled himself. If Hoffmann found one item missing, he might question his own memory. But two major things absent would surely tip him off to what had happened. Instead, Sandy carried the album into the narrow bedroom clothes closet, pushed aside the few jackets, crawled in, shut the door behind himself, and photographed both sides of the ID card. He then placed the original back in the album. Next, Sandy took aim on the birth certificate. From there, as insurance, he went page by page through the album, photographing everything. The Polaroid wasn't perfect but it did produce, for the most part, legible copies. Finished, Sandy stuffed the thirty-six photographs into his satchel along with the camera and all the used flashcubes, which he counted to make certain none had been left in the closet. After straightening the clothes, Sandy returned the leather album to its protective plastic bag, replaced it in its subfloor vault, reset the plywood lid and carpet padding, then flipped down the beige nylon shag before sliding the gargantuan mahogany cabinet back to its original location. He then replaced the drawers and double-checked his work. The room, the chest, and the carpet appeared untouched. He had done well.

Standing up, Sandy glanced at his watch and was shocked to discover that it was three minutes to four; he had been in Hoffmann's bedroom more than two hours. His first thought was for Paula, who must be terrified, having driven around for nearly four hours. But before leaving the house, he forced himself to go from room to room and double-check everything, just to make sure that nothing had been altered that would give Hoffmann a clue to what had transpired.

Only in the kitchen did Sandy find a problem. On the breakfast table, where he'd placed the contents of the freezer, lay a small puddle of water. Tearing off a couple of paper towels from the roll over the sink, Sandy mopped up the liquid and stuffed the wet paper into his tool bag. Moving to the dining room, he completed his work by sliding the glass panes back into the louvered window frame, which he then closed.

Compared with his entry, departing was easy. He simply opened the kitchen door, stuck his head out and checked that no one was watching, then stepped over the threshold and shut the self-locking door behind him. Moving silently, he darted up the side walkway to the garage, where he once again squatted low in the shadows to wait for Paula. Time, which had moved so quickly inside the house, now passed unbelievably slowly. Having done his job, Sandy wanted out of there. As he waited in the dark, his mind began to race over what he had accomplished. Could any court deny a conviction after seeing the Rava Ruska photo, the birth certificate, and Klaus Hagen's SS identification card? With these facts Sandy had the information to write the sort of article investigative reporters dreamed about. All he needed now was for Paula to show up and get him home. *Where the hell was she?*

Headlights moving slowly around the far street corner caught Sandy's attention. Was it Paula finally? Or could it be the cops?

As the two bright circles of light idled toward him, Sandy tried to distinguish between friend and foe. His signal to Paula was one blink of his flashlight, but he didn't want to give himself away if this were the cops. Sandy flattened himself belly down on the ground and watched the headlights move in slow motion toward him. Half a block away, the car was still unrecognizable.

Suddenly Sandy became aware of a living presence directly behind him — something was watching silently. Could it be Hoffmann? The police? A neighbor? An ODESSA killer? Without moving, Sandy concentrated on the observer's mysterious aura.

Surprising himself with his cool reaction, Sandy — the survivor — slowly inched his right hand back beside his body and slipped it into the satchel containing his Smith and Wesson. Releasing the safety and extracting the pistol, Sandy concentrated all his energy on the unseen presence, took one enormous breath, let it out, then moved like lightning, jumping to his feet, spinning around and pointing the barrel of his .38 at the enemy.

The huge emerald eyes of a startled tomcat stared at Sandy from the fence bordering Hoffmann's walkway. With a cavalier arch of his back and one macho hiss, the cat turned and leapt out of sight, into the darkness of the adjacent property. Releasing the grip of his pistol, Sandy reset the safety, slid the hunk of metal back into his satchel, flattened himself up against the side of the house, and once again tried to make out the identity of the headlights closing in on him. Cranked up from the cat-generated adrenalin flowing through his system with the force of a high-pressure firehose, Sandy found his ability to make subtle discriminations seriously impaired. Was it the police or Paula? As he waited and watched, his life seemed to hang in the balance.

Only when the slow-moving vehicle idled under the dim street light adjacent to Hoffmann's house could Sandy see that it was Paula and the Pontiac coming in for the rescue. Yanking out his flashlight, Sandy flashed it once. Paula immediately braked the big machine, turned into the German's driveway, and stopped. One millisecond later the passenger door swung open. Bolting from his hiding place with the speed of an Olympic gold medalist accelerating from the starting blocks, Sandy charged across the asphalt, dove into the passenger seat, and pulled the door shut.

"Go! Go! Go!" he whispered harshly to Paula.

Without panicking and without speaking, she shifted the automatic transmission into reverse, backed out of the driveway, and headed up the block. In only seconds they were motoring at the speed limit, almost out of the tract known as Sea View Estates.

"Sandy, my god, what happened to you? I thought you were never coming out! What took you so long?" Paula spoke quietly, close to hysteria.

"Just keep driving. And be quiet," he ordered as he knelt on the front seat and stared out through the rear window.

"Do you see something?" she squeaked in a whisper.

"I don't know." Sandy studied the darkness all around them. Except for their Pontiac, the road appeared to be empty. But that could just be what the police wanted them to think. It certainly was possible that they were being tailed by squad cars running with their lights off, or even helicopters high overhead. Sandy stuck his head out the window and searched the dark sky above the car.

"I don't see any choppers," he breathed to Paula as he removed his wool watch cap and tossed it on the floor of the back seat. Then, still keeping his eyes on the road, he untied the bags of tools, camera, and gun from his waist, peeled off his surgical gloves, grabbed a cotton towel from the seat, and wiped the grease paint from his face. He not only looked normal again, he felt twenty degrees cooler. If the police stopped him now, he reflected, at least they wouldn't immediately assume that he was a burglar.

Paula cranked the Pontiac around one final residential corner and headed south on the brightly lit main drag leading from Oxnard to the freeway. With the sudden illumination, Sandy could see for blocks in every direction. No cars were moving anywhere near them. As hard as it was for Sandy to believe, it was really beginning to look as if they were homeward bound, scot-free.

Paula accelerated up the wide concrete on-ramp onto the southbound Ventura freeway. When they reached a cruising speed of sixty-five miles an hour, the eight-lane freeway was virtually empty in both directions. At four-thirty on Sunday morning, the world was safely and happily asleep. Only exhausted lovers, a few truck drivers, and the truly desperate were out on the road. Among them were no local police or Highway Patrol. Finally, Sandy felt secure. Turning around, he sat down in his seat, fastened his safety belt, and for the first time took a good look at Paula. What he saw was a rarely exposed aspect of her: exhausted, emotionally remote, hanging on tight to the steering wheel, concentrating on the road.

"You okay?" he asked.

After one glance of suspicion, which he interpreted as fatigue, she nodded.

"You want to know what I found?"

Again she nodded.

In a euphoric monologue that lasted throughout the drive back to her apartment, Sandy gave her a blow-by-blow description of his search of Heinz Hoffmann's house and discovery of the German's true identity. Paula listened, saying little, as Sandy detailed his findings, swooping and soaring with fabulous plans for the article he would write and its consequences on the world.

Even back at her apartment, during a careful examination of the Rava Ruska photograph and the Polaroids, Paula said virtually nothing. Finally, she stacked the thirty-six pictures neatly while Sandy stood staring out the window at the exquisite dawn. It was one of those extraordinary moments to be remembered forever: Finally he had accomplished something impressive enough to ensure his place in the history books. At that moment of triumph, Paula turned to him and spoke.

36

"This is incredible stuff, Sandy. You really did a job in there. You should be proud of yourself. But I've been thinking about this article you want to write, and I'm not sure a newspaper story is the way to deal with this."

Sandy spun around, turning his back on the most beautiful sunrise he could remember.

"What you've found is big, important, and dangerous," she continued. "But I believe you need someone experienced to handle this. What you've got here," Paula gestured to the evidence, "is not just some intriguing facts, but the basis of a full-blown scandal. When you combine what you've discovered with the censored FOIA requests, you've got circumstantial evidence pointing directly at the fact that the U.S. government provided not only safe haven but citizenship for an SS war criminal. You're dragging some very nasty skeletons from some tightly sealed closets. What I'm sure made sense to some anti-Communist politicians and bureaucrats in the early fifties is going to look very bad today. These people aren't going to be happy with your story, and they are probably still in government—people with powerful connections. Some may be senators. Others may work in the State Department, the FBI, or even the CIA. They're going to try to cover their asses. And discredit yours. Sandy, if you publish this article, they're going to come down on you with everything they've got."

"What are you suggesting?" Sandy asked, confused. Her reaction was a total surprise, the opposite of what he would have expected. Something, he knew, was being kept from him.

"I believe you should face reality and turn over all this documentation to someone experienced at taking on this kind of political bombshell."

"Like for instance?"

"Simon Wiesenthal."

"We've already been through this, Paula. The answer is *no*."

"Will you at least talk to him; ask his advice? That's not unreasonable, is it?"

"What do you get, a finder's fee from this guy? Every time things get serious, suddenly you start talking about Simon Wiesenthal." Sandy was angry.

"I don't want to see you get hurt."

"Did you see me get hurt tonight?"

"I thought about it, believe me. Four and a half god-damn hours you were in that killer's house. What exactly do you think kept my mind occupied? That's precisely why I want you to call Wiesenthal."

"I'm not going to argue with you. But that's not the way this is going to be handled."

"Is it the credit you're worried about? If that's what's important, I'm sure Wiesenthal will let you have it all. From what I know about the man he has no ego whatsoever; he just wants to bring war criminals to justice."

"Thank you for your advice. But we have a little difference of opinion here and I'm still going to do things my way. You'll see, it's going to work out fine. Just like it did at Hoffmann's house."

Paula stood up, walked to the window, and stared outside at the fiery dawn light.

"For you, maybe; for me it was horrible. When you didn't come out after the second hour I began to imagine all the things that could have happened to you." She spoke to the window, keeping her back to Sandy. "What if Hoffmann had gotten the flu, stayed home, and let some other captain take his boat on the trip? If he caught you breaking into his house, you'd be sea food — cut up and packed in plastic, ready for the next trip out to Anacapa Island. You and I both saw the guy — it'd be you against a German grizzly bear." She turned to face him, tears forming in her eyes. "While you were in that house I made one of those death-bed deals with myself. If you came out of there alive I promised I'd never, ever — no matter what the reason — let you do something as foolish as risking your life for anything, much less over the exposure of a worthless old Nazi. I want you to swear to me now," she spoke through her tears, "that you'll never do anything like this again. I just can't take it. Will you promise me, Sandy, please?"

Moved by her affection and love, Sandy slipped his arm around Paula and pulled her toward him in an effort to surround her with physical reassurance. But before he could kiss her, she pushed him an arm's length away and held him there.

"I want you to promise me," she demanded fiercely through her tears.

"Paula, the danger's over. There's nothing to worry about."

"It's easy for you to say. I want that promise."

Her reaction to the danger at Hoffmann's house seemed to be the same as her paralysis on board the *Neptune*. This momentarily saddened Sandy, who saw her as being no different from so many other lawyers, living in clean, well-groomed, orderly little worlds in which they were masters of the rules. Those same attorneys, when taken out into the real, physical world of the streets, too often became overwhelmed, panicked, and useless.

"Sure," Sandy lied. "The last thing I want to do is cause you grief." As she relaxed he drew her toward him.

"What about the newspaper article?" she stopped him before he could kiss her.

"What about it?"

"Will you turn over your evidence to Simon Wiesenthal?"

"As you know, I have responsibilities to other people besides myself. First I'm going to write it all down while it's fresh in my mind. When that's done, there'll be a meeting before *we* decide what to do with it."

"But you'll consider what I said?"

"Absolutely. And I appreciate your concern. I know how difficult it was for you to tell me."

"You really do, don't you?" she said sincerely, happy for the first time that night, as she wrapped him in her arms and kissed him passionately.

In spite of the fact that he hadn't slept in more than twenty-four hours, her need for him, combined with his success at Hoffmann's house, awakened enormous reservoirs of sexual energy in Sandy. Upstairs in bed he felt aroused and potent beyond memory. For two hours straight they went at it, humping each other with a ferocity and endurance Sandy wouldn't have believed possible — a fitting end to a truly phenomenal night.

By nine in the morning Paula was spent, asleep in Sandy's arms. But he lay awake. Not since his *Heart of L.A.* days had he felt such unbridled optimism. Despite his exhaustion, he forced himself to stay up in order to enjoy this glorious state of mind. An idea drifted into his awareness. A desire. What he was considering astonished him: marriage to Paula, and children with her. To be able even to contemplate such a risk was in the realm of a miracle. Life was indeed a wonder, Sandy thought, as he fell into a deep and satisfying sleep.

37

Sandy's euphoria proved less enduring than he could have imagined. At eleven o'clock on Monday morning a phone call from Paula obliterated all his new-found joy. That morning he'd arrived at the plant very early, locked himself in his office, and continued organizing the article that he'd begun Sunday night after leaving her apartment.

"How's the world's most wonderful lover?" she whispered happily when Sandy picked up his private line.

"Still tired. But terrific. How are you?"

"For a woman in love and the bearer of exciting news, it could be a lot worse."

"What's happening?"

"Sandy, this is something you're just not going to believe."

"You won your LAPD lawsuit?"

"It's about you." Her voice bubbled with happiness.

"Me?" An edge of suspicion leaked into his voice.

"News isn't *always* bad, Sandy; I'd really like to be able to teach you that."

"You going to tell me or what?"

"Okay. But relax. This is good. I got a call this morning. It was about Uri. From a big muck-a-muck. In appreciation for everything you, as Uri, have done for the community, they want to honor you as the local Humanitarian of the Year. Isn't that fantastic?"

"When do *they* want to do this?" But Sandy had guessed the answer even before asking the question.

"On September 8, at a big fund-raising dinner for Beth-Israel Hospital. You and some businessman are the corecipients of the award." Paula could hardly contain her excitement.

A disaster of catastrophic proportions! September 8 was the date of the dinner honoring Nat at the Beverly Wilshire Hotel. Was it possible, Sandy hoped against hope, that a competing wing of the same hospital had coincidentally organized a conflicting charity dinner?

"Who's the businessman?" Sandy asked after a long hesitation.

"Gee, don't sound too enthusiastic; this is an incredible honor. People are telling you they really care about what you've done. More important than the money you've raised is the fact that you've reached so many young people and excited them about their Jewish heritage. You want to hear what they're inscribing on your award?"

Sandy said nothing, which Paula interpreted as an affirmative answer.

"You've, and I quote, 'inspired the imagination and conscience of the entire community.' Sandy, this is not just a compliment, this is a major *mitzvah* for you; even I'm impressed. And you know what I think about these kind of self-serving charity dinners. In this case they finally chose the right man to honor."

"You going to tell me who's the other guy they're honoring?" Sandy was so choked by fear he could hardly speak.

"It's actually a little funny," Paula said. "He's got the same last name you do: Nathan Klein, a wealthy manufacturer of pharmaceuticals. You know the type. A self-made immigrant who got rich and now in his old age gives away some of his money. For this the community rewards him. He's not by chance a relative of yours?"

"Never heard of the man," Sandy blurted in panic, so overcome with horror that he could hardly think.

"I wanted to ask the same question to the Mister Furgstein who called me on behalf of Beth-Israel Hospital. Sandy, don't you think it's about time for you to drop the Uri business and let people know who you really are? There couldn't be a more perfect opportunity."

"Paula," Sandy spoke forcefully, "I want you to hang up the phone, call this Furgstein back, and tell him thank you, but I absolutely cannot accept the award. Period. That's the end of it. No discussion."

"Sandy," she said sweetly, "you know, you're so predictable. You're like a kid with a new food on your plate; you won't eat it until someone makes you. And then, invariably, you like it. There's no need to call Furgstein back because I already accepted the invitation for you. This is a great honor, Sandy. People spend their entire lives working to get this kind of respect from the community. As your friend, your lover, and god knows what else, under no circumstances will I allow you to turn this wonderful honor down. And that's final."

"I want you to understand something," he raged, "not only will I *not* accept this award, I'm furious with you. You had no right to tell this Furgstein anything without consulting me."

"You really are the King of Stubbornness," she replied, unperturbed. "Ninety-nine percent of the men and women who are honored like this are only wanted because of their money; but you, they choose for the best reason — for your character. After what you've gone through and overcome, no one deserves the acclaim more than you do. How about for once in your life enjoying something instead of throwing it away?"

"Paula, you must have a hearing impediment this morning. I told you I won't even discuss this. I'm not doing it. Period. Final. No! No! And triple no! Just call Furgstein back and tell him you made a mistake. Tell him I'm unavailable. Tell him I'm out of the country on that date. Tell him anything you like but get me out of it, now. Is that clear enough for you?"

"You know," she said calmly, "you sound just like you did about that speech in Anaheim. I'm not going to go through this again unless you tell me why you won't accept this honor."

"Look, it's one thing making speeches to small, out of the way groups," Sandy tried to sound reasonable. "But it's a whole other story making myself into a public figure at some cockamamie bullshit fund raiser for self-serving bigshots. I have to keep out of the public eye; I told you that a long time ago. I'm not supposed to speak in public, as you know too. Even that article about the Nazi, I'm going to have to publish under a pseudonym," Sandy lied. "For me going public is just too dangerous and you're going to have to simply accept that fact. Now call Furgstein back and cancel. There's no alternative."

"No. If you won't reveal your *real* self, then accept the award as Uri. No one will know. Show up, get the award, say a few words and disappear."

"On this particular subject I have no flexibility. Rational arguments won't work. Pressure won't work. Nothing will change my mind. I know what I can and can't do and this is out. 0 . . . U . . . T. Now call the man back and cancel."

"Should I assume," she asked sarcastically, "that if I don't, the police are going to receive another bomb threat?"

Restraining his impulse to lash out at her, Sandy spoke quietly. "You know, given all we've been through the last couple of days I would think you'd have the generosity to stop punching below the belt."

After a long silence, Paula spoke quietly with great intensity. "Remember when you asked me to help you search the Nazi's house?"

Sandy grunted.

"Remember the condition you agreed to when I said I'd help you? I'm calling you on it now. This is an award I want you to receive *for me*. If you're an honest man and you love me, you have no choice but to do it. End of argument."

Sandy felt caught between the battering ram of his family and this steamroller of a woman. Like a trapped animal, he wanted to kill, maim, destroy. "Paula," he said softly, "I know the deal we made, but you're really not being fair with me."

"An agreement is an agreement. I called you with news that I thought you'd welcome as wonderful. And you trashed me. Well, I'm not going to let your pessimism drag me down. This honor *is* something terrific and you're going to see that by showing up and accepting it. And if by chance there's a bomb threat or some other weird last-minute outside intervention that cancels the event—even an act of God—you can just forget my name and forget that you ever knew me." Without another word Paula slammed down the phone, cutting him off.

38

"Dad, can I talk to you a second?"

Nat glanced up from the thick contract on his desk and scrutinized his youngest son standing in the office doorway.

"Sure, what's the problem?" Nat stuck a memo card into the page he had been reading, shut the bound stack of legal-sized papers, turned the contract face down, slid it to the side of his leather blotter, and smiled as if nothing but sincere, affectionate, paternal assistance was on his mind.

The problem, Sandy thought grimly, where do I even begin?

"Dad," Sandy tried to sound matter-of-fact, "I wanted to talk to you about our main speaker for the Beth-Israel dinner. I guess you know that on Friday night Charlie and I missed out on hearing that Uri guy — he got canceled by a bomb threat."

Nat nodded.

"Well, over the weekend I called Uri's lawyer — a woman named Gottlieb — and she made an appointment for me to meet the fellow yesterday in the bar of the Bel Air hotel."

The expression on the old man's face betrayed no hint of the fact that Furgstein had already arranged for Uri to speak and be honored at the dinner.

"I have to tell you," Sandy pretended to be embarrassed by the situation, "the man *is* a disaster. Now I understand why sometimes he gives a decent speech and the rest of the time is terrible, like the night I heard him."

His father maintained his opaque poise, giving away nothing.

"Get this. It's four o'clock on Sunday afternoon. I arrive on schedule; he's forty-five minutes late by the time he shows up with his lawyer. We introduce ourselves, sit down, and order a drink. I have a beer. His lawyer orders soda. And Uri calls the bartender by his first name and asks for *his usual*. From the freezer the bartender pulls out a bottle of iced Stolichnaya that's got a piece of tape across the label which I see reads *Uri*. Boom, our potential speaker takes his first of *four* double shots of iced Russian vodka. And this is the afternoon, remember. When the guy finally left he could hardly walk. Dad," Sandy fixed his father with a profoundly serious expression, "this is a guy we want to forget. I mean this is going to be the biggest evening of your life. The reputation of mother and the family is at stake, as you pointed out. Given what I saw yesterday, Uri's beyond a risk — the man is a guarantee of failure. You don't even want to consider the son-of-a-bitch."

Nat absorbed this information without any reaction. "You're *absolutely* sure of this drinking problem?"

"Dad, I saw it with my own eyes. Eight single shots of vodka in one hour. I was amazed he could even breathe, much less stand up. What he needs isn't a speaking engagement but a month drying out in a psychiatric hospital."

Again, the old man considered Sandy's words without any emotional response. "Let me ask you another question. Is it possible something happened to the man in the morning, like a personal tragedy, that was responsible for the binge? I've heard an awful lot of good things about him."

"The bottle had Uri's name on it; what does that tell you? The bum is a boozer. A fact is a fact. Even his attorney asked me not to spread the story around. What else do you need to know? I mean, we don't want an angry drunk speaking at your dinner. C'mon, Dad, there's just too much at stake here. I don't care how good Uri sounds when he's off the sauce; it's just not worth taking a chance. Think what a nasty drunk would do to our fund-raising. I say we shit-can the idea of Uri and move on; anyone's better than that scumbag."

"I'm afraid we don't have a choice," Nat said flatly.

"How do you mean?"

"Furgstein called me late last night. Woke me up, in fact. Yitzak Alon had just phoned from Tel Aviv. As much as the general would like to speak at the dinner, he's virtually certain now that he can't make it. With the Egyptians preparing for war, Alon has to stay in Israel. This morning Furgstein responded by calling Uri's lawyer and booking him for the dinner. The idea is that we're both going to be honored as Men of the Year. If buying two plaques instead of one raises more money, that's why we're there, right? His lawyer accepted and the press release has already gone out to all the papers. It's a *fait accompli*. What you're telling me about the man is a problem, but you're too late. Sandy, it's twelve-fifteen. You knew about Uri at seven this morning when we both walked into the building. Why didn't you come to me then with this information? *Then* we could have done something about it. *Then* we could have called Uri's lawyer. But now it's too late. Sandy, *you* wanted to be the executive in charge of this dinner. *You* wanted direct responsibility. And I gave it to you. Don't you know the first rule of a leader is to communicate? You could even have called me yesterday from the Bel Air hotel, and we wouldn't have any problem now. You want to be a leader and look how you communicate; what the hell is wrong with you?"

For a long moment Sandy said nothing. Attack, murder, and incinerate were reactions he forced himself to suppress. Instead of showing his true feelings, he made himself speak calmly and rationally. "Dad, as chairman of the dinner my job is not to relay every bit of bad news as soon as I hear it. In fact, since yesterday I've been phoning around trying to line up other potential speakers. I wanted to talk to you about something constructive, not just bring you negatives. But," at this point Sandy raised his voice in a theatrical anger, "since *you* found a speaker, *behind my back,* you obviously don't need me organizing this dinner. Thank you, it's been fun, but you're going to have to find another chairman because I quit. You want Uri, fine. But when he steps up to the podium, bombed out of his mind, and throws up roast beef and mashed potatoes all over the dais, don't talk to me about it because I won't be there." Sandy turned and headed for the door.

"Sandy, wait a minute. I'm sorry, you're right. But you don't know the whole story. Will you listen to me for a minute? It's not what you think. Sandy, come back here and sit down. You owe me the courtesy to at least listen."

Sandy stopped beside the closed door, faced his father, crossed his arms in judgment, and waited.

"Sit down, Sandy. Be reasonable."

But his youngest son didn't budge.

"Okay, have it your way. The rest of the story is this. When Alon called from Israel, canceling, Furgstein went crazy. Not with him but with me. All he could see was his whole cancer research center collapsing and the money drying up. The man panicked and called Uri's lawyer even before consulting me. By the time I had spoken to Furgstein, Uri had already accepted. Believe me, Sandy, when I tell you that this wasn't done to undercut you. You know Furgstein. The man is very emotional. But he cares. *He's* not perfect. *I'm* not perfect. And you know what? *You're* not perfect either. View this as a human error. You're a big enough man to do that, aren't you?"

"Dad, you tell a nice story. But let's get to the bottom line here. Unless Uri gets canceled as speaker, my participation as chairman or anything else ends the minute I leave this room."

"Okay, that's fair enough," Nat agreed after a moment's thought. "You find me another speaker and I'll personally invent a reason to get rid of Uri."

Smiling broadly, Sandy relaxed. "It's not going to be a problem; why don't you call his lawyer right now?"

"Sandy, you've had weeks to find a speaker, and so far you've come up with *bupkus*. The dinner's in less than two weeks. You want me to shit-can Uri—that's okay, I've agreed to that. But you've got 'til six o'clock this afternoon to come up with someone better. After that it's going to be too late to deal with the PR fallout."

"Dad," Sandy's anxiety returned full blown, "six hours isn't enough time. Give me two days."

Nat shook his head. "You want to get rid of Uri, you better find an alternative today."

"You really don't care about being made to look like a fool by that drunk?" Sandy attempted to intimidate his father.

"You're the chairman; I'm leaving it all in your hands."

39

"So, I haven't heard from you. I assume that tells me everything." Nat was speaking from the doorway of Sandy's office at two minutes to six.

Sandy looked up from the pages of handwritten lists spread across his desk. "Dad, I was just about to come to your office. Listen, I made a lot of calls but I've only been able to reach some of the people. If you could give me one more day, I think I could dramatically broaden our possibilities."

"Couldn't find anyone, hm?" Nat asked, unsurprised.

"I don't know," Sandy smiled wickedly. "I wouldn't exactly consider Peter O'Toole and Warren Beatty *nobodies*."

"Movie stars?" Nat was genuinely shocked.

Sandy nodded. "Think of the excitement one of them would bring to the dinner. Who's gonna miss Uri if they can have themselves photographed with the star of *Lawrence of Arabia?*"

"This is crazy; it's a hospital, not a movie premier."

"Dad, I took your advice and went for the bottom line. Don't think *actor*, think of the money that'll be raised."

"This name *O'Toole*. Or *Beatty*. These aren't Jewish, Sandy. Now if you got Eddie Cantor, this I could understand. Or Al Jolson. But a couple of *micks;* no way. We've got a Jewish hospital, a Jewish audience, and a kosher dinner. I think that says everything."

"Dad, if you want Cantor and Jolson we're going to have to have the dinner at Hillside Cemetery. I'm offering you a couple of live speakers — big stars — either one of whom will raise real dollars for the cancer center. That *is* the issue, isn't it? I mean, even King Faisal would be better than your alcoholic Israeli."

"Tell me why an Irish movie star would introduce a Jewish businessman, a complete stranger, at a charity dinner."

"It's simple," Sandy squirmed uncomfortably. "Movie stars need to eat like everyone else. For speaking they get an honorarium."

"Ah hah; an *honorarium,*" Nat spoke with a sarcastic glee. "Now I understand. And just how much *is* this little *honorarium?*"

"Dad, you can't view this simply as cash out of pocket; you have to think about it as an investment. How much do you raise *with* the movie star versus how much *without.*"

Nat nodded. "Yes, I agree with you two hundred percent. But now, just for my own curiosity, tell me, what is the amount, in dollars, we have to pay one of these big-shot movie stars?"

"You know, you really aren't looking at this correctly. It's like buying a new solid gelatin capsule machine; is the cost important in itself, or is the purchase price only relevant in relationship to the income the machine will generate?"

"Sandy, I appreciate the lesson in business principles. But I am not an idiot; I understand these things. What I am asking is a simple question: How much does it cost to have Peter O'Toole introduce me at the dinner?"

"You want a number?"

"That's a good start."

"It's not that simple; it's a proposal."

"Already it sounds too expensive."

"Then stick with the drunk; see if I care." Sandy gathered his notes together as if he were giving up.

"Listen, Sandy, I'm sorry. I want to know. Really. Tell me; I'm all ears."

Leaning back in his chair, Sandy pretended to evaluate his response. "Okay, but don't interrupt me until I give you the whole deal."

The old man nodded.

"This is how their agent at the William Morris Agency explained it to me. For a normal movie, each of the actors gets paid one million dollars. That's for six weeks of work. Per day that figures out to be $33,333. If we were hiring Peter O'Toole for his going rate, which is not what we're talking about here, we'd be flying him out first class from England, putting him up for a night at a five-star hotel, paying for his meals, then flying him back home. For that, his normal fee would be two days' pay plus all expenses, roughly seventy thousand bucks."

"I can't wait to hear the discount we're getting," Nat interrupted. "Seventy thousand bucks for fifteen minutes isn't ridiculous; it's insane."

"Dad, don't I recall you agreeing to hear me out?"

"Look, Son, I don't care how adorable the women find this Mister Peter O'Toole. From a room full of Jews, an Irish Catholic's not going to raise an additional $70,000. This I know for sure."

"You're right, and I couldn't agree more. But Peter O'Toole doesn't need to raise $70,000. You know why?"

The old man shook his head.

"A few years ago while making a film O'Toole was kicked by a horse and spent a week in Beth-Israel. Apparently the doctors were great, and Mister O'Toole agrees that our cause is so good that against the advice of his agent, he wants to cut his fee in half. For us and only for us he'll come out, introduce you, and fly home for the total, all-inclusive price of $35,000. It's a real coup, Dad — an unprecedented opportunity."

The old man nodded, humoring his son. "Sandy, I don't care how much of a pay cut Mister O'Toole is taking to do us a favor; under no circumstances will I give $35,000 so a mick with a cute face can introduce me to my friends."

Sandy smiled. "Okay. I knew this would be your first reaction. But now I want you to think seriously about it. If we publicize the fact that Peter O'Toole's going to be presenting you with the award, it's going to excite every woman coming to the dinner. I don't think you understand how much women love the glamour of movie stars. And Peter O'Toole's the best of the best. Every woman at the dinner's going to want to meet Mister O'Toole and have her picture taken with the man. I guarantee you that if Peter O'Toole makes a pitch for additional contributions, the women are going to press their husbands to come up with far more money than his fee will cost us. You gotta trust me here, Dad, this is something I understand. With Peter O'Toole, we can't lose."

Nat stared at his son. "Do you know how much $35,000 will buy in the real world of research medicine? Forget it, Sandy. I'm not throwing that kind of money away on a pretty face. Uri's free and I'm willing to take my chances. If he's a boozer, for a couple hundred bucks we can hire someone: a broad, a bodyguard — maybe both — that'll keep him off the sauce for twenty-four hours before the dinner. Worst comes to worst and he shows up drunk, Furgstein will introduce me. No matter how you look at it, that's a lot cheaper than $35,000."

Sandy shrugged. "Fine. You want Uri; you got him. I just hope for your sake he shows. Because, as I told you, I don't care. It's not going to be my problem because I'm not going to be there."

"The hell you're not!" Nat erupted in anger. "Sandy, god damn it, you made a commitment to me and you are going to see that commitment through, come hell or high water. So Uri isn't perfect; so what? I ask you again — *are you?* If you're so afraid of him drinking and not performing then *you* spend the day keeping him off the booze. The dinner was *your* idea and you got me involved in it, remember? It's your responsibility to finish it. You have the obligation, no one else. I don't care how you do it but I don't want to hear another word about Uri until I see him, sober, introducing me from the dais. Is that clear?"

"You ever tried to control a drunk, Dad?"

"You're an executive, Sandy — a leader. Your job is not to make excuses but to take charge. So do it." Turning, Nat burst out of the office and slammed the door behind him.

Sandy sat immobile, all of his self-loathing returned in force. He was being squeezed from all sides; he had no room to maneuver. His lies had gone full circle and were imploding in on him. He could never get the article written in two weeks, let alone sell it. Once his identity as Uri was exposed, he'd be humiliated and discredited and his case against Hoffmann would be impossible to present to the public: His work would seem the worthless ravings of a con artist and lunatic. He would be ruined forever.

Only one possibility emerged that would allow him to preserve his dignity. The new plan forming in his mind was a life-
threatening long shot, and just possibly the act of a crazy man.
Desperate times called for extraordinary tactics, he repeated to himself.
To do nothing meant being overwhelmed by events and losing
everything, including Paula. Exposure as an impostor would
bring down such rage and contempt that Sandy had no doubt he
would be better off committing suicide. To be seen as mocking
the Holocaust was perhaps the worst possible social crime, lower
than the anti-Semite neo-Nazis, more disgusting than the muti-
lators of Torahs, beneath the *kapos* and collaborators of Auschwitz. No, unless he preferred death, he needed to perform a
transcendent act.

40

Drums thundered ominously. Cymbals crashed in anguish. Violins shrieked with anxiety, terror, grief, physical torture, random massacres, and violent death. For hours, these sounds had bombarded Sandy as he sat in a mixing booth of the recording studio, watching through the triple-glazed window as Billy conducted fifteen musicians in the hyped-up melodramatic score for Kit Flynn's new horror film *Return of the Hollywood Werewolf*. After what Sandy had gone through that day, the composition took on a heightened personal meaning. It seemed not merely the music for a movie, but a grimly atonal theme to his own life story. Listening as it was played over and over again was agony, but he forced himself to sit through it because Billy was his last, desperate hope.

At 2:10 in the morning, the final track was laid down and the recording part of the process completed. Sandy waited as Billy thanked each of the players for their good work, then disappeared into the adjacent private office for a short meeting with the director. *C'mon, Billy, get your ass out here,* Sandy screamed telepathically.

Ten long minutes later, the door opened and Billy emerged with an obviously pleased Kit Flynn. After a ritual handshake and bear hug, the director departed. Seconds later, Sandy found himself following Billy out the back door, down the alley, and into the bar and grill next door. The all-night private club was packed with strange-looking men and women, all part of the late-night music business scene. At a small table on the edge of the crowded room, the two friends sat down where they could finally talk in private.

"So what did you think of my score?" Billy inquired.

"I was impressed; you've outdone yourself. And I was particularly interested in how you handled all that pressure. You've

293

really grown since the last time I saw you in the studio." Sandy forced himself to appear both calm and reasonable.

"Thank you." Billy shrugged as if it were nothing, but he was obviously pleased by the compliment.

"I want you to take a look at something." Sandy opened the briefcase he was clutching. "This is the result of the work you helped me with." On the table in front of Billy, Sandy spread copies of Klaus Hagen's SS identification card, his birth certificate, and the mass grave photograph linking the Nazi to the atrocities at Rava Ruska. As his friend examined the three incriminating documents, Sandy filled him in on his recent activities. Billy listened, saying nothing, and didn't react until Sandy had spelled out the entire nightmare of his current problem with Paula, Uri, and the shared Man of the Year award at Nat's upcoming dinner.

"You, my friend," Billy said with affection, "are truly in it up to your eyeballs. Can I ask you something?"

Sandy didn't object.

"A month ago you promised you'd tell her the truth; why didn't you?"

Sandy rocked his head backward as if he were suddenly compelled to compress knotted muscles running up his spine. "If I could explain it, I would. I did try. I wanted to. But I could never find the right moment." He straightened his neck, fixing his serious gaze on Billy's tired eyes. "The fact is that I'm where I am today and I'm desperate. I need your help with something. Can I count on that?"

"What sort of something?"

"You're my closest friend. I need you to just go along with me. You do trust me, don't you?"

"Of course I do. But I want to know what I'm getting myself into."

"Billy, c'mon. Don't do this to me. Be a *mensch*. Don't put me through a number. If the tables were turned and you came to me saying, 'Sandy, trust me and jump off this cliff after me,' I'd do it. I know you wouldn't lead me astray. That's friendship."

"Yeah, well," Billy spoke with sudden vehemence, "if we're such great friends how come in the last month you haven't once wanted to get together for dinner, or even for a drink? And how come you wouldn't risk introducing an embarrassment like me to your Miss Auschwitz? How many times have I called you this month? But did you ever phone *me?* I even invited you to the editing room, remember, to watch the rough cut of the movie. I wanted your input. But you were too busy, remember?"

"That night I had a commitment I couldn't get out of to speak in Bakersfield."

"Bakersfield; Durango, Colorado; Paris, France; it doesn't matter, Sandy. You want to pretend to be a victim of the Nazis that's fine; but if you want to be friends you've got to be there for me, too."

"You're really angry with me. I'm sorry." Sandy spoke with humility.

"You're god-damn right. For years we've had dinner together at least once, usually twice a week. We talk. We share our lives. Do things together. Then one night you tattoo your arm. Two nights later you meet a woman and we never have an honest, open conversation again. You call that a friendship?"

"Billy, you're right. I have no excuse," Sandy mumbled in shame. "Again, I swear I'm sorry. I know that saying I went crazy isn't enough, but it's the only explanation I have. I will tell you this: I've learned my lesson. If you help me now, you have my word that I won't ever disappear on you again. That's a promise, if such a thing still has any meaning coming from me."

After some thought and without making a commitment, Billy asked, "What is it, exactly, you want me to do?"

Controlling his sudden surge of optimism, Sandy laid out his plan. "As far as I see it, I have only one way out. I don't have time to write and publish my article, so what I have to do is take direct action. I want to physically capture Hoffmann and present him, alive, at my father's dinner, to the entire Jewish community. Think of the impact that'll have. It'll be like the Israeli capture and delivery of Eichmann. It's risky, I know, but it's the only way I'll be able to make it up to Paula for my lies. Yes, I've kind of misrepresented myself with this Uri business. No question about it. But it was in a good cause, and it wasn't intentional. The genius of exposing Klaus Hagen at the dinner is that my father, the community, Israel, and Paula are going to be so impressed that they won't be able to do anything but forgive and forget my deceptions."

"You thought this whole thing up yourself?" Billy asked, stunned.

"I knew you'd think it was brilliant."

"Sandy, remember a month ago when I told you that you were crazy?"

"Now you see how wrong you were."

Billy nodded. "Absolutely. Compared to this plan, your tattoo, your stories to Paula, and your impersonations as Uri seem like models of sanity. Are you really asking me to help kidnap an American citizen simply because it'll get you out of a jam with your girlfriend and your father?"

Stung by the attack, Sandy went on the offensive. "Hey, give me a break, don't trivialize my problems. We're talking about a mass murderer. A war criminal."

"Do you understand the concept known as *due process of law?* You can't just kidnap someone because you think he's guilty."

"We're not kidnaping the motherfucker; we're only carrying out an iron-clad citizen's arrest. You'll see, the district attorney will thank us."

"Yeah, I'm sure," Billy said, "with an extra helping of dessert in San Quentin. Sandy, you have to understand. I like my life. I have absolutely no interest in spending the next twenty years behind bars getting butt-fucked by psychopaths just because you've gotten yourself in over your head with some woman. Am I making myself clear?"

"Gentlemen, would you care to order?" the waitress interjected, pad and pencil in hand.

After a few disorienting seconds, Sandy ordered coffee, while Billy asked for a half-pound hamburger with mustard, catsup, pickles, onions, and relish, along with a beer.

After the waitress departed for the kitchen, Sandy tried another approach. "Look, honestly, I do understand you not wanting to endanger yourself; I don't want to get hurt either. You may not believe this, but jail really doesn't hold the least bit of attraction for me."

"Given what you're talking about doing, where else do you think you're going to end up?"

"Great accomplishments require risks. Whether you like it or not, it's a fact that capturing and exposing a German war criminal is big stuff. To pull it off would be to really earn yourself a place in history. Wouldn't you like that?"

"Of course. But I already have a place: I write music, remember?"

"You're comparing the capture of a war criminal," Sandy asked sarcastically, "with your score for *Return of the Hollywood Werewolf?*"

Billy shrugged, refusing to respond to that provocation.

"You're talking to someone," Sandy continued, "who knew you when you dreamed of writing symphonies. What happened to the part of yourself that wanted to stretch your limits, to be part of something larger, to strike a blow for greatness?"

"It still sounds wonderful. I mean it. But I'm older and less energetic. You're going to have to face something; I'm less ambitious than you. Maybe once I wasn't, but I am now."

The arrival of their food delayed what Sandy knew in his heart would be the inevitable last rejection of his plea for help. Once again overwhelmed by grief and despair, he was left sipping his coffee while Billy took a huge bite out of his three-inch-thick hamburger. Without Billy, Sandy knew he was doomed; alone, no one, not even John Wayne, could capture Heinz Hoffmann. How could he reach his friend? To end the meal without a commitment would be like a sentence of death. Each mouthful of hamburger moved Billy one swallow closer to the recording studio and Sandy that much nearer to suicide.

What had been trivial background bar noise seemed to grow in volume until Sandy felt himself drowning in drunken laughter, the clinking of glasses, the hollow pounding of leather shoes on the oak floor, all rushing along together to the beat of raucous rock music from the juke box. Worst of all were the noises Billy's white teeth made as they sliced and chewed their way through that pickle, bread, and hamburger. This was a muffled International Harvester in heat threshing its way through a field of ripe winter wheat. *I'm going crazy,* Sandy told himself as he drew slow, deep breaths in the hope of reducing his anxiety. But all he could hear was that hamburger. How could anyone chew with such volume? This was a hallucination, a psychotic break — after holding on for so long, his mind couldn't take it any longer.

Suddenly, without even knowing what he was doing, Sandy reached across the table, grabbed the burger from Billy's mouth, and threw it as hard as he could across the room, where it flew apart, smacked against the wall, and descended slowly to the floor, leaving a trail of mustard, catsup, and onions on the painted plaster.

"Billy," Sandy pleaded, "please, I'm begging you; *I need your help.* Don't abandon me. Please, Billy!"

Stunned both by his friend's action and by his tone, Billy didn't know how to respond.

The reaction from the bar was another story. Once the drunken patrons realized that the flying hamburger was not the beginning of a fight but only the action of a rowdy individual, they broke into applause, whooping loud rebel yells of approval. No one loves crazy behavior more than drunken rock musicians. Unfortunately the waitress had different priorities. She charged toward Sandy's table, enraged.

Before she could say a word, Billy stood to apologize. "Sandra, it's my fault and I'm sorry. It won't happen again, I promise. Now why don't you and the bartender have a couple of drinks on me; have dinner, too. What do you say; will you forgive your old friend Billy?"

Sandra could only stand staring, shaking her head in disbelief.

"And I know this might not be the best time to ask," Billy continued, "but when it's convenient — I mean I'm not in a rush — I'd love another hamburger. This time make it a cheeseburger. And you have my word I'll eat it with both hands. No more ground round Frisbees."

Reluctantly Sandra nodded, then grabbed a handful of napkins and crossed the room to clean the remains of the hamburger off the wall. In seconds the bar resumed its normal hum of activity. Billy sat back down.

"I have no one else to turn to," Sandy said, leaning forward and speaking in a grim, desperate tone. "I'm not exaggerating and I'm not being melodramatic, but without you it's the end for me. This is your oldest and closest friend in the world pleading for help. Alone, I don't have a chance. Planned right, with you, I can pull it off. Help me because you care about me; please Billy."

Sandy's desperation penetrated the shell of Billy's anger. Not to help his friend was unthinkable. Was there some way, Billy wondered, that he could cooperate with Sandy and at the same time steer him toward less insane behavior? Recognizing that Sandy was in a true crisis, Billy understood that he had no choice but to try.

"Okay," he said quietly. "I must be as crazy as you are; tell me what you want me to do."

"You're a real friend." Sandy's expression changed to one of euphoria. "You're great. Let me buy you a drink. Let me buy you ten drinks."

"I want to hear your plan." Billy's tone remained deadly serious.

Sandy nodded. "Just so there's no misunderstanding, you have a commitment from me, here, on my word of honor. After we pull this off, for the rest of our life, whatever it is you ask me to do, I'll be there, at your command. You name it, I'll do it."

"For starters," Billy probed, "how about finding some other way of getting out of this particular jam?"

"Believe me," Sandy smiled, "I'd like that, too. But there is no other way."

41

The next ten days barreled by in a frantic marathon of meticulous planning. Except for his passionate late-night rendezvous with Paula, Sandy's attention remained focused on the details of capturing the Nazi. All his other concerns receded far into the background.

Any other time, the on-going secret family manipulations at Vita-Line would have driven him crazy. Activities at the plant had become so unusual that even an idiot would have known the sale of the business was coming to a head. The clincher was that Charlie — the brother who normally never set foot in the factory — was now in daily closed-door meetings with Ed and Nat. In ten days none of this will matter, Sandy told himself, reflecting on the admiration and glory he would receive for his exposure of the vicious war criminal.

The ongoing meetings with the ballroom manager at the Beverly Wilshire were time-consuming, but a snap compared with the potentially lethal problem of capturing an SS murderer. One after another Sandy made quick, ingenious decisions resolving a host of knotty problems, many of them centering around the temperamental interior designer who created periodic uproars over the budget, the color scheme, the evening's theme, the floral arrangements, the table layouts, the location of the band and dance floor, and even the exact size of the dais. The seating arrangements for the 310 confirmed reservations added a whole new level of aggravation. Not only Sylvia but Nat himself joined in on the endless shuffle of names as virtually every ticket holder called to request front row center tables. Ultimately, the best seats were given to the movers and shakers, the sort of people referred to as "philanthropists." Known enemies, recently divorced couples, and other problem individuals were separated by as much space as possible.

In this mountain of detail, the only item of real importance to Sandy was the actual schedule for the evening's proceedings, which he needed to dovetail with his own plans for Hoffmann. Here, Sandy refused to compromise in his negotiations with the hotel, Sylvia, Nat, and Stanley Furgstein. With astonishing vigor, Sandy whipped his impressive vision of the program into shape. The only significant issue he lost was his last-minute attempt to convince Nat to drop Uri and hire Peter O'Toole. But the old man, like Paula, was obstinate. Uri stayed on the schedule.

The rest of Sandy's working hours were spent perfecting his complicated scheme for the capture and unveiling of the German. The most difficult part of the enterprise was the actual kidnaping. Once those logistics had been sorted out, the question became how to keep such a dangerous man captive for the forty-eight hours until the dinner itself. Sandy hated the idea of imprisoning the Nazi for two whole days, but there was little choice. The last moment the war criminal was vulnerable to capture was the Thursday night before the Saturday dinner. On Friday morning Captain Hoffmann would be gone, out to sea on his three-day weekend fishing expedition.

The abduction itself involved an unbelievable number of challenging and frightening obstacles. Compared with Sandy and Billy, the Nazi had many advantages: physical strength, combat experience, proficiency with a wide range of weapons, and undoubtedly years of well-formulated emergency escape contingencies. In the realm of the brute animal, the war criminal was king. Sandy's bold and clever scheme capitalized on his one asset: the element of surprise.

Despite his promises to the contrary, Billy questioned each decision, attempting to undermine Sandy's faith in the operation. The rationale for this nit-picking and potshotting was Billy's desire to ensure that every potential complication was anticipated and eliminated. As a result, the rehearsals were a war of nerves between the two friends. They accomplished what needed to be accomplished, but only because of Sandy's super-human patience and strength of purpose.

And oddly, for reasons that took some time to become clear, passion between Sandy and Paula escalated to new heights that week.

Only moments after entering her apartment, Sandy would find himself drawn to Paula's half unbuttoned blouse and her firm, eager nipples. Seconds later his fingers would slide up under her skirt, undulate over and inside of her already wet bikini underwear, and go to work on her inflamed clitoris. In the time it took to make a few circular strokes, Paula would begin moaning, thrust her pussy against his hand, and come in a rush. Often she'd then slip off her skirt, yank down her underpants, and make him enter her from behind while she remained dressed in her silk blouse, nylon stockings, high heels, and Italian sports jacket.

Although the phenomena was never discussed, it was clear to Sandy that they were addicted to each other in some mutual, secret way. Eventually he came to understand that their need centered around one word: *death*. Every aspect of their relationship was involved with death. On his arm was *A7549653*, the death camp number. They had met over his near-death in the grocery store. She was preoccupied by the Holocaust and the obliteration of her family at Auschwitz. And now, floating over everything, was the unspoken but palpable danger inherent in capturing the war criminal. Death was the catalyst of their eroticism.

42

On Thursday afternoon, the last half mile up Sunset Plaza Drive was charged with the grim aura of a suicide mission. Sandy felt himself to be the Jewish-American equivalent of a *kamikaze* pilot accelerating down out of the sky at full throttle toward his one and only engagement with the battleship *Missouri*. The sole difference, he feared, between his own mission and the *kamikaze*'s lay in the machine he guided: Instead of a bomb-laden airplane he was behind the wheel of a dark blue 1971 Dodge sedan, once again rented for ten dollars a day and ten cents a mile from Bundy Rent-A-Wreck.

Sandy honked twice as the Dodge rolled to a stop at the bottom of Billy's driveway. Immediately the door of the house flew open and Billy emerged disguised for the kidnaping, completely unrecognizable. Billy was wearing a cheap gray polyester suit, white button-down shirt, dark blue tie, black socks, and freshly polished black wing-tips. His hair, which normally had the inflated, ragged quality of Albert Einstein after a drunken binge, was not only trimmed but slicked down and cemented into place with Dep styling gel. Showered and clean-shaven, he appeared to be an underpaid and overworked Fuller Brush salesman. Billy opened the passenger door, set his regulation Samsonite briefcase on the floor, sat down, shut the door, and fastened his seat belt.

An overwhelming odor set off a surge of terror in Sandy. Billy smelled as if he'd just taken a bath in a fifty-five gallon drum of Old Spice.

"So, do I look okay or what?" Billy mumbled.

"Great, perfect." Sandy assessed his friend. Booze (and the accompanying corrupted sense of judgment) was the most obvious explanation for the industrial-strength stench. Despite his friend's promise to be alcohol-free for two days preceding the operation, Sandy entertained serious doubts.

"I feel like a god-damn fool," Billy said bitterly.

"There's not a person in the world who wouldn't believe you aren't the perfect salesman." Sandy watched his friend for tell-tale signs of drunkeness.

Billy shrugged, betraying nothing but anxiety.

"You have everything with you?" Sandy asked. "The brochures? The Mercedes literature? The Polaroid camera? The . . . ?"

"It's all in the briefcase," Billy interrupted coldly.

"How about, just to make sure, we run through the list one final time?"

Billy glared. "How about we don't. I'm sick of the god-damn list; I've already gone through it six times today. Believe me, I'm too frightened to leave anything out."

"It wouldn't make you feel good to go over it one last time?"

At the limit of his patience, Billy scrunched his eyes into angry slits. "At some point today you're going to have to trust me. I say you start now by driving out of here and getting this lunatic mission over with."

Nodding, Sandy turned the ignition key, put the car in reverse, backed up the long driveway, and headed down the hill to Sunset Boulevard. A left on Laurel Canyon took them over the Hollywood Hills into the San Fernando Valley. Another left elevated the big Dodge onto the northbound Ventura Freeway.

At sixty-five miles an hour with the air-conditioning on full blast, the hundred-and-one degree heat of the smog-ridden Valley was hardly noticeable. On the radio, Alan Price began singing the first bar of his cynical hit song, *O Lucky Man*. Instead of talking, Billy turned up the volume and hummed along. But Sandy flicked the radio knob counter-clockwise, cutting off the music.

"Hey," Billy protested, "if you don't mind, I like that song."

As his friend reached to turn the radio back on, Sandy blocked his hand. "I think it's more important we run through what you're going to say."

"Sandy," he said angrily, "give me a break, will ya? I mean, you and I have gone over this a hundred times in the last week. *Relax.*"

"Just once more. It'll help your confidence."

"Thank you, but my confidence is fine," Billy hissed. "Why don't you just shut up and drive and let me listen to the radio?"

Surprised by Billy's vehemence, Sandy backed down and drove on in silence. As Alan Price once again began to warble through the single speaker, Sandy's anxiety increased ten-fold. Billy is acting too weird, he thought. Out of the corner of his eye he glanced at his sullen friend.

"What?" Billy demanded.

"What *what?*" Sandy feigned innocence.

"You're staring at me."

"Oh, you know how I am. I was just double-checking your appearance."

"Bullshit. You believe I've been drinking; admit it."

"You don't think that's a legitimate concern?" Sandy hedged.

"No, I don't think that's *a legitimate concern,*" Billy mocked him. "You have no reason not to trust me."

"I'm sorry, but with so much at stake today I have to question everything. In case you forget, my life is riding on this."

"Sandy, I know just as well as you do this isn't a kindergartner we're playing with in Oxnard. If he starts shooting, I bleed just the same as you. And if the cops bust us I have a lot more to lose than you do. You *have* to do it; I don't. I'm here because you're my friend and you begged me to help. There's nothing I'd love more than a drink — except maybe ten drinks. But I'm too scared. I don't want to die and I don't want to go to jail. Now are you satisfied?"

"Explain one thing to me. What's with the cologne? You smell like an old whore trying to cover up a two-week orgy."

Blushing, Billy swiveled in his seat and stared out the side window, away from Sandy, at the passing houses below the freeway in Sherman Oaks.

"You're not going to answer me?"

Turning back toward Sandy, Billy spit out the words in a mixture of anger and embarrassment. "You don't know this about me. No one does. But I'm one of those guys who sweats when he's nervous. Not the normal amount—I'm talking *extreme*. It's humiliating. Something makes me anxious and ten seconds later my shirt looks like I've walked through a car wash. I've gone to doctors. I've tried all sorts of medications. Nothing works. *Overactive glands*, they call it. Maybe that's why I'm so thin. Maybe that's why I have such a great capacity for booze. I have an unusual metabolism. That's why I poured on the Old Spice. Maybe I overdid it. But isn't that better than having the Nazi smell my fear?"

Sandy nodded. "Thank you."

Astonished, Billy stared at Sandy for half a minute before speaking. "*Thank you?* I admit something like this about myself and all you can do is dismiss me with a *thank you?*"

"I needed to understand. Now it makes sense. What else is there to discuss?"

"Hey, asshole, how about a little compassion?" Billy was furious.

"Okay, you're right," Sandy admitted after a moment's reflection. "I'm under a lot of stress and I was wrong. I'm sorry. Forgive me?"

"Thank you."

"Can we get back to business now? I want to go over a few details."

The thought of doing another rehearsal was too much for Billy, who rolled his head around on his shoulders in an attempt to dissipate his angry tension. "Sure," he finally said, "but first let's stop for a drink."

"God damn it Billy, I told you . . ."

"Hey, lighten up, I'm only kidding. It's a joke. What happened to your sense of humor?"

"This isn't the time for jokes."

"This is *exactly* the time. Things are so serious right now the tension's going to kill us before we ever get to Oxnard."

"That's why I thought we should run through our contingency plans."

"Do whatever you want," Billy growled. "But do it to yourself. I've got other things to think about." Closing his eyes, Billy slid down in his seat and rested his head against the window, ending the conversation.

Maybe Billy is right, Sandy thought. Maybe I am too tense. Too much is riding on this trip. I'm uptight. My anxiety is creating new and greater problems. Attempting to calm himself, Sandy thought back to the strange and confusing last night he had spent with Paula.

"What I'm concerned about is our future," she had said over the Maine lobster and steamed artichokes he had brought in an attempt to make a festive dinner out of what might easily be their last supper together.

"What about it?" he asked flatly. Sandy had wanted this dinner to be perfect, to stand out in case something went wrong during the kidnaping, he and Billy ended up as fish food, and no one ever heard from them again. In hindsight—after his disappearance—he hoped she might realize that this meal had been his attempt to say good-bye.

It was another interesting idea, Sandy reflected, except that it wasn't working. Paula seemed distracted, anxious, and irritable, barely picking at what he knew to be her favorite dinner. Even Watergate and Judge John Sirica's imminent order forcing Nixon to surrender the incriminating tapes failed to engage her interest. Clearly something even more important was on her mind.

"You do realize," she suddenly announced, "that you never talk to me about the future. I don't even know if you think we *have* a future together."

"This is what's bothering you tonight?" Sandy spoke skeptically.

"Partly."

"What's the rest of it?"

"First tell me if you think we have a future together," she replied hesitantly.

"I've no doubt about it; you're the absolute best thing that's ever happened to me."

"So I'm a *thing?*"

"Paula, give me a break. You know what I meant. I love you."

"It seems to me a person can love someone and still know that they don't have a future together."

"This comes from the woman," Sandy teased, "who's continuously setting conditions and giving me ultimatums. 'Speak at the dinner or I'll leave you. Tell the world about your experiences in Auschwitz or I'll leave you. Tell me about your past or I'll leave you.' It seems to me I'm the one who should be worrying about our future."

She stared at him.

"Why can't you just accept me for who I am and stop judging me? If you really want a future with me, quit threatening to dump me if I don't live up to your standards."

"For us to have a future together, that's all I have to do?" she asked incredulously.

"Simple, hm?" Sandy smiled.

Paula nodded. "Then you won't mind having dinner with me Friday night. I made a reservation at Scandia: a table for four." She hesitated. "My parents are coming to town, and I'd like them to meet you."

He stared at her, too surprised to speak. In his wildest dreams, he wouldn't have anticipated this bombshell.

"The reservation's for eight o'clock. Is that good for you?"

"I don't understand. You've been planning this behind my back and you waited until today to tell me! If you wanted to teach me to trust you, this is *exactly* the wrong way to go about it!" He was hurt and angry.

"They're my parents, Sandy. I didn't find out until this morning that they were coming. I figured why worry you until I knew for sure. It has nothing to do with trust. You say you want a future with me; sooner or later you're going to have to meet my parents."

Before responding, his mind raced over the terrible risks in getting together with her parents the night before the cancer center fund-raising dinner. He knew he would be crazed trying to deal with his Nazi prisoner as well as all the last-minute details of the gala. In the midst of all that chaos and danger, to sit and make small talk with two survivors of Auschwitz seemed inconceivable. Getting through that situation would have been close to impossible in the best of circumstances. It was one thing to deceive college kids about his past; real survivors, he was certain, would spot him as an imposter in two seconds.

"Paula," he said bitterly, "your parents haven't set foot outside Manhattan in twenty years. Now suddenly they're jet-setters, off on a mad fling to Southern California?"

"What can I say; they missed their daughter. It's just a dinner, Sandy." Her voice betrayed an edge of anxiety.

"So they're simply coming out here spontaneously. Okay, I'll accept that story and will totally forget my paranoia if I hear from your lips that they're also *spontaneously* going home on Saturday morning and don't know about the dinner honoring Uri that night."

Tears formed in her eyes. She gave it her little-girl-caught-with-her-hand-in-the-cookie-jar best and smiled submissively. "Don't be angry with me, Sandy, please. They're just two old people who want to be proud of their daughter's boyfriend. Is that so terrible?"

"For them, no. But for you and me, yes. This is a betrayal. It's bad enough I'm exposing myself in public for that idiotic award. But sneaking your parents in; this is unforgivable, Paula. You had no right and you know it. You want them out here to meet me. Fine. I'll agree to that, no problem. But not this weekend. Tell them next week, after the dinner, when I'm not under so much pressure."

"Sandy, in an audience of three hundred and ten, two more people won't even be noticeable."

"I'm asking you nicely. I told you we had a future together. And I told you I was willing to meet your parents. But for god's sake, have some respect for my feelings, too, and get them to hold off their trip for one week."

"But you're receiving this great honor. Think of what it will mean to them, how impressed they'll be. They've read about your public success as Uri and they're proud of what you've done. They're coming out here precisely because of that: They want to meet you. If it weren't for the award dinner, they'd stay in New York and wait for us to visit them. This is an opportunity not just to introduce yourself to my parents but to really impress them from the beginning by getting things started with a real bang."

A real bang is what it will be all right, Sandy lamented silently. Even so, he couldn't deny that Paula's argument made sense — for her. For him, however, it was a different story. As he tried to figure a way out of this new nightmare he felt lost, dizzy, and sinking.

"Am I right to assume you told them that Uri's real name is Sandy Klein?"

"No one else is going to know. I made them promise. And I didn't tell them who you work for. I said you were in pharmaceuticals."

"What about your promise not to reveal my identity to anyone? What happened to that?" he accused.

"They're my parents, Sandy. And I did swear them to secrecy. You have nothing to fear, I guarantee you."

Oh sure, Sandy thought. What a relief to know I have no problems. It wasn't as if he had any leverage over her parents, like he had over Larry Carton. Carton knew that Sandy was Uri; but he also believed that Sandy would think nothing of physically injuring or even killing him if he betrayed Sandy's identity. Dr. and Mrs. Gottlieb, however, would not respond well to such intimidation.

"Paula," Sandy said quietly, making an enormous effort to control his anger, "I'm not saying I don't want to meet your parents. In fact I'm happy to get to know them. But I want it to be *next week,* not tomorrow."

Like a judge, she nodded repeatedly as she considered the request. "I'd like to go along with you. But I need to understand why. I can't ask them to change their plans over nothing."

"You're telling me, that a straightforward request from the man who loves you is *nothing?*"

She shrugged, indicating that her hands were tied and she couldn't help herself; more information was necessary.

To Sandy, the gesture seemed characteristic of everything wrong in their relationship. So much was wonderful between them that he had forgotten the depth of her self-righteous, superlogical, stubborn inability to trust. Would she ever be capable of responding differently? From the beginning, she had been forcing him into behavior that threatened his very life. Her tactics over her parents' visit were no different. The time had come, Sandy knew, for a line to be drawn—a line that she couldn't cross. This had become a state of emergency. As much as he hated to fall back on his big guns, he simply had no choice.

"Paula," he leaned across the table and squeezed her hand in both of his. "You know I love you. You know I trust you. We've already been through so much together. I want you to trust me. I want your parents to trust me. And I definitely want us to have a future together. I know this is kind of an awkward time to say this—I had planned to do something a little more romantic—but you seem to be having such doubts about me that I feel I have to convince you now, tonight, of my commitment to you. I'm sorry to spoil some of the fun by doing it this way but . . ." He stood, walked around the table, and knelt down on the floor by her chair, all without letting go of her hand. "I not only love you, I hope you'll do me the honor of becoming my wife. Paula, will you marry me?"

For quite some time she sat without moving, too shocked to respond. Finally she spoke anxiously. "You're asking me seriously?"

"Absolutely."

"You're not trying to manipulate me?"

"Not at all."

"What about my parents?"

"What about them?"

"You still want them to stay in New York for one more week?"

"This has nothing to do with them. They can do what they want. It's *you* I'm concerned about. It's *you* I want to trust me. Perhaps if you married me, you might. Sometimes, you know, I really think you forget how much I love you."

Paula dropped his hand, stood, and went to the kitchen, where she filled the espresso machine with water.

"You want coffee?" She sounded not just distracted but actually confused.

"That'd be wonderful," he responded. He knew he was manipulating her, but it wasn't as if he didn't want to marry her, he told himself. It was a question of timing. She was the one who had forced him into lying, when all he had wanted to do was remain anonymous. *Everything that's mine is mine; everything that's yours is negotiable,* was her credo. Life had to be on her terms or else it was unacceptable. That kind of love might not be the unconditional love he craved, but it was the only love he had, and there was no choice but to make the best of it. At the Beth-Israel dinner, his own family would have an enormously difficult time swallowing the unveiling of the Nazi. Only the approval of the community would overcome their initial horror and embarrassment at his shocking breech of decorum. For Paula, that same moment would be particularly painful because all his lies would be revealed in front of both her and the public. Ultimately, he had convinced himself, the good would outweigh the bad and she'd come to accept what he'd done. What her parents' presence would do to the equation, however, was an unknown and worrisome quantity.

"Sugar?" Paula called from the kitchen.

"No, thank you," he answered. She knew how he liked his coffee. Was she really that distracted?

After setting a white demitasse cup of espresso on his place mat, Paula sat down across from him and stirred a tiny spoonful of sugar so forcefully into her own cup that Sandy feared the china would fracture.

"Let me ask you something," she said finally. "Do you still want to marry me even if my parents come out on Friday?"

Sandy nodded. "But I'd be a liar if I didn't tell you it'd make a big difference to me if they waited until next week."

"And much as I'd like to please you," she continued, "I just can't ask them to change their plans on one-day's notice. Really, it would be too difficult for them."

"Correct me if I'm wrong." Sandy made an enormous effort to remain calm. "Your parents are retired. They live in a co-op, alone, with no pets or obligations. All they have to worry about is watering the plants. What's so difficult about shifting their plane reservations one short week?"

"Because they know about you, the dinner, and the honor. That's why they're coming. There's no way in the world I can explain *that* away."

"Paula, you're making me feel like I'm talking to a stone wall."

"You should try talking to yourself some time. I still don't understand why I should hurt two old people by denying them the pleasure of seeing you receive this honor. Make that clear to me and I promise I'll do exactly what you want."

Around and around we go, he reflected in despair. It was no wonder he'd resorted to such extreme solutions; the woman was simply incapable of accommodation. "Look, I'll admit there are a few loose ends," he said. "But I promise I'll tell you everything on Sunday. *And* it'll all make sense. Why not go easy on both of us and just accept that fact?"

"Because you know it's not in my nature; I need evidence."

"What about the fact that I love you?"

Paula shrugged.

"Wanting to marry you doesn't count either?"

Paula's silence said everything.

"You are impossible," Sandy muttered bitterly.

"I thought you liked that about me," she teased, sensing victory.

This time Sandy shrugged.

"Do you still want to marry me?" Her tone was both affectionate and seductive.

"Is that a question," he asked sarcastically, "or are you condescending to accept?"

"Neither. I want to think about it."

"What's to think about? You're crazy about me. You want me to meet your parents. So what's the big deal about marrying me?"

"I want to hear about your *loose ends* first. Then I'll give you an answer."

"You really are a very hard woman," he said sadly.

"I can't help my nature," she said without shame.

Having reached a stalemate, both Sandy and Paula sipped the last of their espresso as they contemplated the situation.

"So," he broke the awkward silence, "what did we finally decide about your parents?"

"I told you." She smiled sweetly as if nothing could possibly be the slightest problem. "I have an eight o'clock reservation at Scandia and I'd appreciate it if you'd wear a tie. You know how people are who grew up in Europe before the war — they're very traditional."

"Isn't there any way I can get you to consider changing your mind?" He made one last, weak attempt.

"Sandy," she said gently, "you're going to like my parents. You'll see; they're not nearly as bad as you think. In fact, most people find them very charming. Aside from me and the camps, you do actually share a lot in common. They have the same problem you do with new people and new situations. I'm sure it's the result of what you all went through. I have to do the same thing with them that I do with you and continually remind them that despite their fears, life isn't *always* bad. I mean, look at us, for instance. Would you ever have expected to enjoy yourself like you've been able to do with me?" Paula glowed, savoring her final triumph.

Overwhelmed by the mountain of insurmountable problems he faced, Sandy could only fake a smile as he shook his head.

His response was enough to encourage Paula to come around the table behind his chair, wrap her arms around his rigid neck and shoulders, and begin nibbling on his ear.

"You keep asking me to trust you," she whispered. "You have to trust me too, you know."

Sandy only shrugged.

"Meeting my parents is like when you were first afraid to speak out about your Holocaust experiences. You're going to actually enjoy them. And I know they'll adore you. Like I do."

Unconvinced, Sandy could only nod.

Paula, however, was undeterred and continued to kiss and nuzzle him. "I don't want you to take this as a yes or a no," she purred into his ear, "but I'm very excited about your proposal. In a million years I never would have guessed you'd ask me that. I'm still knocked out by it; I mean it." Her fingers slipped beneath his shirt and playfully began to caress his chest. "Shall we go upstairs?"

As much as he tried to let himself feel sensual, his anxiety prevented him from connecting with his flesh. Once in bed, Paula made a series of valiant efforts, but nothing aroused him. Even her magnificently skilled mouth on his shrunken penis and balls failed to make the slightest difference. He had become a depressed sack of body parts totally disconnected from his mind. It wasn't as if he didn't want to respond to her; more than anything he would have enjoyed linking up with her passion. But he was powerless to stop his brain from ruminating over the next seventy-two hours. Eventually Paula sensed the impossibility of her efforts, rolled over, and contented herself with a simple cuddle.

"Goodnight," she kissed him on the lips. "I'm sorry you're still angry with me."

Sandy gave her a hug. "Sleep well."

Paula nodded, closed her eyes, and in moments was breathing slowly and regularly, fast asleep.

Fully awake, Sandy studied her. Illuminated only by moonlight, she appeared calm, gentle, and lovely. This could be the last time I ever see her, he told himself, trying to fix every detail of her appearance in his mind. I am a true *schlimazel*, Sandy castigated himself. If things went wrong in Oxnard, her last memory of him would be that as an angry lover with a limp, shriveled cock. Why a *schlimazel* and not a *schlemiel*? The distinction was most clearly expressed in an old Yiddish joke. A *schlemiel* is a person who spills his soup; a *schlimazel* is a more hopeless fellow who spills the soup on *himself.*

Stretching out beside her soft, sleeping body, Sandy wrapped Paula in his arms and allowed everything wonderful about her to flood his memory. As he wriggled closer, the warmth of her body relaxed his tense muscles. Soon the familiar ache of sexual longing made its way down his abdomen, stirring the activity she had tried so hard to encourage.

Lying on her left side with her back to him, Paula remained undisturbed, breathing slowly and regularly. As he wriggled his body into a configuration identical to hers, Sandy attempted to make maximum contact and unite every molecule of their flesh. He wanted each individual fiber of his body and soul to connect with her every capillary, artery, and nerve ending. But no matter how perfectly he conformed to her, she remained a separate person, detached and deeply asleep.

Taking a more aggressive approach, Sandy released his grip on her torso, rotated his body a hundred and eighty degrees, crawled head first into the tropical heat under the covers, grasped Paula's ankles, and slowly spread her legs. Then he lowered his mouth onto her vulva and went to work with his tongue on the flesh surrounding her vagina. As the tender tissue began to swell, Sandy curled his lips and tongue around her hard clitoris and quickened the rhythm of his caresses. Stirring noticeably, she nevertheless did not wake up. Perhaps his actions were only stimulating an erotic dream.

Picking up the pace, Sandy alternated his sucking with a gentle raking of his teeth across her clitoris. Despite her quiet moans of excitement, she remained asleep, disconnected. As he continued the skillful work with his mouth he began to feel her familiar passion coming to a head. From her response he knew it would be only moments until she imploded in an orgasm that would leave her drained, satisfied, and even more deeply asleep — exactly the opposite of what he wanted. Suddenly withdrawing his mouth, tongue, and fingers, he left her starved of stimulation. But she surprised him. Stretching her right arm down over her belly, Paula curled her strong fingers around her pussy and manipulated her clitoris and vagina in an urgent effort to satisfy herself.

The sight of this woman so deeply obsessed by her passions instantly jacked up Sandy's own state of arousal. Did it really matter if she were awake or asleep? He was mesmerized by the sight of her hips writhing in languid circles while her fingertips manipulated her damp, swollen pussy. Aroused to the point of bursting, Sandy no longer cared about her state of consciousness. Awake or asleep, he had to have her.

Swinging back around, Sandy hoisted himself over Paula, removed those dexterous fingers from her pussy, and slid his demanding erection deep within the dripping folds of her vagina. Moving slowly in and out, back and forth, around and around, Sandy felt transformed, at peace with the world, enveloped, comforted, and protected. Why couldn't life always be like this?

"Oh Sandy," Paula suddenly commanded, "fuck me with that huge dick of yours."

Paula was indeed awake and more excited than ever as she shifted gears and began to pound the inflamed tissues of her vulva against Sandy's highly responsive pelvis.

"Oh, Sandy, give it to me," she screamed, "fuck me hard!"

At that moment Paula came with such power and passion, thrusting so violently, that all restraint was sucked from Sandy. The sperm which had so fully inflated his prostate now exploded forth.

"Oh that's it. Shoot it *all* into me," Paula commanded as she squeezed his balls and thrilled to the potent spasms filling her.

"Paula, fuck me," he moaned. "Fuck me. Fuck me. Fuck me, I'm coming," Sandy screamed as he thrust himself against her.

In seconds, all blissful feelings had vanished and everything Sandy had feared returned with a new power. After the last orgasmic shudder, despair flooded each cell and crevice of his brain. Once again disaster loomed everywhere, inevitable.

In only seconds, Paula's whole being changed from the essence of sensuality into dead weight, pressing down on Sandy's legs, cutting off the circulation in his right thigh like a tourniquet. *Glug-clunk, glug-clunk, glug-clunk* went his heart in a heavy rhythm, beating out the few remaining moments before his appointment with death in Oxnard.

In one smooth motion Sandy eased off of Paula, stretched out on the bed, and cuddled against her from behind. Feigning exhaustion, he said nothing and she drifted peacefully back to sleep.

Slowly and carefully, in order not to disturb her, Sandy slipped his left arm out from under her head, eased his grip on her body, and sat up, fully awake. Barely legible in the dim light, but compelling nevertheless, was that infernal tattoo—*A7549653,* the source of all his troubles. If only I had cut it off, he fantasized, unable to sleep, as his thoughts vacillated for the rest of the night between the unbelievable consequences of that tattoo and the details of his upcoming confrontation with the Nazi war criminal.

A nasty electronic buzz from the alarm interrupted both his own grim ruminations and Paula's sleep. Frenzied as usual, she raced around the apartment, showering, dressing, making coffee. Only after she had loaded her briefcase and was almost out the door did she notice the exhausted and miserable expression on Sandy's face.

"Hey," she kidded tenderly, "don't take yourself so seriously. You're going to like my parents. Trust me."

Sandy nodded in an effort to placate her.

"I gotta go." She kissed his unresponsive lips. "Don't forget to lock up when you leave."

"Paula," he said with arresting gravity, "there is something I have to tell you. I've got a meeting tonight. It could go very late, so if you try to call and can't reach me, don't panic. I'll talk to you tomorrow. And just remember that no matter what happens, I do love you."

She smiled, misconstruing his meaning. "You're so silly," she teased. "Nothing's going to happen. The dinner's going to be a piece of cake. How could they not fall for someone as lovable as you?"

"You're very sweet," he rose to the occasion. "And very beautiful this morning. I hope we both have a great day."

"Hey, I can't miss," she bragged. "I feel wonderful. And you know why?" Paula grinned broadly. "Some guy showed me a great time last night." Flashing him a seductive wink, she picked up her briefcase, descended the stairs, and was out the front door.

Would he ever see her again? The question only made his drive north to Oxnard that much more difficult.

"Lemme ask you a hypothetical question," Billy interjected out of what seemed like left field. "I mean, just for purposes of discussion."

Startled from his reverie, Sandy glanced from the highway to his friend, who appeared seriously agitated.

"Now don't get angry." Billy gestured with his hands, palms down, for Sandy to remain calm. "I want you to quietly and unemotionally consider something. Instead of looking at what we're doing today as a *fait accompli,* I would like to know what it would take for me to get you to call this whole *mishugena* project off and, you know, like turn the car around, forget the Nazi, and cruise back to L.A., alive, in one piece? Even if you only want to discuss this I'm happy to take you out to dinner at the restaurant of your choice. How does Chasen's sound? Or Le Restaurant? Perino's? Doesn't a nice meal of caviar, champagne, roast duck, and chocolate mousse sound terrific? Think about it; let's talk this out. There's got to be some other way."

Sandy controlled his anger. At this point, a mutiny was the last thing he needed. Instead of reacting, he concentrated on the long hood of the Rent-A-Wreck Dodge. It was a good car, a steady machine: smooth, quiet, and reliable. When he was over his instant of rage, he looked at his friend and spoke carefully.

"You've been doing this to me for a week, Billy, and I simply don't want to hear this sort of thing anymore; it's too late. I'd love it if there were some other way. But there isn't. We both know that I have absolutely no alternative."

"Notice that I'm speaking calmly. I'm not being critical. I'm not trying to get you upset. Things are tense enough without that. But I do have to disagree with your last statment." Billy spoke quietly, as if talking to an irrational child. "No one, not even your relatives the Nazis sent to the concentration camps, had *no* alternatives. I'm trying to get you to do a little last-minute reflection here and really, truly, ask yourself if the benefits of this little outing are worth the risks we're taking?"

"Okay, you tell me. If we don't go through with this today, what happens then?"

"For one thing, we'll definitely be alive."

"And what about Paula?"

"What about her?"

"What do you think she's going to do when she finds out who I really am?"

"Sandy, one way or the other she's got to face the facts. If she can't accept you for who you are then fuck her; you can't spend your whole life jumping through hoops, behaving like Superman just to get some weirdo woman to respect you."

"You really are dumb sometimes, you know that?" Sandy said angrily. "The problem isn't just what she would think, it's me. Let's suppose she accepted everything I've done — which she wouldn't. But if she did, you know how I'd see her?"

Billy didn't.

"She'd have to be nuts. Something would be wrong with her. I've thought about this a lot; if the situation were reversed and she confessed to what I've done, I'd have absolutely no respect for her. That's why I have to do this."

"You know, I thought this plan was sick. But what you just told me is even sicker. Now you really *are* talking like a crazy person."

Without warning, Sandy jerked the steering wheel of the rented Dodge and sped diagonally across all five lanes of the Ventura Freeway. Terrified, Billy braced himself against the dashboard, certain a fatal crash was imminent.

But Sandy had other plans and succeeded at skillfully guiding the big sedan through the maze of honking drivers. With a frightening jolt the Dodge bounced off the freeway onto the shoulder, where Sandy slammed on the brakes, crammed the transmission into park, and turned on his unnerved friend.

"Listen," he said in a menacing tone. "I've had it with you. You made an agreement with me; you knew exactly what I planned to do today. Now either you show some balls and live up to your commitment or you can get out of the car now, *here*."

"All I'm trying to get you to do," Billy pleaded without moving, "is see that you have more options than you think. You're forgetting, *I'm on your side*."

"Thank you. I appreciate it. Now open the door and *vamoose*. When I get back to L.A. I'll let you know how it went."

Confronted with abandonment by and the probable suicide of his best friend, Billy vacillated.

"I'm running short of time," Sandy said quietly. "As a favor to an old pal, don't make this more difficult. Just keep your opinions to yourself and get out."

Billy remained in his seat.

"God damn it!" Sandy screamed. "Get the hell out of this car or I'm going to throw you out!"

After what seemed like an eternity, Billy finally spoke angrily. "I'm a fucking stupid shit-head of an idiot but I can't let you do this alone. Drive the god-damn car." Throwing himself violently against the back of the seat, he tightened his shoulder belt and stared straight ahead.

Nodding as if he understood his friend's conflict, Sandy remained silent as he dropped the transmission back into drive, waited for an opening, planted the accelerator on the floor, and roared back onto the freeway.

43

"Make a Reggie at the corner," Sandy murmured from the back seat to Billy, who was now driving. "It's half-way down the block on the right. The address is 1810."

Perspiring heavily, Billy nodded, made the turn, and idled the big Dodge down Sea View Drive. It was six-forty in the evening, and the most dangerous part of the plan was now underway. Sandy checked for the last time to make sure that every chamber of his Smith and Wesson .38 was properly loaded.

Outside, the sky radiated that lovely burnt orange light characteristic of late-summer California evenings. Photographers called this time the golden hour for the romantic patina that temporarily transformed even Hoffmann's ordinary working class neighborhood into a beautiful vista.

"Any last questions?"

Billy shook his head.

"I just want you to know," Sandy offered, "that I appreciate what you're doing. When I needed you, you stuck with me when no one else would. I'll never forget it."

"Let's hope they don't have to write that on my tombstone. I'd rather be remembered as a composer."

Sandy forced a laugh and gave his friend's shoulder a reassuring squeeze. "You don't have to worry. You're going to be great— I'm convinced. I have total confidence in you."

Billy nodded uncertainly.

"You're four houses away. I'm going to disappear." Sandy, dressed in the same black outfit he had worn during his search of Hoffmann's house, lay down in the back seat footwell and covered himself with a heavy dark gray neoprene tarpaulin. Anyone looking in would have thought the fabric was only an old car cover tossed carelessly on the floor.

"I hope you're settled in," Billy whispered without turning around, "because we're there."

"So far, so good," came the muffled voice through the synthetic canvas.

Billy swung the Dodge into Hoffmann's driveway and stopped by the front steps.

"The light's on," Billy hissed. "Looks like someone's home."

Instead of a response from the back seat, there was only silence.

"Sandy, you okay?" Billy asked in fear.

"I heard you," Sandy spoke almost inaudibly. "It's too dangerous to talk; it's up to you now. Good luck."

Billy took a handkerchief from his jacket pocket and made one final wipe of his palms, forehead, and neck. After stuffing the wet square of linen back into his pocket, he shut off the V-8 engine and left the key in the ignition. Then he gripped his Samsonite briefcase, got out of the car, straightened his jacket and tie, walked up the three flagstone steps to Hoffmann's front door, and pressed twice on the bell. Under the cover of the back seat tarp, Sandy strained to hear each step of Billy's progress.

As he waited, Billy forced himself to take slow, deep breaths in order to appear nonchalant, calm, and businesslike. A quick glance around the neighborhood revealed nothing unusual; the street was empty of cars and people. And the sky, now close to darkness, provided a veil of protection.

From inside the house, the sound of heavy footsteps cranked up Billy's already skyrocketing pulse rate.

"Ya?" a deep voice called through the heavy front door.

"Mister Heinz Hoffmann?" Billy inquired.

"Who wishes to speak to him?"

"I'm an employee of the German-American Travel Agency here to award Mister Hoffmann the grand prize in our travel contest."

For perhaps twenty seconds there was no response. Finally the German-accented voice asked, "And your name is?"

"Steven O'Donnel," Billy told him. "From the German-American Travel Agency."

"One moment, please."

Billy waited as a dead bolt was unfastened, followed by a door chain. Finally the wooden door itself was unlocked and opened just six inches, stopped by the bare foot of Heinz Hoffmann, who took a moment to size up his visitor. The captain had apparently just gotten out of the shower and was wearing only blue jeans. Around the massive neck hung a white bath towel he had been using to dry his thinning hair. Satisfied with the appearance of his caller, Hoffmann swung open the door, giving Billy a full look at his impressively muscular, two hundred and twenty pound quarry.

"Mister Heinz Hoffmann?" Billy asked innocently.

"Ya."

"Hello." Billy gave his best corporate smile and extended his hand. "I'm Steven O'Donnel from German-American Travel, and I want to congratulate you. You're the big, big winner in our 1973 contest."

Unconvinced, the captain played along by reticently shaking Billy's hand.

"Not only are you the recipient," Billy continued, "of an all-expenses paid, round-trip, first-class vacation to Germany, you're also the lucky owner of a brand new Mercedes Benz 450 SEL, to be delivered to you at the factory in Stuttgart for use on your vacation—after which we'll ship it back here, at our expense. Congratulations, Mister Hoffmann."

"This is on the level?" The captain was suspicious.

Billy nodded. "You're a lucky man, Mister Hoffmann."

"This is not some trick, a sales scheme? You're not asking me to pay anything?"

Billy smiled, pretending to be amused—as the captain himself might have said, had the situation been reversed, *about to set the hook.* "I know it must be hard to believe, but you are truly the grand prize winner in the contest of a lifetime. Here, let me show you."

Setting his briefcase on the ground, Billy snapped it open, withdrew a xerox of Hoffmann's contest form, and held it up for the captain to identify.

"You're the same Heinz Hoffmann who sent us this?"

After inspecting the paper, the German nodded.

"Then there's no doubt; you are our big winner. The trip to Germany and the Mercedes are yours. Hold this a second, please." Billy passed the captain a copy of the original travel brochure sent out with the contest forms. "I want to take a few pictures." Billy bent down to his briefcase and retrieved a Polaroid camera, which he unfolded. "It's for our publicity department. If you could hold up the brochure, I need to see the name German-American Travel Agency."

"You wish to photograph me like this?" Hoffmann pointed in astonishment to his bare chest.

Billy nodded. "My instructions are to get a picture of you just as you received the news of your win. The PR people like spontaneous, unrehearsed photos."

"No. Absolutely not. I won't allow it. I must wear a shirt. Excuse me." The captain turned toward the interior of the house.

"Mister Hoffmann," Billy tried to sound formal and official. "I can't let you do that. They want a photograph at exactly the moment you heard you were the winner."

"Are they not going to use such a picture in their advertisements?"

"Of course."

"I can't allow it. I'm sorry. Not without my shirt. It's not dignified. Give me one minute, please. Who's to know I didn't answer the door fully dressed?"

Billy pretended to consider the request.

"I can understand your concern. If it were me, I wouldn't like it either. Go put on your shirt. I'll just figure that's the way you answered the door. Okay?"

Hoffmann smiled broadly. "Thank you. Will you come in? Have a glass of schnapps? Help me enjoy this wonderful moment?"

"Afterwards, Mister Hoffmann. First I have my job to do. I need your picture, out here, by the front door, holding our brochure."

"Of course. Yes, I understand. Give me one minute, Mister uh . . .?"

"O'Donnel."

"Right. Mister O'Donnel. I'll be back in a second."

From the way Hoffmann bounded inside, down the main hallway to his bedroom, Billy could tell that the man had fully accepted the ruse. What else explained the off-key humming of an unrecognizable tune by the tone-deaf Nazi as he searched for a shirt? A few moments later Hoffmann reemerged from his bedroom and strolled proudly back to the front door, this time wearing a staggeringly loud red, black, and violet flowered Hawaiian silk shirt in addition to his jeans, white socks, and loafers.

"Is this not perfect for my vacation?" The German grinned.

"Our PR department will love it," Billy agreed, trying to make sense out of an SS war criminal dressing like an overgrown California surfer. "Now hold up the brochure so that I can see our name."

Complying happily, Hoffmann displayed the rubber-stamped travel folder while Billy focused the Polaroid.

"Is this useful?" The German posed rigidly, like a soldier.

"Perfect. But let's see a little of that happiness you felt when I told you you were our big winner."

Hoffmann dragged his cheeks up in a forced smile.

"C'mon, Mister Hoffmann; that's a grin for grandma. You just found out you're getting a free, first-class vacation to Germany and a brand new, top-of-the-line Mercedes Benz—a prize worth more than $45,000. How does that make you feel?"

The Nazi's smile cranked open a few more degrees.

"Much better. Beautiful. Now hold it."

Hoffmann maintained his smile long enough for Billy to press the Polaroid's shutter and blind the man with the flashbulb. Momentarily disoriented, the German repeatedly blinked his eyes in an attempt to regain his vision.

"No, no, don't move," Billy ordered. "I need to take a couple more from different angles."

Resuming his stiff, artificial expression and pose, Hoffmann endured flash after flash from the Polaroid.

"Thank you. That's good."

The German relaxed.

"Now while we're waiting for the pictures to develop, why don't you pick out the color you want for your Mercedes? And I'll need a photo of you with that brochure too."

Stooping down to his briefcase, Billy flipped through the papers without finding the one he needed. A second search, under Hoffmann's gaze, turned up nothing.

"I must have left the color samples in the car," he told Hoffmann. "Come with me. In fact, I think a photo of you sitting in the company car choosing your Mercedes color would be great."

Turning toward the Dodge, Billy was relieved to sense Hoffmann following him. Around them, the suburban street remained empty. Lights shimmered from inside most of the neighboring houses, but no residents were visible.

Opening the passenger door of the Dodge, Billy pretended to be relieved by his discovery of the Mercedes brochure on the front seat.

"Thank god." Billy picked up the glossy printed folder. "If I'd forgotten this my boss would have killed me. Sit down," he indicated the passenger seat, "and take a look through the color swatches while I get a couple more pictures."

Without the slightest hesitation Hoffmann sat, as ordered, and eagerly examined the Mercedes paint samples under the weak light emanating from the Dodge's overhead light.

"Hold the brochure up about another six inches," Billy commanded as he focused the Polaroid.

Once again Hoffmann did exactly as he was told.

"That's perfect; it's gonna be a great picture. What color looks good to you?"

"In this light it's hard to choose. I need a minute, please."

"Take all the time you want. But while you're looking, tell me what you think of the Mercedes 450 SEL." Billy crouched a little lower, as if the angle might give a better picture.

The Nazi smiled. "Now you ask an easy question. This machine is easily the best automobile in the world."

Billy pressed the shutter button and blasted Hoffmann with the intense light of a flashbulb not three feet from his retina.

"That's a great expression; hold it while I take a few more."

Obedient, the German sat rigidly as Billy came even closer, flashing seven more pictures straight into the big man's eyes.

"Very good, Mister Hoffmann. Now, what color looks best to you?"

As the Nazi moved the chart first away from and then closer to his eyes, blinking frantically, Billy watched Sandy rise up from the back seat, reach around the war criminal's head, and jam the barrel of the .38 Smith and Wesson right between the man's half-incapacitated eyes.

"Don't speak; don't move; don't even blink, Hoffmann," Sandy commanded in his most vicious, uncompromising tone, "or you're going to have a thirty-eight caliber bullet hole straight through your big fucking head."

Disoriented, taken by surprise, the German froze.

Having established the reality of the pistol, Sandy dragged the steel barrel around the side of the Nazi's temple and forced it hard up against the base of his brain stem. "Now, very slowly, put your left arm up over the seat back and let it hang down toward the car floor."

"Who are you?" The German sounded terrified.

"Shut up and do what I tell you." Sandy ground the tip of the pistol barrel into the back of the man's head.

Without another word, Hoffmann did as instructed.

"Now your right arm," Sandy commanded.

The Nazi cooperated perfectly.

"Now press your wrists together."

The German, who was very uncomfortable with his body weight now supported almost entirely by his armpits, nevertheless found the strength to clamp his wrists against each other.

Without diminishing the pistol's pressure against Hoffmann's head, Sandy switched the gun from his right hand to his left, then snapped a pair of handcuffs over the man's perfectly positioned wrists. In a second quick motion, Sandy looped a length of half-inch Dacron yacht braid, already secured at one end to the seat belt bolts, over the chain spanning the handcuffs, yanked down on the line, and tied it off securely.

"Get his feet," Sandy called to Billy.

An instant later, another set of handcuffs were fastened around the Nazi's ankles, then knotted tightly to a short length of line connected to the Dodge's front seat frame. In pain, unable to move, the man was now totally under control.

"Why are you doing this to me?" Hoffmann protested.

Intentionally hurting the Nazi with a further grinding motion from the pistol barrel, Sandy hissed with true menace, "When I told you to shut up, Hoffmann, I meant it. Unless you enjoy pain."

Captain Hoffmann said nothing.

"Get your briefcase," Sandy told Billy, "close his front door, and let's go."

Maintaining a nonchalant demeanor, Billy shut the Dodge's passenger door and strolled to the house, where he closed Hoffmann's front door, automatically locking it. Then he picked up his briefcase from the flagstone entry and quickly scanned the area for any evidence of the abduction. Finding nothing, he walked back to the driver's side of the Dodge, got in, and started the engine.

"We've got a long trip ahead of us," Sandy said from the back seat. "Let's give our guest something to help him relax."

Billy opened the glove compartment and withdrew a pair of wraparound sunglasses, the lenses of which had been painted black on the inside. Once Billy had slipped these into place on Hoffmann's head, the man was in effect completely blind. A strip of four-inch-wide medical tape over the Nazi's mouth eliminated any possibility of verbal protest. The final touch was a fake goatee, slapped on to conceal the tape from passersby on the highway.

Without another word, Billy nodded to Sandy that his part of the job was completed. He then watched as Sandy positioned a disposable syringe behind the large muscle of Hoffmann's upper arm. Without warning, Sandy thrust the sharp needle into the muscle and 300 mg of Seconal began to flow into the Nazi's body. Before the man could react, the syringe was empty and withdrawn. Now total control was only a question of a few minutes.

Billy slipped the transmission into reverse, backed into the street, and drove slowly up the block, out of Sea View Estates. In the rear seat, Sandy swiveled his head in every direction, on the alert for danger. But the drive through the City of Oxnard was uneventful; no one paid them the slightest attention. The only real worries came from Hoffmann, who wriggled in his seat, struggling against the heavy sedation of the Seconal. That moment was the one time in recent years that Sandy was grateful for his pharmaceutical connections. Through the Vita-Line lab, he had access to the company pharmacist's license number and the necessary purchase orders. Obtaining any drug, other than a narcotic, was a simple matter of specifying the desired substance to be shipped to Vita-Line, "to the attention of Sandy Klein."

Within ten minutes the rented Dodge was on the Ventura Freeway and speeding south at sixty-five miles an hour. Despite their apparent success, neither Sandy nor Billy felt safe. Without speaking a single word, both men concentrated as if they were expecting a surprise attack to be launched against them.

With Oxnard safely behind them, then Camarillo, city after city passed without the slightest hint of a problem. Was it really possible, Sandy asked himself, that they had escaped without detection? At that instant, half-way to Los Angeles, just as he was allowing himself a first hopeful thought, a loud growl snarled from the German's nose, terrifying Sandy and Billy.

Cramming the barrel of his .38 hard up against the back of the Nazi's head, Sandy braced himself as the Dodge lurched across two lanes of traffic, out of control, while a terrified Billy jerked on the steering wheel. Only the fact that the freeway was virtually empty saved them from obliteration. After a few deft corrections, the motion of the car stabilized and they were safe. The outburst from Hoffmann was a false alarm: simply a Seconal-induced snore. The man was not just sedated, but actually asleep. Fearful of a trick, Sandy intensified his concentration, monitoring both the German and the road around them.

"What d'ya see?" Billy asked anxiously.

"Nothing."

"I don't think anyone in his neighborhood noticed us. Do you?" This last question was a little lacking in confidence for Sandy's taste.

"Let's talk about it later."

"What do you think the possibilities are that one of his neighbors turned off their house lights and watched the whole thing without us knowing?"

"If that were the case, we'd already be in jail."

"Suppose someone did see us and the cops held off arresting us because they want to see who else is involved. What if they're following us with a helicopter?"

"They're not. I guarantee you."

"How do you know? I didn't see you look for a chopper."

Sandy rolled down the window, stuck his head out, and scanned the sky. After a couple of very uncomfortable minutes, he pulled himself back in and closed the window. "No plane. No chopper. Nothing but stars and clouds. We're going to be fine. Now will you be quiet and drive, please?"

Nodding timidly, Billy did as he was told.

Twenty minutes later the Dodge descended the off-ramp from the Ventura Freeway onto Van Nuys Boulevard. A quarter mile of traffic led to the isolation of Beverly Glen Canyon. Ten more minutes and they were on Mulholland Drive, wending their way down the narrower southern side of the canyon road, nearing Sandy's house. It's not far now, he reflected nervously, more than a little frightened of giving in to the feeling of success. To get excited over his accomplishment meant, in his mind, letting down his guard. Fear had a way of focusing attention, of slowing down his sense of time and keeping him alert, ready at any moment to act; giving in to his wish to celebrate meant getting sloppy. So he buried his growing optimism by forcing himself to study every shadow, driveway, and corner for unexpected danger.

Eight minutes later, in spite of Sandy's paranoia, the Dodge rolled to a halt inside his garage. After killing the engine and setting the brake, Billy got out and swung the garage door shut.

With a flip of a wall switch, the overhead fluorescent light illuminated the firetrap of floor-to-ceiling cardboard boxes where Sandy stored every issue and all the records of *The Heart of L.A.*

Slipping quietly out of the back seat, Sandy opened the front passenger door and untied the rope holding Hoffmann's ankle cuffs to the seat frame.

"C'mon over here and take his feet. I'll get the shoulders."

Billy nodded obediently, slipped around the back of the Dodge, and readied himself to hoist the German's legs.

After untying the wrist cuffs from the shoulder belt bolts, Sandy attempted to lever up the dead weight of the unconscious Nazi in order to slip the manacled arms back over the seat. With Billy's help, the wrists finally made it up and the snoring man twisted sideways, clearing the backrest. Too top-heavy to control on the way down, Hoffmann slipped from their arms and bounced off the steering wheel, terrifying both Sandy and Billy by landing on the horn, not once but twice, first with his nose and then with his shoulder, before collapsing across the front seat.

Gun in hand, Sandy leapt from the back and pressed the barrel of his .38 against Hoffmann's skull. But the German didn't stir.

"Shit," Billy whispered, "just when we were doing so well. I'll bet the whole fucking neighborhood heard the horn."

"So what?"

"What do you mean, *so what*? Someone'll probably get pissed off and call the police."

"Over two lousy horn honks? Give me a break. One Sunday last summer, five houses up the block, some drunk started shooting squirrels out of his avocado tree with a twelve gauge shotgun and no one called the police." Sandy flicked on the safety and thrust the pistol into his waistband. "Let's get this sucker inside."

From the driver's side, Sandy grabbed the Nazi under his armpits and dragged him out of the car. With Billy lifting the feet, together they were able to hoist him over the connecting threshold into the house.

Resembling two sweating laborers from Bekins carrying a rolled-up Persian rug, Sandy and Billy hustled the dead weight of Hoffmann through the kitchen, across the living room, down the hall, and into the carefully prepared second bedroom.

"Of all the Nazis you might have picked," Billy wheezed as they set the sleeping body down on the oak floor, "you couldn't have found one that was a skinny midget; I mean, this guy's the original brick shithouse."

"Let's get him into the chair," Sandy panted.

Together the two men heaved Hoffmann up into the seat of an old oak chair of Spanish design built in the days when furniture was constructed with enough strength to act as the foundation of a four-story apartment building. While Billy held the German upright, Sandy used two additional sets of handcuffs to lock the man's ankles to separate legs of the chair. Then, using two sets of handcuffs per arm, Sandy secured the Nazi's wrists and forearms to the four-inch oak armrests. Further control came from an eight-foot bicycle chain, which Sandy doubled around Hoffmann's body and the seat back. When he regained consciousness, the man would find himself immobile. The final touch was a stainless steel marine cable, which Sandy wound twice around his prisoner's neck before threading the ends through holes drilled in the headrest extension and locking them together. Having bolted the chair itself to the floor joists, Sandy was confident that even Houdini wouldn't have been able to escape.

After double-checking his work and finding it flawless, Sandy removed the sunglasses from the Nazi's face and tied a black opaque blindfold over his eyes. Peeling off the goatee but leaving the surgical tape gag completed the operation. Hoffmann was clearly under control.

Sandy checked his watch. The time was a little after eleven o'clock on Thursday night, leaving almost forty-eight dangerous hours before the war criminal could be turned over to the authorities. Two solid days was a long time to be the jailer of such a clever and capable killer. Thanks to the Seconal, the first part of the plan had gone smoothly. Just as the Physician's Desk Reference had predicted, reliable old Seconal had worked like a charm to knock out the powerful Nazi. However, Seconal lasted for only three to six hours and soon, Sandy knew, he'd have to switch to Tuinal, a much longer-acting barbiturate.

As he triple-checked every detail of Hoffmann's restraints, it began to dawn on Sandy that he had, in fact, accomplished something magnificent. Not only had he succeeded in unearthing and capturing an SS war criminal living comfortably in Southern California, but he had pulled it off with grace, skill, courage, and efficiency. No one had been hurt. No property had been damaged. And other than Billy, no outsider had been involved in the operation. Hoffmann wouldn't be missed until early Friday morning, when the passengers and crew of his boat would wait in vain for their captain. Finally, Sandy told himself with pleasure, after years of despair, failure, and unending humiliations comes an undeniable, stunning, overwhelming, personal and historical success. The implications of this insight reverberated throughout Sandy's brain, penetrating and exciting uncounted millions of long dormant neurons. Sandy felt the rush of a great, unbelievable, fucking-amazing, hydrogen bomb of a success. He had realized the miraculous, attained the impossible.

"What the hell are you doing now?" Billy's voice radiated fear.

"Take a look at this." Sandy had rolled up the sleeping Nazi's shirt sleeve, revealing a small scar — a circular burn — perhaps two inches in diameter, not far below his shoulder.

"So?"

"You don't know what that is?" Sandy asked with some surprise.

"It's a scar," Billy stated, as if it were irrelevant.

"This," Sandy pointed to the shiny, half-dollar-sized area, "is where the Germans tattooed every member of the SS with the double lightning bolt insignia. If you read the transcripts of the various war crime trials you'd be amazed at how many German 'farmers' and ordinary 'frontline foot soldiers' had scars in exactly this shape and location."

Billy nodded and said nothing, but it was obvious that his state of mind was far from tranquil.

"What do you say I make us some coffee?" Sandy hoped to lighten his friend's mood. "I don't know about you, but I'm wiped out."

"Sure."

"Hey, you don't have to if you don't want to."

"I'd rather have a drink."

"You're going to have to wait 'til Sunday." Sandy handed Billy the .38 and gestured to the Nazi. "Don't take your eyes off the son-of-a-bitch."

Billy nodded, took the pistol, and stood guard while Sandy disappeared into the kitchen. Five minutes later he returned, carrying two steaming mugs of coffee.

"To the future and all the great things it's going to bring our way," Sandy proposed euphorically, clicking his cup against his friend's.

Billy nodded and took a tiny sip of his coffee.

"So are you going to tell me what's wrong, or what?" Sandy demanded.

"Why do you think something's wrong?" Billy stalled.

"Oh, I don't know," Sandy teased, "it has something to do with the expression on your face. You have the look of a man who's just been told he has brain cancer."

Billy shrugged. "That's pretty close to the way I feel."

"What could be so bad? The hard part's over. We've got Hoffmann. No one was hurt. Everything went exactly as planned."

"I keep thinking about what's going to happen at your dad's dinner. Sandy, I've given this a lot of consideration, and I'm convinced it's not going to work."

"What's not going to work?"

"They're not going to understand. They're going to think you're crazy."

"Who?"

"Those three hundred over-dressed big shots at your old man's dinner. Why do you think they're showing up at the dinner? I guarantee you it's not because they want drama. These are people who believe in the conventional. They want the reassurance and security that come from being pillars of the community. When you present them with your Nazi war criminal, you'll not only be disrupting the whole evening, you'll going be scaring the holy shit out of them. They are there to hear Uri. You tell them *you're* Uri — you, the son of Nat Klein. That's crazy enough. But then you're going to serve them a Nazi for dessert. Sandy, that group of people is going to go nuts and call the police; they aren't going to give a damn about your noble intentions. You're going to be behind bars for kidnaping before you can say *boo*."

"So what are you suggesting I do?"

"If you really have to, present your evidence at the dinner in the form of poster-size blow-ups of the photograph at Rava Ruska and the SS identity card. Even take a picture of Hoffmann if you think that'll help. And be sure to send copies of it all to Simon Wiesenthal in Austria. And to that other person, Serge Klarsfeld in Israel. Let *them* handle all the complex bureaucratic and legal issues. You'll still be the guy who gets credit for it. It may not be as dramatic, but at least you'll be able to go on living."

"What about our friend here?" Sandy pointed to the sleeping Nazi.

"We'll wait until three in the morning, drive the fucker up Canoga Park Avenue to Mulholland, and dump him in the boondocks. He has no idea who kidnaped him. Or even why. With his past he can hardly go to the police. By the time the Seconal or whatever wears off and he's awake, he might not even remember what happened. Like you and your drinker's blackout. The beauty of the plan is that, criminally, you're out of the woods and yet you can still use what you've uncovered to overcome your problems with Paula and your family."

Sandy shook his head. "I'm sorry, but holding up a few photographs at the dinner isn't going to do it. They'll laugh me off the stage."

Billy shook his head in disagreement. "It's all in how you present it. I'll help you with the speech."

"Forget it, Billy. If I present the photographs and the evidence and the police investigate, Hoffmann will be in Paraguay faster then you can spell ODESSA."

"You won't even consider my idea?"

"If I'd followed your advice in the car this afternoon, you know where I'd be right now?"

Billy said nothing.

"A suicide. Can't you see that you're just flat out wrong? I mean, Billy, you're not talking to a loser here. This is a big-time accomplishment, and on Saturday night the world's going to sit up and take notice. Mark my words."

"Honestly, Sandy, I admire what you've done. It's impressive, more than I ever would have guessed you were capable of. But I've never been so frightened as I am right now. Guns, needles, Nazis, mass murderers — this is all too serious for me. Please, before this gets out of hand, let's dump Hoffmann out on Mulholland like I just said. I know it's not quite what you had in mind, but as you keep saying: Trust me; I know what I'm talking about here."

"I seem to recall," Sandy's voice once again conveyed more than a tinge of menace, "that in the car this afternoon you made a commitment to me. Doesn't your word mean anything anymore?"

"Hey, am I still here? Did I not do everything I promised? I'm trying," Billy spoke angrily, "to get you to change your mind to save your fucking life. Or are you too hard-headed now to even listen to your only friend's opinion?"

In a move that made Billy blanch, Sandy crossed the room and, with his right thumb and forefinger, grabbed a chunk of the German's sagging cheek and pulled it like putty, stretching it away from the man's face. "What is it exactly that you think we have here? An old fisherman? A sleepy Bavarian sausage maker? A nice middle-aged European cabinet maker?"

Billy knew enough not to say anything.

"This organism is not some poor little victim of a deranged kidnaper. This, Billy, is an unpunished mass murderer, a world-class sadist. *It* may look like a human being. *It* may talk like a human being. *It* may even walk like a human being. But you know what? *It* isn't one. This thing is nothing more than living garbage, a blight on the world's moral ecology. If we don't clean up this kind of pollution, who will? Like it or not, history has assigned us this job. It's as simple as that."

Before Billy could answer, a muffled groan reverberated from Hoffmann, scaring both of them. The Seconal was wearing off. Sandy let go of the Nazi's cheek — flesh flopped back against his bone like a damaged rubber band.

"Keep the gun on him," Sandy commanded his friend. "I'm getting the Tuinal."

Terrified, Billy aimed the .38 at Hoffmann's head and watched as the big German began to struggle against his restraints. Hoffman was coming off the Seconal disoriented and panicked. If the Nazi were frantic enough to break his bonds, Billy wondered if he would be courageous enough to shoot the man. Like it or not, Billy reflected angrily, the commitment he had made to his friend now extended to the act of killing.

Carrying a syringe filled with 300 mg of Tuinal, Sandy entered the room and knelt beside the Nazi's writhing body. Using a cotton ball soaked in alcohol, he wiped the back of the man's arm not far from the site once marked by the SS tattoo.

Hoffmann's muffled voice issued from behind the gag in a ghostly, incomprehensible groan. Without trying to understand or speaking, Sandy once again inserted the sharp needle of the disposable syringe. In thirty seconds the war criminal's muscle had accepted every drop of the heavy-duty, long-lasting barbiturate. Setting down the empty syringe, Sandy used the cotton ball to wipe a dribble of blood from the puncture hole in the back of the German's arm. To Billy's great relief, his own sudden nausea — needles always made him queasy — ended along with the bleeding.

For perhaps ten minutes Sandy crouched on the floor and waited, ignoring the continuous stream of unintelligible protests, until gradually the Tuinal took hold and drove the Nazi back into the limbo of dreamless sleep.

"This should keep him under for somewhere between six and twelve hours," Sandy told Billy. "We should use the time to get some rest. Want me to take the first watch?"

Billy shook his head. "I couldn't sleep if I tried."

Sandy stood. "If there's the slightest problem — I don't care how unimportant — I want you to wake me. This is not a time to take chances. And remember, if something really terrible happens — which it won't — and you have to stop him with the gun, do it. This is not a man who's going to give us a second chance."

Billy nodded, understanding only too well.

Following the second hand of his watch, Sandy clamped his hand around the German's wrist, timed the man's pulse, then removed the taped gag, allowing him to breathe with less effort.

"The old ticker's pumping along at a nice, steady seventy-two. Just to be sure I didn't overdose him, check it every half hour. And if he starts talking, tape his mouth shut again, okay?"

Again Billy nodded.

"I'd like a solid three hours of sleep if that's possible. Can you stay awake that long?"

For the third time, Billy bobbed his chin up and down.

"Don't look so worried," Sandy assured him. "It's all going to work out perfectly. The worst is over."

Billy smiled mechanically, unconvinced.

"You'll wake me if you have the slightest question?"

"Of course."

After a final check of the Nazi's restraints, Sandy washed his face, flopped down on his bed, closed his eyes, and for the first time in almost forty-eight hours, fell asleep.

44

"Sorry to wake you, but Hoffmann's up and he needs to take a crap."

Sandy rolled over and opened his eyes. Instead of the darkness he had expected, bright sunshine blazed in through the window. How could that be? He had gone to sleep around midnight; the latest Billy was supposed to wake him was three A.M. What the hell had happened?

Sandy sat up. "What time is it?" he demanded.

"Six-thirty."

"What the shit! You were supposed to wake me at three. Why didn't you? Were you drinking? Did you fall asleep? I want the truth, Billy." Sandy was out of bed, on his feet, ready for a fight.

"Listen, asshole," Billy said, "for once in your life I want you to give me a break. At three o'clock when I came in here to wake you, you were sleeping like the dead. I shook your shoulder and you didn't budge. Fuck it, I told myself. You were exhausted and obviously needed sleep. And I still felt pretty good. Hoffmann was out, snoring. The night was quiet. And after all the craziness of Oxnard everything finally seemed so peaceful. You know, being a night watchman isn't bad; it gives you a lot of time to think. So I left you alone. With tomorrow being such a big day for you, you're going to need all the energy you can muster. The only reason I woke you now was because I want your help. We have to get Hoffmann to the can."

"Did he say anything to you?" Sandy asked as he pulled on his pants, shirt, and shoes.

"Just that he needs to take a crap."

"When did he wake up?"

"Five, six minutes ago."

"How's his mood?"

"He sounded scared."

Sandy smiled. "And right he should be. Go back and watch him, I'll be there in a minute."

Billy did as he was told, and Sandy quickly washed, shaved, and used the toilet himself. Clean and rested, he made his way into the second bedroom. What he saw renewed his optimism.

Hoffmann sat shackled to the chair exactly as he'd been six hours earlier. The accomplishment wasn't a fantasy, as Sandy had feared on and off throughout the night. In his sleep, he'd had vivid, terrifying dreams of an empty room, an unoccupied oak chair, empty chains, and no one on guard duty. But the reality was more than reassuring.

"Let's do his feet first," Sandy told Billy.

"Who are you?" the German suddenly shouted. "Why are you doing this to me? I'm a human being. This is a free country. I demand an answer."

"Hoffmann, I want you to shut up," Sandy ordered. "We're going to take you to the toilet. If you're not absolutely quiet — if I hear one more peep from you — we're not moving you one inch and for all I care you can shit in your pants and sit in it all day long. If that's clear I want you to nod your head."

Limited by the neck restraint, Hoffmann made a tiny bob of his chin in Sandy's direction.

"Good, then we understand each other." Gesturing to Billy, Sandy said quietly, "Okay, shall we?"

Together the two friends unlatched the shackles holding the Nazi's legs to the chair, leaving only the set of handcuffs locking the two ankles together in the manner of a hobbled horse. Next they removed the stainless steel necklace, freeing the man's head. However, before disconnecting any of the other restraints, Sandy fitted a nasty-looking leather and metal collar tightly around the war criminal's muscular throat.

"What this is, Hoffmann," Sandy explained, "is an electronic dog-training collar. It works on a simple principle: You do something we don't like and I press this little button on my handset here and you get a cattle-prod dose of electricity into your neck and head. You want to see how it feels?"

"No, please, I believe you," the Nazi muttered.

"I thought I told you not to speak." Sandy sounded very disappointed. "Well, I'm going to be nice just this once. If you say another word, though, here's what's going to happen to you."

A short press of the button on his radio transmitter handset sent a searing blast of electricity into Hoffmann's neck and spine.

"For one tap of the button," Sandy said calmly, "it's pretty effective, wouldn't you say?"

Sweating profusely, the German was too uncomfortable even to nod.

"I'm sorry to have to hurt you," Sandy continued, "but I did want you to know exactly what you're dealing with here. According to the manual, this battery is good for fifteen continuous minutes, if necessary. Imagine how that would feel. Of course, I wouldn't lock the button down unless you decided to be uncooperative. I think we understand each other, don't we?"

Still trying to catch his breath after the searing pain, Hoffmann nodded.

"What we're going to do now is disconnect you from the chair, lock your hands behind your back, and march you to the bathroom. Ready?"

Again the German nodded.

Sandy gestured to Billy, who unlocked the Nazi's left arm, twisted it behind the man's back, and handcuffed it to a hole drilled through the chair. Removing the right arm's restraint, Billy rotated the shoulder, twisted that arm behind the chair, and shackled it to the other wrist. After uncoupling the chain surrounding the captain's trunk, Billy unfastened the temporary handcuff connecting the left wrist to the back of the chair. Hoffmann was now fully disengaged from his seat.

"Okay, you can stand up now," Sandy commanded the prisoner.

Obediently, Hoffmann rose.

"Now, very slowly, walk straight ahead."

As directed, the Nazi shuffled across the floor, his gait heavily impaired by the ankle cuffs.

"You're doing fine. Keep moving."

Almost like a voice-controlled robot, the Nazi obeyed Sandy's directions, working his way down the hallway and into the bathroom, where Billy slipped down the man's pants and underwear before helping him onto the toilet.

"Okay, Hoffmann," Sandy told him, "it's all yours."

Despite what must have been a serious insult to his modesty, the urge to relieve himself overcame the German's inhibitions and within moments he succeeded in emptying his bowels into the toilet.

"If you're finished, nod." Sandy took two steps backward, out of the bathroom, where he drew deep breaths of uncontaminated air.

Hoffmann waited a moment more, sensed the end of his intestinal activity, pointed his head in the direction of Sandy's voice, and nodded.

"Stand up, please," Sandy ordered from the hallway.

The Nazi obeyed and Billy had the odious task of wiping—using grapefruit-sized handfuls of toilet paper—the man's ass. Finished (and after more than a few nasty glances in the direction of his friend), Billy pulled up Hoffmann's underwear and pants, then guided the war criminal back to his oak chair and the security of multiple handcuffs and chains.

"You're going to be here for a while, Captain Hoffmann," Sandy said with authority. "I'm considering bringing you something to eat; nod if that interests you."

Restricted by the steel cable once again wound around his neck, the German bobbed his chin affirmatively.

A gesture from Sandy brought Billy into the hallway, out of Hoffmann's earshot.

"If you watch him, I'll make breakfast. How does scrambled eggs, bacon, toast, and coffee sound?"

"Yes to everything but the coffee; after I eat, I'd like to get some sleep."

Nodding that he agreed, Sandy handed Billy the .38.

As Billy returned to guard duty in the prisoner's room, Sandy went to work in the kitchen. As he broke the eggs into the mixing bowl a profound sense of well-being bubbled up through his already self-confident mood. Absolutely everything was working out exactly as he'd anticipated. He wasn't just on a roll; he was blasting upward through the rarefied stratosphere of human accomplishment. Good-bye grief. So long pain. Adios misery and humiliation. Everything imaginable that was good was about to descend on him in a wave and obliterate the traumas of his past. What he was about to experience, Sandy was convinced, wasn't merely a stunning success but the rebirth of his long-truncated life. Along with public acclaim would come full acceptance by Paula and, finally, the beginnings of a real family.

As he cooked the eggs, Sandy imagined himself surrounded by adoring children excited by the sight of their father whipping up a delicious Sunday morning breakfast. How many kids should they have? Once upon a time he had wanted two. Now he had a desire for five — three boys and two girls. With Paula the mother, the whole scene made a beautiful picture, bringing to life long-suppressed, achingly desirable dreams.

45

Sandy's morning passed in a blaze of energetic efficiency as he worked the phone, effortlessly fielding a whole spectrum of problems that any other day would have left him paralyzed. With Billy asleep and Hoffmann still succumbing to the Tuinal, Sandy operated on cruise control, whipping through seemingly impossible situations, starting with Paula. Her parents had indeed arrived and were looking forward to meeting him that night at Scandia. Instead of the last-minute fight he knew she had expected, Sandy was a model of generosity and charm, too self-assured to allow any mundane annoyance to compromise his mood. To a man who could single-handedly engineer the capture of a vicious war criminal, one lousy meal with an old couple from New York would be a breeze.

More complicated (but no more difficult for Sandy to handle) were the myriad questions arising over the preparations for the cancer center dinner. With unending patience, Sandy kept everyone at bay until noon, when he awakened Billy, put him back on guard duty, and drove to the Beverly Wilshire Hotel for a serious meeting with Hugo, the frantic maître d'. To everyone's surprise, Sandy was a font of calm, coming up with brilliant, decisive solutions to a seemingly endless number of crises. This resulted in an unprecedented rush of well-orchestrated labor and allowed Sandy to slip out late in the afternoon and run two essential errands.

His first destination was Western Costume on Melrose Avenue, down the street from Paramount Studios, where a complete outfit—a part of the cancer dinner plan—awaited his pick-up. After another stop at the House of Uniforms for a rented tuxedo, Sandy headed back to the hotel for one final, potentially dangerous family meeting: Nat, Sylvia, Ed, and Charlie were descending in unison on the main ballroom for an inspection of Sandy's efforts.

To the surprise and disappointment of Sandy's brothers, Sylvia and Nat were honestly impressed. As much as they all had expected to find fault, Sandy's work survived the most critical scrutiny. Delayed by the Friday afternoon traffic, he was ten minutes late, arriving at the main ballroom to find his father and stepmother strolling through the cavernous room with uncharacteristic smiles on their faces. Nat greeted his youngest son with a bear hug and the admission that the beauty of the room exceeded his highest expectations.

Sandy responded to his father's and Sylvia's compliments with an almost aristocratic graciousness, disguising his boredom with the ballroom's decor. The color scheme, in the official blue and white of the Israeli flag, was an attempt to reflect Nat's desire to connect the evening to "Jewish history throughout the ages." The old man wanted to place both himself and the cancer center squarely in the middle of Jewish culture, to make the point that he was not just an important person within the community but a contemporary biblical figure, a philanthropist to be remembered forever.

The simple fact that the old man had been pleased was sufficient for Sandy. What difference did the color scheme really make? The immediate problem was the upcoming dinner with Paula and her parents. Leaving Nat and Sylvia to one final review of the ballroom, Sandy went home to change clothes for the evening.

Any other time, dinner at Scandia might have been truly enjoyable. The restaurant had a world-wide reputation for its superb Danish cuisine and gracious service. But on that particular night, driving east on Sunset Boulevard, all Sandy could think of were the unsettling aspects of his situation: the sedated war criminal at home guarded by Billy, the cancer center dinner coming up, and the threat of premature exposure by Paula's parents. At least the radio hadn't mentioned anything about a missing charter boat captain. The big story that day was the indictment of John Erlichman for conspiracy, burglary, and perjury in connection with the break-in of Daniel Ellsberg's psychiatrist's office.

Pulling into the driveway of Scandia at twelve minutes after eight, Sandy ran a comb through his hair, turned the Volvo over to the parking attendant, opened the carved wooden door of the restaurant, and entered the dim, mahogany-paneled foyer. If I pull this off, he told himself, I'll know I can succeed at anything.

The maître d' informed Sandy that the rest of the party had already been seated, and led the way across the all-white dining room to a small square table adjacent to the white, trellis-covered windows where Paula sat opposite an older couple.

"Hello, sweetheart," Sandy touched both of Paula's shoulders with his hands. "I'm sorry I'm late; there was an accident on Sunset and the traffic was a nightmare." He lied to cover the fact that he'd driven slowly in order to listen to the local newscast.

"Sandy, we were just starting to worry." Paula stood and turned her face in such a way as to allow only the most formal, asexual kiss — the greeting of a friendly business associate. Unlike her usual masculine office attire, she was dressed in a lavender and white floral print, bare-shouldered, summer frock that made her appear European, formidable, and distant.

"You look terrific; I love the dress."

"Thank you," she responded coolly. "Sandy, I want you to meet my mother, Charlotte Gottlieb. And my father, Ira Gottlieb." To her parents, she then introduced, "Sandy Klein."

"A pleasure to finally get the opportunity to meet you," Sandy smiled as he shook the mother's surprisingly firm hand. "Paula has told me so much about you, I almost feel like we've met before," he addressed her father before extending his hand toward the man's limp unimpressive grip.

Both parents' response to Sandy was chilling. Their faces bore the same skeptical, contemptuous expression he had endured all his life from his own father and brothers. Paula's mother and father were clearly well trained in the school of hanging judges; the look they gave him was the familiar "death sentence without appeal." To survive the evening, Sandy knew he had no choice but to change his strategy. Humor wouldn't work. Charm certainly wasn't going to suffice. Nor would small talk do the job. No, these people were professional assassins when it came to protecting their daughter. They had a job to do and that job required the preemptive exposure, humiliation, and destruction of Sandy Klein before he could seduce their only child one inch further from the embrace of her parents.

To make it through the evening and retain Paula's love, Sandy knew he would have to shift from his low-key, passive plan to an inspired course of action that would allow him to take control.

All kinds of wild and weird ideas came bubbling up into Sandy's frantic brain. Getting them drunk was the first possibility that occurred to him. Perhaps, as Europeans, they were into wine. Scandia's *sommelier* was certain to recommend a whole battery of superb California vintages the Gottliebs wouldn't be able to resist. Perhaps a little vino would take the edge off their killer instincts!

"What do you think?" Sandy addressed Paula in his most upbeat, cheerful tone of voice as he sat down. "Since your parents are in California, shall I order one of our own wines? I don't know if you're familiar with our wine industry," he turned to her mother and father, "but in some of the recent European blind tastings, a few of the better boutique vineyards in Napa have been producing both Chardonnays and Cabernets that have beaten the best of the Montrachets and Mouton Rothchilds. I think it'd be fun to try one of each, don't you?"

"Thank you," Paula's mother spoke. "That's a very nice idea. But Mister Gottlieb and I don't drink. Please, don't let that stop you from enjoying yourself."

Grinning pleasantly as if that information were no problem, Sandy turned to Paula. "What do you feel like: white or red?"

"Soda's fine, thank you." She pointed to the glass of ginger ale in front of her. "Order whatever you want."

Oh boy, am I in trouble, Sandy reflected. As far as he could see, Paula had regressed into a little girl totally under the influence of her dominating parents. No wonder she had moved three thousand miles from them. Paula had a bigger problem than Sandy had imagined. Could she *ever* liberate herself from them? Would she be able to tell them both to go to hell and stop meddling in her life? No surprise she was so obsessed by the concentration camps; she was as much a psychological victim of the Nazis as the actual survivors of Auschwitz.

"Paula was kind enough to send us your clippings, Mister Klein. My husband and I found them very interesting." The woman was the quintessential European wife — short, stocky, and tough, as if all joy had been drained from her life. She obviously trusted no one, least of all a stranger who was trying to take away her one and only daughter. Knowing that the old lady had been both ruthless and clever enough to survive two years in Auschwitz, Sandy could hardly blame her for a bleak and controlling outlook.

Smiling politely, Sandy turned to Paula. "They really do have a superb wine cellar here; how about if I order one of those great Haut Brions that you like?"

"I'm happy with ginger ale, thank you."

Two down and nowhere to go, he lamented silently, wondering what to do next. Paula had opted out and was letting him dangle in the wind, raw meat for her parents' scrutiny.

"Tell me," Ira Gottlieb broke the silence, "from what we've read, we can't figure out when it was, exactly, that you were in the *lager*." A sharp nod from the wife confirmed her interest in this mystery.

Paula's father appeared to have been treated even less generously by time and genetics than his wife. No more than five foot seven, Mister Gottlieb wore a charcoal, chalk-striped, Saville Row suit that, despite its expensive tailoring, failed to conceal his bowling-ball stomach and sticklike limbs, neck, and chest. It was obvious to Sandy that the man had long ago abandoned the realm of the physical for the cerebral. All that was left of Ira Gottlieb's life was skepticism, suspicion, distrust, and the compulsion to protect his daughter from danger. Why else had he flown to Los Angeles? For what other reason was he zeroing in on the time Sandy had spent in Auschwitz?

Sandy answered Ira's question with a grin that managed to be both enigmatic and polite. "There'll be plenty of time for that later," he said, dismissing the inquiry about Auschwitz. "How was your flight out here?"

After a brief exchange of eye contact between the couple, Charlotte answered. "Neither of us enjoys being locked inside an airplane. But it could have been worse."

Sandy nodded as if he understood. "I take it you haven't been to California before."

Charlotte shook her head. "When Ira and I were young we did enough traveling, thank you very much, to last us for six life-times. By the time we were twenty-eight we'd moved from Germany to France to Belgium and then Holland before the SS sent us to Poland. After liberation we went to Sweden, then Canada, until finally we came to the United States. We were never interested in California; as far as we're concerned New York has everything a person could want. That's why we were so surprised when Paula took this *temporary* job in Los Angeles. Except for Disneyland and smog, what does this city have that's better than Manhattan?"

Sandy smiled broadly. "Me."

The blatantly provocative statement acted as a bombshell on Paula, her mother, and father — a true conversation stopper. At least, Sandy noted with pleasure, it shifted the subject away from concentration camps.

"Have you ever been to New York?" Ira finally inquired.

Sandy nodded. "I love the city."

"You were never tempted to live there?"

"My work is here."

"Paula told us you import and export pharmaceuticals."

"That's correct."

"For which companies? I guess you know I'm a physician. I was curious."

"We're wholesale distributors; we work with everyone — the usual business. Pharmaceuticals *are* interesting. But you know what's *really* fascinating?" He asked this last question with great excitement, once again changing the direction of the conversation.

Not knowing where he was leading, no one responded.

"The news today; did you hear it?"

They hadn't.

"This morning, down at the L.A. county jail they booked John Erlichman, charging him with conspiracy, burglary, and perjury for his role in the break-in of Daniel Ellsberg's psychiatrist's office. I think that's really bizarre, don't you?" He addressed his question to Ira and Charlotte.

Having no idea what Sandy was talking about, they could only wait for him to continue.

"Look, instead of our country drowning itself in this self-righteous witch hunt, we should grow up and face facts. Obviously Nixon is behind all of this; that's a given. The question that no one wants to address is *why*? The man was reelected president by one of the largest margins in history. What does that tell us?"

Again no one answered.

"The country hated and feared George McGovern. Almost no one but the radical left and the street people wanted him to be president. Nixon didn't have to do anything illegal to beat the man; so what he *did* do looks pretty stupid, in hindsight. But compared with having McGovern as president, Nixon's mistakes weren't earth-shattering crimes but regrettable misdemeanors —political parking tickets."

"Sandy," Paula inquired with noticeable embarrassment, "are you suddenly a Nixon supporter?"

Pleased that his diversion was working, Sandy continued. "I think it's important to look at the big picture—the real world. What would have happened if McGovern had won the presidency? I don't know about you, but with what I've seen of anti-Semitism in Eastern Europe I certainly don't get excited by the idea of socialism. And I *definitely* don't get worked up by Mister McGovern's enthusiasm for Jews and Israel. No, Nixon isn't my favorite guy but he's not a right-wing Nazi and he's not a socialist. Instead of persecuting him for his minor warts, we should be thankful that he's in office and not that left-wing idealogue from the sticks of South Dakota. Don't you agree?" Sandy looked for an answer from Ira and Charlotte.

But Paula's parents were too shocked too respond. Just as Sandy had expected, they were died-in-the-wool liberals, identi-

fying with the down-trodden, even if it was to their own disad-
vantage. They would have described themselves as in favor of
"enlightened self-interest" but were, in reality, so insulated by
the repository of political fantasies known as Manhattan that they
couldn't distinguish between their own long-term interests and
the rosy-sounding liberal ideas that might lead to another
Holocaust.

"How about ordering dinner?" Paula attempted to change the
subject.

A gesture from Charlotte summoned the waiter and menus,
absorbing minutes of trivial food-related questions before the
meals were selected and the four of them once again faced the
difficult privacy of a table without a waiter.

"So what do *you* think about Watergate?" Sandy asked
aggressively, prodding the conversation toward a useful area of
controversy.

"Neither my parents nor myself are crazy about Nixon,"
Paula replied. "Until this minute I didn't know you were either.
Did something fall on your head today, or have you suddenly
changed your opinion a hundred and eighty degrees?"

"I've been giving this a lot of thought lately, and I've come to
the conclusion that we're looking at the whole situation in the
wrong way. Nixon isn't the first president to tape his meetings.
Kennedy did it too. And Johnson. At times, all of them lied. All
of them played political tricks on their opponents. Nixon got
caught. I mean, none of us at this table believes that this is a *nice*
world we're living in, do we?"

Ira, Charlotte, and Paula said nothing.

"Okay, so it's a grim, vicious, nasty, unjust world, then, right?"

Again there was no response.

"Sometimes unsavory tactics have to be used to preserve
important ideas and institutions. For example, we have the
police."

"Don't tell me you're suddenly a fan of the LAPD too?" Paula
spoke with undisguised sarcasm.

"C'mon, Paula, have an open mind. This isn't a debate but a
discussion. Okay?"

She didn't answer.

"The point about the police is that we need them because, despite how we might like society to function, we still have murders, robberies, and rapes — crimes up the kazoo. If we want our community to advance, we've got to keep the criminals under control. So we train police, give them guns, radios, cars, motorcycles, computers, crime labs, handcuffs — the works — and encourage them to arrest and jail people who trample on the rights of the majority. Every society does this. And I think that's honestly how Nixon, Haldeman, and Erlichman viewed the consequences of George McGovern as president. If the senator from South Dakota had been elected, it would have been like putting the crazies in charge of the asylum. If we had any guts, instead of persecuting Nixon, Haldeman, and Erlichman we'd be honoring them."

Assigning such noble intentions to President Nixon broke the ice and opened the flood gates of argument. Paula spearheaded the rebuttal in her finest courtroom manner, debating with Sandy, totally supported by her parents. For the next two hours, nothing was discussed but the details of Watergate and the effects of Nixon and his men on society.

Under attack for his opinions, Sandy was happy. His outrageous position overshadowed any questions about his past or present and allowed Sandy to skate through the dinner without committing himself to even one compromising lie. The only drawback of this strategy was its effect on Paula, who was caught in the impossible position of trying to demolish Sandy's argument without demeaning him in the eyes of her parents. Socrates and Plato would have found this a difficult task. For Paula it was exhausting, frustrating, and confusing. By the dinner's end, she had run out of patience. The only positive impression Sandy made on her parents came when the waiter presented the check, which he grabbed and paid without discussion. His one admirable quality was incontestable: He was not a freeloader.

In the parking area, Paula helped her parents into the rented Chevy, then turned to Sandy, who was still waiting for his own car to be brought up from the lot below.

"Thank you so much," she said with quiet sarcasm. "You didn't have to do that. You could have been nice."

"So could they."

"What are you talking about?"

"C'mon, Paula, you saw the way they looked at me when I sat down; on sight they hated my guts."

"You're crazy."

"Am I?" Sandy spoke softly.

"I'll tell you one thing for sure: You really disappointed me tonight. I'm their only child. Of course they were going to be more than casually interested in you; but you didn't have to bait them. Do you really believe all that crap you were spouting?"

Sandy shrugged. "It's worth thinking about."

"I couldn't believe you were serious about it," she said unhappily. "Why did you argue with us like that?"

"Why did you let them run their judgmental magnifying glass over me?"

"Your car, señor." The parking attendant gestured to Sandy's Volvo, which was up and ready to go, blocking two other diners' cars.

"One minute, please," Sandy growled at the man, silencing him.

Paula smiled coolly. "We'll continue this another time. But I want you to think about something, Sandy: Tomorrow night you've got one more chance. Be smart and make an effort."

"Are you threatening me?"

Paula shook her head. "I'm simply telling you the facts."

"Well thank you, Amy Vanderbilt. While you're so free with the advice, why don't you slip a few of those 'facts' to your parents? Tell them this isn't New York but California and they're on vacation. Let them know that this native here," he pointed to himself, "is friendly. Inform them that I'm a lovely human being, that you're more than fond of me, and that they have no choice but accept me."

The honking of a car blocked by the Chevy, and the Volvo prevented any further argument.

"Remember what I advised you," she glared at him. "See you tomorrow night." Without so much as a peck on the cheek, Paula spun angrily on her heel, slid into the driver's seat of the Chevy, and drove out into traffic, disappearing from Sandy's sight in the direction of Beverly Hills.

46

Once home, Sandy's earlier euphoric fantasies dissolved, sending him into an emotional free-fall. How could I have been so stupid? he lambasted himself. Why am I such a clod, an imbecile, an unimaginative jerk? Why couldn't I have figured out some reasonable way to deal with Paula and her parents? Why did I have to pick such a hostile and offensive solution? Am I crazy? Is my judgment going?

"I put in a few calls while you were out," Billy interrupted his thoughts. "I hope you don't mind."

"Fine." Sandy, too distracted by his self-loathing to seriously consider what his friend was saying, pretended to concentrate on the hamburger, broccoli, and potato dinner he was preparing for Billy and the half-awake Hoffmann.

"You're not even interested in who I called?"

"As long as it wasn't the police or the papers, I couldn't care less," he mumbled. Why hadn't Paula intervened to ease the tension? Sandy ruminated. Why had she sided so totally with her parents at the expense of the man she supposedly loved? Was she telling him their relationship was nothing, that when push came to shove, he meant that little to her? Deep down she was daddy's girl. A mommy's girl. A spoiled princess.

"How about Vienna?" Billy inquired.

"Vienna?" Sandy looked up from the frying pan. "Vienna like in Austria?" he asked, confused. "Why Vienna?"

"Simon Wiesenthal."

Simon Wiesenthal. First Paula had yearned for the Austrian; now it was Billy's turn. Apparently neither of them had the guts to face life on their own. "You spoke to Wiesenthal?" He was furious.

Billy shook his head. "I only talked to his answering service. Vienna information gave me the number." He looked at his watch. "It's now eight-fifteen in the morning in Austria. The

356

service told me Wiesenthal usually comes in by eight. I think you should phone him. This is what you dial." Billy pointed to the long row of numbers written across the bottom of the paper he waved in front of Sandy.

"A great idea. Truly. Thank you." Sandy crumpled the paper and tossed it into the trash basket. "Now hand me that plate." With a spatula he lifted the first of the two hamburgers out of the frying pan.

"Look, is it so terrible to bring in an expert? Think of Wiesenthal as a consultant. So far, you've been right. I admit it. But tomorrow the problems are going to get much more complicated. Political. Legal. The State Department. This is an area where Wiesenthal's had experience. The man has been there. Would it really be so terrible to have someone of Wiesenthal's stature on our side?"

"You going to hand me that other plate or what?"

"I am not an idiot, Sandy. At the very least I deserve an explanation of why you won't call Austria," Billy said stubbornly. "I mean, I really don't understand how it could hurt."

"It's not necessary." Sandy spoke flatly.

"You call that an explanation?" Billy asked in exasperation.

"You said yourself that so far I've been right. The rest of my plan is going to succeed perfectly, too. Explain to me why your mind works overtime on ways to fuck everything up?"

Glaring at his friend, Billy controlled his urge to lash out in anger. "Set that spatula down and come with me for a second. I want to show you something." Without giving Sandy time to refuse, Billy left the room.

Sandy put down the spatula and followed Billy into Hoffmann's room.

"What do you see here?" Billy asked, pointing to the Nazi, who sat chained, shackled, handcuffed, drugged, and blindfolded like a vision from the Spanish Inquisition.

After momentarily considering Billy's question, Sandy turned to his friend. "I'm going to get the hamburgers off before they burn," he said, heading to the kitchen.

"To you," Billy explained while Sandy removed the food from the stove, "the man in that room is an SS officer. But this is California and to the district attorney that American citizen in there is a victim of assault, kidnaping, burglary, breaking and entering, criminal conspiracy, and gross violations of his civil rights. It's just possible that tomorrow night *we're* going to be the ones with the legal problems, not Hoffmann."

Sandy smiled, apparently unaffected by this logic. "I really think you should eat something. Over the years I've observed that some of the worst ideas in the world occur to people with empty stomachs. It has to do with sugar levels. All your hormones get out of balance and it affects the mind. Here," Sandy handed him a plate of food. "Eat, and I guarantee you'll feel a whole lot better about the situation."

"Well, okay, then. Since you're not jumping at the idea of talking to Wiesenthal, why don't *I* give the guy a call? I could even do it anonymously. You know, like tell him what we've done and what we've planned for tomorrow and see if he has any suggestions. What's the worst that could happen?"

Ignoring his friend's plea, Sandy loaded a second plate with dinner. "I'd prefer it if you'd do something practical and feed this to Hoffmann."

Billy reluctantly picked up the plate. "Okay, but on one condition. You come with me and watch the man while he eats. Try to see him as he's going to appear to a jury. Yeah, he has a slight German accent. But you know what those twelve men and women are going to see? A nice old lobster fisherman, straight from a feature spread in *Life* magazine. Hoffmann looks like a classic old-world grandfather. And his defense team's going to try to prove what all those war criminal trials go after. What you call evidence they'll regard as the product of brilliant Soviet fabrication — KGB forgery. That's if the ID card and picture aren't ruled by the judge as inadmissible because you stole them instead of obtaining them legally with a search warrant. By the time we go to trial, the German-American immigrant groups are going to be screaming bloody murder. Backing them up will be the ACLU who'll support Hoffmann with the best lawyers in the country. All this, while we have to defend ourselves at our own expense. Think about it, Sandy; what do you have to lose by one call to Vienna?"

"Quit being such a gutless wonder and go feed the son-of-a-bitch."

"Isn't there any way I can persuade you to call Wiesenthal?"

Without the slightest hesitation, Sandy shook his head. "I don't want anything to diminish the impact of surprise tomorrow. When I march the Nazi into that dinner I want that room full of people to be shocked. If we tell Wiesenthal what we're going to do, we might as well take out a front-page ad in the *B'nai Brith Messenger*. Wiesenthal is tied into the leaders of every Jewish community in the country. If I talk to him now, by the time we show up at the dinner tomorrow half the police in the city will be there waiting for us, which would obliterate the impact of our accomplishment. If you were Wiesenthal and a couple of guys called from California and told you what we are planning to do, you wouldn't believe us for one second. As soon as you hung up you'd be phoning Los Angeles to warn the authorities. We could be psychotics. PLO Terrorists. Neo-Nazis. You name it and he'd think it was a possibility. The last thing we want is to have the hotel ringed with police."

"I guess you have a point." Billy's voice sagged with defeat.

After unshackling the drugged Nazi and seeing him through the awful ritual with the toilet, Billy and Sandy tied him back in the chair, fed him, then injected him with another 300 mg of Tuinol. Moments later, Billy ate in silence while he watched Hoffmann succumb to the effects of the powerful depressant. With the situation totally under control, Billy jotted a few characters on a piece of paper and slipped the note into Sandy's shirt pocket before disappearing into the bedroom for a few hours of long overdue sleep.

Once again on guard duty, Sandy observed that Hoffmann did resemble a lobster fisherman from a *Life* magazine cover. But so what? Billy was wrong. No jury would be deceived by his appearance. The man wasn't a Teutonic Santa Claus. He wasn't even a true Homo sapiens. Hoffmann was morally subhuman; below the level of a rabid dog.

Remembering the paper in his shirt pocket, Sandy lifted out the note, unfolded it, and read the short sentence: "In case you change your mind, Simon Wiesenthal's number is two two two . . ." Without a second thought, Sandy crumpled the message into a ball and tossed it out of the room onto the floor of the hallway.

Hang tough, Sandy told himself, and tomorrow all of them, Paula included, will understand how much they've been underestimating you.

47

After nearly seven hours, Sandy awakened Billy with a freshly brewed cup of black coffee. The time was six o'clock on Saturday morning. But even eight ounces of the caffeine-rich liquid didn't elevate Billy's dark and depressing mood. Quickly showering and shaving, Billy dressed and got ready for guard duty without speaking one sympathetic word.

"I purposely didn't sedate him," Sandy whispered to his friend after they had successfully shepherded Hoffmann to the toilet and back to his chair. "I want the drugs out of his system so he can walk tonight without wobbling or tripping. So I suggest you watch him particularly carefully. If he gives you any trouble, wake me immediately."

Billy nodded and took his place in the prisoner's room, sitting opposite the shackled and blindfolded Nazi.

Exhausted, Sandy washed his face, brushed his teeth, and flopped down on his mattress, fully dressed. Within seconds of closing his eyes, he drifted off to sleep.

"Sandy! Get up!" Billy was yelling what seemed to be only a few seconds later. "C'mon, quick. Get up — I think Hoffmann's having a heart attack!"

Propelled by a surge of adrenalin, Sandy sat up, fully awake.

"He's moaning, breathing real strange," Billy continued, "complaining of pain in his left shoulder, arm, and chest. It hurts so much he's having trouble talking. Even his skin looks green. I think we should call an ambulance."

"Are you fucking crazy?" Sandy jumped to his feet and bolted for the prisoner's room.

"Okay Hoffmann, so what's the problem?" Sandy spoke in his flattest, most unsympathetic tone of voice.

"Pain," the Nazi groaned. "In the chest, neck. Very bad. Uhhh!" he moaned. "Waves of pain, like an elephant crushing me," he whispered, writhing against his restraints.

"Sandy, we really should get this guy to a hospital."

Whirling around, enraged at the mention of his name in front of the Nazi, Sandy grimaced with a threatening expression as he silently mouthed the phrase, "Shut your fucking face," effectively communicating his feelings and intentions.

Frightened by this degree of rage, Billy nodded meekly.

"Have you had this pain before?" Sandy asked Hoffmann.

The German nodded. "Two years ago. Uhhh," he groaned, taking deep breaths. "The doctors said it was a heart attack."

"That's what you think you're having now?"

The Nazi nodded, sweat dripping down his pale face.

"Did they give you medication to take?"

Nodding, Hoffmann opened his mouth but no sound emerged — apparently the pain was too great for him to speak.

"I'm going to call the paramedics," Billy announced.

"Don't you so much as fucking move," Sandy yelled.

"Hey, the man could die. What kind of good is he going to do anyone in that condition?"

"Shut up and don't worry about it," he commanded.

Billy nodded.

"What kind of medication did they give you?" Sandy asked Hoffmann.

Again the German tried to speak, but the intense pain apparently prevented him from forming words.

"Were you taking medication at the time of the first heart attack?"

Hoffmann shook his head. "But you take medication now, daily?"

The Nazi nodded, letting out a pitiful, pain-induced groan.

"Sandy, if the man dies here," Billy sounded frantic, "not only does it not do you any good but it's going to mean a murder charge. Let's call the paramedics, please!"

Infuriated by a second use of his name, Sandy swung around, grabbed Billy by the front of his shirt, and literally dragged him out of the room into the hallway, where he slammed the door shut to exclude the Nazi from the conversation.

"Number one," Sandy hissed. "You say my name again in front of Hoffmann and I'm going to make you wear a fucking gag over your mouth, do you understand?"

Frightened by his friend's outrage, Billy nodded.

"Good." Sandy released Billy's shirt. "The other thing you gotta get through your head is that the man in there is no dumb-shit Kraut. When he was an SS officer he was in the situation we're in now, hundreds if not thousands of times. Maybe some-one once faked a heart attack when he was on guard. So he decided to try that one out on us. He's pretty convincing, isn't he?"

"But what if he's *not* faking it?" Billy pleaded. "If he dies, we're really in deep shit. At least if we call the paramedics he'll live to stand trial as a war criminal."

Sandy shook his head. "The son-of-a-bitch is faking it. You know how I know?"

Billy shook his head.

"The night I searched his house I went through every nook and cranny of his medicine cabinet. I found aspirin, cough syrup, Mylanta and Valium. Nothing else. *Not one other prescription.* And let me tell you, a man taking medication for a heart condition has a hell of a lot more than that in his medicine cabinet."

"What if he keeps his heart medicine someplace else?"

"I went through everything. And I guarantee you someone with an illness doesn't keep medicine he takes daily in a secret, inaccessible location."

Billy couldn't refute this logic.

"Do me a favor now. Not only do I never want to hear my name mentioned, I also don't want you to talk to him. Instead of answering his questions, come get me. If he groans in pain, let me deal with it. Say nothing to him, do you understand?"

Billy nodded. "And if he is having a heart attack and dies? I mean, let's take the worst case. Then we dump the body on Mulholland. If the police somehow trace it to us, what are you going to tell me when we face the gas chamber instead of ten to twenty years in the can?"

"I'll testify in court that at gun point I stopped you from calling the paramedics. I promise I'll never, ever reveal I even had an accomplice. You help me through the rest of this and you're off, scot-free. Of course you won't get any of the glory. But I'm absolving you totally from the downside risk. That's what you want, isn't it?"

"What if someone identifies me?"

"Like who?"

"Like Hoffmann."

"If he dies of a heart attack, that's going to be pretty unlikely."

"And if he doesn't die?"

"It's his word against mine—and he's the war criminal, remember? So now that you're free of all responsibility, will you relax and quit worrying?"

Billy said nothing.

"C'mon, I'll show you something that'll make you feel a lot better. If this were County Hospital, what I'm about to do would make medical history. And no talking, remember?"

Billy nodded.

Sandy opened the door, revealing the Nazi still squirming in apparently uncontrollable spasms of pain so severe his face had flushed the color of sweet and sour cabbage.

"So," Sandy inquired, "you're having this heart attack because you left your medication at home?"

The German nodded between labored breaths.

"It's in your medicine cabinet, I suppose?"

Again Hoffmann bobbed his head up and down affirmatively, causing Sandy to flash an *I told you so* smile at Billy.

"Well I don't believe you, Hoffmann. I know you're faking. But let's suppose I'm wrong and this heart attack of yours is real. What's going to happen is that you're going to die. Because I'm *not* going to call the paramedics. You're *not* going to the hospital. And I'm not even going to try to get your medication." Sandy addressed Billy. "Tape his mouth shut again."

"You're sure?" Billy asked, still not convinced that Hoffmann was faking it.

"You really want to keep hearing all these grunts and groans? This guy sounds like a fucking sow in a slaughterhouse."

"But with tape over his mouth, how's he going to breathe?"

"Who cares?" Sandy spoke for the benefit of the Nazi. Billy cut off a six-inch strip of the heavy adhesive and slapped it across Hoffmann's mouth, once again silencing the man.

"Now, isn't that better?" Sandy asked with relish.

Uncertain, Billy studied the German, wondering how the diminished air supply would affect his breathing.

"Listen, it's still only nine o'clock." Sandy spoke with bravado. "I'm going back to my nap. If he dies, don't wake me because it doesn't matter; we can't get rid of his body until it gets dark."

"I understand," Billy grimaced.

Pretending to leave the room, Sandy walked behind Hoffmann to the threshold and slammed the door to convince him he was now alone with Billy. Gesturing with a finger to his lips, Sandy leaned against the wall and watched the German.

In no more than a minute, the Nazi's breathing returned to normal, his tortured writhing ceased, and his complexion resumed its former suntan.

So much for the heart attack, Sandy grinned as he stepped out into the hallway and returned to his bedroom, where he once again flopped down on his bed.

Pleased with himself, Sandy tried to relax. But with all the problems plaguing him, sleep was impossible. He wanted the Beth-Israel dinner to go as smoothly as his solution to Hoffmann's heart attack. He wanted Paula to be on his side, not her parents! He wanted the world to appreciate his accomplishment for what it was. The list of possible complications grew exponentially by the minute and he felt like a little kid wishing on a star. No one ever knew what the future would bring. The only thing that remained certain was that in less than twelve hours, all mysteries would be resolved. In the meantime, Sandy told himself, the one good thing he could do was sleep. But at nine-thirty, the phone started ringing.

Hugo, the Beverly Wilshire's grand ballroom maître d', was the first in an endless series of frantic callers demanding immediate solutions to last-minute problems. The lilies hadn't arrived; what other flowers could they substitute? Five minutes after Hugo came a question from the old man himself about reworking the order of speeches. Then it was Charlie, followed by Stanley Furgstein. Sylvia called with a couple of seating changes. Hugo phoned again, hysterical — the band leader was threatening to quit if he wasn't allowed to move his musicians from behind the dance floor to a more visible location, which required that the entire seating arrangement be reorganized. Negotiating an end to that idiocy took nearly half an hour, after which the assault of phone calls went into high gear. No one seemed to be able to make a decision without Sandy. Nat, Charlie, Ed, Sylvia, Hugo, Furgstein, Hugo again: It was a madhouse with Sandy as the warden, keeping everyone calm and everything moving. What a strange reversal, he told himself in the middle of all the craziness; I'm the one with the truly bizarre scheme, yet they all expect me to be the model of cool reason.

By eleven o'clock, Sandy had completely given up the idea of sleep. Three hours later, to stay alert, he was chugging coffee at the rate of one cup every fifteen minutes as the endless stream of problems continued.

By five o'clock, all the organizational fires had been extinguished, the phone calls had ended, and it was time to begin the last stage of the operation. After seeing Hoffmann through yet another repulsive toilet ritual, Sandy fed the German a light meal of scrambled eggs and toast, helped Billy change the man's clothes, then took a shower himself.

A few minutes after six, he had finished dressing and was standing in front of the bedroom mirror inspecting his appearance. Decked out in a well-tailored tuxedo, he appeared to be the perfect young executive, so slick and well-groomed as to make even a suspicious and skeptical father like Nat suspend his judgment and glow with pride. Sandy was the vision of the dutiful son, ready for an evening honoring his generous, loving, supportive, wealthy philanthropist father and pillar of the community.

48

By six-thirty Sandy surged with self-confidence. Behind the wheel of a rented 1969 Buick Electra, he had become in his mind a force of nature, a human tidal wave. Not fifteen minutes away — down the canyon and across Beverly Hills — lay his magnificent destiny. Talk about making a splash. What would occur at the Wilshire would be nothing less than an apocalyptic debut, a *bar mitzvah* into the legions of the famous. This was Carnegie Hall, Broadway Opening Night, and a Klieg Light Major Studio Premiere, all rolled into one. It was the perfect play, with the ideal cast, presented to the ultimate audience, the hit of hits — a once in a lifetime moment in the world spotlight. Throw out the old, Sandy told himself. Life was going to change, now and forever. *I am unstoppable!*

Of course he said none of this to Billy, who rode in the back seat of the car, or to Hoffmann, who sat in the front passenger seat. Sandy's object was to remain calm and appear as inconspicuous as possible. So far, he observed as he turned left from Beverly Glen onto Sunset Boulevard, it's working perfectly. No one in a passing car gave them a second glance.

Sandy, in his tux, looked formally conservative. Billy, sitting low in the back, wasn't visible. And Hoffmann appeared to be an English businessman wearing his London Fog raincoat and crumpled Irish wool cap. The only even marginally incongruous item — which no stranger could have noticed — were the sunglasses the German wore: The lenses were opaque, covered on the inside with black enamel. Even the tape silencing the Nazi's mouth was once again concealed by the fake goatee. The shackles on his ankles, the handcuffs binding his wrists, and the rope locking him to the seat itself were of course invisible outside of the Buick. Even a passing police car, Sandy congratulated himself, wouldn't look twice at them — just three normal, middle-class citizens out for a night on the town.

The drive to the hotel was uneventful. The episode with the faked heart attack seemed to have tranquilized both Billy and the Nazi, as if they each had given up resistance in the face of Sandy's superiority. For Billy, the drama was nearly over. Another hour and he would be gone, not just from the Wilshire but from the country with a confirmed ticket on an-over-the-pole flight to Paris, courtesy of Sandy. This was a gesture of gratitude that Billy had been delighted to accept — he couldn't wait to put as much distance as possible between himself and the scene of the crime.

Hoffmann's capitulation was another story. Was the war criminal's cooperative behavior a ruse to lull them into complacency and make some new escape plan possible? Most likely, Sandy reassured himself, the German had given up. After forty-eight hours in chains, blindfolded and shot full of Tuinal, the Nazi's will to resist had no doubt been severely compromised. Psychologically, the man was like a Jew after one week in a cattle car to Auschwitz. Resistance was impossible, rebellion unthinkable. Cooperation was the best alternative.

Heading south from Sunset, the cruise down Whittier Drive took no more than three minutes before the big Buick crossed Wilshire and arrived at the entrance to the Beverly Wilshire Hotel. As he flicked on the turn signal and braked, Sandy could feel the excitement shoot through his gut, hardening his belly with tension. Rehearsal time was finally over; the moment of achievement had arrived.

As the Buick idled into the multistory parking lot, the logistical nightmares that had plagued Sandy for more than a week evaporated into harmless irritations. The worst that could happen was some feeble physical resistance from Hoffmann. But what could he do? Moan and perhaps thrash his upper body a foot or so from side to side. Controlling that wouldn't be difficult, thanks to the electronic dog-training collar, which was now tied like a jockstrap under the German's underwear, tight up against his balls.

After a complete circle of the lot revealed no evidence of police or security, Sandy parked the Buick in a secluded spot adjacent to but not visible from the side hotel entrance and parking elevator.

By carefully positioning the car between a wall and a concrete column, Sandy and Billy could see everything around them without themselves being observed.

"Just remember," Sandy spoke to Billy for Hoffmann's benefit, "if he causes you any trouble, shoot the bastard."

Sandy got out and opened the trunk. After triple-checking the German's bonds, Billy followed.

"How do I look?" Sandy handed his friend the car keys and one of the two walkie-talkies he'd retrieved from the space next to the spare tire.

"Like you're supposed to." Billy spoke with a grim lack of enthusiasm.

"Well, I feel fucking-A great. And so should you. You sure you don't want to change your mind and stick around for the speech?" He rotated the dial on his walkie-talkie, producing a satisfying crackle.

"I've done my part, thank you. I'll take my chances with the food on Pan Am."

"You're going to miss something sensational," Sandy whispered as he continued to scan the parking lot.

Billy shrugged. His mind was made up.

"I'll call you and let you know how it goes. *Before* you read about it in the papers. You came through for me when no one else would. You're the only one who cared; I won't forget that."

Billy nodded, unable to conceal his terror. "Good luck, Sandy."

"See you in a few minutes. And turn on your radio." He pointed to the walkie-talkie in Billy's hands, gave his friend a grin and a wink, and headed for the hotel's entrance.

"Can you hear me?" Sandy asked over his handset.

"Roger," crackled back Billy's voice.

Sandy disappeared through the doorway marked "Beverly Wilshire Hotel, Lobby Entrance."

Billy closed the trunk, got in the front seat of the Buick, put the key back in the ignition, closed the door, and waited for the next transmission from his walkie-talkie.

49

To Sandy's mind, all that was missing from his entrance into the hotel was a regal fanfare of trumpets. The grandeur of the lobby, which only the day before had seemed garish and pretentious, welcomed him into the select company of those who deserved head-of-state treatment. From the scarlet and gold brocade carpeting to the massive crystal chandelier, the architecture and interior decor promised a larger-than-life reception.

"I'm about to enter the main ballroom; how's the signal?" Sandy transmitted over his walkie-talkie.

"Loud and clear," Billy responded without the least static or interference.

Sandy strolled past the two long tables of elegantly dressed volunteers who were organizing their alphabetized list of guests. Passing Miss A-D, he smiled. Miss E-G shuffled her lists. Sandy stopped in front of Miss H-L. The sequin-gowned socialite glanced up, delighted to serve her first customer of the evening.

"Name?"

"Sandy Klein."

"Table number one," she informed him, checking off his name.

More perfection, he glowed, strolling through the open fifteen-foot doorway that would have adequately honored the entrance of Moses, Abraham, Isaac, Jacob, the Golden Calf, and the Pharaoh himself.

Activity in the Grand Ballroom had shifted into overdrive as a swarm of hotel employees swirled through the cavernous room in a frenzy of last-minute activity. At the bar area by the entrance, bartenders clad in tuxedos lined up rows of sparkling glasses. Sandy picked up a tumbler of soda water and surveyed the situation.

Five steps down, the room spread out into an enormous multilevel dining area. At the far end, on a small stage, stood the speaker's podium. Fanning out from this central point, like the circles on a peacock's tail, were round tables of ten, seating a total of two hundred. The other hundred and ten guests sat in the charity ball equivalent of Siberia at tables flanking the outer boundaries of the hall.

Descending onto the main floor, Sandy dodged the white-jacketed waiters rushing to double-check the silverware, reposition the huge blue and white floral centerpieces, fill the water glasses, bring bread, add dishes of green and black olives, or replace missing blue and white gift-wrapped bottles of Israeli perfume. To the left of the podium and behind the dance floor, the ten-piece orchestra tuned their instruments while the lighting crew made things difficult for everyone by whipping beams of focused spots back and forth across the room in a last-minute test of their equipment. No question about it, the place was humming. Regardless of what happened with Hoffmann, no one would ever be able to say that he, Nat Klein's youngest son, hadn't done a superb job as the dinner's chairman. If only my mother could be here to see it, Sandy lamented.

"How's the reception now?" He spoke into the mouthpiece of his walkie-talkie while inspecting table number one, directly in front of the podium.

"We're getting a lot of cars driving through, a lot of tuxedos walking by. You sure you don't want to change your mind and dump this living shit up on Mulholland?" Billy answered, clearly anxious.

"What's with dumping shit on Mulholland?" Nat's voice growled from behind, startling Sandy, who swung around to see his father standing with Sylvia not ten feet away.

"Dad, Sylvia. You both look great."

"Yo. Hello," Billy's voice crackled over the two-inch speaker. "Do you hear me?"

Gesturing for his father to wait one second, Sandy spoke into his transmitter. "I appreciate the offer," he improvised, "but we're not dumping anything until I meet with the Health Department inspector tomorrow. I don't care what the scumbag from Hoffmann Meat Packing claims, he's not going to be paid one lousy nickel. Keep the meat just the way you've got it and we'll go exactly according to plan. Now I gotta get back to work." Before Billy could answer, Sandy flicked off the walkie-talkie, then turned to his father. "Can you believe it; we got a special deal on some prime filet and the kitchen told me the meat wasn't what it was supposed to be. They supplied something a couple of notches below choice — USDA Grade B shoe leather. Fortunately the chef spotted it this morning; smart guy, huh?"

"What're they going to serve?" Sylvia asked anxiously.

"Not to worry; another wholesaler sent over a superb cut. You're going to be very happy. So tell me; what do you think of the room?" He gestured around them in an effort to change the subject.

"Sylvia and I were just talking about that." Nat beamed as he turned to his wife. "Why don't you tell Sandy what you said to me?"

Smiling graciously, Sylvia appeared to be sincerely proud of her husband's youngest son. "I was telling your father that I've been to god knows how many affairs in this room and I've never seen the place look this lovely. You did a wonderful job."

"Thank you," Sandy answered modestly.

"I agree with Sylvia two hundred percent; I only wish your mother could be here to see it," Nat confided.

Ignoring the momentary chill radiating from Sylvia, Sandy nodded in agreement as he reassured his father, "I'm sure somewhere she sees and knows, Dad. And I'll bet she's pleased."

"Nat! Sylvia! You both look won-der-ful."

Everyone swung around as Stanley Furgstein hustled toward them, dragging his bleached blond wife. With them was a small, trim, dark-haired, sad-faced man in his early fifties, distinctly military in bearing, wearing an impressively tailored European tuxedo.

"Isn't the room beau-ti-ful?" Furgstein enjoyed dragging out his compliments. "Of course not as lovely as you, Sylvia. How *do* you do it?"

She smiled at the flattery.

Sandy had to admit that in this instance Furgstein *was* telling the truth — Sylvia had never looked better. She was stunning in her new Chanel gown. Who wouldn't be? At five thousand dollars a shot, even Hoffmann would get compliments wearing the Paris original. The god-damn dress cost more than the average Oldsmobile.

"And look who flew in after all, just for tonight, for your dinner," Furgstein continued in his hyped-up promotional voice. "Sylvia, Nat, you both know Yitzak Alon, Israel's Minister of Defense."

"Ex-minister — I'm just an advisor now, remember?"

Nat thrust out his hand, genuinely touched by the man's unexpected appearance. "Yitzak — they kept telling me you couldn't make it."

"As I told Stanley, only a war could keep me from honoring an old friend like Nathan Klein." Alon spoke in a heavy Israeli accent as he warmly shook Nat's hand. "Hello, Sylvia." Yitzak turned, smiled, and kissed her on both cheeks. "You are truly a vision tonight."

"I don't think you've ever met my son, Sandy," Nat interjected.

The old Israeli warrior and politician extended a hand in his best, most impersonal manner.

Sandy ignored the snub. "Thank you so much for coming. From what I read in the papers I'm surprised you could get away; it looks like another war with Egypt could start maybe even tomorrow."

Nodding his head gravely, Alon spoke sadly. "If only you weren't right; the Arabs never seem to learn. Why more Jews have to die to remind them we're in Israel to stay I'll never understand."

The serious manner in which Alon spoke cut through Nat and Sylvia's playful ebullience, and for a moment killed the conversation.

"Yitzak, Sylvia, Nat," Stanley interrupted in his most upbeat tone, "we can't do anything about that part of the world tonight. But we are making a contribution here — a big, important one at that. Come." He took Nat and Yitzak by the elbows. "There are some people I know you'll enjoy meeting." A born fund raiser,

Furgstein directed the group away from the stick-in-the-mud youngest son toward a cluster of new arrivals by the bar.

Without the slightest apology, the five of them took off across the room, leaving him to stand alone by the head table — the family fool. Sandy switched his walkie-talkie back on. "Are you still there?" he inquired.

"Affirmative," came the answer. "What happened to you? Your radio went dead after that meat-packing comment. What the hell is going on?"

"Not a thing," Sandy spoke quietly. "Everything is humming along perfectly. You know how they treat you in Beverly Hills; you're missing a truly great evening. Sure you don't want to change your mind?"

"Hello stranger," a female voice teased from behind Sandy's back. "Long time no see."

Whirling around, Sandy was caught off guard by the stunning beauty of Vikki, who wore a daringly low-cut black silk gown which prominently displayed her finest assets. Standing beside her, holding Vikki's hand, was the man who had accompanied her to the screening of Kit Flynn's horror movie.

"Sorry, but no thanks," Billy's distorted voice sputtered from the walkie-talkie's speaker.

"Listen," Sandy spoke hurriedly into the transmitter. "I can't talk now. People are arriving. Don't answer; just stay tuned for instructions. Over and out." Sandy immediately turned down the volume on his speaker and smiled pleasantly at the new arrivals. "Vikki, you look wonderful. What brings you out to this circus?"

Vikki flashed Sandy her most angelic expression, indicating the man beside her. "Allen," she answered simply. "You two met outside the Director's Guild Theatre, remember? As I recall, you described the movie as *garbage*. I think your judgment was a little off that night, Sandy: That garbage turned out to be the sleeper hit of the summer."

Grinning politely, Sandy rose to the occasion. "One man's meat is another man's garbage, isn't that the expression?" Extending his hand to Allen, Sandy added, "Nice to see you again."

Uncertain of Sandy's meaning, Allen shook hands as if no insult were intended.

"Funny, Sandy. Very funny," Vikki grimaced. "You know, you and Allen have more in common than you think; you're practically in business together."

"Oh, and how is that?" Sandy challenged.

"Does the name Allen Strachen mean anything to you?"

"That's you?" Sandy indicated the man holding Vikki's hand.

"Very good," she mocked him. "Now tell me you don't know who he is."

"This is a little out of context. You want to give me another clue?"

"Okay. Can you think tax attorney, like in international law?"

"Vikki, I hate to spoil your game but I have a lot of responsibilities tonight. I'm a little distracted. Can you just tell me straight out what you're trying to say?"

"Sandy, you're no fun at all," she teased, giving her boyfriend's arm an affectionate hug. "Allen is *the* Allen Strachen, the attorney representing the British investors buying your family's company."

Sandy was speechless. Everything he had guessed was true. The good news, he told himself, is that now, finally, the reality of the betrayal is out in the open, incontestable. As the rage built within him, he felt stronger, cleverer. Revealing nothing of his real reaction, Sandy pretended to be amused. "Oh, yes. You're *that* Allen Strachen. I'm sorry to be so stupid. It was hard to connect you to Vikki and this dinner. Now I understand why you're here."

"Exactly," the man beamed.

"Tell me, honestly," Sandy spoke like a conspirator. "When do you really think the deal's going to close?"

"That's what your father just asked me." Allen smiled professionally. "The syndicate met today and as I understand it—I haven't seen the paperwork yet—those last few niggling details have finally been wrapped up and everyone's happy. Barring any last-minute problems, a messenger should deliver the signed contracts, amendments, and check to me on Monday. We'll do one final review of all the documents, then turn everything over to the escrow officer, hopefully late afternoon on Tuesday. So by Wednesday, god willing, the deal will be closed."

"Finally." Sandy tried to sound informed. "I can't believe it took so much time."

Allen shrugged. "As your father likes to remind me, important deals never happen fast. To do it right you have to dot every *i* and cross every *t*. That way there's no confusion and both parties are absolutely certain about exactly what was bought and sold. In my clients' case, we have some particularly careful individuals who only involve themselves in first-rate investments. Doing things meticulously means avoiding problems and unwanted publicity. They like getting the job done the right way without a lot of hoopla and BS. I don't know if you've had an opportunity to get to know them yet, but once you see how they think and do business you're going to find it's a real pleasure working with them."

"I'm looking forward to it," Sandy answered blandly, wondering how such cautious, careful, and publicity-shy British investors were going to react to the evening's unveiling of the Nazi. Talk about controversial! If a Nazi war criminal at a Jewish fundraising dinner didn't arouse publicity, nothing would. Perhaps it was all for the best; if the investors were Jewish themselves, they couldn't help but be impressed by their new partner's youngest son. And if they weren't impressed and his actions rattled the deal, fuck 'em, Sandy thought. I am being screwed out of my rightful share of the family business; who gives a shit what the investors or my father and brothers think about my activities?

Before Sandy could pump Strachen for further information, a waving arm up by the bar caught his eye: Paula and her parents had entered, accompanied by Larry Carton. Shit, Sandy cursed to himself, things were complicated enough without that dumb-ass lawyer involved. Was he here as a subtle threat, a covert message from Paula? See how a nice Jewish boy behaves, she was telling him. See how civil and well-mannered he is. See how much my parents like him. Yeah, well, Sandy wanted to yell at her, see what a worthless, fucking wimp that fat-ass lawyer really is. You want him, you can have him.

Refocusing his gaze on Vikki and Allen, Sandy closed the conversation. "You know I'd love to talk with you more about this but I have a lot of responsibilities tonight; I'm the chairman of this affair."

"Along with that affair, too?" Vikki indicated Paula across the room.

Sandy laughed, pretending to be amused by her game. She knew nothing and was only probing. Some other time her jealousy might have been flattering, but at that moment Sandy had too much on his mind.

"Gotta go, Vik. Allen. Enjoy the evening." Without waiting for a response Sandy made a beeline across the now crowded ballroom toward Paula, her parents, and Carton. The moment Sandy had dreaded for so long was now inevitable: He had to tell her the truth about his real identity before it was unveiled in front of the whole community.

"Still there?" Sandy asked into the walkie-talkie as he wended his way through the mob of designer gowns and well-pressed tuxedos.

No answer. Panicked, Sandy stopped walking, pushed the transmit button, and tried again. "Hello. Are . . . you . . . there?"

Again there was only silence.

Paula waved a second time. Sandy held up his finger, indicating one minute. What was wrong? Had Billy let the German go? Could the Nazi have talked his way to freedom? Maybe someone had spotted the shackles and called the police. There were so many possibilities that Sandy didn't know where to begin. Talk about a nightmare! Every black possibility descended on him like a ten ton block of concrete. Controlling his sudden flare-up of hysteria, Sandy checked his walkie-talkie and realized that the volume control was still off. Turning on the knob, he spoke into the mouthpiece. "Hello, do you hear me?"

"Of course I hear you; what do you expect?" Billy's voice sounded testy.

"We're still on schedule. The big P just arrived with her parents. Wish me luck." Sandy spoke with relief.

"Hey, I guess you haven't been listening. For the last three days all I've been doing is wishing you luck."

"Yes, you're right. Thank you. Okay now, the next call will be when I need you. Whatever you do, don't shut off your set, understood?"

"I'm with you and I'm ready. Give 'em hell."

Without turning down the volume, Sandy slung the walkie-talkie over his shoulder and once again headed for Paula. The fact that Billy was still in place instantly restored Sandy's self-confidence. Rocketing up from the depths of despair, he crossed the room with the grace and assurance of a lion running down his prey. The feeling was primordial, the strength of the hunt. Now certain of success, the risk involved in telling Paula the truth seemed minimal. In the face of such an achievement, what could she say? Who else did she know who had singlehandedly captured a Nazi war criminal? Compared with that, Carton was nothing but a fat joke!

Snaking his way through the crowd of philanthropists, Sandy felt plugged in to the center of life itself, carried along by the river of fate. Nothing could stop him now. Soon everyone in the room would be astounded by him, in awe of his bravery. Depression, despair, alienation, and self-contempt would all be mental states of the past, gone forever.

Sandy floated the final twenty feet to Paula. He was Babe Ruth, making his way from third base to home plate after hitting home run number sixty. He was Neal Armstrong setting foot on the moon — "one giant leap for mankind." The world was his; he was untouchable, unstoppable, finally assured of his rightful place in history.

"Paula, darling, how wonderful to see you," Sandy purred, wrapping her in his arms and kissing her rigid lips. "You are truly the most beautiful woman in the room, isn't she?"

This last remark was addressed to her parents who, instead of answering, only scrutinized Sandy with their contemptuous, high-powered judgment meters, rating him a solid zero on their hundred-point scale.

"What happened to your Uri outfit?" Paula asked, startled by his sudden self-confidence.

He shrugged his shoulders cavalierly. "I thought about what you said last night in the parking lot at Scandia, and I came to a decision. Tonight I'm cutting out all the bullshit, going to be myself, tell the truth, and let the chips fall wherever."

Stunned by this major reversal of his behavior, Paula didn't know how to respond.

"What's with the radio?" Carton gestured to the walkie-talkie.

"They've got a director for the program tonight up in the control booth." Sandy pointed in the direction of the balcony-level spotlights. "He wanted to be able to talk directly with the speakers in case there were any last minute changes."

Carton nodded.

"So," Sandy addressed the older Gottliebs and Carton, "if you'll excuse me for just one minute, I'd like to speak with Paula."

She looked at him with suspicion.

"There's something important I need to discuss with you alone, about tonight. It won't take long."

Clearly conflicted, she hesitated, then finally turned to her parents. "I'll be right back."

Both parents nodded gravely as Sandy took Paula's hand and led her down the carpeted stairs toward the relative quiet of the seating area. But once out of her mother and father's earshot, she stopped him abruptly with a yank on his arm.

"Sandy, hold it a minute."

He turned to face her. Visible from the bar area, making matters more difficult, Mister and Mrs. Gottlieb stared down at them. Were they lip readers? Sandy wondered. Couldn't they just leave him alone for five minutes?

"They're watching us, aren't they?" Paula asked.

"Is the Pope Catholic?" Sandy spoke without moving his mouth.

"Before you tell me anything," she said angrily, "there's something I want you to know: You, Sandy, caused me a lot of grief today. *A lot of grief.*" Paula emphasized this last point just in case he had gone deaf. "My parents are beside themselves. Nuts. All because of your ridiculous attitude last night. Why couldn't you have been nice? It's not like you can't be charming. Do you have any idea what they put me through today because of you?"

"Paula, you know what *you* think about me; you don't need their approval."

"That's not the point. They're my parents. They're old. They've had a very difficult life *and* they've made plenty of sacrifices for me. The least I can do is be nice to them in their last years. Or is that concept too difficult for you to understand?"

"In case you've forgotten, it wasn't me who wanted them here tonight."

"Yeah, well," she growled, "you almost got your wish. They didn't want to come either. All day they were hounding me to drive them to the airport and put them on a plane back to New York. I practically had to threaten suicide to get them to stay through tonight and see you accept this award." She stopped and studied him, seriously considering her words before speaking further. "Sandy, what I'm about to say is not something I want you to take lightly. This is very important, and I'm not kidding. If you want a future with me you'd better make a great speech up there and make us all proud of you tonight."

"Another ultimatum?" Sandy asked.

"I'm counting on you. Are you going to come through or not?"

"Both and neither," he grinned, to her confusion. "There are a few things occurring here tonight that are going to be something of a surprise. That's why I wanted to talk to you alone. I'm not sure how you're going to take it. Before I tell you about it I want you to know something. With or without your parents, I accept you even if you are often impossible. Yes, there are parts of you I'd like to change. But overall, I love you *just as you are*. I hope you feel the same for me. Now, what I want you to know is . . ."

An electrified drum roll from the band blared through the room, cutting off Sandy's confession.

"Ladies and gentlemen," the band leader bellowed through the loudspeakers, "please take your seats; we'd like to begin."

Paula shifted her attention from Sandy to her parents and Carton, who were being swept along by the flow of the crowd, down toward the seating area.

"Paula," he said urgently, "I need you to listen to me. I'm not the person you think I am. You don't know everything about me . . ."

"Give me a break, Sandy." Her attention remained distracted, on her mother and father. "That's exactly what I've been telling you for weeks. And after last night I particularly don't know who the hell you are. The truth is, if you want me to be who you think *I* am, you'd better straighten up your act, and real fast. Now I'm going back to my parents. A good way to start would be trying to be nice to them at the table. Hm?"

"I'm not sitting with you; they put me at the head table."

"Terrific," she said sarcastically, turning away as her parents and Carton approached.

"Paula, please, I need five more minutes. I *have* to explain something to you . . ."

Another drum roll preceded a second announcement from the band leader. "Everyone, you're requested to take your seats quickly; dinner is served."

"Larry, Mom, Dad, this way," Paula waved over the heads of the passing tuxedos and designer originals.

"Paula, it's very important we talk. I listened to what you had to say; can't you hear me out for five minutes?"

Shrugging her shoulders to indicate that this was impossible, she smiled. "Give a great speech and we'll talk afterwards." Kissing him quickly on the cheek, she slipped away and headed through the crowd toward her parents and their seats, located in the outer ring of the lower level, a long way from the head table.

Well, I tried, Sandy shrugged to himself. At least she's prepared for something out of the ordinary. Rather than letting his inability to get through to her depress him, Sandy took the point of view that it was all for the best: She would feel the impact and drama of his accomplishment at the same time as everyone else in the room.

His energy restored, Sandy made his way to the head table, where he found his place card and sat down. In a few moments, he was joined by Nat, Sylvia, Ed and his wife, Charlie and his wife, the Furgsteins, and Yitzak Alon. An extra seat had been placed at the table for Uri, whose empty chair was on Sandy's right.

Through the fruit salad, Sandy concentrated on his speech, ignoring the waves of self-important community leaders and business associates who trooped up to the head table to congratulate Nat. By the time the filet mignon had been served, the clamor of BS and flattery had diminished to the point that Furgstein had time to react to the empty seat beside Sandy.

"What happened to Uri?" Furgstein asked.

Nat swung around to hear his son's answer.

"Not to worry." Sandy communicated not the slightest concern. "I spoke with him myself. He's here, outside in the hallway. All I have to do is go get him when it's time for him to speak."

"Wouldn't he like some dinner?" Furgstein asked suspiciously.

"What can I say?" Sandy shrugged. "This is the way he wanted to handle it."

"He's in condition to speak? You remember your promise to me," Nat threatened.

"He's as sober as a judge. There's nothing to worry about. Enjoy yourself and you'll see; Uri will do fine."

"I don't want *fine*; I expect *brilliant*." Nat jabbed his knife into his steak.

"He'll be that, too; I guarantee it."

Nat nodded, unconvinced, and turned back to his latest well-wisher, toward whom the old man extended a hand and a broad, affectionate greeting.

It figures, Sandy told himself, I do all the work and I still get all the shit.

After the ice cream parfait and coffee had been served, the ballroom lights were dimmed and a brilliant spot focused on the elevated podium, where Stanley Furgstein silenced the room with his presence.

"Excuse me a minute," Sandy whispered across the table to his father, "I'm going outside to check on Uri."

Nat nodded as Sandy got up and, hunched low beneath the spotlight, hurried across the ballroom and up the aisle past Paula, who watched with concern as he disappeared into the hotel lobby.

"Señor, you there?" Sandy spoke into his walkie-talkie.

"Yes, boss," replied Billy's familiar voice.

"The show's starting. We need you and your friend." Sandy studied the crowded hotel lobby but saw no indication of danger. It was business as usual on this Saturday night — families getting ready for a late dinner, honeymooning couples returning for an early evening in bed, conventioneers waiting for an inspired idea to waste time and money, and a busload of package tour travelers departing for the airport and a red-eye flight back to New Jersey.

"We're on our way." Billy's voice carried no emotion.

"Any problems?"

"Not on my end."

"Great, keep it that way. I'll see you in a few minutes. Remember, don't come into the ballroom. I'll come out to get you."

"Roger."

Sandy slipped the walkie-talkie back over his shoulder, took one final look around, and returned through the big doors to the ballroom. After giving his eyes a few moments to adjust to the darkness, Sandy edged his way around the perimeter of the seats and descended the stairs not far from Paula. His quick wave was hardly enough to reassure her. But with Furgstein already speaking, there was not much more he could do.

Making his way to the head table, Sandy sat down in time to hear the bulk of the fund raiser's long-winded, humorless introduction. That the audience even put up with guys like Furgstein never failed to amaze Sandy. Here was a room full of intelligent, sophisticated, articulate individuals who would have walked out of any movie or play that was even faintly repetitive. How could they sit still while a world-class bore delivered the same speech they'd all endured hundreds of times over the years?

In one word, the answer was *vanity*. Furgstein specialized in telling the community exactly what it craved to hear. Unlike the rabbis at temple, Furgstein's view of goodness and nobility was easy to understand and even simpler to achieve: All they had to do was give money to charity. The bigger the gift the better the person. Donations to the hospital overrode all other considerations of character. Sandy remembered attending a posh fundraising dinner in honor of a man who'd actually served time in prison twenty years before. His crime? Embezzling huge sums of money (a portion of which he later gave to charity) through the sale of bogus insurance policies to widows and orphans.

It was no surprise, Sandy thought, that the audience listened so carefully to Furgstein, who thanked "each and every one of them" for their assistance to humanity. As a result of their "noble generosity," one of the world's great cancer clinics was about to be built, another testament to their enlightened commitment, providing the community with the nation's finest medical care. The speech had all the subtlety of a French farmer force-feeding pâté-bound geese.

As Sandy glanced around the room, he realized that Furgstein was also delivering a narcoticlike reassurance of social and political superiority. In a well-fed, beautifully dressed, and self-satisfied state of mind, all the problems of life temporarily receded. The nightmare of Vietnam disappeared over the moral horizon. President Nixon was forgotten along with Watergate, John Dean, Haldeman, Erlichman, and the other anti-Semites. Issues such as world hunger, political oppression, the rumblings of war in the Middle East, and that universally feared eventuality — death itself — were all erased by the effusive flattery of Stanley Furgstein.

After enjoying an enthusiastic burst of applause, Furgstein finished with a florid and obsequious introduction of the ex-minister of defense from Israel. As Yitzak Alon stepped up to the podium, enjoying the spotlight and public welcome, Furgstein returned to the head table where Nat enthusiastically pumped his hand in gratitude for the "magnificent speech."

Finally the room went silent and Alon prepared to speak. This was the moment the people had paid their money to hear — the presentation of the Beth-Israel Man-of-the-Year Award to Nathan Klein. In a run-down of his life that was better than anything Nat could have written himself, the Israeli politician poured forth the details of the eldest Klein's progress from the *shtetels* of Germany to his endless string of business triumphs in the United States. Woven in with this tale of financial wonder was the tragic story of Florence Klein, cut down in her prime by cancer after an exemplary life as wife, mother, business advisor to Nat, and dedicated philanthropist. As good fortune would have it, Yitzak Alon continued, a remarkable second chance at happiness had presented itself to Nat in the form of the lovely and gracious Sylvia, "who has done so much in her own right for her family and the community." To conclude, the Israeli read an impressive list, itemizing Nat's long record of social and charitable contributions, which "in themselves sum up succinctly the activities of a truly great man of whom the community can be proud."

In spite of Sandy's efforts to stay engaged with the Hebrew-accented rhetoric, his mind drifted to the more gripping reality taking place in the parking lot. This was the only part of the operation that Billy was to carry out completely on his own. All he had to do was remove a folding wheelchair from the trunk of the Buick, roll it into position beside the passenger door, slide Hoffmann (still covered with the oversized raincoat) into the seat, handcuff his ankles and wrists to the polished metal tubing, wrap him from ankle to shoulder with a thin cotton blanket, and push him through the hotel lobby to the tall entry doors of the Grand Ballroom. Sandy knew there wasn't much that could go wrong. No one would get near enough to Hoffmann to notice the fake goatee, taped mouth, and opaque sunglasses. But now that success was so close, just the possibility of an unpleasant surprise was enough to distract Sandy from Alon's presentation of his father's award.

The massive wave of applause from three hundred pairs of clapping hands jolted Sandy out of his reverie. At the podium, Yitzak Alon had finished his extravagant introduction and was holding up, for the audience's appreciation, a three-foot-square walnut and bronze plaque: the Beth-Israel Man-of-the-Year trophy. This was the signal for Nat to bound enthusiastically up the few steps into the spotlight. An ear-to-ear grin announced to the room that this was truly one of the old man's greatest moments.

The audience reacted to Nat's joy with a standing ovation. This of course caused the honoree to respond with a show of even more gratitude as he lifted the impressive walnut and bronze prize over his head in the style of Sonny Liston winning the heavyweight championship of the world.

As the whistles, clapping, and cheers swelled, Sandy couldn't help thinking about the contrast between the self-important artificiality of this presentation and the reality of the Nazi just outside the ballroom. More than a few of these lightweight philanthropists are about to experience one hell of a shock, Sandy told himself as he contemplated his presentation of the SS mass murderer. Compared with an endless mass of repetitive, tax-deductible charity dinners, this would definitely be one evening that would stand out forever in everyone's memory.

"It has always been my belief," Nat intoned to the hushed group, "that a man who gives generously to the community receives back in the long run far more than he spends. Your honoring me tonight confirms that belief. What we hope to accomplish with the Florence Klein Cancer Research Center cannot be measured in dollars. It cannot be measured in numbers of beds nor in hours of work. The only real standard for the Florence Klein Cancer Research Center will be in the relief of pain and suffering for which, as we all know, there is simply no price. That's why you're here tonight. That's what we're going to accomplish together. And for that, I thank each and every one of you from the bottom of my heart." Nat paused, soliciting more applause.

While the audience responded with a nice wave of self-congratulatory clapping, Sandy reflected on his father's rhetoric. Yes, Nat certainly did hope to accomplish something worthwhile with the cancer center — that part wasn't a lie. But it wasn't the old man's main purpose; he also wanted to see the name *KLEIN* bolted in enormous bronze letters to the front of the cancer center building for the entire world to admire and envy. So important was this part of the deal that the major sticking point in the negotiations with the hospital board of directors had been the location and size of the sign: *Florence Klein Cancer Research Center.*

The old man's demand — a take it or leave it proposition — was that the building be oriented in such a way that everyone driving along both Olympic Boulevard and 26th Street (thousands each hour) be clearly able to see the family name. This whim added over a hundred thousand dollars to the cost of the project. Despite the opposition of the architects and the board of directors who wanted to put the hundred grand to a better use, Nat's condition was accepted in the end.

"The Florence Klein Cancer Research Center," Nat continued, "owes its existence to more than just our collective financial contributions. Nothing so magnificent could possibly come into existence without the participation and vision of a whole host of dedicated individuals."

Sandy grinned with pride. This was himself the old man was describing. Nat was finally softening in his old age — if not in sharing money, at least in publicly acknowledging credit for work well done. Hadn't his father and Sylvia made a point, both alone and in front of Sandy's brothers, of telling him what a wonderful job he'd done on the ballroom?

"First on the list, of course," Nat continued, "is Stanley Furgstein, who spearheaded the drive to make my dream a reality."

First on the list! Sandy was jolted back to reality.

"Assisting him tirelessly were all three of my sons, of whom I'm very proud." As Nat waved in the direction of the head table, a spotlight briefly followed his gesture. "And last, but certainly not least, is my wife, Sylvia, who put so much time and thought into every detail of the project. This award tonight," Nat once again held the plaque up over his head, "belongs not just to me but to every one of you who has contributed so much to the Florence Klein Cancer Research Center. Thank you."

While Nat nodded humbly, soaking up the explosion of applause, Sandy remained paralyzed, stunned by his father's speech. *All three of my sons?* What the hell is the old man talking about? What about me? What about my work? What the hell did Ed and Charlie do except try to engineer my failure? How dare you act as if I don't exist! Sandy glared at his father. Well, I want to see you fucking dismiss Heinz Hoffmann! You can treat me like a piece of shit, but I dare you to ignore the mass murderer I'm about to bring you, straight from the death camps!

"Sandy, c'mon, stand up," Ed hissed from across the table.

Jolted from his fantasy of revenge, Sandy realized that everyone in the room except him was on their feet, bestowing another standing ovation on Nat. Rising up, Sandy joined in the applause, disappointed in himself for almost creating a problem that might have disrupted the impact of his surprise.

Still at the podium, Nat lowered the heavy award, smiling humbly, obviously enjoying the applause.

In a touching but fake gesture of friendship, Yitzak Alon returned to the microphone, wrapped his arm around Nat's shoulder, and led the seemingly overwhelmed vitamin magnate back to his family. Followed by the spotlight, the old man headed for Sylvia who, to the audience's cheers and further applause, threw her arms around her husband and embraced him in a showy display of affection.

The spotlight returned to the podium, where Stanley Furgstein once again waited to address the audience. "And now," he said after Nat had shaken the hands of everyone at his table and returned to his seat, "we have another very special award to present — an honor to a man most of you have heard about and who I know you're all eager to welcome."

This was the moment Sandy had been waiting for. His whole life was about to change. Now he would be unstoppable, finally triumphant, free of his family.

"He calls himself simply *Uri*," Furgstein told the audience. "But who is Uri? He's a courageous and articulate man who time and again has come forward to tell of his experiences as a survivor who carved out an heroic existence in the center of that indescribable hell hole of the Holocaust — Auschwitz. Uri tells it like it was and *how* it was to go through everything Hitler's henchmen could devise. Yet Uri isn't depressing but inspiring; in talk after talk he has brought the memories and feelings of Jewishness to enormous numbers of our children. Not only have Uri's stirring accounts of the suffering and sacrifices he endured aroused the sleeping energies of the community, but he has raised an unprecedented amount of money for the organizations to which he has so generously given his time. As a man and as a survivor, we honor Uri tonight for his immeasurable contributions to Judaism. Ladies and gentlemen, I present to you, Uri — recipient of the Beth-Israel Humanitarian-of-the-Year Award."

On cue, the audience applauded with enthusiasm.

From the podium, Furgstein smiled and held out a welcoming arm toward the ballroom's entrance, where Uri was expected to enter from the lobby. The lighting director followed Furgstein's lead and aimed a powerful quartz spot at the fifteen-foot entry doors. Swiveling in their seats, the audience turned in expectation. But no one came in. At first perplexed, then anxious, Furgstein shifted his gaze to Sandy. Nat swung around, angry. This is your responsibility, the expression on his face seemed to accuse his son, you better produce the son-of-a-bitch.

Without saying a word, Sandy stood up and straightened his tuxedo as the lighting director swung the powerful spotlight onto him.

"What the hell are you doing?" Sandy heard his brother Ed cry out contemptuously.

"Shut up, sit tight, and you'll see." Sandy spoke with calm authority as he strolled around the table and headed for the podium.

"I think he's gone nuts." Ed addressed the entire family, summing up their collective viewpoint.

50

"Where the fuck is he, Sandy?" Furgstein's hand was clamped tightly over the podium's microphone.

"Sit down." Sandy, speaking calmly, gestured to the head table. "Relax and let me use the mike. You'll understand everything."

Furgstein hissed viciously, "Are you telling me that Uri's not here?"

"Stanley, stop making a scene. Sit down and you'll hear the whole story."

"Where is he?" Furgstein didn't budge.

"He asked me to say something on his behalf to everyone in the room."

"Does that mean he's here or not?"

"He's definitely here."

"Where?" Furgstein glanced around the dark hall, but the spotlights illuminating the podium prevented him from observing anything.

"If you sit down, you'll see."

"Why didn't you tell me this before?"

"Because it's what Uri wanted, okay? Now sit down, Stanley. This conversation is going nowhere, and I think the audience would like to hear what I have to say."

Another quick glance around the ballroom made it clear to Furgstein that the room full of philanthropists was growing restless. The applause ended and the hall was silent as people sensed something unusual and problematic.

"This isn't going to embarrass your father? Or the hospital?"

"Trust me, Stanley."

This was out of the question for Furgstein. "All I have to say is that this better be good."

"You won't be disappointed."

Resigned to the inevitable, Furgstein removed his hand from the microphone, smiled his broadest, phoniest grin, and spoke to the audience. "To introduce Uri, I turn you over to Nathan Klein's youngest son, Sandy Klein." Nailing Sandy with a final nasty glance, Furgstein stepped off the podium and bolted for his seat.

Alone at last in front of the audience, Sandy stared out into the cavernous darkness. Because of the brilliant spotlights, he could see nothing beyond the faces of his family at the nearby head table. This was unfortunate because he'd hoped to get a glimpse of Paula's reaction to the shock of Furgstein's introduction. Now she knew. Finally the truth was out. Most likely she would be too confused to say or do anything. The audience was absolutely still, as if they too understood that this moment was serious beyond anything they'd been prepared for.

Here we go, Sandy said to himself as he held out his left arm for everyone in the room to see. In one dramatic move, he used his right hand to slide the sleeve of his tuxedo jacket up beyond his elbow. Then he unfastened the tiny gold stud that secured his French cuffs around his wrist and rolled back the sleeve until his unbandaged tattoo was clearly visible in the bright light of the halogen spotlights.

"Most of you know me as Sandy Klein," he said gravely. "But only a few of you recognize me as Uri, *A7549653.*"

A low-level blast of whispers ricocheted throughout the ballroom, a buzz of anxiety and confusion. From the head table, through the glare of the lights, Sandy caught the paralyzed faces of Nat, Sylvia, Ed, Charlie, and Furgstein staring, horrified.

"Yes, I'm really Uri. And yes, I'm also Sandy Klein, Nathan's son. 'How could he have ever been in Auschwitz?' you must be asking since many of you know that I was born in Los Angeles in 1941. Since I wasn't *actually* in Auschwitz, you must also be wondering why I tattooed this number on my arm, disguised myself as Uri, and told so many people I'd been through such terrible experiences. You might think I'm crazy. I'm sure that's what my father thinks, who just this moment found out that I am Uri. I'm sorry, Dad, to have to tell you like this." He addressed Nat, who could only stare back, wide-eyed.

"And I'm also sorry for my lawyer and fiancée, Paula Gottlieb, who's here tonight and knew nothing about any of this. You must be furious," Sandy spoke out into the darkness to her, "but please listen to the rest of what I have to say and maybe then you'll forgive me.

"There is a real and valid reason," he addressed the crowd, "why I've done all this. It's the same reason that I believe you all gave money and came here tonight in support of my mother's cancer research center. You and I have the same motivation, which is to do something worthwhile for the Jewish community. Yes, I impersonated Uri. However, the stories Uri told weren't invented. While they didn't happen to me, they certainly happened to others, to real survivors of the camps. And obviously those stories did an enormous amount of good — otherwise why would you have chosen to honor Uri? So, when you think about my deception, consider my accomplishments, and balance them off, I'm sure you'll see that the benefits outweigh the drawbacks. But that isn't why I came here tonight."

As Sandy paused, the entire ballroom remained so attentive that only the emphysemic breathing of a few old men in the back could be heard through the enormous room.

"No, I could have avoided the embarrassment of revealing this impersonation by refusing to accept this award. Uri could have simply, without explanation, moved to Europe, address unknown. But more important issues are at stake here. With your contributions to the Florence Klein wing you hope to root out cancers from the body while I, acting as an agent of the community, have uncovered a killer of Jews far more deadly than a simple cellular malignancy.

"Over the last few months I've conducted a secret investigation and found proof that living anonymously and comfortably within fifty miles of this dining room is a Nazi war criminal, an SS officer from the infamous *Einsatzgruppen* — the mobile killing squads who murdered over one million Jews in the German-occupied territories of Eastern Europe. My proof is this." Sandy withdrew the small printed card and Rava Ruska photo from his jacket pocket and held them up to the light. "I know you're too far away to see these, but what I have in my hand is the man's SS identity card as well as a photograph of him in uniform clutching a pistol, standing over a mass grave of naked, murdered Jews. Along with the evidence, I have the man himself, whom I captured two days ago and am going to reveal to you tonight."

No one in the room moved or even seemed to breathe as Sandy slipped the ID card and photo back into his jacket pocket.

"His real name is Klaus Hagen. For the last twenty years, with the full approval and protection of the U.S. government, this Nazi killer has been living in Oxnard under the alias of Heinz Hoffmann. Ladies and gentlemen, Dad, Paula, sit quietly for one minute and I will present to you, in the flesh, Klaus Hagen of the *Einsatzgruppen,* a man personally responsible for the deaths of thousands of our European relatives."

Without a moment of hesitation, Sandy left the podium and, followed by the circle of halogen spotlight, charged through the ballroom, headed for the doors in the back of the hall. He was on an emotional rocket ship, blasting high above the mundane concerns of the off-balance and anxious audience. Sandy felt invulnerable, stronger than any comic book Superman, unstoppable. Even the reaction of embarrassment and frantic terror he saw on the faces of Paula and her parents didn't make a dent in his surging optimism. Beyond those doors, he told himself, is the key to the future. This was his moment of glory, a memory to cherish for the rest of his life.

Flinging open the double doors, Sandy disappeared from the spotlight into the relative darkness of the lobby. Behind him the spring-loaded doors swung shut, leaving Sandy alone with the disguised and unrecognizable Billy, ready with Hoffmann in the wheelchair.

"Okay," Sandy commanded, "we've got to move fast. Get him up and then you can get out of here."

Without speaking, Billy unshackled Hoffmann's ankles while Sandy unlocked the handcuff holding the German's right arm to the wheelchair. After yanking the blanket and raincoat off his shoulder, Sandy twisted the man's arm and locked it to the back of the chair. Next came the left arm's handcuff, the removal of the raincoat from that shoulder, and then a double handcuffing of the two wrists behind his back. The entire operation took only thirty-two seconds.

To the forty or so people milling around the lobby, Sandy and Billy's strange activities with the man in the wheelchair became the focus of curiosity. Everyone from businessmen to bellhops stopped what they were doing and stared, unable to make sense of the situation.

"Stand up, Hoffmann," Sandy commanded.

The German didn't move.

"We don't have time to screw around, Hoffmann. Get your ass up, now."

Attempting to undermine whatever plan he was part of, the war criminal remained immobile in the wheelchair.

"Okay, just remember I tried to get you to do it the easy way." Sandy grabbed the radio transmitter for the dog training collar and pressed the button. This sent a searing blast of cattle-prod proportions deep into the German's gonads. Not surprisingly (yet much to the shock of the watching bystanders) Hoffmann leapt to his feet and danced what appeared to be a short but wild Irish jig.

"Hat," Sandy ordered Billy, who removed the fearsome object from the pocket in the back of the wheelchair and placed it in position on top of the sweating, panting, but now docile German's head.

"Gun," Sandy demanded in an authoritative voice intended to scare the Nazi.

But his tactic frightened far more than Hoffmann. As Billy handed the Smith and Wesson .38 to Sandy, the crowd's curiosity turned to terror — what they were witnessing wasn't a theatrical act like a singing telegram but something far more ominous.

"Hoffmann, stand at attention," Sandy shouted.

This time the German obeyed immediately. With a yank, Billy pulled off the now capelike raincoat, revealing Hoffmann dressed in the rented SS uniform, complete with jackboots, gloves, and hat. Sprouting from the shoulders, chest, and visor peak were a splashy array of death's head insignias and regimental medals. Anywhere, anytime, such a figure would have been a terrifying sight. But here, in the middle of Beverly Hills on a warm September night, the man in the lobby was a living nightmare.

In one swift move, Sandy ripped the goatee and taped gag from the Nazi's mouth and, without disturbing the opaque sunglasses, pressed the barrel of the gun against the back of the man's skull. The whole operation had taken less than ninety seconds.

"Open the doors," Sandy commanded.

"Are you sure, Sandy? There's still time to reconsider."

"Open the doors and get the hell out of here, mister," Sandy yelled at his friend.

Billy nodded. "Just remember, I tried to talk you out of it." With a yank, Billy swung open the ballroom doors.

The crowd in the lobby drew back, frightened, as hotel security men, armed only with walkie-talkies, came nearer, trying to make sense out of the situation. Already, frantic calls were going out over the airwaves for police reinforcements.

"I want you to walk straight ahead and say nothing," Sandy hissed into the Nazi's ear, "or your brains are going to leak out all over the floor through a .38 caliber bullet hole. Is that clear?"

Hoffmann nodded.

"Okay then, move."

As Sandy pushed the German forward through the open doorway, the crowd and the security men inched after them, still uncertain about the meaning of this event. In the confusion, with people running in every direction, Billy slipped through the mob and disappeared unnoticed out the side exit of the hotel.

51

Sandy's entrance into the ballroom had an impact beyond any-thing he could have imagined. The moment those enormous doors opened, over three hundred people ceased their nervous whispering and stared at the incarnation of horror that Sandy was pushing toward them at gunpoint. What had been a noisy, anxious crowd suddenly became a room full of mutes who could only recoil in terror at the approaching SS nightmare.

This was a Jewish dinner, a Jewish fund raiser for a Jewish hospital. Until Sandy had stepped to the podium, it had been a perfect evening. Now, in an instant, the gala event had been turned upside down into a horrible and frightening drama. A Jew holding a gun to the head of a man dressed like a Nazi. Was Sandy crazy? Where was it going to lead? This looked like something more than just an embarrassment; it held all the ingredients of violence and death. With each step the Nazi took, vivid fears flashed through the collective memories of every Jew present: Auschwitz, Dachau, the Warsaw Ghetto, Treblinka, Bergen-Belsen, the endless Arab attempts to destroy Israel, the massacre of the athletes at the 1968 Munich Olympics, terrorist attacks on Jews of every nationality. Coming down the aisle, brilliantly illuminated in halogen spotlights, was the living image of death, terrifying to every Jew in the room.

At the doorway, the hotel security guards held their positions without entering the ballroom. They were in over their heads and they knew it; instead of acting rashly, the men waited out of range of Sandy's gun until experts from the police could arrive to handle the situation properly.

With his left hand gripping the chains connecting the Nazi's wrists and his right hand pressing the .38 against the war crimi-nal's brain stem, Sandy guided the German down the five stairs, onto the floor of the seating area. The SS uniform had an amazing effect on the philanthropists, Sandy observed. The waves of motion in the room resembled Moses' parting of the Red Sea, as well-dressed men and women bounded out of the way, clearing a twenty-foot-wide pathway for the Nazi and his guard.

Passing Paula's table, Sandy momentarily diverted his attention from Hoffmann in an effort to see her reaction. He wasn't able to learn much, but what he did observe was far from encouraging. Instead of the amazement and admiration he had expected, she appeared to be grim, terrified, and ashamed — just like her parents and Larry Carton beside her. Was this her real response, he questioned, or was it only the momentary facial expression of a person caught off guard?

For Sandy, the strangest part of the long march to the podium was the noise level in the room. The hall pulsed with a stillness so profound that for a minute he wondered if something had gone wrong with his hearing. How could more than three hundred guests and at least a hundred waiters and busboys make absolutely no sound? As one step followed another, all that Sandy heard were the creaks and groans emanating from the Nazi's heavy leather boots. Against the background of silence, this unusual sound reverberated with a frightening familiarity, like an amplified racial memory. Across the ballroom, the squeaking and rubbing of jackboots penetrated the souls of the philanthropists. How many millions of Jews, Sandy wondered, had heard the stretching and creaking of thick leather boots as their last audible memory before the Nazi in charge had given the order to shoot, stab, club, whip, or gas them to death?

Approaching the podium, the Nazi hesitated. Because of the opaque sunglasses, Hoffmann couldn't see the blue and white Israeli flags standing on either side of the raised platform, but Sandy wondered if the German somehow sensed them. A firm screwing of the Smith and Wesson's blued-steel barrel against the back of the man's head convinced him to get moving again, ascend the three carpeted steps, turn a hundred and eighty degrees, and face the audience and the microphone.

Maintaining a firm grip on the pistol, which was now jammed firmly between the Nazi's left eye and ear, Sandy leaned toward the microphone. No one in the room moved, not even the hotel security people safe in the rear. They, like everyone else in the hall, had no idea what Sandy was about to do. Given the bizarre, unpredictable situation, anything could happen: If Sandy had pulled the trigger and executed the war criminal on the spot, nobody in the ballroom would have been surprised. As he prepared to speak, Sandy felt a rush of excitement. He had done it! Signed, sealed, and delivered, this was one live Nazi war criminal for the community to digest! *What a triumph!*

"Ladies and gentlemen. Paula. Dad. May I present to you S.S. *Hauptsturmfuhrer* Klaus Hagen of the *Einsatzgruppen.*"

In shocking contrast to the massive wave of applause Sandy had expected, the cavernous Grand Ballroom thundered with silence. No one moved. Not a single person responded. At the head table, which Sandy could only barely see through the glare of the multiple spotlights now focused on the podium, Nat appeared to be frozen in his seat, shocked by his son's actions. Both Ed and Charlie had slid down in their chairs, their posture crying out the message, "Don't look at us; we had nothing to do with this mess." Stanley Furgstein was in worse shape. The sky was falling and his career with the hospital was in jeopardy. The only person who seemed calm and unaffected was Yitzak Alon, who sat quietly, showing no emotion, a simple observer. This was hardly the worst drama that the experienced Israeli military commander had witnessed.

The silence from the head table seemed to spread in waves of paralysis throughout the ballroom. Shaken and confused by the astounding turn of events, the audience took the lead from the Beth-Israel Man-of-the-Year and remained frozen, waiting.

Up on the podium, the crowd's reaction felt to Sandy as if someone had suddenly turned the air conditioning up full blast. A chill from over three hundred benefactors radiated off the brocade fabric on the walls and bounced down from the enormous, iciclelike crystal chandeliers. This frigid reception was amplified by contempt from the grim souls at the head table, his family, bomarding Sandy with an emotional jet stream of condemnation straight from the heart of the community.

No matter how he had rationalized his actions up to that moment, despite the nobility of his intentions, Sandy knew now that he hadn't simply made a minor error and been a little too optimistic; this was a gross misjudgment, a mistake of the most serious proportions, a true fuck-up, a total misreading of the temper of the times. One of his major delusions centered on the notion that the community would be outraged. He had anticipated that they would be infuriated when they realized that the U.S. government had not just tolerated but had actually sanctioned a Nazi living in their midst. What Sandy had failed to understand was that these same powerful community leaders considered *themselves* to be the government. To them, World War II and the Holocaust were ancient history, something to be studied, useful for fund raising, but not anything to ever really worry about again. Israel, yes, that was always in jeopardy. The Arabs were now, and forever, distinctly a worry. But as far as life in the United States went, the community felt comfortable and safe, finally free after thousands of years from pogroms. The last thing in the world that any of these leaders wanted was the sort of scandal Sandy had just thrown in their faces. Their reaction wasn't unlike that of the solid Jewish burghers in Germany during the 1920s and 1930s who couldn't believe that the government of which they'd been citizens for three hundred years, could ever turn on them. Just like those German Jews, the audience in the Grand Ballroom didn't want its complacency shattered. Instead, they responded like over-indulged Romans: Rather than rise up in rage over the message Sandy was delivering, they preferred to kill the messenger.

Sandy understood the seriousness of his error too late. Instead of reassuring and congratulating the cancer center's contributors for their generosity, he had exposed them to some painful truths that they had labored for decades to deny. They were Jews. They were in danger. Their government protected their enemies, and they preferred being comfortable to doing anything about it.

These grim facts, Sandy realized, were both embarrassing and threatening. To insulate themselves from this dark reality, they'd erected endless barriers: Tudor mansions in Beverly Hills, massive charitable edifices like the Beth-Israel Hospital, top-level positions on the boards of national corporations, the newest Mercedes sedans, jewelry from Harry Winston, summer cruises of the Greek Isles, Ivy League educations for their sons and daughters. But this nightmare image of the storm trooper on stage screamed to the audience just how vulnerable they really were. In the flash of a saber, their lives could be reduced to slave labor and gas chambers. Not all the fine oak paneling, the sophisticated Italian furniture, the elaborate home security systems, the marbled sirloin from Jurgensen's, the face lifts, tummy tucks, designer jeans, fur coats, Jaguar XKEs, not all the noble words of reassurance from the community's business leaders would do the slightest bit of good against the lethal, irrational fury of anti-Semitism.

To the members of that audience, Hoffmann uncorked the most deep-rooted, uncontrollable terror, a sense of helplessness in the face of a primitive, unforgiving brute power. Standing in front of those silent philanthropists, Sandy understood the message Hoffmann's presence blasted to every Jew in the room. *You are doomed. You will be enslaved. The world not only hates you, they'll gas you, rip out your children's expensive orthodonture to extract gold, make whores out of your women, mules of your men, and when you're worn out and dying they'll melt you down and turn your flesh into cheap bars of soap which the murderers will use to wash their crimes from their hands.*

Still holding the pistol to the side of the Nazi's head, Sandy finally realized that he had screwed up on a monumental scale. If only someone would applaud. If only the room wasn't so cold. The faces of his family stared up in frozen embarrassment and horror, mirroring the feelings of everyone present. If only one person would come up with a little support, Sandy thought, it would get the ball rolling in his direction.

Suddenly, without the slightest warning, chaos exploded from every doorway, window, and corridor as armed soldiers wearing camouflage uniforms burst into the dining room and sprinted toward the stage, where they shoved aside terrified, shrieking philanthropists, tilted tables sideways for cover, and took secure positions behind the heavy wooden bar, the piano, the ceiling's concrete support pillars, and above the stage behind Sandy's podium. It was the LAPD at its finest: the military-trained, heavily armed, Special Weapons and Tactics team. Within seconds, the business ends of about fifty M16s were aimed at Sandy's vital areas from every sector of the ballroom.

"Mister Klein," a deep voice bellowed through a portable loudspeaker from the back of the room, "throw down your gun and surrender your hostage."

Without removing the pistol from the Nazi's skull, Sandy squinted through the light, spotting the detective giving the commands from behind the heavy oak bar in the back of the room. "You can't be talking to me," Sandy spoke over the microphone, in disbelief. "You fellows have it all wrong. I'm the good guy here. This," he indicated Hoffmann, "is a German war criminal and a mass murderer. He's the one you want."

"I am an innocent American citizen," Hoffmann cried out into the microphone. "This man is a kidnaper and a lunatic. Help me, please!"

"Shut up, Hoffmann, or no one will be able to help you." Sandy dug the end of the revolver barrel into the bone just above the Nazi's ear.

In pain, terrified, Hoffmann said nothing.

"I'm asking you once again," the voice through the police loudspeaker commanded, "throw down your weapon and release your hostage. Make it easy on yourself, Mister Klein."

Standing absolutely still in front of a room full of hostility, the target of god knows how many high-powered weapons, Sandy's perspective began to unravel and implode. The situation had progressed beyond a serious miscalculation and gone over the brink, past all recovery. What should have been a resounding success had for reasons that were now obvious become a potentially lethal catastrophe. Clearly, the automatons in camouflage didn't have a clue what he had accomplished with the Nazi. Could he explain it to them here and now? Or did it make more sense to surrender and try to discuss the situation with the district attorney under less pressured conditions? No, it was hopeless, Sandy realized. If the leadership of the Jewish community couldn't understand what he'd done, how could the law? If he gave himself up, it was obvious what would happen. First, Hoffmann would immediately disappear to South America. Then the State of California would throw the book at Sandy, starting with kidnaping, which in itself carried the possibility of the death penalty. The list of related charges now that the SWAT team was involved put Sandy up for a solid twenty to thirty years at the very best. Surrender just didn't make any sense. It would in effect guarantee safe haven for the Nazi and life in prison for himself; the exact opposite of justice.

"You don't understand," Sandy protested passionately into the microphone. "This is a Nazi war criminal. He's killed thousands of men, women, and children. I have proof. That's why I brought him here. I made a citizen's arrest. He's the man you want. Point your guns at him."

"Mister Klein," the detective called through his loudspeaker, "we understand completely. But until you put away your pistol and turn your hostage over to us, we can't sit down and discuss this with you. Put away your gun; then we can talk."

Okay, fuck you, was Sandy's first reaction. I understand what you think, you tricky fucker. It was like negotiating with Yassar Arafat over the recognition of Israel: "You give us the entire country," the *schmuck* of a PLO thug says with a straight face like the detective's, "and then we'll clearly and unambiguously recognize Israel." A deal only a *schlimazel* would be stupid enough to accept.

"Uh, I'm having a little trouble thinking clearly with all these weapons pointed at me," Sandy said, attempting to take charge. "I need some time to myself. Please clear an aisle so SS *Hauptsturmfuhrer* Klaus Hagen of the *Einsatzgruppen* and I can walk out for some air."

"Mister Klein," the voice bellowed again through the loudspeaker, "we'll give you all the air and all the time you need to think. But right here. You're not leaving this room until you release your hostage and surrender that pistol."

The police were playing hardball. Reduce the options, then

reduce them further until the criminal had no choice but to give himself up.

"For God's sake, Sandy," Nat yelled to his son, "do as the officer says and drop that gun. So what if you made a mistake? If you do what they say, no one will get hurt and we can work this out later."

Nothing could have convinced Sandy to take a tougher stance than this appeal from his father. The thought of spending the rest of his life in jail, dependent upon Nat for pocket money, was enough to make Sandy try anything, no matter what the risk.

"Unless you want a dead hostage on your hands — and I'm prepared to shoot this Nazi right here — " Sandy spoke with deadly calm into the microphone, "give me room because, like it or not, I'm coming through."

Without waiting for an answer, Sandy grabbed the chain linking Hoffmann's handcuffs, yanked the man's arms up, urging him forward, and pushed with the barrel of the Smith and Wesson against the back of his head. Descending from the podium, the two of them slowly shuffled across the parquet dance floor in the direction of the distant entry doors. The police wouldn't shoot, Sandy reasoned, because there were so many important people in the vicinity. If one stray bullet hit a VIP, the LAPD would be in court for years. Sandy's other reason for moving out of the ballroom came from something he had learned during his news-paper days: To remain in the room and negotiate was certain death. While talks were supposedly proceeding, the SWAT team would clear the hotel and quickly take well-fortified sniper posi-tions against which Sandy would eventually be defenseless. Over-coming such tactics required unpredictable action, keeping the police off-balance, unable to execute their normal game plan.

Sandy pushed the Nazi up the aisle, using the German's body as a shield, while from every direction the SWAT team followed each step through the sights of their automatic M16s. As he and Hoffmann approached, nearby philanthropists ran for their lives, diving for cover out of the line of fire. If the situation had not been so tense, it would have been almost funny, Sandy reflected as he watched sixty- and seventy-year-old dowagers slide for safety behind overturned tables in moves out of some geriatric World Series.

"Mister Klein," the detective called through his electric bull-horn, "that's far enough. Stop where you are."

Ignoring the order, Sandy directed the Nazi up the five stairs to the bar level toward the exit.

"Sandy, please," Nat shouted across the room. "Do what the man says. Be reasonable for once in your life!"

Make the fucking SWAT team be reasonable, Sandy raged to himself without slowing. It was far too late to be reasonable. All he could do was stay close to Hoffmann, keep the .38 hard up against the back of the German's skull, and pray that none of those trigger-happy cops screwed up and fired accidentally.

As one philanthropist after another bounded out of harm's way, a bizarre thought stuck in Sandy's racing mind. In a sick perversion of fate, a twist on his original intentions, he had finally achieved his place in history. He would be remembered as that infamous legend, the champion fuck-up and greatest embarrassment in the history of Los Angeles' Jewish community. Shooting for the big time, Sandy had not only come up empty-handed, but had hurt everyone close to him and destroyed anything he might have accomplished. No matter how the standoff with the police resolved itself, he had no doubt that all his bridges were burned.

From his days as a reporter, Sandy knew that the local media would have a field day with the story. *The Home Town Screw-Up. The Klein Calamity. Vitamin Executive Loses Mind.* No one would ever forget this night. At best, his future would consist of an expensive, negotiated plea of legal insanity, the prelude to a life-long stay in a mental hospital. Even burdened with the considerable expense, his brothers would love it. For the rest of his pitiful life, Sandy would be officially, medically, certifiably crazy — the incarcerated, hopeless son.

This vision of the future left him with no alternative but to use Hoffmann as a hostage for real: War criminal or not, the man still had value as a bargaining chip. How absolutely weird, Sandy thought, after all of this *mishegas,* I am now a Jew who's holding a Nazi hostage and using the slimebag as my ticket to freedom. It's like something out of the Middle East, a reversal of a PLO airline hijacking.

This insight suddenly made clear to Sandy his next major objective. Only one country in the world regularly faced up to the sort of life-and-death dilemma in which he found himself. There was only one way out, one great leap that promised a solution to all of his problems. He needed a homeland where he would be appreciated, understood, and granted permanent political asylum. As a wanderer without roots, a man without a country, he would exercise his cultural and genetic claims and apply for emergency citizenship. *Israel, here I come!*

"Mister Klein, do not open that door," the voice cried through the nearby police bullhorn. "Stop right where you are, put down your gun, and surrender your hostage. This is an order."

A quick glance around the room confirmed everything for Sandy. What had earlier been an ordinary gala evening now resembled a twisted scene painted by a modern Hieronymus Bosch. More than a hundred of the formally dressed guests cowered in silence on the floor, hiding behind overturned tables, waiting for Sandy's decision. In every sector of the room, SWAT team commandos moved into new positions, taking aim at the Jewish man in a tuxedo who stood by the door holding a hand-cuffed Nazi storm trooper at gunpoint. This painting might have been titled *Good Intentions Gone Bad.* Without question, this was the most exciting fund-raising dinner the community would ever attend. Warren Beatty or Peter O'Toole wouldn't have been nearly as interesting.

"Sandy," Paula's voice called out over the silence, "don't be stupid. Give yourself up. Drop the gun and release Hoffmann. These men aren't here to fool around."

"She's giving you good advice, Sandy. Listen to her," the police negotiator bellowed through his bullhorn.

Thank you, Paula, he lamented silently to himself. If even you buy the SWAT team's act, I'm totally lost. Israel was now really his only alternative.

"Move away from the door," Sandy commanded the two cam-ouflaged cops aiming automatic rifles at point-blank range.

"Drop your weapon, Mister Klein. You have to the count of five," the negotiator threatened.

"I'm going to give you two choices," Sandy shouted. "Either open the door and give me room or you're going to have a very dead German on your hands. *You've* got to the count of five, Mister." With his thumb, Sandy pulled back the hammer on the Smith and Wesson. "One . . ." he counted slowly.

It was obvious to everyone that even a feather touch on the trigger would blow a fatal hole through the German's brain.

"Two . . ." Sandy called out for the room to hear, pressing the gun firmly against the Nazi's skull.

"Okay, Mister Klein. Stop. We'll let you go through the doors. *Give the man room,*" the negotiator commanded.

Like robots, the two cops obeyed.

"Move it twenty feet farther," Sandy shouted without resetting the pistol's hammer.

The cops looked to their boss, who was still crouched behind the bar.

"Do what he says; give him twenty more feet."

As commanded, the police moved back.

Kicking the door open, Sandy pushed Hoffmann out of the Grand Ballroom into the lobby, to be greeted not by the fusillade of bullets he feared, but by a huge crowd of spectators jockeying with the hotel security guards for the best angle to observe the action. The police couldn't do anything now, Sandy observed, overjoyed. Again, they wouldn't risk even one sniper shot with so many innocent civilians around. Thank god I moved fast, he congratulated himself, before the SWAT team had time to take control of the whole area.

"Clear the corridor," Sandy yelled at the police, indicating the side route out to the parking lot.

Shoving back the circus of bystanders, the cops opened up a clear run to the lobby's exit.

Using the Nazi as a shield, Sandy moved quickly across the foyer and down the hallway, followed at a respectful distance by the police and SWAT team, the hotel security guards, and many of the curious, excited hotel lobby loiters.

52

The journey toward the garage resembled one of those snakelike conga dances fashionable in Europe during the 1960s. At the head of the line was the jackbooted Nazi followed by Sandy — the brains of the beast — who maintained a threatening pressure on the back of Hoffmann's skull with the .38. After a fifty-foot gap came the body of the monster, an undulating, snarling line of SWAT team members, detectives, and regular police. Bringing up the tail were security guards struggling without much success to stay in control of the unruly mob of voyeuristic tourists.

"When I go through that door," Sandy shouted behind him to the police negotiator, "I want you to give me thirty seconds before you follow me. I *do not* want you in the stairway as we walk up to the top level of the parking garage. Is that agreed?"

As soon as the negotiator nodded, Sandy pushed open the steel door and hustled the Nazi into the concrete garage.

"He's heading for the top of the parking garage," the police relayed over their walkie-talkies as they used the thirty seconds to plan their strategy.

However, by the time the platoon of police burst into the garage and began charging up the concrete staircase, Sandy had crossed the few feet to his rented Buick, stuffed Hoffmann into the passenger seat, reanchored the prisoner to the seat-belt mounts, reshackled the German's feet, pulled the ignition key from where Billy had left it under the floor mat, and started the engine. Still holding the pistol against the war criminal's head, Sandy eased the hammer back against the firing pin, then used his left hand to shift the transmission into reverse and back the big Buick out of the parking space. At that moment, he was spotted by the police. But by then he was already accelerating toward the ramp, only two right turns away from the exit.

"Mister Klein," the loudspeaker resonated through the parking structure, "stop your car, throw out your gun, and release your hostage. This is your last chance!"

Without the slightest hesitation, Sandy cranked the wheel of the Buick to the right and descended in the direction of the exit.

"If I were you," the German volunteered to Sandy, "I'd obey the police; this is only going to make it harder on you later."

"My concern is *now*, Hoffmann. The next word out of you is going to be your last. It's not like I have a lot to lose."

Frightened by the rage and desperation in Sandy's voice, the Nazi went silent.

Completing the tight right turn, Sandy steered the Buick out of the narrow, low-ceiling ramp to find himself surrounded by armed SWAT team members aiming their weapons at him. Holding his right arm straight out, Sandy made it clear to the police that his .38 was still in position against the German's skull, implying that if they weren't careful he would turn the situation into an American version of that famous photo of the South Vietnamese police chief shooting a civilian Viet Cong suspect in the head.

Without slowing, Sandy made the second right turn and headed for the exit. In his side mirror he could see the police, SWAT team, and reporters running across the garage toward their cars parked on the street outside. It would be close, Sandy knew, but if he kept his speed up he could maintain his lead. The only immediate obstacle was the barrier controlled by the parking attendant in the adjoining kiosk. If he stopped, or even slowed down, a police sharpshooter could get off a clean, point-blank shot from the protection of the booth. His only course of action, Sandy decided, was a full-throttle acceleration through the wooden barrier.

Planting the gas pedal to the floor, Sandy steered for the wooden arm. As the big Buick's carburetor kicked in all four barrels, the parking attendant looked up at the source of the noise, spotted the mammoth machine bearing down on him, realized the inevitable, and protected himself and his equipment by punching the button that raised the wooden arm before bailing out of his kiosk.

Speeding past the empty ticket booth at over forty miles per hour, Sandy slammed on the brakes and skidded out onto the private connector street joining the hotel to both Wilshire and Santa Monica boulevards. From the entrance of the hotel itself, heading Sandy's way, came a siren-screaming, accelerating line of police cars and Harley-Davidson motorcycles, all flashing their red emergency lights. With Wilshire obviously not the way to go, Sandy cranked a hard left, then a fast right, and blasted west down Santa Monica Boulevard. Within seconds, the clamorous herd of twenty-five police cars and motorcycles surrounded Sandy's Buick, jockeying for position to get close to him.

Positioning the heavy .38 plainly in sight against Hoffmann's head, Sandy drove west, trying to block out the distractions while contemplating his next move. What he needed was some time and distance from the chaos — somehow he had to carve himself out a little breathing room. Passing Westwood Boulevard, he had an idea.

Forcing his way into the right-hand lane, Sandy drove one more block and then, without warning, whipped a hard right into the street running between the Standard Oil station and Leo's Stereo. Accelerating at full throttle up the narrow north/south lane, Sandy was now in the lead, followed by a long single-file line of police cars.

At Ohio, Sandy again turned right, sped east half a block, then ducked left into the narrow alley paralleling the shops along Westwood Boulevard. A few more lefts and rights, in and out of narrow streets and back alleys, spread the cops out farther and farther behind him, making it easier for him to weave and dodge through Westwood Village without opposition. By Sunset Boulevard, the nearest cop was almost a quarter of a mile behind him. Fortunately for Sandy, traffic was unusually light for a Saturday night, and he had no trouble running the stoplight at Beverly Glen, turning left, and rocketing north up the canyon.

On his own turf now, Sandy drove at such a frightening speed that he was able to gain even more distance on his pursuers. At least two solid curves ahead of the nearest cop, Sandy braked hard and skidded, unobserved, into the narrow, steep street leading to the relative safety of his house and open garage.

By the time the police were able to retrace their path and find their way to his home, Sandy had already dragged the Nazi out of the car, shackled him to the oak chair in the second bedroom, covered his mouth with a fresh gag of surgical tape, closed all the shades and curtains, double-checked the locks on every door and window, and turned off all the lights inside the house. When the fleet of motorcycles and squad cars finally roared to a halt outside, Sandy took cover behind the two-inch-thick oak dining table he'd tilted onto its side in the living room.

Thanks to all the flashing lights and police high-beams, enough illumination penetrated the shades and curtains for Sandy to write a note, which he taped to a heavy metal ashtray. Beside him, on the floor behind the safety of the oak table shield, lay his loaded .38 and an open box containing nearly fifty rounds of ammunition.

"Mister Klein," the police bullhorn blared, "we know you're in there. We've got you surrounded. There's no way you can escape. Throw out your weapon. Release your hostage and give yourself up. You have no alternative, Mister Klein."

After rereading the message he had written, which said, "I will only speak to Yitzak Alon, the defense minister of Israel, who should still be at the Wilshire Hotel," Sandy folded the note. Then, using a second piece of tape to secure it to the ashtray, he crept out of the protection of the table and across the living room floor to the front door. In one quick motion Sandy opened the door less than a foot and lobbed the ashtray at the police across the street. Slamming the door and double-locking the dead bolt, Sandy scurried back to his refuge behind the table while the police outside hit the deck, flattening themselves to the ground in response to what they assumed was a bomb or a hand grenade. When the metal object landed with a clatter and did nothing but sit quietly on the asphalt, the ordnance expert, using binoculars, identified what had really been thrown at them and sent a volunteer out to retrieve it.

Moments later, over a loudspeaker, the voice of authority called to Sandy, "Mister Klein, we're trying to reach Alon for you. But in the meantime I want you to think about something. You don't have anywhere to go. We've got you surrounded with a hundred well-trained, armed men. You don't have any options. You're going to have to surrender. Why not make it easy on yourself by tossing out your weapons and releasing the hostage? This is the end, Klein. Come out and talk to us. You're a smart man; I know you understand what I'm saying."

Negotiating with the cops was not the plan Sandy had in mind. Nothing could be gained by speaking with them. Cops weren't politically astute. They had no sense of the big picture. History, culture, philosophical ideas — everything subtle and progressive was lost on these men in blue who only understood courts, concrete walls, iron bars, guns, and the gas chamber. They lived and worked in the sewer of society and could dispense only bullets, violence, and prison. Even to begin discussing the question of trading the Nazi for free passage to Israel would be a waste of time. The issue was political, requiring the sympathetic reasoning of men with both vision and power. Sandy needed an advocate, someone who understood what had actually been accomplished. If the local community couldn't see the nobility in his capture of Hoffmann, then he would have to appeal to a higher authority, Yitzak Alon. Who in Israel, Sandy reflected confidently, wouldn't understand and approve of his handling of the war criminal? The country could hardly refuse to help him. Wasn't that why Israel had been created? Wasn't its purpose to act as a haven, a homeland for any Jew facing persecution? If I don't deserve political asylum, Sandy told himself, then no one does.

Just the idea of Israel boosted Sandy's self-confidence. Instead of treating him as a common criminal, that little democracy in the Holy Land would embrace him as a hero. In his frantic state, the contrast between American and Israeli political perspectives seemed bizarre. Yet the fact was that America had a lot to lose by his exposure of the war criminal. Roosevelt and the state department had done nothing to stop the Nazis from murdering millions of Jews, despite self-serving official statements to the

contrary. Shielding themselves behind the 1943 Bermuda Con-
ference and other anti-concentration-camp PR, the U.S. government had made infinitely greater efforts to save Germans from
"the horrors of Communism" immediately after the war. This
was the reality that Israel recognized and that modern day
America ignored: No one truly cared about the survival of the
Jews but the Jewish nation itself.

The same people in the U.S. government who had worked on
behalf of those German anti-Communists (while ignoring six
million dead Jews) were still very much alive, prominent in
public life. For those politically prestigious people — U.S. senators and congressmen — to be brought on the carpet and
punished was going to be close to impossible. From these
powerful men's perspective, Sandy was the one requiring arrest
and elimination. *"Baruch atah Adonai, elohenu melech haolum.
Praised be the Lord our God, King of the Universe.* Thank you for the
existence of Israel," Sandy found himself suddenly praying.

The sound of his living room telephone jolted him out of his
reverie. Allowing it to ring four more times, Sandy tried to calm
himself. Then, crawling below the level of the windows, he
crossed the living room to the coffee table on which the telephone rested. Without lifting the receiver, he carried the whole
instrument back to the safety of the thick dining table before
finally picking up the handset.

"Hello?" He spoke with impressive calm.

"Is this Sandy Klein?" an Israeli-accented voice inquired.

"Yes."

"This is Yitzak Alon. The police said you wished to speak with
me."

"Mister Alon. Thank you for calling." Sandy paused for a
moment and carefully considered the words he was about to
speak. The strange background tone of the phone and the
formality of Alon's voice made it obvious that other interested
parties were listening in and recording their conversation. "I
need your help."

"How can I help you?"

"You understand the situation I'm in. And you can see how the police regard my citizen's arrest of a Nazi war criminal. Here I accomplished what you Israelis did with Adolf Eichmann. Yet the police want to arrest *me* and send *me* to jail. Mister Alon, if I work out a way to get myself to Israel, can I count on getting political asylum?"

Instead of an immediate answer there was a long silence from the other end of the phone. Alon had obviously put him on hold while consulting with someone else. Who could that be? Sandy wondered. Was the ex-defense minister with other Israelis? Perhaps phoning the consul for advice? Or was he surrounded by Los Angeles authorities urging him to help capture the Jewish lunatic?

"Mister Klein?" Alon finally returned to the line.

"Yes," Sandy responded, a little too eagerly for his own taste.

"I would like to be able to give you good news. Believe me, I do understand and sympathize with your position. If I had any doubt at all I would talk on your behalf to my government. Even to Golda Meir. But there's no point in doing that because I'm one hundred percent certain of their answer. Under the circumstances you are *absolutely not* a candidate for political asylum. I'm sorry."

"I'm not sure I'm hearing you correctly," Sandy responded, too shocked to face the implications of Alon's direct refusal. "You're saying Israel *won't* give me asylum?"

"That's correct."

"But I'm a Jew and I'm being persecuted." Sandy attempted to sound calm and reasonable. "I have a *right* to Israeli citizenship. You *can't* refuse me."

"As a Jew you have an automatic right to citizenship, that's true. But at the moment you're in legal trouble for criminal actions committed in the United States. Israel has an extradition treaty with the U.S. government. Even if you somehow were able to smuggle yourself out of this country and land in Israel, my government would be forced, by law, to arrest you and turn you over to U.S. authorities. You have to understand, Mister Klein, that Israel is in too precarious a position to allow itself to be viewed as a haven for terrorists, no matter what their intention. And unfortunately, what you've done falls into that category. Like the United States, Israel lives under the rule of the law, which you've broken. If you really want to live in Israel, I suggest that you surrender yourself now, resolve your legal situation, and at that point come to the consulate and apply for citizenship. That's the most help I can give you."

"You call that *help?*" Sandy erupted in anger as despair and disaster once again overwhelmed him. "That's the kind of help that sent six million Jews to the gas chambers. You want to help, call Golda Meir and ask her to intervene personally. You can't be sure you're right. You're a soldier. This is politics. You say you want to help, *then help:* call her and ask. The worst that will happen is nothing."

In response to Sandy's outburst, Alon spoke softly. "If I thought that there was the slightest chance of success I would. I'm sorry."

"Instead of being sorry," Sandy shouted, panicked, "pick up the fucking phone and call her. Yes, I know you're an Israeli government official and you know the laws. But you're also a Jew; don't you care about bringing a killer like SS *Hauptsturmfuhrer* Klaus Hagen of the *Einsatzgruppen* to justice?"

"Of course I do, Mister Klein." Alon continued to speak in an unhurried, reasonable manner. "But at the moment Israel faces much graver problems than a tired, frightened old Nazi who's been hiding for twenty-five years. I know you read the papers. As we speak, Egypt's army is marching toward the Suez Canal, about to attack Israel. Our country is in an emergency, preparing for another war which could start any day. Even if it did make sense to call Golda Meir, I couldn't. The woods are on fire, Mister Klein, and there's no time to deal with your problem. As much as I might admire you for your courage, there's nothing I can do. This is an impossible moment even to consider discussing asylum. My honest advice to you is to give yourself up. You just don't have an alternative. I mean it."

His mind frozen, Sandy could not respond. What Alon said made sense. It was all so logical. Everything was exactly as the

Israeli had claimed. Yet it was he, Sandy, who was being obliterated — one more Jew led to the dungeons. Surrender was unacceptable. Accommodation was the equivalent of death. There has to be another way, Sandy told himself. There was always another way. What he needed was time to think it through.

"Someone here wants to speak to you, Mister Klein. Hold on one moment."

Was this Paula? Sandy wondered, his hopes soaring once again. Yes, she had turned her back on him at the hotel. Obviously the shock of his revelations had thrown her off balance. But underneath her panic — and who could understand and sympathize with the consequences of panic better than Sandy — the woman loved him. Now, after thinking about it, and realizing her priorities, she was finally rallying to his defense with a brilliant plan. After so many ups and downs, he told himself, she recognized the truth of their relationship. Why had he ever doubted that she was his ally?

"Sandy?" the familiar voice sounded in the receiver. "This is your father here. Sandy, listen to me. I'm standing here beside the chief of police. I've already talked to the district attorney and the mayor himself. They all understand that what you did, you sincerely believed was correct. Not only are they sympathetic, they've promised to help. You've got the chief of police, the district attorney, and the mayor all on your side. They're good people, Sandy. But for them to go to bat for you, you've got to demonstrate that you're willing to work with them. What they're asking you to do, Son, is to throw out your gun and give yourself and your hostage up. That's not much. It's not so difficult. Just go to the door, toss out your pistol, and that's it. It's over. No one will be hurt."

"And then what happens?"

"I don't think anyone knows. We'll let the lawyers handle it. And believe me, I'll hire the best — Edward Bennett Williams! Sandy, I'm your father. I love you. Listen to me. You've got to be reasonable; these men all want to help but you have to understand, they're not fooling around."

"What do *you* think about what I've done?"

"I believe you should surrender. You don't really have a choice."

"You have no sympathy for what I've accomplished?"

"I'm not sure what you have accomplished other than embarrassing many, many people. I said this to you already and I still mean it: For once in your life, behave reasonably. Surrender. This is crazy, Sandy. If you won't surrender for yourself, do it for me. I promise you, weeks or months from now you'll thank me."

In a letter from jail, Sandy despaired. Talking to Nat was nothing but destructive and demoralizing. What he was offering wasn't a solution but a grim and hopeless prophesy: the end of Sandy as a man.

"Dad, thanks for the advice. I know you mean well. But I've got to get off the phone now. I'm sorry about your embarrassment. I'd hoped you'd be proud — my mistake. You'll just have to forgive me." Without waiting for a response, Sandy set down the phone. Can everything really be as final as it now seems? he wondered, appalled and frightened by the paucity of his options.

"Mister Klein," the bullhorn thundered from the street, "if you're going to surrender, the first thing you should do is toss out your gun."

Surrender my ass, Sandy growled, enraged, to no one in particular; *leave me the fuck alone!*

Of course the big question, for which he had no answer, was: What the hell to do? Slithering across the living room floor, Sandy peeked out through a crack between the shade and the window frame. Outside, the normally dark, narrow street looked like something out of his concentration camp nightmares. For hundreds of feet above and below Sandy's house, the area was cordoned off and the surrounding structures evacuated. From shielded positions on adjacent rooftops, behind parked cars, and in the windows of the houses directly across the street, the barrels and scopes of high-powered rifles protruded from virtually every opening. Arc lights powered by portable generators illuminated the area to the brightness of a summer day. All that was missing to recreate the full Auschwitz effect were Gestapo officers carrying whips and walking rottweilers. Enjoying the

charcoal briquette implants, the perfect companion to the torchlike pain in his lungs.

Dragging himself from room to room in search of breathable air, Sandy made his way by Braille. What had started as a white-out became a thick, dark gray cloud as the police continued to fire tear gas bombs at a rate that would soon have filled the AstroDome. Every fiber of Sandy's body radiated with a pain that screamed to him: *Run outside and surrender — anything is better than this torture.* But he stopped himself from giving in to such weakness. To walk back out the front door would only begin a lifetime of emotional humiliations infinitely more painful than the physical torture of tear gas.

Blinded and near collapse, Sandy bumped against an unexpected obstacle — the bathroom door, which was closed. Reaching upwards, he twisted the knob, slipped inside, and slammed the door shut behind himself. The room, located on the side of the house blocked from the sharpshooters by an untrimmed California live oak, was gas-free and surprisingly cool. Grabbing towels off the bathtub rack, Sandy soaked them with water, then stuffed these wet cotton plugs into the small gap between the door and the white tile floor. After sitting for a few seconds and enjoying the relief of breathing uncontaminated air, Sandy washed his eyes out with cold water.

Still in pain, but at least able to see and breathe to a limited extent, he opened the double-hung wooden bathroom window and contemplated his next move. Would it be possible to slip through the narrow opening, shinny up the long-neglected tree, climb over the neighbor's fence, and drop down into the adjacent yard? The problem with this plan, he realized, was that the fence and the yard next door were both perfectly visible to the sharpshooters on the back hill. Should he try to escape by this route, the marksmen would shoot him off the fence without the slightest difficulty.

If he couldn't yet figure a way to get out, he reminded himself, at least he could see and breathe. But did that really matter? Short-term relief wasn't success; only the postponement of disaster! He couldn't spend the rest of his life sitting in a ten-foot

by twelve-foot toilet. Nor could he leave Hoffmann tied up and
gagged, only able to breathe through his nose. Given the quantity
of gas with which the SWAT team was bombarding the house, it
would be a miracle if the Nazi survived even a few more
minutes.

Who gives a shit if the German chokes to death, Sandy raged, *it's not
as if the fucker doesn't deserve it!* At that moment, a startling
revelation about his own character entered Sandy's consciousness: He, Sandy Klein, was thinking and behaving exactly like a
Nazi! "Beware what you pretend to be, for that is what you
become," Nietzsche warned. Out of desperation, he had hard-
ened himself to accomplish the tasks of capturing and holding
the Nazi. But in the process, Sandy realized, he had become
exactly like the people from whom he had most wanted to be
different: not just the Nazis, but his father and brothers.

This insight led him to an even more painful realization. It
wasn't his father, or his brothers, or his mother's death, or
Rachael's death, or the divorce from Anne, or even Fate, that had
caused his trouble. Instead of accepting responsibility for participation in his own problems, he had blamed everything on
people and forces outside himself. This was no different from his
father blaming all of the family problems on Sandy's inade-
quacies or Germany blaming the Jews for every difficulty. "Liq-
uidate the Jews, eradicate them from the face of the earth," the
Nazi philosophy had trumpeted, "and all the economic, political, and cultural problems of the German people will be solved
forever." No one accepted responsibility for his own fate. Everyone simply wanted to find a scapegoat. And he, Sandy Klein, was
behaving no differently. What he had fought so fiercely, he had
now become.

The difference between himself, his family, and the Nazi was
that he now recognized his own failure. He had begun his quest
for the noblest of reasons: to bring a criminal to justice. Along
the way, he'd come very close to losing everything, but he still
had his humanity. The one honest alternative left to him was to
act on that realization. *He, Sandy Klein, was not a killer.*

What he would do, Sandy decided, was to make an example of his own humanity by surrendering both the Nazi and himself. He would walk out with his head high. They could imprison him or lock him away in a mental institution. Neither sentence would matter. What counted was his behavior. When revenge seemed the only solution, when death and destruction appeared inevitable, he had stood up and declared his humanity. *I am not a killer.*

Grabbing the wet towel from the floor, Sandy pressed the cool cloth against his nose and mouth. In one rapid move he opened the door, slipped out into the hallway, and slammed the bathroom door shut behind himself to maintain one room as a gas-free refuge. Dropping back down to his knees, Sandy was shocked by the dramatic change throughout the house. In the few minutes he'd been isolated from the tear gas, the visibility had diminished to zero. In place of the gray fog was an atmosphere dense with black toxins. Were the police only trying to drive him outside, or were they actually out to kill him? A sudden series of explosions from the firing of more canisters made matters even more desperate. Despite the towel, the vicious airborne irritant penetrated Sandy's mouth and nasal passages and once again torched his lungs.

Crawling as close to the cool floor as he could manage, Sandy coughed his way down the hall, navigating solely by feel. Other than the occasional bright flash of an exploding gas grenade, nothing was visible but the opaque veil of super-saturated black CS fog. Finally the familiar contour of a door jamb identified the entrance to the prisoner's room. This must be what it was like at Auschwitz, Sandy reflected as he crawled to Hoffmann's chair. Nearing the German, Sandy suddenly realized something that further terrified him: *I'm in the fucking gas chamber with a dangerous Nazi and I don't even know where my gun went!* Had he left it in the bathroom, or was it out in the living room, beside the box of shells? Did it really matter? What could the war criminal do in the state he must be in?

Eighteen inches from his face, Sandy identified Hoffmann's leather jackboot. Searching through his own pockets, Sandy found the correct key and unlocked the ankle shackles, freeing the Nazi's legs from the chair. In agony, Sandy stood up and ripped the taped gag from the war criminal's mouth. Removing the towel from his own face, Sandy draped it over the German's head, allowing him to breathe through the imperfect but nevertheless cool moist filter of densely woven cotton. Locating the keys for the locks securing the body and neck chains was delayed by the nearby explosion of another canister of CS gas fired in from the hill behind the bedroom. Virtually blind and in devastating pain, Sandy finally freed the German from every restraint except the handcuffs connecting the man's wrists to the chair.

Should I really do it? Sandy asked himself. *Can I not do it?* he responded. He had wanted to go down in history as someone of substance — a hero. Once he unlocked those handcuffs and surrendered, he'd be remembered only as an embarrassing freak and mental case. Yeah, Edward Bennett Williams and a whole team of brilliant lawyers might make a difference. The fact that he hadn't left the Nazi to asphyxiate would count for something. But no matter how impressive the legal defense, Sandy knew that his own life, as he'd once imagined it, was now at an end. No dreams, no future, no final escape from his family. All he had left was the dignity that came from acting with humanity. He might have created a tactical disaster, but in the big picture of life he had behaved with courage and achieved what he hoped would eventually be regarded as a true moral victory. Wasn't it possible that after both he and Hoffmann were taken to jail and the police understood all the evidence against the war criminal, he, Sandy, might just be forgiven?

Whipping the towel off the Nazi's head, Sandy pressed it up against his own eyes, nose, and mouth, seeking a momentary release from the excruciating pain.

"What are you doing?" Hoffmann wheezed.

"It's over. I lost. I'm giving you up."

Sandy unlocked the handcuff restraining the war criminal's right arm. Now all that connected the German to his jail was the shackle on the man's left wrist. Pulling the opaque glasses from his face, the Nazi watched as Sandy unlocked that last handcuff.

"C'mon, get up, you're free," Sandy shouted over the explosion of another tear gas grenade.

Hoffmann, whose face was right up against Sandy's, appeared overwhelmed and terrified, as if this were all a nasty deception, exactly the kind of thing the Nazis carried out themselves. First the SS relaxed their victims by pretending that there was no threat and then, when their backs were turned, shot them in the head.

"You're really letting me go?"

Sandy nodded. "We're going to walk out the front door together." He coughed in pain.

"Why?" Hoffmann remained seated, unconvinced.

"*Because I'm not like you!*" Sandy screamed in fury. "Now get your ass up and let's get out of here while we still can."

Reassured by this spontaneous, obviously sincere outburst of emotion, Hoffmann stood. "Thank you," he said. "I really must thank you very much. I don't know why you're doing this but you have my admiration forever. You are truly an extraordinary man."

After everything Sandy had been through, it struck him as bizarre that the only person who acknowledged and appreciated him was the war criminal SS *Hauptsturmfuhrer* Klaus Hagen of the *Einsatzgruppen*. So much for the Klein family, Paula, and the rest of the community to whom he, Sandy, was only contemptible garbage. At least someone values what I've done, he reflected with a surprising moment of happiness. *"Thank you very much. You have my admiration forever. You are truly an extraordinary man."*

Another CS grenade smashed through the last remaining window pane in the living room, ricocheted off the wall, and exploded directly on top of the open cardboard box of .38 caliber shells, raising the temperature of the primer loads above their ignition point. The cartridges in the box exploded, blasting bullets and shell casings in every direction in an uncanny semblance of machine gun fire. In terror, with no idea of who was doing the shooting, Sandy and Hoffmann dropped to the floor and attempted to press themselves down against the oak boards, below the line of gunfire.

To the SWAT team outside, the source of the gunfire was no mystery; they knew exactly what to do. Giving the signal to open fire on the house, the team commander finally issued the order he had known was inevitable. From every sector of the perimeter, fifty trained gunmen with automatic M16s began emptying clip after clip of .223 bullets into the dense cloud of tear gas obscuring the house. The canyon's acoustics were such that the police had no way of determining whether the shooting was now coming from their own forces or from inside the house. Having no real idea what they were up against, the SWAT team had little choice but to protect themselves by blasting Sandy's bungalow with every round of ammunition in their possession. The rationalization for the frenzy of hatred was simple: Anyone stupid enough to fire on the SWAT team deserved anything they got.

For ten whole minutes the house was assaulted with thousands of rounds of deadly fire. Not even the cockroaches could have survived. Finally, a .223 bullet cut through the supply line to the water heater and quickly filled the garage with highly inflammable natural gas. The inevitable spark from another bullet's collision with a nearby metal shovel ignited first the gas and then the far more lethal fumes from the leaking fuel tanks of the bullet-ridden Volvo and Buick. The resulting explosion resembled a dynamite bomb, ripping through and obliterating Sandy's small bungalow in a raging inferno of flame and deadly fumes. If the original gunfire hadn't accomplished the SWAT team's purpose, the incineration of the house removed all doubt. Sandy's struggle to be a part of history had finally come to an end.

53

In September of 1974 — one year after the conflagration — Nathan Klein gathered his family, friends, fellow philanthropists, Stanley Furgstein, the mayor of Los Angeles, the city councilmen, and select members of the press to witness the unusually emotional ground-breaking ceremony dedicating the Florence Klein Cancer Research Center.

The outdoor event drew almost a thousand spectators. Despite rosy speeches promising the eventual cure for cancer, the tone of the gathering was somber, more like a funeral. Complicating matters was the curious crowd of strangers who had been drawn by the recent newspaper account of the official investigation of the Klein/Hoffmann catastrophe.

Three weeks before the dedication, a blue-ribbon committee of police, politicians, and experts had presented their report — nearly ten months in the works — on the circumstances leading up to the shooting and fire that had eventually consumed all twenty-six houses on the narrow canyon street. Because the inferno wiped out virtually all physical evidence, the investigators had drawn their conclusions from the ashes of Sandy's house. In fact, the report concluded that it was only because of the nearby forest–fire-fighting equipment and aerial water bombers that the firestorm hadn't spread throughout the Beverly Glen and Bel-Air canyons.

The committee's report proved only one item of importance, and that had made headlines around the country. A thorough search of Heinz Hoffmann's Oxnard residence turned up evidence conclusively establishing the German as SS *Hauptsturmfuhrer* Klaus Hagen of the *Einsatzgruppen* — a war criminal who had, indeed, emigrated illegally into the United States as a result of what the committee members called "bureaucratic incompetence." Sandy's death was officially judged to be "justifiable homicide," even though the committee found that the SWAT team had "over-reacted in the confusion of the moment." The only critical item never discovered was the identity of the accomplice known to have assisted Sandy at the Beverly Wilshire Hotel.

Rebuilding of the canyon homes was publicly funded, and life for virtually everyone involved continued much as it had before the horrible event. The long-negotiated sale of the Vita-Line Corporation went through on schedule, and ownership transferred to the British investors. The only change in the deal involved Sandy's share of the proceeds. Since his youngest son had left no heir, Nathan decided to donate Sandy's money to fund a permanent research chair in the Florence Klein Cancer Center. Although this gift wasn't substantial enough to warrant Sandy's name going up on the outside wall in big bronze letters, at least — in the consensus of the Klein family — it was something positive to be remembered for.

Not in attendance at the dedication was Paula Gottlieb, who had moved back to New York with her parents only days after Sandy's funeral. Refusing to discuss her relationship with Sandy — even with the investigating committee she successfully protected her privacy by cloaking herself in the client-attorney privilege — she swore to herself never again to set foot in Los Angeles. In a generally successful effort to forget Sandy and her humiliation, she followed her therapist's advice and threw herself into her new job, working sixteen hours a day as an underpaid but much-appreciated lawyer for the Manhattan Center for Holocaust Survivors.

The most stirring part of the cancer center dedication was Billy's contribution. When the litany of boring, self-serving speeches had finally reached its conclusion, a twenty-piece orchestra played the first movement of a symphony based on the pentatonic scales that Billy had written in honor of his friend, entitled *Blue Numbers*. Despite the Klein family's lack of interest in serious music, the considerable throng of strangers seemed remarkably sympathetic and greatly appreciative. In fact, as the newspaper account of the dedication stated: "At the conclusion of the orchestra's performance the teary-eyed crowd gave Billy Hoyle and, by inference, Sandy Klein a sustained, enthusiastic, and moving standing ovation".

Even Uri would have been pleased.